THE ONLY AMALEKITE CONVERT

THE ONLY AMALEKITE CONVERT

R. E. D. RICHARDSON

BONNEVILLE BOOKS
An imprint of Cedar Fort, Inc.
Springville, Utah

ISBN 13: 978-1-4621-2157-1

Published by Bonneville Books, an imprint of Cedar Fort, Inc.
2373 W. 700 S., Springville, UT 84663
Distributed by Cedar Fort, Inc., www.cedarfort.com

LIBRARY OF CONGRESS CATALOGING-IN-PUBLICATION DATA

Names: Richardson, R. E. D., 1980- author.
Title: The only Amalekite convert / R.E.D. Richardson.
Description: Springville, Utah : Bonneville Books, an imprint of Cedar Fort, Inc., [2017] | Includes bibliographical references and index.
Identifiers: LCCN 2017049945 (print) | LCCN 2017053224 (ebook) | ISBN 9781462128655 (epub, pdf, mobi) | ISBN 9781462121571 (perfect bound : alk. paper)
Subjects: LCSH: Lamanites (Mormon Church)--Fiction. | Book of Mormon. Alma--Fiction. | LCGFT: Religious fiction. | Book of Mormon stories.
Classification: LCC PS3618.I34484 (ebook) | LCC PS3618.I34484 O55 2017 (print) | DDC 813/.6--dc23
LC record available at https://lccn.loc.gov/2017049945

Cover design by Katie Payne
Back cover design by Shawnda T. Craig
Cover design © 2018 by Cedar Fort, Inc.
Edited and typeset by Erica Myers and Kaitlin Barwick

Printed in the United States of America

10 9 8 7 6 5 4 3 2 1

Printed on acid-free paper

FOR MY BROTHER JOSEPH.
SOMEDAY YOU MAY READ THIS.
I LOVE YOU AND I MISS YOU.

Author's Note

In a way, this entire book comes from a single verse of scripture. In Alma 23:14, we learn that one solitary Amalekite was converted in all the fourteen years of missionary work done by the sons of Mosiah. That is the only mention of this person and the only thing we know about him (or possibly her). In fact, there's even more mystery to the whole thing because the Book of Mormon doesn't say where the Amalekites came from, except that they had dissented from the Nephites. There's no mention of when, how, or why they dissented, and we can only assume they were led by someone named Amaleki or possibly Amalek.

So, I hope this single Amalekite convert will forgive me for making up his (or her) story for myself and using it to tell the story of the mission to the Lamanites from a different perspective. I may have gotten it all entirely wrong. In fact, I probably have. But someday, after this life, I intend to track this person down and find out what really happened. I'm confident it's going to be one excellent conversion story.

You may notice I've translated into something more like everyday English for those times when the Book of Mormon actually gives me dialogue to quote. It was either that or write *all* dialogue in formal, scriptural language so the real quotations didn't stand out. This seemed the better method.

And these are the names of the cities of the Lamanites which were converted unto the Lord; and these are they that laid down the weapons of their rebellion, yea, all their weapons of war; and they were all Lamanites.

And the Amalekites were not converted,
SAVE ONLY ONE;
neither were any of the Amulonites; but they did harden their hearts, and also the hearts of the Lamanites in that part of the land wheresoever they dwelt, yea, and all their villages and all their cities.

ALMA 23:13–14

ONE

VILLAGE OF ANI-ANTI, 90 BC

THE FIRST TIME MIKIAH SAW HIS FUTURE, HE RAN RIGHT PAST IT.

He might have stopped, if he hadn't been in such a hurry. Two men speaking to a crowd beside the central well of a small village—a snatch of a sentence about angels—his eyebrows drew down in a scowl. That kind of talk didn't belong in Lamanite lands, and neither did that accent. But the news Mikiah carried couldn't wait, so he ran on, his feet hitting the dirt lightly in a ground-devouring pace he could keep up for hours at a time. He'd reach Jerusalem before sundown.

CITY OF JERUSALEM, 90 BC

"*WHAT?!*" KING ASHORAM BELLOWED, HIS FACE TWISTING WITH fury as he jerked out of his throne. He glared at Mikiah. "Say that again," he commanded, his voice a deadly whisper.

"Lamoni is lying to you," Mikiah repeated, facing his king's rage without blinking. An echo of that rage tinged his voice and burned in his gut, furious that the Lamanite would dare insult Ashoram this way. "He's playing along to see how much he can get out of you, but he'll never give you his daughter. He doesn't want her marrying so far away." His mouth quirked in something that wasn't a smile. "He even offered her to some Nephite who wandered in one day.

Just because the man said he wanted to live there." Mikiah shrugged slightly. "Temisah *is* his favorite daughter."

Ashoram paced once around the throne room, his feet smacking onto the stone floor, his leopard-skin cloak swirling behind him. Jerusalem was still a young city, but Ashoram's palace already matched even the most ancient Lamanite buildings in opulence. The floor was polished black stone, gleaming in the late sunlight that poured in through the tall windows. Colorfully embroidered tapestries covered the walls, and thick wooden beams sent the thatched roof soaring high above their heads. The sound of the sea filtered constantly through the room, waves crashing against the base of the cliff on which the building stood.

King Ashoram himself—young, clever, full of energy and ambition—was more than a match for King Lamoni's self-indulgent pride. The Amulonite king of Jerusalem showed his mixed ancestry in his black hair and in the hazel-green eyes that flashed disconcertingly from his dark complexion. The king's skin was several shades lighter than the Lamanites', but far more bronzed than Mikiah's own Amalekite pallor.

Ashoram scowled at his thoughts as he paced, and Mikiah could almost feel the rush of his king's mind speeding through possibilities. Mikiah thought he knew what the Amulonite king would do next.

"Could you get her for me?" King Ashoram demanded suddenly, swinging around to pin Mikiah with a calculating stare. Mikiah nodded, winning the mental bet he'd placed with himself. He knew how the Amulonites had stolen their wives in the beginning, and family history would have its say, after all.

"Definitely, if she came willingly," he said. "If not . . ." He took a few seconds to consider, then nodded again. "Still possible, but I'd need some extra hands."

Ashoram waved that away. "Take whoever you want. I *will* have Lamoni's daughter, and I don't care if she comes smiling or screaming," he growled. "Do whatever you need to. Just get her here."

Mikiah nodded. "We'll leave first thing tomorrow," he said, bowing. "We'll bring her back for you." A small smile twitched at his lips, hungry for the adventure.

This was going to be fun.

The Only Amalekite Convert

Mikiah hurried down the palace steps, his feet beating quickly over the risers like the wings of a hummingbird. The guards standing at the bottom merely nodded in response to his cheerful wave, and he allowed himself a wolf's grin as he broke into a loping run. The sun was lowering toward the sea in the west, the sky beginning its purple descent into star-specked darkness, and he could taste the moisture of oncoming night in the warm air.

Mikiah was twenty-one years old, and he'd been in continuous training for the past five years, constantly honing the skills he needed to serve his king. But no one, not even his family, knew what it was he was truly training for. Oh, they knew he was King Ashoram's message runner, and that was true enough. It made an excellent cover, allowing him to go almost anywhere Ashoram needed him. His true purpose, however, wasn't to carry messages but to use his eyes and ears and mind, to see the things his king needed to know. Sometimes that meant seeing things that other rulers didn't want him to know. Sometimes it led him into trouble.

Mikiah had become King Ashoram's favorite spy because he'd turned out to be very—*very*—good at trouble.

His grin faded a bit as he neared the synagogue of the Nehors. The imposing structure had been erected on the same high bluff above the sea, only slightly lower than Ashoram's palace. It was positioned to catch the last rays of the dying sun, and it seemed to glow with the light that streamed in its windows and reflected off the polished walls inside. There should have been a steady trickle of people coming out by now; crowds of Lamanites, Amalekites, and Amulonites scattering toward their homes; clumps of family and friends chatting comfortably as they went. But the street was empty, and Mikiah could see the press of people still crowded in the open door. Curious, he drew nearer and heard a voice raised in exhortation over the muted grumble of impatient worshipers.

Mikiah came to a stop in the doorway, his long legs giving him the height to peer in over the heads of the crowd, and what he saw sent a jolt of fear and anger through him. The crowd's grumbling wasn't caused by impatience, and the raised voice had nothing to do with the order of the Nehors.

"A *Nephite!*" he whispered to himself, and felt he'd dirtied his tongue with the word. The pale-skinned man stood at the front of the synagogue, and the accent of the Nephite city of Zarahemla was clear in his raised voice. Mikiah's eyes flew over the crowd, hoping desperately—but no. Even as he thought to look, Mikiah's father was already on his feet, his thin body trembling with repressed rage.

"What are you saying?" Minek called out, his strident shout cutting through the Nephite's words. Pale wisps of the old man's hair stood out around his head, lifted by his burning fury. "You've seen an *angel?*" Mikiah's father's voice dripped scornful disbelief, but the Nephite preacher only nodded calmly. Minek's eyes flashed at such obvious lies. "If you've seen an angel, why hasn't anyone else seen one? Why haven't any of our people? Or are you saying your people are *better?*"

A round of loud, angry shouting answered that, the general murmur of the crowd growing in volume and hostility. Mikiah dove into the press of people, pushing frantically to reach his father. There were too many, too closely packed, and Minek was near the front. Mikiah shoved through with no thought for courtesy, desperate to get to Minek, to stop him before—

"He says we have to *repent,*" Minek jeered, riding over the Nephite's attempts to speak. "He's been here less than a day, and he thinks he knows us—thinks he can judge us? What do you know about us, *Nephite?* How do you know we're not a righteous people? We built this synagogue, didn't we? And we're gathered here to worship God, aren't we? We believe God will save all men. What do we have to repent of?"

Supporting yells came from the corners of the room.

"Call *yourself* to repentance, Nephite!"

"Nephite liar!"

"Repent yourself!"

Mikiah had made it halfway across the room when the preacher, flushed with some unreadable emotion, finally managed to make himself heard. "Do you believe that the Son of God will come?" he asked. "That He'll redeem mankind from their sins?" He was speaking directly to Minek now, but pitching his voice so the whole synagogue could hear, and Mikiah felt a stronger stab of fear and rage. Why couldn't the man leave them alone?

"That old fable!" Minek yelled, and Mikiah was close enough now to see the vein throbbing in his temple. "You can't prove that! You can't prove any of it, any more than your fathers could! No one can see the future! It's a stupid superstition! You don't *know* it's true! You can't! Because it's *not!*" Minek was screaming now, shaking his fists in fury, and Mikiah thought his father might have tried to physically attack the Nephite if Mikiah hadn't reached Minek just then and grabbed him.

"Father, stop!" he hissed, shaking Minek's arm urgently. "Calm down!"

"I *won't* calm down!" Minek shouted, jerking his arm free and glaring at his son. "Not while this Nephite liar is standing there spreading his—his stupid lies! Expecting us to just—to just take—" He stuttered to a halt, clutching his chest as his breath heaved in and out.

"I know, Father," Mikiah said soothingly, reaching out to support the old man. "But no one's listening to him. No one here believes all that nonsense." He heard the Nephite trying to say something about the prophet Isaiah, but the crowd wasn't listening. Other voices were raised now, angry and mocking. If the Nephite wasn't quick getting out of there, he was going to end up carried out in a box. *And so much the better!* Mikiah thought savagely. *Bringing his lies here, of all places!* "It'll be all right," he murmured, wrapping a strong arm around Minek's shaking shoulders. "Let me take you home now. You need rest."

Minek nodded jerkily, his eyes squeezed shut now as he rubbed at his chest, letting his son guide his faltering steps. "Yes," he whispered. "That'll be good. I'll be fine after I lay down. Just for a little while. Yes . . ."

Carefully threading their way through the increasingly angry mob, Mikiah and his father left the synagogue in the blue dusk and made their slow way down the dark street, the furious, baying shouts still echoing behind them. As he walked alongside, half-supporting the old man and watching his shuffling feet to be sure he wouldn't stumble, Mikiah felt angry tears prick at his eyes. This shouldn't be happening. Minek had always been so strong, so full of fire, a loving giant in his son's eyes. He shouldn't be reduced to this—hunched and weak and trembling with pain. It wasn't right. Mikiah wished he could turn back and join the mob, drive the Nephite from the city, punish him for bringing his father to this weakness.

Mikiah's sister Nabeth was waiting for them when they reached home, warm lamplight shining from the open door as she stood looking expectantly down the street for them. The golden light turned her long chestnut curls to burnished bronze and gilded one plump cheek. She'd inherited her looks from their father, and her darker complexion might have almost been mistaken for part Lamanite. Mikiah was more like their mother with his pale blue eyes and long tail of brown-blond hair hanging past his shoulders. Mikiah had loved his mother, but he wished he hadn't gotten her coloring. Mikiah's pale skin wouldn't have stood out in the heart of Zarahemla, the Nephite capital, and he'd been teased mercilessly about it as a child—at least until he learned how to fight.

Nabeth grinned when she saw her brother walking beside Minek. "Mikiah! You're back!" she cried, and threw herself at him, nearly knocking them all down with an exuberant hug. Mikiah staggered theatrically, grunting as he absorbed the weight of the joyful sixteen-year-old.

"Ooof! Not so hard, Nabeth," he said, massaging his ribs. "I bruise easy."

Nabeth laughed, slipping her arm around him as he escorted Minek into the house. She didn't notice their father's weakness. She never had, and Mikiah worked hard to make sure she never would.

"Hah! You bruise about as easy as a boulder," she retorted, giving her brother a sharp jab in the midriff. "Come sit down. I wasn't expecting you for supper, but I *think* we have enough to feed your worthless carcass."

Mikiah laughed, but the laughter was mostly to cover his anxiety as he helped his father to one of the soft pallets at one end of the large room and made sure he was lying comfortably. Some of his worry eased as he saw the old man drop almost immediately into sleep, his breathing deep and steady. Surely that kind of sleep would bring healing.

"It was a longer meeting than normal," he explained when his sister raised an eyebrow at him. "He just needs a quick nap before supper."

Nabeth hesitated a moment longer, and Mikiah could see the thoughts almost forming behind her eyes before she dismissed them with a shrug. "Well, *I'm* hungry now, and I've already been waiting." She quickly set out a container of hot stew, a plate of fruit, and a skin of wine, grinning impudently as she grabbed half of a yellow-skinned cherimoya fruit and took a large bite, licking up the juices that dribbled from its white flesh.

Mikiah snorted. "You've got no respect, young lady," he said, glowering, but the effect was spoiled by the upward twitching at the corners of his mouth. "Let's just remember to save some for Father, shall we?" He reached across her for the stewpot. Mikiah had to admit his sister did cook a fine meal. Someday she'd make some man very lucky—and possibly very fat.

As he ate, Mikiah's mind drifted back to the synagogue. What had the Nephite preacher even been doing there? He had to know how dangerous it would be to spread his lies in Lamanite lands. *Especially* here, where people knew better. The full-blooded Lamanites might have forgotten what the Nephites had done to them, the hatred dimming with time. This was Jerusalem, though. This city had many more Amulonites and Amalekites, like Mikiah and his family, and for them the memory of Nephite oppression was far more recent. Some of the very old men even remembered when they'd left the Nephites, unable to live any longer under the lies and hypocrisy and self-serving superstitions of their so-called religion. Liars and thieves, the whole lot of them, and Mikiah hated the idea that he was in any way related to them.

It struck Mikiah as suspicious that he would have encountered two Nephites in as many days. First the man who'd wandered into King Lamoni's court and nearly taken King Ashoram's bride, and then the preacher who'd caused so much trouble at the synagogue. Then he remembered the two men beside the well in Ani-Anti. He scowled. Four of them. He knew he should have stopped to hear what those two were saying.

"There was a Nephite in the square today," Nabeth said in an uncanny echo of his thoughts.

Mikiah nearly choked on his mouthful. "What?!" he snapped, and Nabeth looked startled by his glare.

"I—I just said—"

"I heard you!" Mikiah interrupted. "What was he doing there? What were *you* doing there?"

Nabeth recovered enough to make a mocking noise in the back of her throat. "The same thing I'm doing there every day, idiot!" she snapped back. "The same thing *everyone* is doing. It's the *square!*"

"All right, all right." Mikiah spread his hands, waving away the argument. "I didn't mean to snap. It's just—there've been a lot of Nephites around. I don't like it." He glowered at the wall.

His sister shrugged. "I don't see what there is to get so worked up about," she said, taking a sip of wine. "He was just talking. What harm can that do?"

"A lot," Mikiah told her, his voice coming out in a low growl, "if people believe him." He gave her a sharp look. "You didn't, did you?"

"What, all that stuff about angels and the Son of God?" She laughed. "Of course not. Although . . ." She gave a small sigh. "I can understand how someone might want to. It's a pretty kind of fantasy." Nabeth shrugged again when she saw her brother's horrified look. "Anyway, what does it matter to you what anyone else believes? *You* hardly believe in anything."

The hot retort died in Mikiah's throat as he saw Minek stir restlessly, but their father only turned over and slipped back into sleep, making small snoring noises. Mikiah let out a relieved breath. "Look, Nabeth. I'm not going to argue with you. Just—don't talk about the Nephites, all right? Especially not in front of Father. Trust me. It's better if you don't."

Nabeth leaned over to nab a papaya, the subject apparently already forgotten. "Fine. So . . . what grand adventure is our worthy king sending you off on next? Delivering a birthday present to his dearest friend's wife's great-nephew in farthest Shemnilom?" She grinned, her broad cheeks going round and dimpled, and Mikiah glared at her teasing. But when she looked away, he let that faint smile creep back behind his eyes. If only she knew.

Early the next morning—so early it hadn't quite stopped being last night yet—Mikiah tapped gently on a stone windowsill, ignoring his friend Shehum's sleepy yawns coming from the predawn darkness behind him. Shehum hadn't been hard to awaken. The Lamanite was an orphan, raised by his grandfather, who was nearly deaf with age. Shehum might yawn and shiver at the early morning chill of the air, but at least Mikiah hadn't needed to worry about waking anyone else in the house. He'd dragged Shehum out of bed and through the deserted streets to the home of the third member of their trio. Here, they had to be more careful. Eliah was one of a large family of Lamanites, and Mikiah had no desire to deal with a barrage of questions from a range of younger siblings. He tapped again, hoping his friend would wake quietly. "*Eliah!*" he whispered.

A small moan of protest came from inside, and a few moments later, Eliah's thin face appeared in the window, blinking and squinting in the starlight. He groaned when he recognized Mikiah and Shehum. "What's he want this time?" He rested his arms on the windowsill and laid his head down on them. "And why does it need three of us?"

Mikiah poked him. "Because you'd never forgive me if I didn't let you in on this one," he said. "Now get your stuff, and let's go!" When Eliah didn't move, Mikiah prodded him again. "If you don't get a move on, I'll tell Nabeth you're lazy as a bear and you snore like one, too. See how interested she is then."

Eliah opened one eye enough to glare. "That's fighting dirty."

"You might as well give in," Shehum said, his deep, quiet voice even softer and more stolidly calm than usual. "He's in one of those moods." He stifled another yawn. "Although I don't know why it can't wait till dawn, at least."

"I'll tell you." Mikiah grinned and beckoned Shehum closer, leaning in to whisper so only they could hear him. "We're going to steal a wife for King Ashoram."

They stared at him for a moment in shocked silence, their eyes suddenly wide rather than half-shut with sleep. A slow grin stole over Eliah's face. "Lamoni's daughter?" he whispered, and went off into a peal of silent laughter when Mikiah nodded. "Just let me get my pack!"

Eliah disappeared from the window on silent feet, still snickering, but Shehum was frowning thoughtfully, chewing on his lower lip. "That's not going to be easy, Mikiah," he said, studying the confident tilt of Mikiah's head. "You have a plan?"

Mikiah smiled. "I always have a plan."

TWO

VILLAGE OF ANI-ANTI, 90 BC

THEY LEFT WITH DAWN JUST BEGINNING TO TINGE THE PALE GRAY OF the sky with pink. The ostensible reason for the journey was to deliver yet another precious gift to sweeten King Lamoni's mood, one more step in the dance of negotiations for Temisah's hand. Mikiah let his feet fall into rhythm with his friends as they made their way down the road toward Ishmael, enjoying the alternating sensations of warm morning sunlight and cool tree shadows across his shoulders. By now he knew the path very well; he'd gone over it several times in the past few months as Lamoni intentionally dragged out Ashoram's courtship. The first village they'd reach would be Ani-Anti, before the sun was halfway to its peak, then across the land of Midian, reaching the city of Midian itself around noon. They'd have to stop the night at the border between Midian and Ishmael, but they should see the walls of Lamoni's city fairly early the next day. Most importantly—especially for a runner—the road joined a river not long after it left Ani-Anti and followed its course well into the land of Midian, so they'd have a ready source of water whenever they needed it.

Which meant there was no real reason for them to stop at the well in Ani-Anti—except that Mikiah recognized the Nephite preacher from the night before sitting on the ground beside it. Another Nephite—one of those he'd seen talking as he ran past yesterday—was just settling down next to his friend when Mikiah jogged into the square. Mikiah wondered where the third Nephite was; there was no sign of him. He turned on a moment's impulse, ignoring the puzzled looks of his friends as he made a great show of puffing up to the well and gulping water as if he was dying of thirst. He wanted to hear what these two said to each other.

"Anything?" he heard one of the Nephites ask, but not as if he had much hope.

The other shook his head. "When they ran us out of Helam, we thought maybe a smaller village, people might be more open." He sighed. "But I think we've spoken to every single person in this place. None of them'll listen to us."

His companion echoed the sigh. "Where's Muloki?"

"Exploring one last possibility."

Just then, a door across the square slammed open and the third Nephite stumbled out, propelled by the fist of the large man who followed him, shouting, "Think you can make fools of us! Take your lies back to your own spineless dreamers!" He hit the Nephite again, knocking him to the ground, and the other two jumped to their feet. "If you come back here, I'll cave your head in, you hear me? See how smart you think you are then!" The man waved his fist threateningly one last time and slammed the door shut with such force that it rattled in the frame.

Mikiah watched out of the corner of his eye as the two Nephites hurried to help their friend. Muloki let them pull him to his feet, leaning dizzily against their supporting arms for a moment. "I'm all right, Ammah," he said, jerking away from the hands trying to examine his darkening black eye. "But I don't think we should stay here any longer. Aaron?" He gave the third man—the one Mikiah had seen in Jerusalem—a questioning look. Apparently, he was the leader of the three.

Aaron blew out his breath, studying the ground at his feet as if he could find some kind of answer in the grass-lined cobbles. "Further south," he said finally. "Past the dissenters. Maybe the true Lamanites will listen." He gave the other two a sudden wry grin. "Look at it this way: the worst they can do is kill us, right?"

To Mikiah's astonishment, Muloki and Ammah actually laughed at that. He watched, dumbfounded, as the three Nephite preachers turned to take the southern route that ran up through the pass toward Middoni. "Religion just turns a man's brain to mush!" he said softly, staring at the three retreating figures.

"Thanks a lot!" Eliah hit his shoulder lightly, pretending to be offended.

"You don't count," Mikiah told him. "Your brain was already mush."

"Anyway," Shehum added, "we don't get to the synagogue more than once or twice a month. That probably limits our exposure to the brain-mushing elements. And the Nephites' religion sounds a lot more irrational than the Nehors'."

Eliah snorted. "The Son of God will come to save us!" he mocked, dancing around with his hands in the air. "If it feels good, it must be sinful! You can only be happy after you're dead!" He dropped his hands and spat on the ground. "Some people will believe anything."

"I doubt they'll have any better luck in Middoni," Shehum said thoughtfully, and Mikiah agreed with him. King Antiomno wasn't likely to put up with that kind of nonsense. Still . . .

"Who cares? Come on, already!" Eliah called, grinning as he ran backward, facing his friends. "It'll be nightfall before we even reach Midian at this rate!"

THREE

CITY OF ISHMAEL, 90 BC

MIKIAH EYED THE LAMANITE "HERDSMEN" AROUND HIM WITH carefully concealed disgust. They filled the wood hut, oblivious to the smoke that hung heavy in the air from the guttering fire in the center of the floor, the organic stench of badly tanned hides and unwashed bodies, the swarms of flies that flew in to feast on puddles of spilled wine.

"How do we know this isn't some kinda trap?" their leader asked, narrowing his eyes to black slits and bunching up his mouth obstinately. Mikiah hid a frustrated sigh.

"Look, Tubal," he said, keeping his voice friendly and strangling the exaggerated patience that tried to creep in. "How many times have you done this? If King Lamoni was going to set a trap for you, he'd have done it ages back, right? Instead he just keeps blaming his servants. I'm just asking you to do something you've done a dozen times already—but at a specific *time.* I mean, you were going to do this again anyway, weren't you?"

"Don't trust 'im," Tubal's brother grunted. "'E's a Nephite."

Mikiah glared. "Say that again, and I'll take out what's left of your teeth," he growled. Tubal might not have been the brightest specimen, but he was positively incandescent compared to his brother.

"I'm an *Amalekite,* not a Nephite. Even you should be smart enough to know the difference, Hem."

Hem, staring into that blue-eyed glare, saw something there that made his dark skin go several shades paler. He looked away after a second, muttering something unintelligible, and Mikiah turned his attention back to Tubal. "So, can I rely on you?"

Whatever Hem had seen in the Amalekite's eyes, when Tubal looked into them, he found something that reassured him, something he could understand and trust in. He gave a sharp nod. "Yes," he said. "We'll be there."

Once they had Tubal and his men set up, Eliah headed for Lamoni's palace kitchen. "Special gift for the king's table," he sang happily, holding a small basket out for Lamoni's young, buxom cook to examine. Eliah was dressed simply, with nothing to identify him as Ashoram's messenger. He might have been anyone, and today he was one of King Lamoni's dutiful subjects, sharing the fruits of his labors in the hope of pleasing his king, or at least the king's pretty cook. In this case, the "fruits of his labors" were a couple dozen bright, red-fleshed strawberries.

"Oh, my!" the cook exclaimed, cradling the tiny basket in both her flour-dusted hands, almost clutching it to her ample bosom. Behind her, a tray of round loaves sat cooling beside the large cement oven. Basins of vegetables soaked in water, waiting for chopping, and several small, skinless carcasses hung in the cool closet. But Eliah knew his humble offering would bring more delight than all of those everyday delicacies put together. "The king's daughters will love these! Wherever did you find them?"

"Now, now. If I told everyone my secrets, there wouldn't be any left for me to gain the king's favor with," Eliah chided. "But I'll tell you what." He lowered his voice and leaned in conspiratorially, his eyes dancing. "If you give me a kiss, I'll give you a hint."

"You rascal!" She smacked him sharply on the shoulder. "I should turn you out with a sore head and an empty belly." She glowered at him, but he could tell her heart wasn't in it. And that she *really* wanted to know. Mikiah had been right again. "All right, then," she said finally. "Hint first."

Eliah pouted. "You don't trust me? I'm heartbroken!" He sighed theatrically. "Well, if you must know . . . I found them in a grove of trees down by the waters of Sebus."

He grabbed her before she could escape, wrapping her in his arms and kissing her for all he was worth. Then he ran, laughing, dodging away as she took another swat at him.

"Don't let them go down there!" Shehum cried a few minutes later, running into the paddock where Lamoni's servants kept his flocks. He dashed up to the head herdsman, Ladon, gripping the startled man by both shoulders. "As you value your life, don't take them out! Not yet!"

"Wh-what?" Ladon stammered. "Why not?"

"The thieves are back!" Shehum gasped. "At the waters of Sebus! They'll steal the king's flocks!"

"But—but the flocks *have* to have water," protested the herdsman. "We can't just—"

"Are you mad?" Shehum demanded, shaking him again. "Don't you know what happened to the *last* group of servants that let the flocks be scattered?"

Ladon paled, his dark eyes widening. It had been over a year ago, but that kind of thing stuck in the mind. "They . . . were put to death," he whispered, finally catching up with Shehum's feigned panic. "But what'll we do? There's no other place to—"

"No, it'll be all right," Shehum said, comforting now that he'd gotten his mark properly frightened. "We'll wait them out. The flocks can go thirsty for an extra hour or two. Better thirsty than stolen, right?" He patted Ladon's shoulder. "The thieves will get bored and go away if we don't come on time. I'll go and watch. I'll let you know when it's safe. You just wait here."

He slipped out again, leaving the man standing nervously in the middle of an increasingly restless herd.

Mikiah sat on a small hill overlooking the waters of Sebus, watching the brisk wind rippling over the long grass around him. So far, everything had gone according to plan. From his vantage point, he could see the group of about twenty thieving herdsmen hidden down by the water's edge. Looking down the other side of the hill, he had an equally clear view of King Lamoni's daughters, strolling happily toward a nearby copse, berry-picking baskets over their arms. They had a few men with them, but Mikiah thought that was mostly for show, seeing the carefree way the guards walked, weapons held loosely in lax hands. As he watched, the youngest of the girls—not more than eight years old—ran ahead of the group, laughing as she flung her arms out and spun around and around, turning her face up to the clear blue sky. Mikiah made a mental note to—if possible—avoid scaring the life out of her.

"Here they come," Eliah said, nodding toward the city gates. Sure enough, the king's herds were pouring out into the open, the impatient beasts picking up their pace as they smelled the water ahead.

"There's Shehum," Mikiah said, narrowing his eyes against the bright sunlight. His friend would have waited until the king's daughters were well on their way before telling the herdsmen that the thieves had gone. Mikiah and his friends had needed to delay everything until the young women innocently took the bait. That had been the trickiest part of the plan, but now the only worry was that the animals would be so thirsty the thieves might have a hard time scattering them. "Get ready," he said to Eliah. "And stay on plan, right?"

"Yeah, yeah," Eliah muttered. "Chase the cattle toward the girls, 'find' the girls, pretend to be evil, smelly brigands, steal the girls. How hard can it be?"

"*Girl*," Mikiah corrected him. "Just the one. I catch you laying a finger on any of the others, I'll tie it in a knot."

Eliah gave him a long, measuring look. "You know, you're no fun when you're on the job," he said.

"Well, it'd be fun for *me*."

A horrific, many-voiced howl broke the peaceful scene, echoing from the throats of Tubal's men as the flocks neared the water's edge. The king's servants cried out in terror, stumbling back at the sight of the horde of large, filthy men running toward them. The thieves brandished clubs and long sticks, poking and beating at the animals to send them running in every direction, and the panicked bleats and bawls of the protesting animals nearly drowned the servants' frightened, despairing wails. Mikiah ignored them, his heartbeat quickening as excitement flowed through him. His eyes glowed. Several of the beasts were headed straight for the grove of trees where the girls were searching for Eliah's strawberry patch.

"That's our cue," Mikiah said. He started trotting down the hill after the fleeing animals.

"Don't just stand there crying about it!" The strangely accented voice rang out cheerfully above the noise of frightened people and animals, and Mikiah froze in his tracks. *It couldn't be!* But the unmistakable Nephite accent continued. "If you don't want to be killed, let's go get them back! Come on!" Mikiah could see the man now, his pale skin standing out among all the dark-skinned Lamanites. The Nephite rushed away across the meadow, waving enthusiastically for the others to follow.

"Utterly mad, the lot of them," Mikiah said, shaking his head as he saw the man's bright and joyful expression. Whatever insanity the Nephite carried, it was obviously contagious. The other servants took off after him, spreading out as he directed them to head off the scattering flocks. The animals Mikiah had been relying on didn't even make it halfway to the trees.

Beside him, Eliah breathed a curse, his voice almost awed. "I don't think they lost more than a handful," he said, watching as the herdsmen drove their cattle back into a single large herd. The animals milled around one another, confused, frightened, and still thirsty, but the herdsmen didn't dare let them go to the water. Tubal and his men were still planted firmly on the shore, screaming insults and taunts, ready to do it all over again.

Impasse, Mikiah thought. *And now what do we do?*

Three groups stood frozen, waiting for someone to make the first move. Out of the corner of his eye, Mikiah saw Shehum slip out of the city gates. The Lamanite walked only a few steps before he saw what was happening and stopped, caught in the same immobility that held the others. Mikiah wasn't sure what would happen next, but he made a mental bet with himself on who would be the one to start it.

"Y'can't hold them forever!" one of the thieves yelled. "Them beasties need—" There was a sharp *crack* and the man fell, blood welling up between his staring eyes. A round, gray stone fell to the wet earth beside him with a faint thud. The dead thief's comrades stared at him, shocked into silence by the suddenness of it. That silence was broken by the rhythmic, buzzing hum of a loaded sling.

"Ammon, no!" one of the other herdsmen cried as the Nephite stepped free of the crowd of animals and his fellow servants, sling spinning in his hand, and Mikiah won his bet. "They'll kill you!"

"I'll be fine, Ladon," the Nephite said calmly. "You all stay here and make sure the flocks don't scatter. I'll deal with these men."

That got a howl of laughter from the brigands gathered on the shore, and even Mikiah and Eliah snorted in disbelief. One man against twenty? He'd be nothing but a red smear in the mud.

Mikiah didn't even see the Nephite's hand move. One moment, Ammon was standing, just twirling his sling. The next moment there was another *crack* and one more of Tubal's men fell dead. The howl of laughter turned to a howl of outrage.

"Get him!" Tubal bellowed. "Bring him down!" Several of his men pulled out their own slings, fitting stones into leather pouches. It should be an easy target, Mikiah thought, and felt a faint sense of anticipation. Ammon wasn't even trying to dodge or retreat back into the protection of the flock. The first stone sped at him, humming through the warm morning air straight at his head—

And fell short, plowing into the earth several paces away.

Mikiah's mouth dropped open. It was impossible! He'd *seen* the trajectory, the speed of the stone. There was no way it could have missed!

But it had, and the second slinger fared no better than the first, his stone burying itself only a few inches beyond its brother. The third one flew straight over Ammon's head before dropping several paces behind him.

Crack, crack, and *crack!* Three more dead bodies dropped, leaking blood into the pond weeds. The flight of stones that came back never got within arm's length of the Nephite, tracing utterly improbable paths to ground themselves in soft, grassy dirt.

Tubal had had enough. He wasn't about to back down from a single man, no matter what uncanny force protected him—but it was obvious even to Tubal's sluggish thought processes that throwing rocks was only working in one direction for some reason. He shook his club above his head, rallying his band with a wild yell, and charged.

Ammon had just enough time to empty his sling once more and send one last attacker sprawling face down in the mud. Then, still with that air of infuriating calm, he tossed the sling to one side and drew his sword. The Nephite wasn't standing still any longer.

Mikiah watched, filled with a fresh surge of disbelief, as one man *ran* to confront fourteen huge, club-wielding, enraged thugs. The Nephite barely even paused for the first man who reached him. The bandit wasn't exactly a martial genius—he was broadcasting every move he was about to make and seemed to think that brute force was the only thing he needed. It was also possible that he'd never heard of the concept of dodging. He raised his club high over his head and brought it down toward his intended victim. Ammon's sword flashed, blurred into a circle of bright metal, and the club flew over his head, the hand that was holding it still attached. The thief screamed, staring bug-eyed at the stump of his right arm. Without even sparing him a second glance, Ammon whirled his sword back to the ready and continued his sprint.

The next men were smart enough to learn from their comrade's fate. They held back, came at Ammon in a coordinated group, three on one side, two on the other, while three more circled around to come at him from behind. It was a smart move, and it should have done them much more good than it did. Mikiah lost sight of the Nephite for a moment in the confusion of bodies, but he could still see the results. Two more men, and then a third, fell or staggered away, clutching at the remains where their arms used to be.

He's not killing them! Mikiah marveled. *Eight against one, and more on the way, and he's not even killing them! He doesn't* have *to!*

He could see Ammon again now, twisting, ducking, slashing in the midst of the shouting men and swinging clubs. The skill of the

Nephite amazed him. Landing a solid blow on an opponent's body was hard enough, and the body was a larger, slower target than the arm. It was sometimes possible to take an arm by accident, if someone blocked with it rather than be killed. But to actually aim for and consistently hit the relatively small and quick-moving targets of attacking arms—and not just to deliver flesh wounds but to lop them off completely like so many waving grass stems! It was something Mikiah had never even imagined was possible.

Six severed arms lay scattered across the grass now. The Nephite's sword whirled again as a club came at him from behind. Another arm flew away, and the seventh man fell to the ground, screaming and writhing like the others. The rest of Tubal's men had slithered to a halt, and the two attackers who still had both arms were scrambling over themselves to get away from this unearthly demon. They dropped their clubs as they ran, rather than risk his vengeance. Tubal, seeing his men crumpling before the Nephite, his own safety at risk, turned and fled, the remains of his band trailing behind him.

Ammon ran after them, sword still at the ready. One man, *chasing* a half-dozen ruthless bandits. He hardly even looked winded—and he was catching up. The two who'd thrown down their clubs fell to the grass as they felt him bearing down on them, cowering away from him with despairing cries. He passed them without a glance. Two of their companions, he simply tripped, hooking their legs from under them with the flat of his blade. Mikiah could have sworn he saw the Nephite grin impishly as the two men fell behind him.

But there was no trace of humor as he caught the bandit leader's shoulder and pulled him around. "Face me, leader of cowards!" Ammon snapped, his eyes flashing. Tubal stumbled, nearly falling as the implacable hand dragged him about. He was nearly twice Ammon's size, and his eyes widened as the Nephite somehow overruled him without apparent effort.

But he *was* bigger—a great deal bigger—and Mikiah, watching his face, could see the anger, fear, and his carefully nurtured sense of his own invulnerability squashing whatever amount of better judgment he might have had. Tubal had always preyed on those weaker than himself, and so he had never been beaten. He'd told himself he *couldn't* be beaten, and securely complacent in his own superiority, he'd believed it. Now, faced with the impossible truth that he'd been wrong, he simply couldn't accept it. Tubal bellowed like a wounded bull, swelling with rage, and used the speed of the turn to add extra strength to his swinging club, intent on smashing this impudent fool who had dared to insult him, who had dared to make him fear.

Ammon jumped back out of the club's path, and his sword swept viciously forward. Tubal's arm, thick and meaty with solid muscle as it was, fared no better against that invincible blade than his followers had, and he screamed as he saw it go spiraling away from him. But Ammon didn't stop there—not this time. His sword arced back around, and Tubal's anguished scream cut off with sickening finality. The lifeless body fell backward, landing in a broken heap on the damp earth.

Ammon flipped his sword back to his side, setting his feet and raising the blade back into a defensive position, holding it and himself ready. But the thieving herdsmen had had more than enough. Not even Hem was stupid enough to come back to try to avenge his brother. The uninjured men ran for their lives. Those who couldn't run were staggering away toward the city gates, hoping to find a healer who could help them. Ammon gave the scenery one last, searching look, and finally lowered his sword, bowing his head for a moment before he raised his hand to beckon to the other servants with a calm smile.

The impatient flocks were so thirsty by this time that they didn't even balk at the smell of blood in the air. They headed for the water in a great, unstoppable mass, bawling their displeasure. Mikiah let out a breath he hadn't realized he'd been holding as the Nephite turned to help. Mikiah could have sworn that Ammon had stared right at him for several seconds as he'd scanned the area, and those deep brown eyes had seemed to see right into his mind and heart, to know everything about him within the space of a breath.

"Well, that was . . . unexpected," Shehum remarked drily as he strolled up the hill to finally join his friends. "I hope you have a backup plan, Mikiah, because I don't think we'll get within shouting distance of the king's daughters at this point." He nodded toward the grove, where the men King Lamoni had sent to guard his girls were standing with drawn swords, arrows on strings, set to high alert by all the screaming and yelling.

Mikiah gritted his teeth. It had been such a *good* plan. "Something will come to me."

Lamoni sat in the late afternoon splendor of his palace. The walls had been formed of golden sandstone, hung with tapestries in warm earth-tones, and when the sunlight poured in through the windows the room looked like it was filled with warm honey. Lamoni himself, with his bronzed complexion and deep brown eyes, often dressed himself in colors to match the golden glow of his hall, turning the room itself into an extension of his power and personality. But just now the effect was lost, as the weight of the chief herdsman's words seemed to press down heavily on the king's shoulders. The severed arms of eight men lay in an untidy pile on the stone floor.

"He can't be human," Lamoni murmured finally, when the last of the herdsmen had given his account of Ammon's battle with the bandits at the waters of Sebus. "Could he—is it possible he could be the—the Great Spirit? The power he has—it's like the punishments the Great Spirit sends. For our murders." The last words came out in a low voice, and the king tried to hide a shudder, but his eyes suddenly looked old and haunted.

Mikiah, Eliah, and Shehum stood watching unnoticed in a corner of the room, hidden by the crowd of herdsmen and household servants. Even the young cook had left her pots to boil dry if they would, and Mikiah could see her across the room, unconsciously gripping the fingers of one hand tight with the other and staring with wide, frightened eyes at the pile of arms. Though the king's daughters hadn't been in a position to see anything, with the hill and the trees blocking their view, they'd been so excited by the snatches of the story they'd picked up as their guards hustled them back to the city that they'd invaded the throne room and refused to leave. Mikiah himself wouldn't have been anywhere else for a big pile of gold. As soon as the flocks were watered and Ammon had gone, the other herdsmen had broken into a buzz of conversation, wild speculation, and general astonishment. When Mikiah had seen some of them start to gather up the fallen arms, he'd known what was about to happen—and that he *had* to be there to see it.

"My king, we—we don't know what he is," Ladon answered. He sounded frightened also, but more confused. "He might be a man, he might be the Great Spirit, as you say. All we know for sure is that he can't be killed. And when he's with us, those thieves can't scatter your flocks. Maybe . . . maybe that means he's your friend? But whether a man could have done all that or not"—he gestured at the bloody fruits of Ammon's labor—"well, we're not sure. But—we don't think so."

The last sentence drew a murmur from the crowd, and the king drew his hands over his face, scrubbing at his eyes with his fingertips. "He *is* the Great Spirit," Lamoni said, and Mikiah could hear the hidden tremor in the king's voice. "He must be. He's here to keep me from killing any more of you." Lamoni's hands clenched together in a white-knuckled ball, and his lips were pressed tight against his teeth. Mikiah could see him fighting to hold back an all-consuming terror.

Mikiah didn't know whether to be amused or disgusted, and he clamped an iron-willed control over his expression lest he betray either emotion. He knew Lamoni believed in a Great Spirit simply because his father had taught him to, and that neither one of them had ever before in his life considered whether his Great Spirit would think what he did was good or bad. Now Lamoni was writhing under the fear of a punishment he'd never even worried about before, and Mikiah couldn't help a feeling of wry humor at the irony of the king's situation. Gods weren't nearly so comforting a fantasy when they could get directly involved in people's lives.

But at the same time, the king was just setting himself up for the Nephite, and Mikiah fully expected to see Ammon play this for everything it was worth. Mikiah himself had no doubt that Ammon was nothing more than a man—a highly skilled and excessively well-trained warrior, perhaps, but certainly nothing supernatural or divine. His mind shied away from the memory of slung stones falling in impossible angles. He must have missed some variable that accounted for it, or just been at the wrong vantage point to see it properly. Yes. He couldn't be remembering it right. And as for everything else—well, Tubal's men were bullies and thieves, not real warriors.

Once you'd learned the trick of lopping off arms, it was probably easy against such poor opponents. All it took was a bit of rational thought, and all Lamoni's worries could have been erased. Mikiah personally thought King Lamoni had taken punishment a bit too far, executing his servants when thieves raided the flock, but that was for *Lamoni* to decide, not some unknown god somewhere, looking down in judgment. Or, more likely, some fake preacher pretending to speak as the voice of their judgmental god.

Angry words pressed at the back of Mikiah's throat, and he longed to let them out, to denounce this Nephite charlatan for what he was, to make Lamoni see how he was being fooled. His fists clenched with the effort of holding his tongue. When Eliah gave him a questioning glance, he shook his head sharply, willing both of his Lamanite friends to silence. They didn't dare jeopardize their mission.

Lamoni drew in a deep breath, his dark face paler than it should have been. "Where is he now?" he asked.

There was some shuffling of feet and passing of embarrassed glances among the herdsmen. Finally, Ladon cleared his throat nervously. "He's—um—he's preparing your horses and chariots, my king, as you commanded."

Lamoni's mouth dropped open, and Mikiah's eyebrows lifted in surprise as well. "He—he remembered?" Lamoni stammered. "Even after—all that?" He copied Ladon's gesture at the arms. "Any of my other servants would have figured they were owed some time off, after that," the king muttered, as if to himself, and Ladon ducked his head, biting his lower lip. Mikiah was relieved to hear a bit of the normal King Lamoni showing through, but he was just as surprised and confused as the king. He couldn't believe Ammon wasn't just waiting to capitalize on his success, and he couldn't do that by going back to the servant's role. He should be here already, or at the very least be lurking nearby to see how the king reacted.

"That proves it. He *must* be the Great Spirit," Lamoni repeated, and Mikiah suddenly understood. It brought a bitter taste to his mouth, but he gave the Nephite extra points for cleverness. Of course, anyone who *was* trying to trick the king into trusting him would have been there to make sure it took. But Ammon would have known that, and probably guessed that Lamoni would realize it too. So he'd done the exact opposite and made his success all the more certain. "I wish . . ." Lamoni continued, but trailed off, gnawing uneasily on one thumbnail.

"What do you wish, my king?" Ladon prompted after a long moment.

Lamoni shook his head, an almost despairing gesture. "I was about to send one of you to call him in to see me." He gave a deep sigh, shaking his head again. "But I don't dare to."

So they waited, the king huddled miserably in his throne, waiting for whatever judgment had been pronounced upon him, his servants standing around him echoing his nerves. They waited while the sun slid lower and lower in the sky, and the severed limbs leaked blood across the golden stones. Mikiah wondered if Ammon was actually feeding all the horses and getting them harnessed up all by himself, while the king and all his household sat waiting for him. The murmur of quiet conversations slowly died away, and silence wrapped itself around the room. The buzz of a wandering fly, the vague chirrups of birds outside the windows, served only to highlight the silence.

"*He's coming!*" The stir by the door and the quietly intense whisper jerked Mikiah awake, and he only then realized that the quiet warmth had lured his wandering thoughts into a doze. The silence of the room seemed to congeal at the sound of approaching footsteps, holding the crowd frozen. Lamoni watched the sun-limned doorway with poorly concealed dread. A shadow split the square of light that fell across the floor, and then—finally—the man himself entered.

The crowd drew back from him, clearing a wide path to Lamoni's throne, afraid to let even the edge of his clothing touch them. A look of confusion flitted across the Nephite's face as he saw their reaction, and then he looked up the cleared path to the king. Lamoni flinched as he met Ammon's brown eyes, and the Nephite drew in a sharp breath, his own eyes widening as his eyebrows climbed his forehead. Mikiah had to admit, it was a masterful performance. The man seemed genuinely surprised. He walked into the room and bowed low, still casting confused looks from the corners of his eyes at his fellow servants. When he arose, he gazed expectantly at the king, waiting for his master to speak first, as a servant should. Lamoni opened his mouth, but no sound came out. Ammon stared at him for a moment, glanced around at the crowd of people, so obviously only a short step away from cowering before him, and pursed his lips, his brow furrowing thoughtfully. He started to say something, then stopped himself with a shake of the head. He cast one more questioning look at the king. When he got no better response, he bowed low to the king once more, and turned to go out again, looking faintly hurt by the rejection.

Ladon was the first to regain the power of speech. The chief herdsman put out a tentative hand, almost but not quite touching Ammon's shoulder. "Rabbanah," he said softly, using the highest honorific he knew. "The king wants you to stay."

Ammon turned again, looking hopefully at Lamoni, but the king still seemed unable to get his voice working. After a moment, Ammon dropped to his knees before Lamoni, eyes and head lowered subserviently. "What may I do for you, O king?" he asked simply. Mikiah thought that single act had probably terrified Lamoni more than anything before it. If he hadn't already been scared speechless, this would have done it twice over. Bad enough to suspect that one had a deity pretending to be one's servant, but to be outright asked to give that deity *orders?* It would have frightened the wits out of greater men than Lamoni.

The room waited, breathless and still, hanging on the question. They waited for a long time. Lamoni could not or would not answer.

Finally, Ammon looked up again. "My king?" he asked once more. "What do you want of me?"

Lamoni tried to speak, but only a faint squeaking noise escaped him.

Suddenly, Ammon smiled, a sweetly innocent smile, and the room seemed to breathe again, something like a sigh of relief. "It's that your servants told you about what happened at the waters of Sebus, isn't it?" he said, and Lamoni looked stunned that Ammon knew what he was thinking. Mikiah couldn't help a soft snort of disgust at the king's credulity. It was hardly a huge leap of the imagination, after all, especially with that pile of arms just sitting there on the floor. They were beginning to emit a faint but persistent smell. "But why does that surprise you?" Ammon continued. "I'm just a man, and I'm your servant. If you ask me to do something, and it's right, I'll do it."

Lamoni stared at him for another moment, a sheen of cold sweat beading his face. He gulped in a deep breath and gripped the arms of his throne with white-knuckled fingers. "*Who—are—you?*" he said hoarsely. "Are you—are you the Great Spirit?"

"The Great Spirit!" Ammon reared back on his knees, his eyebrows going up in shock. Then he smiled again, that same sweet, compassionate smile. "No," he said gently. "I'm not the Great Spirit."

"But then . . . how did you know what I was thinking? And how did you defeat so many of those men all by yourself? Tell me, and I'll—I'll give you anything you ask." Lamoni might or might not have believed Ammon when he denied being the Great Spirit, but he obviously still felt he was dealing with something supernatural, something that might need to be placated. "I'd set my whole army to keep you safe, if you needed it. Not that you do. Obviously." His eyes had strayed to the severed limbs again. "But whatever you want, I'll give it to you."

Mikiah stifled a groan. The idiot was just *asking* to be sheared like a sheep!

Ammon hesitated for a moment. "Will you . . . believe what I tell you? That's all I want."

It wasn't the answer Lamoni had expected, but he'd already committed himself. He gave a short nod of the head. "Yes. I'll believe you." Standing unnoticed in his corner, Mikiah gritted his teeth. He was starting to wonder if King Ashoram shouldn't reconsider marrying this man's daughter, just in case this kind of gullibility was hereditary.

The Nephite drew in a deep breath and a sort of joyful light seemed to kindle behind his eyes, but when he spoke, it was in a calm voice, hiding any hint of triumph that his trick had worked. "If you want to know how I did those things, I'll have to start with something else," he said. He met the king's eyes with the same intense gaze Mikiah had seen from the hilltop, as though he was searching Lamoni's soul. "Do you believe that there is a God?"

Lamoni shook his head in confusion. "I don't know what that means," he said, and Ammon smiled gently.

"Do you believe that there is a Great Spirit?" he amended.

"Yes."

"That's God. Do you believe that the Great Spirit, or God, created all things in heaven and earth?"

Lamoni was still looking a little lost, but he answered as well as he could. "Well . . . yes, I believe He created the earth, but I don't know anything about heaven."

Ammon nodded as though he'd been expecting this. "Heaven is where God lives, and all His holy angels." Mikiah sighed. He'd been sure the Nephite would get angels into the conversation somehow.

"Is heaven above the earth?" Lamoni asked.

Ammon nodded again. "Yes, and God watches over all of us. He knows our thoughts and desires, because He created us in the beginning."

Lamoni took a long moment to consider that. "I believe you," he said finally, studying the Nephite's face intently. "Are you . . . sent from God, then?"

Here it comes, Mikiah thought, but to his surprise Ammon was shaking his head. "I'm just a man," the Nephite said. "Man was created in the image of God, in the beginning. And the Spirit of God called me here to teach your people, so that they'll know the truth. A part of that Spirit stays with me, giving me knowledge, and also power, if I ask for it and have enough faith in God."

"And that's how . . ." Lamoni's awed voice trailed off, his eyes wide with wonder.

So that's his game, Mikiah thought. Who needed wealth when you could influence the wealthy instead? By setting himself up as God's messenger to the Lamanites, Ammon could have all the luxury and power he wanted, with none of the bothersome responsibility of ruling or managing his own riches. If it worked, he'd be living *better* than a king before the week was out.

The next hour was perhaps the worst of Mikiah's life, as the Nephite trickster poured out his lies, and Mikiah didn't dare open his mouth to refute them. His jaw clenched tighter and tighter, holding back the angry words that built up inside him like the pressure of lava building in a volcano. The effort of silence probably would have killed his father, and that thought only made him even more angry. He tried not to listen, but his eyes flashed as phrases like "Fall of Man" and "Great Plan of Redemption" went floating past his ears. The Nephite also trotted out that old lie they'd used for years, claiming that *they* were the rightful rulers of the people, even though they *admitted* that Laman had been the eldest son. Oh, but of course, Laman was *unrighteous* so God had chosen—not Lemuel or Sam, who should have been next in line—but Nephi. Mikiah snorted softly. It was easy to accuse a brother of wickedness when a kingdom was at stake. Mikiah sometimes wondered why Nephi hadn't just killed his older brothers and been done with it, if he was going to steal their birthright like that. Probably because he was a pipsqueak little coward who couldn't stand up to Laman in a fair fight. It sickened Mikiah to think that his own ancestors had followed such a man, a man who only ever gained anything by theft and trickery.

But the worst part was watching Lamoni just *swallow* it all without question. The king hung on Ammon's every word, rapt and fascinated. Mikiah nearly snarled aloud at Lamoni's dumb credulity. Looking around the room just made it worse. There was doubt and skepticism on most faces, but not anger, and that told Mikiah that no one would even protest when Lamoni handed the kingdom to the Nephite. Even the king's son looked more convinced than not, and it was *his* birthright Lamoni was risking. How could anybody be that blind? How could anybody *follow* someone that blind?

"Take it easy, Mikiah," Shehum murmured softly, pulling his friend out of the increasing whirl of rage-laced thoughts. Mikiah turned to look at him, meeting Shehum's concerned look with a sharp glare. "Calm down," the Lamanite insisted. "Or you'll give us all away."

Mikiah drew in a deep breath and held it, turning to his training to help him tune out the hateful words that beat at him. He let the breath out slowly and evenly, counting silently. When he'd reached the count of thirty, he was back in control of himself. He gave Shehum a thankful nod.

"We've got to get out of here," he murmured to his companions, speaking low so no one else could hear them. "Lamoni is buying every bit of this tripe. He's going to do exactly what the Nephite tells him to. Ashoram needs to know about this."

Shehum nodded sharply in agreement, but Eliah looked disappointed. "What about her?" he asked, indicating the cluster of the king's daughters on the far side of the room with a small inclination of his head. Temisah was listening intently to what Ammon told her father, and her eyes shone in a way that Mikiah didn't like.

Mikiah opened his mouth to say that this was more important than Ashoram's matrimonial adventures, but just then Lamoni lurched off his throne. Falling to his knees on the golden sandstone, the king lifted his eyes to heaven and cried aloud.

"Oh Lord, have mercy!" he said fervently. "According to the abundant mercy which thou hast had upon the people of Nephi, have upon me, and my people!"

He knelt there for a moment, his eyes still upturned, his face full of his newly found, misguided faith. Then he drew in a sharp breath and toppled over, collapsing to lie limp and motionless across the floor in front of his own throne.

There was a brief, shocked silence, broken by a wordless shout of denial. A confused babble rose all around Mikiah and his friends, increasing to near hysteria within seconds. The king had fainted. The king was dead. The Nephite had killed the king. The Nephite's God had struck the king down for presuming to address himself to deity. The true Great Spirit had punished the king for turning to a false god. The Nephite was an angel. The Nephite was a monster. The babble rose to a frightened tumult, and—most importantly—*every guard in the room had rushed forward to protect the king.*

Which meant that no one was paying any attention to guarding the rest of King Lamoni's household.

Mikiah smiled, thinking quickly. "Looks to me like we'll be taking her with us," he said. In spite of everything, Eliah grinned in anticipation and Shehum's eyes sparkled.

Mikiah had spent a lot of time in King Lamoni's court. Enough to know, for instance, that the king's daughters loved strawberries and would reliably go out hunting for them if they happened to hear a rumor about a new patch. Admittedly, he'd never seen the court in this kind of uproar—the death or near-death of a king by possibly supernatural means was a singular occurrence—but he knew the people there well enough to guess at what they would do. As far as he could tell, the most likely explanation for the king's collapse was simply the combination of terror and hysteria caused by the Nephite's deception. Possibly Lamoni had a weak heart, like Minek, in which case the extreme excitement and whiplashed emotions had most likely been the death of him. No one was making any official announcements, of course, but Mikiah wouldn't have been surprised. Whether he was dead or near death, though, Temisah *was* his favorite daughter, and she honestly and devotedly loved her father. Mikiah had gotten to know her, as was only appropriate for his king's future wife. He knew that Temisah wasn't the kind of girl who was capable of mourning publicly.

So when she ran into her bedchamber less than an hour after her father's collapse, weeping violently, Mikiah and his friends were already there, waiting for her. Mikiah's arms closed around her from behind before she'd even realized they were there, one elbow crooked tight against her throat. He only had to hold her for a few struggling seconds before she went limp in his arms, blissfully unconscious. He lifted her easily and carried her to lie on her bed.

"The rope," he whispered to Eliah. "Remember, tight enough she won't get away, not so tight it hurts her. This is Ashoram's bride, after all."

"And we can't have her all sore and swollen about the wrists and ankles on her wedding day," Eliah agreed. He wound the rope deftly around the girl's slender wrists, tying her securely but not harshly. "I can see why he's going to all the trouble," Eliah continued, eyeing Temisah's delicate beauty. Lamoni's daughter was petite, her triangular face and gently pointed chin framed by a long fall of sleek, black hair. Her high cheekbones and small nose gave her an almost child-like look, but the long-fingered hands were already skillful in every womanly task. Although her eyes were closed now, Mikiah could remember their liquid, deep brown color, like staring into the depths of a forest pool. Those eyes would go dark with rage when she woke up and discovered what had happened to her—which would probably make her even more attractive to Ashoram.

"Keep your eyes to yourself," Shehum said, smacking Eliah sharply on the crown of his head. "And your hands too, for that matter. How long do you think she'll be out, Mikiah?" he continued, eyeing the girl himself with a more calculating air, though Mikiah saw a hint of the same admiration there as well. "Should we use the drug?"

"I think so," Mikiah said. "It'll take some time to get out of the city. After that, she can squirm all she wants, but we want her quiet till we're well on our way."

Shehum nodded agreement, pulling at the string of a wine skin he kept slung at his side. The wine it contained was heavily laced with the extract of a rare plant, and would keep the girl quietly dreaming for at least an hour. Mikiah knelt down and gently held Temisah's mouth open while Shehum poured a measured dollop down her throat. Once Eliah had wrapped a muffling gag over her mouth, she was as ready for the trip as they could make her. Of course, they couldn't just carry an unconscious girl away from the king's palace without someone noticing, which was why Mikiah had mostly emptied the clothes chest he found at the foot of Temisah's bed. It was a large box with rings set into the sides for the lifting poles. They lowered the girl gently into it, curled on her side on the last layer of dresses with her hands bound behind her, and layered a thick blanket on top of her. There was still a good amount of space available on top when they'd lowered the lid and locked the hasp down, which was just what Mikiah wanted. If Temisah had known what he planned for the next step, she probably would have been just as glad to be unconscious for it. Things were about to get messier.

"You three! What're you doing in here?"

Mikiah nearly jumped at the guard's barked question, although he'd been half-expecting something like it from the moment they entered the throne room. He put down the arm he was holding and straightened to meet the man's challenge. Eliah and Shehum ignored them, continuing their gruesome work.

"We're moving these things," Mikiah told the guard, stepping forward to keep him from coming too close. "Just in case it was some effect of their putrefaction that struck the king down." That caught the guard's attention, and he backed a step. The box was now full to the brim with severed arms. They'd been sitting in the late afternoon heat for many hours now, and gave off a rank and sweetly nauseating smell. The guard raised a hand to cover his nose. "We'll take them out into the country and burn them properly," Mikiah continued. "Even if they weren't what made the king sick, we don't want them laying around stinking the place up."

The guard hesitated, but there was nothing he could argue with. He glowered at the box, and at Eliah carefully tucking in a limp hand that dangled over the edge. Mikiah could see the relenting in his eyes before he spoke. "Yes, all right," he said gruffly. "Get it out of here, and be quick about it."

"Right away!" Mikiah said, slamming the lid down and deftly securing the hasp. Eliah and Shehum stepped in between the bars at either end and quickly lifted them to their shoulders. The three spies jogged out of the throne room and down the palace steps, heading for the city gates and the open countryside. It was lengthening toward dark now, and they wanted to be past the farmlands and well into the forest before they stopped that night.

Four

Wilderness, Land of Midian, 90 BC

Mikiah lifted the lid of the box and stepped back quickly. Shehum was already nursing a splendid black eye from the last time they'd let the girl out. They'd taken the layer of arms out well before she woke and left them somewhere just inside the forest. At least now she had more room in there and didn't have to breathe in that stench, but they couldn't just leave her to starve and lie in her own filth for the two days it would take to get back to Jerusalem. They'd learned to be more cautious about it, however. Even tied up, Lamoni's daughter knew how to kick!

He looked down at her, meeting her dark-eyed glare with a calm interest that only seemed to infuriate her all the more. As he'd guessed, she *was* even more attractive when she was enraged.

"You're thirsty," he said finally. "Don't try denying it. It's hot and you've been in there for hours. I'll let you get away with starving yourself if you want, but you need water." The glare increased by several notches of intensity, but she granted him a jerky nod. He knelt beside the box and reached out to pull the gag down around her neck. It was awkward, holding the water skin up for her. With her hands tied behind her, she had a hard time propping herself up enough to drink, and a few times she had to let the water pour over her chin because Mikiah couldn't tell when she needed to stop for air. Finally, she turned her head away when he offered her more. Even with the gag off, she refused to speak to them, as if that rejection of what was happening would somehow make it all just a dream she could wake from.

"I don't know what good you think you'll do yourself by getting so upset about this," Mikiah told her, reasonably. "It's not like you're the first woman to be stolen for a wife, and the Amulonite women don't seem to have minded much in the end. Ashoram is a good man—and a good king. You'll be his queen. Your children will rule Jerusalem. And you have to admit a man would have to love a woman deeply to go to all this trouble to get her."

She snorted, disdain and incredulity mingling in her chocolate-brown stare. It was the closest she'd come to actually speaking.

Mikiah's eyebrows drew together. "If you're upset about the travel arrangements, you can blame your father for that. If he'd negotiated in good faith, you would have taken this road in a litter, surrounded by servants and handmaids and attendants. But Ashoram won't be made a fool. Your father should have known that."

Temisah drew in a hissing breath. If she'd been able to kill Mikiah with her eyes, he would have already burst into flame. "My father!" she snarled, and his eyes widened at the venomous hatred in her voice. "Don't you *dare* talk about my father! He might be dead now, and you dare talk like I should be *happy* to be stolen away while he lay dying?! Your Ashoram is a *pig!* He doesn't love me! He doesn't even know me! And a man who loved me certainly wouldn't treat me like this—like I'm just some kind of precious prize to be stolen and bundled into a box and carted home!" Mikiah opened his mouth to say something—he hardly knew what—but she rolled right over him. "I don't care what you say, and I don't care what *he* does. I swear by heaven I will *fight* you both to my dying breath, with every weapon I possess. I would rather die than be married to the king of swine!" She stopped, panting with rage, her brown eyes sharp as daggers, her long hair seeming to crackle around her with the force of her fury.

Mikiah met her anger with a studied tranquility, fighting his own rising temper. "You should calm down," he said evenly, but now there was just the slightest edge of threat in his voice. "You might do yourself a mischief, getting all worked up like that. Do you want some food?"

She turned her face away from him. He waited a moment longer, to see if she would change her mind. When she just continued to stare off into the trees, he reached out to tug the gag back into place.

Swift as a striking serpent, her head twisted and her teeth sank into the flesh of his hand, nearly hard enough to draw blood. He jerked back before she could bite any harder, and his fist flew in pure, instinctive response. He managed at the last second to turn it into a vicious slap rather than the brutal punch it started as, but the force of it slammed her back against the side of the box, whipped her head sideways, and split her lower lip against her own teeth.

He started back a step, staring in horror at what he'd done. Temisah lay curled in her box, her whole body shaking. But the shaking was—laughter. She was laughing at him—great, racking sobs of laughter. She turned her face to him, grinning up at him—a predator's grin with blood-stained teeth. "Every. Weapon," she told him again. This time he believed her.

"Eliah! Shehum!" he barked, calling his friends from resting beside the river. His hand throbbed angrily. "We're running through tonight," he told them when they scrambled into view. "There's a full moon; it should be bright enough. We can be in Jerusalem by dawn." He met Temisah's hate-filled glare with a challenging stare of his own. "Let's get this wildcat into the hands of her tamer."

Shehum frowned, staring at the blood on Temisah's lip. The Lamanite's hands twitched toward his satchel and the ointments and bandages he carried, but then he shook his head. He absentmindedly touched the dark bruise Temisah had given him, but the look he gave Mikiah was far too close to an accusing glare. Mikiah pushed his guilt down and glared back.

Eliah raised an eyebrow, noticing the bite mark on Mikah's hand and the girl's defiant, jaw-clenched snarl. "Well, if Ashoram wanted adventure in his marriage, I think he's got it."

FIVE

CITY OF JERUSALEM, 90 BC

"AND HE *BELIEVED* IT?" ASHORAM'S HAZEL EYES CHANGED TO GREEN sometimes, in response to strong emotion. They'd been the color of spring leaves when he saw Temisah carried in, struggling and spitting defiance, but his at last. Mikiah's report had taken his mind momentarily away from his approaching nuptials, however, and the green had been darkened and muddied by this new worry.

Mikiah nodded in response. "Swallowed it whole," he confirmed. "Didn't even chew on it first."

Ashoram grimaced, and Mikiah could see the king's mind twisting through all the convoluted political considerations. Mikiah himself was gifted when it came to tactics and tricks, predicting behavior and using it to his advantage. But he'd never developed the mind for long-term strategy as Ashoram had, and he watched the turning wheels with interest, wondering where they'd end up. He guessed it wasn't going to be anywhere good—not with Nephites involved.

"Sheer luck or wild coincidence," Ashoram said finally. "Lamoni won't dare attack me when I have his daughter."

"*Attack* you?!" Mikiah echoed, shocked. It wasn't a thought that had even crossed his mind.

Ashoram gave him a wry smile. "Of course. What else do you think the Nephites are doing here? Oh, they'll try to conquer us with conversion if they can, but if that doesn't work?" He made a tossing gesture with one hand. "The Nephites want to rule this land completely. They always have. And if they can get enough converts among the Lamanites to form any kind of army . . ."

"They'll have us pincered," Mikiah finished the thought, catching up with his king's foresight. "The Nephites attack from Zarahemla in the north, while their Lamanite dupes come at us from the south."

"But thanks to your efforts, even if Lamoni recovers and agrees to help the Nephites, *I've* got the perfect hostage. And if he dies, his son won't want to risk Temisah's life either. Especially not if it means facing us in open war. King Laman wouldn't like that, not at all." Ashoram gave his spy a wolf's grin. Lamoni's father was king over the land of Nephi, which had been the Nephite capital until the Lamanites conquered it several generations back and forced the survivors to flee for their lives. The name could be a bit confusing, but Mikiah had always appreciated the subtle taunt, a constant reminder to the Nephites that the Lamanites had taken their homeland. From the city of Nephi, King Laman ruled all the other kings of the Lamanite lands, and he wasn't known to be a very forgiving man, even with his own family. In fact, he'd been known to be downright bloodthirsty when he felt the occasion called for it. A son or grandson who started an internal war without the king's permission would soon find out that there were much worse things than losing a mere girl to a forced marriage.

"Still, even with that advantage, we'll want to keep an eye on the situation," Ashoram mused. "Did Lamoni survive? That's the important question. And if he did, did his conversion survive as well? It could be that he just needed some kind of jolt to bring him to his senses, in which case he'll be rid of the Nephite preacher as quick as he can. If he didn't survive, the Nephites'll have his son to deal with, and the boy'll probably blame this Ammon for his father's death. Problem solved. Or at least avoided for the moment."

"Maybe I should go back to Ishmael?" Mikiah suggested. "Make *sure* the problem is solved?"

But Ashoram shook his head, his eyes thoughtful. "No, not you. You're getting too well known there. I'll send one of your friends for that. Probably Shehum; he's quieter. I'll need to inform Temisah's family about our marriage, anyway. No, I've got another problem for you to solve."

"What's that?"

"These other preachers, the ones you saw in Ani-Anti. You said they were headed south?"

Mikiah nodded, and Ashoram scowled.

"That makes them a threat as well. Possibly a greater threat, since we don't know where they are or how much success they've had." His hazel eyes met Mikiah's, challenging. "I need you to find them, Mikiah. Find them and stop them, however you can. This land will *not* fall to the Nephites—not if I can help it—and you're the best I have to send."

Mikiah bowed his head, a hungry anticipation stirring. "As you wish, my king," he said formally. He turned to go, already imagining what he could do to the Nephites when he caught them.

"Oh, and Mikiah?" Ashoram called him back, and now his voice was almost hesitant. "There's one other thing you could do for me." The king's smile was a mixture of pride, amusement, and a hidden worry. He looked strangely vulnerable, and Mikiah remembered suddenly—as he rarely did—that his king wasn't all that much older than he was. "It's—well, it's Temisah. I think, maybe, she needs some time to . . . adjust." Obviously, that first sight of his wildly ferocious intended bride had given Ashoram some second thoughts. He'd said he could handle her smiling or screaming, when he'd sent Mikiah off to fetch her, but perhaps he hadn't counted on a wife who might well try to kill him at the first opportunity. "Do you think your sister would be willing to come spend some time with her? Sort of help her come to terms with—with everything?"

Mikiah offered his king a wryly compassionate smile. "I think we could arrange that."

He let Nabeth go in by herself to meet the future queen. "I think you'll have a better chance with her if I'm not there," he told his sister.

Nabeth gave him a reproving look. "Mikiah? What did you do to the poor girl?"

"Nothing!" Mikiah protested automatically, and then remembered his hand striking her cheek and felt his face go red with shame. "Well, nothing on purpose. Aside from—I mean, she didn't really want to come here, and I'm one the one who brought her, so . . ."

"So she probably never wants to see you again in her life," Nabeth finished for him. "It's barbaric, you know, the way kings trade their daughters around like livestock. Has she even *met* Ashoram before today?"

"Umm . . ." Mikiah wondered if the first time Ashoram had seen Temisah counted as a meeting. It had been almost exactly a year ago. King Laman had commanded all the rulers of his people to join him in the city of Nephi for a great feast, and Lamoni had brought his daughter. Mikiah didn't know if Ashoram had actually talked with the girl then, but he'd certainly *seen* her. His eyes had still been glowing with the sight when he came home afterward.

"I thought so," Nabeth said, taking his hesitation as an answer. Her eyes glinted angrily at him. "Men! I don't think I'd *let* you come in with me, even if you wanted to. Between you and Ashoram, you've caused enough grief already." She flapped her hands at him. "Go on, shoo! Go do something masculine with your friends, like grunting and comparing the size of your clubs. *If possible,* try to make it something I won't have to clean up for you afterward."

She turned her back on him and strode into Temisah's room, her feet pounding against the polished stone floor as if she had a grudge against it, her back straight and tight. Mikiah grinned after her, not believing for a moment that she was as upset as she pretended to be. His sister never insulted him when she was *really* angry; she was too busy projecting a freezing, silent fury that he could feel from the other side of Jerusalem. All the same, he almost wished he could be there to witness the meeting between the two women. He suspected their temperaments were very similar, and he was curious whether they'd clash or connect to start out with. If they did end up combining their talents, he wasn't sure the city would still be standing when it was all over.

But he wouldn't be there to find out, not even how this first meeting would go. He had a trio of Nephite preachers to find, and they already had several days' head start on him. He had no time to waste if he was going to prevent the war Ashoram saw coming.

Six

City of Middoni, 90 BC

The path of the Nephites turned out to be ridiculously easy to follow. They hadn't exactly been hiding, after all, spreading their lies in every city, village, and farmstead they came to. Tracking them was a simple matter of asking around to find out which way they'd headed once they learned that people weren't inclined to listen to them. They hadn't been moving very quickly, either, so when Mikiah reached the city of Middoni, he was only a few hours behind them.

He found them preaching in the market near the city gates, and they'd found a new way of doing things. Aaron was the one doing all the talking this time (and now that Mikiah had had a chance to take a close look at them both, he was almost certain that Aaron was Ammon's brother), but Muloki and Ammah lurked nearby. Mikiah had to sit and watch them for quite a while before he figured out what they were doing. For the most part, the people of Middoni ignored Aaron. Some stopped to argue, and many who were too polite to say anything gave him looks that clearly showed the kind of things they *wanted* to say. But every so often—maybe once in an hour—someone would pause to listen, and something like wonder or curiosity would flicker across their faces. Then they would move on. Their curiosity wasn't enough to risk the ridicule of the crowd by stopping for more than a moment. When that happened, Aaron simply went on preaching, but Muloki or Ammah would casually push off from the wall they leaned against and follow the curious person for a little way. Once they were out of the public glare, the Nephite would stop them and have a short conversation. About half of these ended with frowns and shaking heads, but the other half didn't, and that was half too many for Mikiah's peace of mind.

As the sun puddled itself on the distant horizon, casting long shadows across the market, Aaron finally gave it up. He'd been talking loudly all afternoon without stopping, and Mikiah couldn't understand how he still had a voice left. The Nephites weren't exactly jubilant as they walked past the closing market stalls, but there was an air of tempered satisfaction about them, as if they thought their new plan might just work. They didn't notice the shadow that followed them, flitting down the narrow streets silently as a ghost.

Mikiah came to rest in the darkness outside a long, narrow building in one of the less pleasant areas of the city. He watched the light of a feeble lantern drift from window to window and followed it, crouching finally where it stopped. The sounds and smells coming through the window were enough to tell him what kind of building it was.

"If your father could see this!" he heard Ammah say. "A king's son sleeping in a cowshed."

"Yes, well, he doesn't know, and he's not going to know," Aaron replied mildly. "I had a hard enough time convincing him to let me come in the first place."

"We could have stayed at the inn," Muloki offered, but Aaron snorted.

"No, we couldn't. Not unless we wanted to lie and say we're Amulonites or Amalekites. The inns here don't cater to Nephites. Are you prepared to lie, just so you'll have a comfortable bed to sleep in? You think that's the way the Lord would want us to behave?" It sounded like Muloki gave a regretful sigh, but they both must have shaken their heads because Aaron continued, "I didn't think so. And what do we have to complain about?" His voice brightened cheerfully. "We've got a roof over our heads, enough to eat, soft hay to sleep in, and—most importantly—tomorrow we'll be able to go and teach people in their own homes. And if even some of them believe us, this whole trip will have been worth it. We're finally getting somewhere!"

Mikiah growled to himself. *Not if I can help it, Nephite,* he vowed silently. *Nephite, son of a Nephite king.* Ashoram must have been right, he thought. If the Nephite king was sending his sons here, this must all be a Nephite ploy to gain control over the Lamanites—to rule the whole land as their ancestor had wanted to do from the beginning.

Mikiah presented himself formally to the guard at the palace gates early the next morning. "Message for King Antiomno of Middoni from King Ashoram of Jerusalem!" he said crisply, holding up his message satchel as evidence.

The guard frowned at him. "What, did you run through the night?" he asked incredulously.

"It's a very important message," Mikiah said, with just a hint of reproach in his voice. It wasn't a lie, even if it wasn't the answer the guard thought it was.

"All right, all right," the guard grunted, unimpressed. "Give it to me; I'll get it to the king."

"It's a *very important* message," Mikiah repeated, as though shocked at the very suggestion. "I have to deliver it in person!"

The guard sighed, recognizing the slicked-down keenness of a man who would obey instructions to the last iota, regardless of how inconvenient it was for everyone else. Mikiah felt an inward smile. There were very few people who could out-stubborn a true stickler, someone who followed rules simply because they were rules and never thought about *why*. Most guards wouldn't even try, not without a very good reason. Resigning himself, the guard waved for Mikiah to follow and trudged into the palace to look for King Antiomno.

The king was still at breakfast when Mikiah was ushered, with exaggerated formality, into his presence. The room was small, but bright and airy, with large, soft cushions and an ornately carved wooden table covered with rich dishes. The king barely even glanced up from his plate at their entrance. "All right, hand it over," Antiomno grunted, biting into a banana. "Let's see what Ashoram thinks is so all-fired important that a man can't even finish his meal."

Mikiah started to reply, but then stopped himself and glared dramatically at the guard who'd followed him into the room. The man snorted derisively, but gave a casual shrug and left this troublesome messenger alone with the king to deliver his *very important* message.

"Well, what is it?" Antiomno asked again. The king of Middoni was a stout, round-faced man, his black hair just beginning to go gray at the temples. Sitting there with a sumptuous meal spread before him and half-eaten, he didn't look very awe-inspiring as a king, but the flash of his black eyes was familiarly demanding. Perhaps his lax manner was just a show.

"I don't actually have a written message for you, O king," Mikiah admitted, dropping the act. "I've come to warn you."

Antiomno's eyebrows jumped upward. "Warn me? Of what?"

"Treason, O king," Mikiah told him grimly. "Treason and sedition being spread among your people."

"I find that very difficult to believe." Antiomno settled back, regarding Mikiah with measuring eyes. "My people are generally content and well provided for. I'd say they annoy me more with throwing too many parties than with complaints. What makes you think such a thing is happening?"

"Because I've seen it," Mikiah insisted. "I've heard them with my own ears. It isn't your people, though. They're outsiders—Nephites. I've heard them questioning your right to rule." Well, if the Nephite version of history didn't count as that, he didn't know what would. "And there are those who are listening to them."

The king's face darkened like the sky before a storm. "How many?" he asked, and his voice held the threatening rumble of approaching thunder.

"Not many. Not yet. But you know how that kind of thing spreads. If even one of your people believes . . ."

He could see the idea worrying at Antiomno's composure, but still the king hesitated, suspicious. "How do you know all this?" he asked. "Why did Ashoram send you here?"

Mikiah smiled grimly. "Sometimes a messenger's job is to listen instead of speak and to see instead of being seen."

Antiomno grunted. "So you're a spy."

"But not spying on you," Mikiah agreed, raising an eyebrow. "I've been watching these Nephites, and they are devious. You might almost think they actually believed their own lies." Mikiah grimaced. "But one of them is the son of the Nephite king." He nodded at Antiomno's sudden look of intense calculation. "That's right. Why would a king's son be here, if not in the hopes of expanding the kingdom he'll inherit one day?"

"I see," Antiomno said, and now his dark eyes were hard and determined, with no trace of self-contented indolence. "I do see indeed."

"How many people do we *need* to take on three stupid Nephites?" the captain of Antiomno's guard groused. Jubek and twenty of his best men were following obediently at Mikiah's heels through the gloomy streets, but that obedience obviously didn't keep them from voicing their thoughts. And Jubek's thoughts revolved around just how overcautious—or some might even call it cowardly—it looked to send twenty men, armed to the teeth, after a mere three religious preachers. In normal circumstances, Mikiah would have agreed with him. But these weren't normal circumstances.

"Don't be overconfident," he warned the captain. "One of these men has a brother who killed and disabled fifteen men single-handed. If any of these have the same kind of training . . ." He trailed off grimly, but Jubek gave a bark of laughter.

"Oh sure," he said derisively. "Fifteen men, was it? Hah! Stories like that always grow in the telling. More likely it was two men and a lame dog!"

Mikiah whirled on him, grabbing one arm so he could pull the Lamanite close and glare straight into his surprised eyes. "Are you questioning my word?" Mikiah hissed. "I was *there.* I *saw* it happen. I still don't know *how* he did it, but I'm telling you he did. And I know it was fifteen because I helped gather up their severed arms afterward. That's not something you forget, and it's not something you need to exaggerate. It happened," he finished, his voice flat and unequivocal.

Jubek stared at him, shocked. "He cut off their *arms?*" he finally asked.

Mikiah nodded. "On purpose. And walked away from it without a scratch. I don't even think he was breathing hard. Now be quiet." He turned and stalked toward the final turning. "We're nearly there."

Mikiah had followed the Nephites around all day as they made their visits, marking in his memory the houses that had welcomed them in and listened to their lies. They'd need to deal with those people later. But for now, the Nephites had returned to the makeshift shelter of the stable, probably already drifting toward sleep. If one of them *was* another Ammon, it was the perfect time to take them, unaware and unprepared.

"All right, captain," he said as the stable came into sight, its windows thankfully dark. "They'll be in there, probably somewhere in the center where the hay is stored. How do *you* think we should take them?"

Jubek studied the stable in the moonlight, and Mikiah was pleased to see that he looked more worried than he had been. He might still have doubts about Mikiah's story, but at least he'd been warned, and he seemed prepared to *act* like it was all true, whether he believed it completely or not. He gathered his men around him with a gesture and gave his orders in a whisper. "Pay attention, boys," he said. "We're going in silent and soft, all right? Pretend you're tracking a bear in there. Move carefully and keep your weapons ready. Don't take a step until you're sure what you're stepping on. Those of you with the torches, keep them dark, but ready to light at a moment's notice. We'll stay dark either until I give the word or until they notice us, whichever comes first. Everybody got it?" A soft murmur of assent came out of the darkness. "Then let's go."

As they moved off, Mikiah heard one of the guards mutter, "Only an idiot tracks bear at night," but he couldn't tell who had said it.

It was almost black inside the stable, even with the moonlight shining in through the windows. Mikiah slipped in through a window near one end of the building, lowering himself slowly and carefully into one of the pens. The animal inside didn't even wake up as he moved past it. The other guards were making their own ways into the building, moving silently as shadows, avoiding the beams of moonlight that might offer a betraying gleam. Creeping and cautious, the silent tide of men moved farther in, closer to their goal.

"*Muloki! Ammah!*" The startled shout rang through the darkness, and Mikiah cursed. He didn't know what had given them away, but they weren't close enough. Even caught unprepared, the Nephites would have time to arm themselves while the Lamanite guards ran at them.

Torches flared around them, giving light to pounding feet. It came too late for at least one of the guards—Mikiah heard him trip over a bucket and fall on his face half a second before the light hit him. But they still outnumbered the Nephites seven to one and had the advantage of surprise. "Get them!" Jubek shouted, and the guards rushed forward, prepared to swarm the startled Nephites.

Mikiah was near the front and had a clear view of Aaron's face. He saw the Nephite preacher's eyes dart around, flicking over the torches, the running men, the animals, the brandished weapons shining in the firelight. Then, strangely, Aaron shot a glance down at the ground he stood on—or rather the hay he stood in, for the Nephites had obviously been curled up in the soft fodder to sleep.

"Hold on!" Aaron yelled, dropping the sword he carried into the hay and raising his hands.

It was such an unexpected thing for the Nephite to do that several of the guards did pause in their wild charge. The others began to slow as well, turning to look at Jubek for instructions. The captain hesitated a moment, but raised a hand to halt his men. He cast a puzzled glance at Mikiah, but Mikiah could only shake his head. He didn't know what the Nephite was doing either.

"If we fight in here," Aaron called, once he saw that he had their attention, "someone will drop a torch. The hay will catch fire, the animals will burn to death, and possibly so will we."

"So, you want to take this outside?" someone said, mocking, and there was a small outbreak of sniggering.

Aaron gave them a tiny half-smile, but he shook his head, and Mikiah could see that his eyes were grim. "No," he said. "We don't want to kill any of you, either, and we'd be just as glad if you didn't try to kill us." He turned to his companions. "Muloki, Ammah, drop your swords. If King Antiomno wants us arrested, we'll go peacefully."

Mikiah saw several mouths drop open as the other two Nephites also abandoned their weapons to the straw at their feet and raised their hands. He felt the hollow singing of disappointment in his chest, and his eyes narrowed, studying Aaron with a calculating gaze. *What game are you playing, Nephite?* he wondered, watching as Aaron and his companions meekly allowed themselves to be bound hand and foot, hoisted onto the guards' shoulders, and carried away.

Early the next morning, Mikiah had part of an answer. He stood in the center of the bare room, glowering into an empty corner with his arms crossed tightly over his chest. There should have been people there. A whole family had lived in this room the day before, a family that had let the Nephites in and listened to them. Now they were gone, bag and baggage, just like all the others.

Growling an oath, Mikiah turned on his heel and stalked out into the street. The Nephites must have warned them—somehow. Or even worse, this could all be part of their plan. Those people might have been *sent* somewhere, sent with a purpose to help the Nephite invasion. Maybe to spread their lies even further, to turn more people to their way of thinking. The Nephite religion was like a willow tree: cut it down and it just grew back even more thickly.

The prison was a stout, ugly building in the poorest part of the city. Its walls were built of thick, gray stone, windowless and cold. The guard on the single door let Mikiah inside without question, and Mikiah stepped into the stinking, torch-lit cell. He paused just inside for a moment, peering into the shadows, before he saw the three hunched figures in one corner.

The Nephites had been stripped. The ropes that held their wrists and ankles were drawn cruelly tight, biting deep into their flesh, and their bound wrists were secured to metal rings set in the wall. As his eyes adjusted to the darkness, Mikiah could see clear signs that some of the guards had been expressing their displeasure with the three prisoners. Half of Muloki's face was dark with bruising, one eye swollen shut, and Ammah was curled around himself, listing to one side as he favored cracked ribs. Aaron was the worst off, though. He lay half-sprawled—as much as the ropes would let him—barely conscious, a bloody gash across one side of his head. His breath made an unnatural fluttering sound in his chest. The other two did their best to get between him and Mikiah when they saw the Amalekite. Mikiah snorted at their stupidity. That very protectiveness was probably what had inspired the guards to pay special attention to Aaron.

Mikiah was glad the guards hadn't given all three the full treatment. It was probably just an extra dollop of psychological cruelty, leaving the other two fully alert and unable to help their friend. Mikiah didn't particularly care what happened to any of the Nephites—in trying to conquer the Lamanites, they'd more than earned whatever they got, and he hoped to see them stopped, permanently. But that was for later. Right now, with frustration and anger boiling inside him, what he wanted were answers—and the chance to beat those answers out of this scum with his own hands.

He stood a moment, looming over the prisoners with the torchlight at his back, a black shape glowering down at them. "Where are they?" he asked, his voice a harsh growl.

There was no answer. Ammah and Muloki simply glared at him, their lips pressed shut.

"*Where are they?!*" Mikiah snarled, snatching Ammah up by both arms and slamming him back against the stone wall. The Nephite cried out in pain, but said nothing. "*Where?!*"

"I don't know what you're talking about," Ammah gasped, struggling to free himself from Mikiah's painful grip.

Mikiah dropped him and rammed a fist into his weak side. He cried out again, falling, but Mikiah slammed his shoulders into the wall once more. "Don't lie to me, you sack of dung. You warned them somehow. Or you sent them off to do more of your dirty work. *I want to know where!*"

"I don't know what you're talking about!" Ammah insisted.

Mikiah's fist lashed out again, and Ammah let out a strangled scream.

"*Who?!*" Muloki's desperate, croaking shout brought Mikiah whirling toward him, letting Ammah slump back to huddle on the stone floor. "Where *who* are?" Muloki asked again, his speech slurring around swollen lips. "We don't know who you mean!"

Mikiah growled, advancing on the other prisoner now. "Your mud-sucking *converts,* of course! Where did you send them?"

Muloki's good eye widened. "But—but we don't know! I swear we don't know!" He cowered away from Mikiah's wrath, obviously terrified. "We didn't tell them to go anywhere!"

Mikiah growled again, but in frustration this time. He was a spy, which meant he observed people, and he'd seen honest fear enough to know the Nephite wasn't acting. Mikiah wished he could convince himself otherwise, but both the surprise and the fear were genuine. Muloki truly hadn't known that the people he'd talked to the day before were gone, or where they might have run off to, and he was terrified the Amalekite wouldn't believe him. Mikiah—utterly unexpectedly—felt a flash of something almost like compassion. To be tortured for information that one did not, in fact, have, and therefore *couldn't* betray . . .

With a muffled oath, Mikiah whirled away, stalking back toward the door. He left the Nephites huddled in the dark, and as far as he was concerned they could rot there. It *wasn't* compassion that made him go, he told himself, it was just common sense. He wasn't a torturer—he didn't have the skill or the stomach for it—and he didn't want to accidentally kill them before they'd been wrung dry of information. He'd leave that part up to Antiomno.

By the time he got back to the king's palace, he'd almost managed to convince himself that the flicker of unwelcome emotion had never happened at all.

The rippling, metallic snarls echoed from the sides of the pit. Lithe black shadows twisted and curved in the depths, impatiently pacing the circumference of their prison or stretching up against the sides, reaching with sharply clawed paws toward the light.

"They're always bad tempered just before feeding time," Antiomno said placidly. He pitched a hunk of meat over the edge. The offering was greeted by a chorus of growls and shrieks as the panthers fought over the morsel. Antiomno threw in another handful. "To tell the truth, they're bad tempered most of the time. That's one of the reasons I like having them around." He listened to the reverberating growls for another moment, then shrugged and planted his foot on the haunch of wild peccary, shoving it over the edge. "So no luck?" Antiomno asked, leaning slightly over the edge to watch the big cats feed.

"No." Mikiah didn't like admitting it, and the word came out full of frustration. "Half a dozen families just up and disappeared. I can't find any trace of them."

"And the guards at the city gates?"

Mikiah sighed. "They're supposed to watch for people coming in, not going out. They didn't see anything."

"They would have noticed if a large group left at once, though," the third man at the edge of the pit offered. He was also watching the panthers intently, actually sitting on the brim with his legs dangling over, bouncing his bare heels off the stone wall. He was an older man, possibly in his late forties, his dark skin weathered by years of sun and rain, his hands scarred by bow and arrow, spear and sling and knife. "They must have gone out in bits and pieces, one or two at a time." The man grunted, a short bark of almost-laughter. "If I find them, I'll make sure they come back in bits and pieces too."

Antiomno smiled drily. "Mikiah, this is Cherom. He's my . . . hunter."

Cherom turned and met Mikiah's eyes for a moment, and Mikiah didn't need the significant pause to know exactly what Cherom was. He recognized the calculation behind the genial mask, the hidden awareness of everything around them, and knew he was meeting his Middonite counterpart, Antiomno's chief spy. He gave the man a wary nod of recognition, one professional to another, and received the same nod in reply.

"What about the Nephites?" Antiomno continued, when it was obvious the two spies weren't going to start chatting anytime soon.

Mikiah lifted his hands. "They claim they know nothing about it. And—" He gave a frustrated growl. "For what it's worth, I believe them. I doubt they'll be able to tell you anything you don't already know." Now Mikiah took his own turn looking down at the grisly meal taking place below them. "Possibly we can find a different use for them. Those cats certainly are hungry, aren't they?" he said with a significantly raised eyebrow.

Antiomno laughed. "Well, that's one solution."

"But probably not the best one," Cherom said quietly. "Even if they don't know where our people have gone, they may be able to tell us something else, like exactly what the Nephite king is planning. Give me a few days with them; I'll see what I can find out."

"What did you have in mind?" Antiomno asked.

"Oh . . . starvation, perhaps. It might take a bit longer, but it's much less messy. Less chance of unfortunate mistakes, you know. And even if they don't know anything, they might still be useful. Hostages. Ransom, maybe. Death is just so permanent." He gave his king a cheerful grin that was, in context, a bit frightening.

Antiomno nodded slowly. "Good point. Yes, we'll keep them alive for now. No point in rushing things. And anyway, the cats have just eaten. If we feed them too often, they get fat and lose their edge, and then they're no fun anymore." He pouted, and Mikiah was sure now that it was an act for his benefit. "So we'll have to keep our guests at *least* until feeding time tomorrow. Maybe watching one of them go down a panther's throat will loosen the tongues of the others."

"As long as the one you choose isn't the one who knows everything," Cherom said, and Antiomno gave a deep sigh.

"Fine, have it all your way!" he said, tossing his hands. "But you realize we'll have to take the time to fatten them back up after you're done starving them if we're going to satisfy Mikiah here."

Cherom grinned at Mikiah's sour expression. "I'm pretty sure we can afford the delay."

Mikiah growled. "Just make sure they don't convert the prison guards in the meantime," he warned. Cherom gave him a sharp, hard look, and Mikiah bit down on the inside of his lip, worried that the Lamanite spy had thought he was being disrespectful. He bowed to the king. "Forgive me," he said formally. "It shall be as you wish, O king."

"Hmm, yes," Antiomno said easily, but his black eyes were hard and there was an edge to his voice. "It usually is."

The sun was gone behind the mountains on the horizon, but the memory of it still lingered in the bright sky and the warmth of the breeze along the streets of Middoni. Mikiah paced the streets just inside the city walls, scowling at nothing. He felt like one of Antiomno's panthers, circling the confines of his prison, but he couldn't help it. Frustration drove him to move; unfulfilled duty pulled him back. The Nephites were still alive, in spite of his best efforts, and still stubbornly silent. Their converts were still missing. Much as he racked his brain, Mikiah could think of nothing he could do to change either of those things.

He looked up as he neared the intersection with the broad street that passed through the city gates. It widened into a plaza here, just inside the walls. In times of war, it allowed soldiers more space to defend the gates. In times of peace, it turned into a market. Mikiah slowed, habit keeping him in the shadows of the side street as his gaze passed over the stall keepers beginning to close up for the night, the last few shoppers hurrying between the stalls and trays and blankets laid across the paving stones.

Mikiah almost stumbled, drawing in a sharp breath as he ducked sideways out of sight. There was a boy at one of the stalls, no more than ten or eleven years old, haggling with the vendor over the last few baked sweets. Mikiah knew his face, recognized the way he stood and the excited gestures he made with his hands. He didn't know the boy's name, but he did know exactly where he'd seen that face before. The boy was one of a large family—a family that Mikiah had seen welcoming the Nephite preachers into their home.

If their son was here, could the rest of his family be far away? And if one family of Nephite sympathizers was still in Middoni, perhaps all of them were—hiding, waiting for their chance to escape when everyone was convinced they'd already gone.

Mikiah's eyes narrowed as he watched the boy finish his business and trot away, his hands full of slightly stale sweet bread. "I've got you now," Mikiah whispered. He slipped out of hiding and walked casually after the child who would lead him to his quarry.

It wasn't a difficult pursuit; the boy paid more attention to balancing his burden than he did to anything around him. Mikiah walked softly through the deepening shadows, but took care to pretend he had no particular interest in the boy. They just happened to be going in the same direction, of course. By the time the child reached a perfectly normal-looking house in a slightly rundown area near the walls, it was dark enough for Mikiah to see the golden glimmer of light around the edges of the closed door. He quickly rounded a corner and stopped in the shadows as the door opened and a stream of light fell out across the pavement.

"*Jeromihah, where have you been?*" a voice snapped. For all its intensity, the voice was hushed. Mikiah had to concentrate to make out the words, but the street was quiet enough for him to hear everything. "Get inside! Now!"

"But I brought—" the boy said.

"And is that treat worth all our lives?" the adult voice interrupted. "What were you thinking? You might have been seen!" A face peered around the edge of the door, scanning the darkness, and quickly drew back again.

"You worry too much, Uncle Cherom," the boy said. "Nobody's gonna—" The door shut, muffling his continued protests, but it was already far too late.

Mikiah stood in the shadows, frozen with shock. Cherom. *Cherom!* King Antiomno's most trusted spy! Mikiah could hardly believe it, but he'd recognized the voice, seen the man's face when he looked out into the gathering dark. Even without his nephew calling him by name, Mikiah would have known. *Cherom,* who'd seemed so casually bloodthirsty—a Nephite sympathizer! So many things made sense now. All that talk about starving the Nephites into submission—he was just playing for time, trying to keep them alive as long as he could. The vanished converts—Cherom must have been the one who warned them, who helped them escape.

Mikiah scowled, gnawing on his lower lip. King Antiomno needed to know about this . . . but would he believe it? *Mikiah* had a hard time believing it, and he'd just met the man. Cherom had served Antiomno for years. Antiomno trusted him, relied on him, probably even more than Ashoram trusted Mikiah. If Mikiah made this kind of accusation, it was possible that the result would simply be *Mikiah's* expulsion from the city, and he could say goodbye to any chance of dealing with the Nephites permanently. No, he couldn't just walk into Antiomno's throne room and start pointing fingers. This would take caution, and planning, and time.

Blue dusk hung low from the darkening sky as Mikiah silently slipped away along the deserted street and headed back toward the palace, his thoughts churning. One thing he did know—if Cherom knew that Mikiah suspected him, Mikiah's job would become a great deal more difficult, if not impossible.

He was only a few streets away from the palace when he became aware that someone was following him. This close to the center of the city, there were still people about, making their way home through the gathering night, but Mikiah felt the itch on the back of his neck that said one of those people wasn't what he seemed. Mikiah paused, glancing casually around him as though he was merely stopping to enjoy the cooler evening air, but didn't see anyone obviously out of place. Whoever this was, he was good. Mikiah strolled on, unconcerned, until he rounded the next corner.

A few seconds later, a man came around the same corner and stopped, confused. The street was empty, filled with nothing but shadows. He took a few hurried steps, then paused, turning a complete circle, scanning the encroaching darkness. There was nothing there.

The man jumped several inches, making an undignified squawking noise, as a deep voice spoke from inches behind him. "Hello, Shehum."

"Well, you can't blame a man for trying," Shehum said later, reclining comfortably on the cushions in Mikiah's room. "And I did manage to follow you for nearly three streets before you noticed."

"Hmm. I'm getting sloppy," Mikiah agreed. "All this soft living." He gestured around the chamber Antiomno had provided. It reflected the Middonite king's normal lush style, with thick carpets and soft cushions layering every available surface. The furniture was of fine wood, worked with gold. The fabrics were soft and closely woven. One of the tables held a bowl of fruit, lavishly decorated with geometric patterns. A full wineskin was perched on another table, and even there the leather of the skin had been delicately tooled in a floral design. It was an *ostentatiously* rich room, and Mikiah would never feel quite at home there.

"So," he continued, settling himself on the cushions across from his guest, "I suppose you've got all the news from Ishmael. Did Lamoni ever wake up?"

Shehum grimaced. "Oh yes," he said grimly. "And unfortunately, he woke up right on schedule."

Mikiah's eyebrows rose. "What's that supposed to mean?"

"The Nephite actually *predicted* it." Shehum sighed. "I mean, Lamoni was next best thing to dead for two days. Half of everyone thought he *was* dead. In fact, a bunch of them were strongly suggesting to the queen that he ought to be buried before he started getting all bloated and wormy. She wouldn't listen. She called the Nephite in, and he took one look at Lamoni and told her he'd be back on his feet the next day. And she decided to believe him."

Mikiah groaned. He'd almost thought the situation in Ishmael couldn't get any worse.

"So, next day, Lamoni wakes up as promised—and don't ask me how the Nephite pulled that one off," Shehum continued. "And then *Lamoni* starts preaching, just like the Nephites! He actually converted his entire family, *and* all the servants."

Mikiah dropped his face into his hands. "What next?" he groaned.

"It doesn't get any better," Shehum warned. "One of the servants was already a convert—had been for years, apparently—and she decided to go out and get as many people as she could to come in and see the 'miracle.' And most of *them* seemed to think that anything good enough for the king was good enough for them." He sighed again. "Especially after the *second* miracle."

Mikiah raised his head to stare at his friend. "Another one?"

"Yeah. You know your friend Tubal had a brother?"

"Hem? What's he got to do with it?"

"Well, he came in with the rest, and apparently he decided this was a good time for a little revenge. He tried to kill Ammon, stab him while he wasn't looking. I wasn't there to see it, but everyone agrees he didn't even get close before he dropped. Ammon didn't even touch him. Some of the stories say Ammon was actually unconscious at the time, but that sounds like some kind of exaggeration to me. But they all agree that Hem was just *dead*, all at once. And once Lamoni started telling everyone it was because the Nephite's god was protecting him . . ." Shehum shrugged dejectedly. "Let's just say he had a very receptive audience. Even when I told him Temisah ran away to marry Ashoram because she hated the Nephite influence Lamoni was allowing, even that didn't bring him to his senses. It hurt him, but it didn't shake him. I think at this point, Lamoni would believe Ammon even if he told him the sky was made of iron and held up by four giant rabbits."

Mikiah drew in a deep breath and let it out in a long, weary sigh. "Ishmael is lost, then. King Ashoram can't have been happy about that."

"He wasn't. Especially with—" Shehum broke off with a grimace, and Mikiah's eyebrows drew together over a piercing blue gaze.

"All right, now you're going to tell me what you've been avoiding," he said, and there was an ominous note of command in his voice.

Shehum took in a deep breath and held it for a moment. "Temisah tried to run away," he said.

Mikiah grunted, dismissive. "Big surprise. And I notice you say 'tried,' so it obviously didn't work. What else?"

Shehum toyed nervously with the tassel on one of the cushions. "It—ummm—it looks like Nabeth was helping her."

"*WHAT?!*" Cushions scattered as Mikiah rocketed out of his seat, his eyes blazing, but Shehum just watched him, nodding sadly.

"That's what it looks like," he repeated. "And Temisah's come right out and announced she's a convert to the Nephite religion. Nabeth won't say one way or another, but she's been accused of Nephite sympathies. Even conversion. Ashoram locked Temisah up in his palace," Shehum said, scowling darkly, "but Nabeth . . ." He broke off, shaking his head, unwilling to meet Mikiah's eyes.

"Prison?" Mikiah whispered, and felt his heart sink when Shehum nodded. He settled back into the cushions, cradling his head in shaking hands. "Curse that girl," he said to his knees. "And curse me too for not warning her." He looked up, his eyes full of hurt and fear, expecting the worst. "What about my father?"

"Minek?" Shehum looked confused. Not many people knew about the old Amalekite's fragile heart. "I didn't stay long enough to find out. Why?"

Mikiah dropped his head back into his hands, squeezing his eyes shut, trying not to imagine what something like this could do to his father. He should have warned Nabeth. He should have stopped her. He should have made her *think*. Foolish, thoughtless, selfish girl; why couldn't she have *seen?*

"I have to go home," he breathed, raising his head again and climbing to his feet. Cherom, King Antiomno, the Nephites—none of it mattered compared to this. "Right now. I have to go." He started stuffing his things into a small pack.

Shehum scrambled up beside him. "It's not a *huge* rush, Mikiah," he said. "I mean, it's not like Ashoram will let anyone mistreat Nabeth. He knows she's your sister. And the Nephites here are still—"

"*Hang* the Nephites!" Mikiah cut him off savagely. "Here or anywhere! They can rot until I get back, if Antiomno doesn't feed them to the panthers first. Let Cherom do his best! I am going home. *Now.*" The last words were like boulders thumping down, the foundation stones of what must be.

Slinging his pack over one shoulder, Mikiah turned and ran from the room, not even pausing to find out if Shehum would follow. And if King Antiomno was going to be offended at his guest's sudden departure, at that moment Mikiah just couldn't bring himself to care about it.

SEVEN

WILDERNESS, BORDERS OF MIDDONI, 90 BC

OF COURSE IT COULDN'T BE THAT EASY, MIKIAH THOUGHT AS HIS STEPS slowed in the dust of the road. He felt the anxiety gnawing at the back of his throat, wanting to come out in impatient screams. *Move! Get out of the way!* But he swallowed it back. Shouting at heavily armed men, no matter the provocation, was something he generally tried to avoid, and he wouldn't get back to Jerusalem any faster by getting into a fight.

The road from Middoni to Jerusalem meandered down through a line of sharp hills here, joining with several other roads to pass down a narrow canyon. It was just his luck that someone had decided to set up a tent in the middle of the road and set guards on either side to enforce the sanctity of their claim to the space—and done it in one of the many areas where the hills on the sides of the road were impassable walls of rock. There were already two or three travelers—merchants and traders by the look of it—lined up and fuming silently in the shade of the tree-lined cliffs.

"Must be someone important," Shehum muttered. "The peddlers aren't shouting."

Mikiah nodded, threading his way around the waiting men so he could approach one of the guards. "What's going on?" he asked, and with a huge effort managed to sound no more than politely interested rather than near-frothing with impatience.

The guard gave him a dismissive glance. "King Laman is having a discussion with his son," he said, and his tone indicated strongly that asking more questions would be a bad idea. Mikiah took the hint and moved back.

"King Laman?" Shehum said in a low voice. "Definitely someone important. I wonder if it's Lamoni in that tent with him."

"Can't think of anyone else he'd come out this way to see," Mikiah replied. "They must have met on the road, though who knows where Lamoni was headed at the time." He shook his head. "I think I actually feel sorry for him, poor deluded fool. If King Laman learns his son is a Nephite convert, he'll just kill him right there and have done with it." An irritated growl rolled around the back of his throat. "At least then they might clear the road and let us through."

Even as he spoke, an enraged bellow sounded from inside the tent. Mikiah and Shehum turned to stare as King Lamoni came stumbling past the door flap into view, closely pursued by his father. King Laman was a big man, tall and square-shouldered. He was getting on in years, his black hair faded to iron gray, but his age had never diminished the strength of his arm—or his temper. He had a reputation for being implacable as winter and merciless as stone. He never bothered to hold grudges because anyone who might have offended him was thoroughly and quickly punished for it. The sight of the king in such a towering rage was enough to make strong men tremble.

"Lamoni, you fool!" King Laman roared as his son finally lost his balance completely and sprawled on his backside in the dust of the road. "You want to save these *Nephites,* these sons of a liar? Isn't it enough that he robbed our people in the beginning? Now his children come and try to trick us out of what's ours! I won't have it! And I won't have my own son helping them steal from us!" He reached down and hauled Lamoni to his feet. "You're coming straight back to Ishmael with me. Right now. But first . . ." Laman reached out and grabbed the stunned Lamoni's sword hilt where it hung at his side, pulling the blade free with an ominous hiss, like a snake about to strike. He pressed the hilt into Lamoni's hand, his black glare boring into the younger man's eyes. "You will kill your Nephite dog."

Unnoticed by anyone, Ammon had stepped into view, though whether he'd been inside the tent or hidden on the far side of it, Mikiah couldn't have said. He'd been too wrapped up in watching the unfolding scene. At the sight of the Nephite, he felt a thrill of . . . something, some unknown emotion—anticipation, fear, anger, or all of them mixed into one. He just knew what he wanted to see happen next—and knew he was going to be disappointed.

Lamoni looked at the sword in his hand as if he'd never seen it before, then turned his wide eyes to Ammon, who met his gaze levelly, without a trace of fear. That simple assurance was enough. Lamoni's lips firmed and he shook his head sharply, slipping his sword back into its sheath. "No," he said simply. "I won't kill Ammon. I doubt I could even if I wanted to. And I'm not going back to Ishmael with you, Father. I'm going to Middoni to convince Antiomno to let Ammon's brother and his friends go free. It doesn't matter what you think of them; I know they're good men. I know they are prophets of the true and living God. They aren't here to steal from us at all, Father," he said, his voice taking on a note of pleading. "They're here to save us. If you'd just—"

The backhanded blow cracked across Lamoni's face, sending him tumbling into the dirt again. King Laman's own sword was in his hand half an instant later, whistling down upon his disobedient offspring.

"*NO!*" The shout echoed off the surrounding walls at the same time as a loud, metallic *clang* of sword against sword. Again, Mikiah hadn't seen him move, but Ammon stood now between Lamoni and King Laman, his sword ringing with the blocked blow. Ammon's brown eyes blazed, but not with anger or hatred. Mikiah almost thought—just as he had when he saw Ammon take down Tubal's men—that there was a strange kind of joy there. "You won't kill your son," Ammon told the king. "If you do, you'll be shedding innocent blood. You'll lose your soul. And I won't let you do that."

King Laman glared at the Nephite, his breath coming in short, angry bursts. "You're right," he spat. "Lamoni isn't to blame here. *You're* the one who's trying to destroy him!" He swung at Ammon with vicious speed, but Ammon was faster still, his sword meeting the king's stroke for stroke, filling the canyon with wildly ringing echoes.

"*Oh no . . .*" Mikiah breathed. He was moving before he thought, as if his feet and legs knew for themselves how deep a disaster it would be for King Laman to face the Nephite in battle.

"Woah, hey!" the guard said, grabbing Mikiah roughly by one arm and hauling him back. "You can't—"

"The king needs help!" Mikiah jerked free, but the guard caught him again.

"I think the king can handle one single Nephite on his own," the man said scornfully.

"Not *this* Nephite!" He sent the guard reeling with a single, well-placed blow, his feet already moving into a run as the man crashed to the road behind him.

He was already too late.

King Laman, drunk with anger, lunged toward Ammon, obviously hoping to overpower the Nephite with his greater bulk and reach. Ammon simply swayed to one side, leaving the king overbalanced and off guard, while Ammon's own sword came whirling in from the side. He could have had Laman's arm off just as he'd taken the robbers', but instead his blade struck with the flat. Laman cried out in pain as the blow cracked the bones of his forearm, and his sword flew from his hand, spinning end over end through the morning air until it hit the canyon wall and clattered down. It landed in the road with a muffled thud, much too far away to do the king any good, even if he'd been able to pick it up. Ammon planted a kick squarely in Laman's stomach, knocking him to the ground with an anguished grunt. Mikiah skidded to a horrified halt as the Nephite leveled his sword point at Laman's throat, the deadly blade poised above the fallen king.

Laman stared up the length of the blade into a brown-eyed glare, and his dark face paled as he realized his own helplessness. He clutched his injured arm with the other hand, but he appeared too shocked even to recognize the pain of it yet. He glanced swiftly around, but all of his guards were as frozen as Mikiah, held by Ammon's blade. Laman's eyes found the Nephite's again, and now there was desperation in his face. "D-don't," the king whispered. Mikiah felt his insides twist. There was something terrible about the sight of a strong man begging for his life. "Don't . . . please. I—I'll—"

Ammon drew his sword back, but only to get a better angle for the death stroke, the lightning thrust that would pierce the king's heart. "I'll kill you," he said, his voice grim with utter sincerity, "unless you let my brethren out of prison."

"Yes! Anything!" Laman gasped, his eyes wide with terror. "Half the kingdom, if you want it! Just let me live!"

Mikiah groaned. All his hard work, undone in the course of a few minutes! Curse this meddling Nephite! But there was nothing he could do to stop it.

"Anything?" Ammon considered that, relaxing the hovering sword just a bit. "All right. I want my brethren out of prison." He glanced aside where Lamoni stood, tense and shaken. "And I want you to let Lamoni keep his kingdom. Don't be angry at him anymore; let him do what he chooses. Do that, and I won't kill you."

King Laman gaped at him. "That's—that's it? That's all you want?" His mouth dropped even wider at Ammon's firm nod, and then, slowly, he began to grin. "Yes! Yes, absolutely!" He sat up, struggling to climb to his feet while favoring his sword arm, and Ammon and Lamoni quickly moved to help him. The king swayed for a moment as he stood, leaning heavily on his son, but he was still grinning. "Of course my son can keep his kingdom. And more than that, from now on it'll be his entirely." He gave Lamoni a sharp, playful blow on one shoulder. "No more answering to your old father, my boy!" Lamoni matched his father's grin but wisely said nothing. "And—yes—tell Antiomno I said to let those men go free." He met Ammon's eyes again, and some of the jovial exuberance faded from his expression, replaced by a confused wonder. "And you—and your, um, brethren—you come to the land of Nephi. Come see me in my kingdom and my court. Perhaps . . ." The look of confusion increased. "Perhaps I've misjudged some things." And then, in a voice so low that Mikiah might have imagined it—and hoped he had—Laman murmured, "Perhaps . . . everything."

EIGHT

CITY OF JERUSALEM, 90 BC

THE SIGHT OF HIS FATHER DROVE THE LAMANITE KING FROM Mikiah's thoughts entirely. Minek seemed to have shrunk since Mikiah had seen him last. Laying in his bed, he looked shriveled, fragile, crushed by the weight of the blankets that covered him. His face held a grayish-blue pallor, but his eyes were fever-bright, glistening in the watery daylight that drifted in through the open door. The rain had started just as Mikiah and Shehum were entering Jerusalem, a heavy, blustery downpour that reflected Mikiah's fears.

He ran a hand over his face and hair as he came in out of the rain, slicking the water away, but he still left damp footprints as he crossed to kneel beside Minek's bed. "Father?" he said, his voice hoarse and hesitant.

To his horror, Minek's eyes filled with tears. "My boy," the old man whispered. His hand sought Mikiah's, gripping it feebly, and Mikiah could feel the bones beneath the chilled skin, fragile as spun glass. "They took her, Mikiah," Minek said, tears spilling over and etching down his cheeks. "My little girl. They took her, and I couldn't stop them."

"I know, Father." Mikiah squeezed the thin fingers gently. "But don't worry. I'm here now. Everything will be all right."

"You have to get her back!" With more strength than Mikiah would have believed, Minek lurched half out of his bed to grab his son's shoulder with his other hand, his eyes wild and desperate. "You have to, Mikiah!"

"I will, Father," Mikiah soothed. "This is all just a misunderstanding. Nabeth will be back home by the end of the day." He pushed the old man back into the bed, pulling the blankets back into place and tucking them around the shaking shoulders. "Trust me. I'll take care of everything."

Minek's eyes clung to him with a frightened vulnerability that twisted Mikiah's heart. "Promise," the old man commanded, but his voice was a flimsy thread of a whisper, and his eyes sank closed as he spoke, too weary to stay open any longer.

"I promise," Mikiah said, infusing as much confidence into his voice as he could, speaking around the tears that pushed at his throat. "You rest now, Father. Rest, and I'll go bring Nabeth home."

He sat at the bedside for a long moment, watching Minek sink jerkily into a restless sleep. Then Mikiah drew in a deep breath, and his jaw firmed, the grief in his eyes tempered with determination. Wearily, he climbed to his feet and walked back out into the drenching rain. He had a promise to keep.

For whatever good it would do now.

Mikiah paused in the doorway. It was dark inside the prison, the stone walls built out from a natural cave and unbroken by windows. With the door closed, it would become an utterly black pit, cold and damp and filthy. But it wasn't the darkness that slowed his steps and left him feeling like he was groping for solid ground.

He didn't know what to say to his sister, how to tell her what needed to be told, how to talk to her about it at all. How could he bear to tell his bright, cheerful, opinionated Nabeth that her actions had doomed their father? That she had thoughtlessly caused the final failure of his weakened heart? That he would never recover? A few days ago, when Shehum had first told him the news, he'd been angry with her, but now he couldn't stand his own anger, the harshness of the words he might have said. The thought of it sickened him.

He could see her now, his gaze shaping her huddled form out of the gloom of one corner. That withdrawal might have looked like despair to anyone who didn't know her well, but Mikiah could see the outrage in the set of her back, in the tension of the arms resting on her upraised knees, in the white-knuckled fists. He could feel the cold fury radiating from her, silent and fierce.

With a weary sigh, he sank down to sit with his back against the wall beside the door. He leaned his head back, closing his eyes as he allowed himself a brief moment to truly *feel* the grief. Very soon—far too soon—Nabeth would be all he had left. He wouldn't lose her, too. But what to say?

"You're angry," he finally observed quietly. "I assume you're angry about Temisah." There was no response, but he didn't really expect one. His sister's rage had always been silent. "I won't argue with you, Nabeth," he said. "You can call me a brute and a coward. You can say I shouldn't have stolen her—and especially not just *then,* when her father was—was maybe dying." He choked on the word, forcing it out past the lump in his throat. "I *definitely* shouldn't have hit her. I wish I hadn't. I didn't mean to." He sighed deeply, scrubbing a hand through his damp hair, the sandy blond strands tangling his fingers. Temisah's bite on his hand had nearly healed by now, but the mark was still visible. "But Ashoram asked me to get her for him, and I did it. You can think what you like of me for that. I won't say you're wrong." He risked a glance at her and saw that she had at least unbent enough to turn her head and look at him. He couldn't see her expression in the darkness, but he hoped her attention was a good sign. He drew in a deep breath. "But you need to come home now."

There was a moment of stunned silence, and then Nabeth broke her long muteness with a derisive laugh. "Come home? Just as easy as that?"

"Yes," he said simply, encouraged that he'd gotten her to speak. "It's not that difficult, and you know it. All you have to do is denounce the Nephite religion, and King Ashoram will let you go."

"Oh, that's *all,* is it?" She turned away from him again, staring stubbornly at the dark cave wall beside her.

Mikiah's eyebrows rose. "Yes, that's all. You're not telling me you actually *believe* it, are you?"

"And what if I did?" Nabeth hissed. "What would you do then? Let Ashoram kill me? Or would you do it yourself, if he *told* you to?" Her voice dripped with scorn, and he could feel her glare even in the darkness. "You're such a mindless toady, Mikiah, doing whatever Ashoram wants and never even *considering* whether it's right or not. You'll believe whatever he tells you—and what gives him the *right?*"

"He's the king."

"Oh sure, and his word is law." Nabeth's hands flew in the air and then dropped like stunned birds. "But laws are for actions. Even for words. You *can't* make a law that actually affects what people *think*. *Nobody* can control what people believe. Nobody should try!"

Mikiah made a rude noise, momentarily forgetting his promise not to argue with her. "Isn't that exactly what the Nephite preachers are doing? Coming into our land, telling us what to believe?"

"Trying to convince and trying to control are two very different things, Mikiah, and you would know that if you weren't being pig-headed. The Nephites aren't doing anything but talking. People don't have to listen if they don't want to."

"That Nephite in Ishmael wasn't just 'talking,'" Mikiah replied quickly. "He killed and maimed over a dozen men, Nabeth! These Nephites are dangerous!"

"He was doing his job!" Nabeth protested. "Don't assume just because I wasn't there that you can spin it however you want. Temisah told me what happened. Ammon was just protecting Lamoni's property, and from what I hear, those men were no great loss anyway."

"No, they weren't," Mikiah admitted with a sigh, pinching the bridge of his nose and pushing the anger back down. "But it was still uncanny, watching one person take them apart like that. And it doesn't mean he isn't dangerous."

"And the fact that some Nephite is good with a sword doesn't mean Ashoram should be able to tell Temisah what she can and can't believe!"

"Ah. So that's it," Mikiah said wearily. "It *isn't* that you believe. It's that Temisah does, and you think she should be allowed to."

Nabeth said nothing, crossing her arms tightly over her chest, her lips pressed together stubbornly.

Mikiah sighed again. "Nabeth, you know I love you," he said quietly. "And normally I'd let you carry your crusade whatever way you want. But this time, you're going to have to decide which is more important to you—your principles or your family."

Nabeth gave a disbelieving grunt. "Why? Is Father threatening to disown me?"

"No," Mikiah said, and his voice had dropped to a whisper, the sound drained from it by the pressure of tears pushing insistently at the back of his throat. "Father is . . . dying." It was the first time he'd admitted it out loud, and it nearly undid him. He breathed deeply, head down, not daring to look at his sister. He knew if he looked at her, the tears would spill over and never stop.

Nabeth was perfectly still for several breaths. "How?" she asked finally, and Mikiah could hear the beginnings of creeping fear in the word.

"His heart," he answered gently. "It's been getting weaker for a while now. Did you really never notice?"

"I . . . didn't want to." She said it so quietly that Mikiah might have imagined the words. There was a long silence. Nabeth's voice broke it, soft out of the darkness and trembling with shattered rebellion. "Tell Ashoram I'll do whatever he asks," she said. Then she put her head down on her knees and wept.

"Do you renounce the Nephite religion?"

"Yes."

The first voice was loud and harsh, echoing angrily from the polished black stone of the floor, from the pillars and high rafters. The second was small, broken, almost lifeless, and it twisted like a knife in Mikiah's heart.

"Do you swear never to join that religion, or give help or aid to any who profess it?"

"Yes."

Mikiah was watching closely, and saw his sister's eyes flicker as she answered, glancing sideways to where the king's unwilling bride stood as witness, held between two guards. Temisah's jaw was firm, her chin held high, and her eyes flashed with anger as she saw her one-time ally turning away from her. There was something awful about the whole scene—Ashoram in his triumph, Temisah in her betrayed trust, Nabeth with her head bowed and hands clasped before her, her round cheeks still silvered by tears. There was a horrible, empty feeling in Mikiah's gut as he watched.

Ashoram suddenly stepped forward, the leopard skin cloak falling back from one shoulder as he reached out to grasp Nabeth's chin and jerk her head up so she was forced to look into his glaring hazel eyes.

"Do you swear loyalty and obedience to me and me alone as your king and lord?"

Nabeth hesitated for just a moment, fresh tears spilling from the brown pools of her eyes. "Yes," she said finally.

Ashoram held her for a moment longer, searching her face. Then, abruptly, he released her, turning away in a swirl of spotted fur. "Take her home, Mikiah," he said dismissively, "and see that she behaves herself. Take care of your father. And then—" Mikiah couldn't see his king's face, but he heard the sudden grimness of his voice. "Then I want you back here with your report. There are things we must discuss."

"Yes, my king," Mikiah said, bowing. He put a gentle arm around his sister and led her from Ashoram's throne room. He noticed her last, parting glance toward Temisah, a look filled with regret and shame, but he chose not to mention it. There were other things that were so much more important.

Nabeth paused just outside the door. The rain still fell, and both of them were drenched, but she hesitated in the downpour and Mikiah wouldn't go in without her. The water glistened on Nabeth's pale face and darkened her hair nearly to black, sending wet tentacles of it across her cheeks and forehead. She looked up at her brother, blinking as raindrops tangled in her eyelashes, and her eyes were full of hurt and pleading.

"Will he be angry with me?" she whispered.

"No," Mikiah told her softly. "I don't think so."

She bit her lip, still frightened, and Mikiah reached out to take her hand. It was icy cold, small and helpless in his grip, and he gave it a reassuring squeeze. For a moment, she looked like she wanted to say something, but she swallowed it with a gulp, gave him a jerky nod, and together they stepped over the threshold.

There was a darkness in the room that seemed to envelop them as they entered, though watery daylight still came in at the windows. Mikiah, who had seen death before, recognized it approaching now. Minek lay unmoving in his bed, unaware of his children's presence, and only the shallow rise and fall of the blanket over his chest showed that he still drew breath. He had very little time left. Possibly the hope of seeing his daughter was the only thing that had kept him here this long.

With a tiny sob, Nabeth dashed to her father's bedside and fell to her knees beside him. Her fingers trembled as she lifted his hand, fragile as old parchment over bird bones. "Father," she whispered, pleading for a response, a little girl begging her father to make everything all right again.

Minek's frail fingers stirred against hers and his eyelids fluttered open. He stared around for a moment, unfocused and confused, as if he didn't know where he was or who had woken him from the edge of his eternal sleep. "Father," Nabeth said again, and the old man's eyes found hers. He smiled at the sight of her, a sweet, vulnerable smile that forced Mikiah to swallow the lump in his throat before he could speak.

"I brought Nabeth home, Father," he said hoarsely, coming up to kneel beside his sister. "Just like I promised."

Minek nodded, a tiny movement of his head against the pillow. "I'm . . ." He was forced to stop, to draw in a gasping breath. "Glad," he finished. The fingers of his other hand stirred, and Mikiah reached to hold it, feeling the rapid beat of his father's pulse through the delicate skin. "Nabeth," Minek breathed. "I'm glad. I'm proud . . . you're my girl." He paused again, panting shallowly. The effort of speaking was obviously too much for his waning strength, but he continued anyway, his gaze moving to find his son. "Mikiah. You're a . . . good man." A single tear trickled from the corner of one eye and etched a shining path across Minek's skin. "I've done my best," he said, and his voice now was nothing but the faintest thread of sound, as though he was already far away, leaving them forever. "Be . . . good to each other," he breathed, and then his eyes sank closed again.

"I love you, Father," Nabeth said, her voice choked. Mikiah wanted to echo her, but couldn't make any sound come from his throat. He mouthed the words, anyway.

For a few more minutes, the breath rustled in Minek's throat, the weak, rapid pulse beat against Mikiah's fingers. Then Mikiah's father breathed out, and didn't breathe in again. Mikiah had seen men die before, but he'd never noticed the change so clearly. One moment, his father was there. The next, it was as if something—some kind of light or strength or motion—had gone, and all that was left was a dead shell wearing the mask of a familiar face.

With a cry of grief, Nabeth threw herself across her father's body, pillowing her head in his chest as she sobbed. Mikiah, still staring into Minek's motionless face as though expecting some sign of life, reached out and laid a hand on her trembling shoulder, stroking down the length of her wet hair over and over. He felt the hot tears spill over, silently adding their wetness to the rain that still lingered on his cheeks. He felt as though the whole world had changed with his father's death, had shifted into something strange and horribly wrong, and it could never go back. Minek was gone forever, and the world would never be right again.

The funeral bonfire sent orange sparks drifting high into the darkness, trying to replace the stars that were still obscured by a thick layer of cloud. The rain had stopped, but the clouds hung low enough to reflect the glow of the fire, bloody light against black. Mikiah stood beside Nabeth, watching the glowing flames dance, the bright points of light drift away from him. He felt the heat of the fire beating against his face and chest and legs, reminding him of the edges and limits of his own body, shaping it out of the night. But the heat had no power to warm his heart, and the flying sparks couldn't lift it.

Nabeth's small hand insinuated itself into his, clutching tightly, and he squeezed it in return. There were other shapes around the fire, other mourners standing there, indistinct in the darkness, but they seemed distant and unreal, like ghosts or illusions. Nabeth was the only real thing left in the world. The only right thing in a world gone wrong. The two of them were stuck, trapped together in this moment that never should have been, and it just went on and on. The fire burned, the clouds lowered, the sparks jumped into the sky, and the weight of Mikiah's heart chained him down. He had a sudden, strange fancy that he would never leave this place and this moment—that he would be trapped here with the endlessly burning fire for all eternity.

One of the ghosts materialized out of the darkness, standing close beside him, and a warm arm settled around his shoulders. Mikiah glanced sideways, startled, and found Shehum there, his dark face set in grim lines, his eyes glistening in the ruddy light. Eliah came up on Nabeth's other side, and at his touch she turned jerkily to bury her face in his shoulder, though she never relinquished her brother's hand. Eliah's arms cradled her there, and he stroked her hair, leaning down to whisper soothingly in her ear.

The four of them stayed there until dawn, watching the fire consume its fuel, as the flames slowly died down from leaping gold to flickering red to sullenly glowing embers. When the last embers had turned gray-black in the rising light of the sun, Eliah took Nabeth home to find what comfort she could in sleep. Mikiah and Shehum went to give their report to the king.

Ashoram was stalking around his throne room again. Mikiah's eyes sank closed as he related what he'd seen and done, too heavy with grief and sleeplessness to stay open. He could hear the king's footsteps ringing against the black stone and echoing from the walls. The sound made him feel slightly dizzy in his exhaustion. It was hard to focus on what he was saying, though he was aware—distantly—that the king was being driven into a fury by his words. Eventually, he wound down, not at all sure he'd remembered everything or managed to report it coherently.

"Blast them!" Mikiah jerked awake at Ashoram's enraged shout, surprised to find that he'd dozed off on his feet in the brief moment of silence. "A Nephite *prince*, no less, and he's got his hooks buried in King Laman!" Ashoram whirled around, his hands punctuating his anger, and glared into Mikiah's red-rimmed eyes. "Why the devil didn't you *stop* him?!"

"I couldn't interfere," Mikiah said hoarsely. "The Nephite would have killed the king."

Ashoram's hand flew, landing a savage, backhanded blow across Mikiah's cheek, and the Amalekite staggered back a step, eyes wide in shock. "Idiot!" hissed the king. "Half-witted, sentimental *child!* It would have been better to kill King Laman yourself than to let him fall under the influence of the Nephites!"

"But—" Mikiah shook his head, trying to get his scattered mind to work again.

"But, nothing!" Ashoram snapped. "If you hadn't been my best spy—*up until now!*—I'd send you after your father!" Mikiah drew in a sharp breath as his king's anger flicked against the raw wound of his grief, but Ashoram went on inexorably. "Yes, and I'd send your sister off with you, the traitorous, double-faced shrew!" The king was shouting now, his hazel eyes wild and mad. "Get out of my sight!" he screamed. "You go find King Laman, and you *fix this!*"

Mikiah stood in stunned immobility for only half a moment, a deep hurt burning in his eyes. Then he turned on his heel and fled, and he felt some part of himself broken and bleeding inside his mind as he ran away from the king he had idolized.

He ran.

He had no supplies, no water, no money, nothing but what he was wearing. He couldn't remember the last time he'd slept. He hadn't even said goodbye to Nabeth.

He simply ran, blindly, feeling the wind push the tears from his eyes, feeling the sharp impact of each step against the ground jerking through his whole body. He didn't know where he was going, and allowed his feet to find their own way. He ran through the streets of Jerusalem, past houses and shops and people who called out after him, but none of it could hold him. The city walls loomed ahead, and he passed through the gate at a dead sprint. His breath heaved in his chest, tearing at his throat as it passed, but he didn't stop and he didn't slow. He knew this speed was far beyond what he could maintain over a long journey, but he didn't care. He pushed himself to go even faster. Speed. Speed was what mattered now. If he ran fast enough, maybe he could outrun the memories, the misery. Maybe he could run fast enough to slip into the past, where things would be right again.

Maybe if he ran fast enough, he would die of it.

NINE

WILDERNESS, BORDERS OF JERUSALEM, 90 BC

A FALLEN TREE BRANCH SAVED HIS LIFE BY CATCHING AT HIS FOOT and slamming him face down into the hard-packed dirt of the road. He panicked as his lungs forgot how to breathe for a moment, as he tried to breathe in and couldn't. Then—air, coming in a great, sobbing gasp. He lay there in the dirt, gasping and panting, feeling the air burn his lungs, with tears still tracing muddy tracks down his face. Something trickled from his nose, and he wiped at it, coming away with a bright red smear across his fingers.

With a groan, he rolled over onto his back, closing his eyes against the tree-speckled sunlight as he pinched the bridge of his nose. As he lay there, something like rational thought began to seep back into his mind. He thought of Nabeth then, left alone with her mourning, left without a clue where he'd gone or when he'd return. He thought of Shehum and Eliah. He thought he remembered running past Shehum on his way out of the king's palace, remembered his friend's face, wide-eyed and frightened as he tried to stop Mikiah's headlong flight. The Lamanite must have heard what Ashoram said. Screamed. Surely, he'd tell Nabeth . . . something.

Mikiah groaned again as he cautiously raised his head and looked around. He'd run for hours before he'd fallen, and Jerusalem was far behind him. The thick trees that lined the road blocked any view of the surrounding landscape, but it didn't matter. Mikiah had run this way often enough to know every turn. He lay his head back on the hard earth, feeling the grit of sand against his hair and stray pebbles digging into his scalp. He'd taken the same road he'd come in on a day ago, the road that would lead back to the scene of his great failure. Back to Middoni—or farther on, to the city of Nephi and the court of King Laman.

If he went on at a more reasonable pace, he could get to the city of Nephi in five days. He'd cut at least half a day's journey off the time already with his wild sprint, but now he was exhausted, on the edge of collapse. He doubted he'd be able to hold even to his normal jogging pace. Without food, and with only the water he could find as he went, he'd be in poor shape after five days, but he could do it.

If he went on . . .

And what then? Perhaps Mikiah would be able to turn King Laman against the Nephites, but what if he failed? Ashoram had been clear on that. Better dead than in thrall to the Nephite lies. And if Mikiah did kill King Laman?

He'd never get out of Nephi alive.

Who would take care of Nabeth then? Ashoram certainly wouldn't. Mikiah remembered the way Eliah had stood the night before, his arms around the weeping girl. He'd known his friend was developing an interest in Nabeth for a while now, and it seemed Nabeth wasn't entirely opposed to the idea. The thought cheered him slightly. Nabeth could certainly do worse, and Eliah couldn't possibly do better. He wished he could know for sure that his sister would be protected and provided for. He wished he'd taken the time to arrange the match himself. He'd thought they had time to wait, to let things progress as they would.

Heaving a weary sigh, Mikiah finally winched himself to his feet. His legs trembled beneath him, his knees ached, and the soles of his feet felt bruised. His lungs still protested every breath, and he felt a constant desire to cough. At least the flow of blood from his nose had stopped.

Slowly, painfully, Mikiah prodded his exhausted body into a walk and then a foot-heavy jog. He had only one chance—to live, to find out if his sister would marry his friend, to redeem himself in the eyes of his king. To take that chance, he had to get to the city of Nephi and find King Laman.

He only hoped he was in a fit state to do anything about it by the time he got there.

WILDERNESS, BORDERS OF NEPHI, 90 BC

Mikiah stopped in the middle of the road four days later, his eyes darting from one side of the tree-lined path to the other, every sense suddenly on high alert. Something was wrong. He wasn't sure exactly what it was that had set his instincts ringing the alarm, but he had enough experience to trust them. There was something there—no, *someone*—hidden in the thick, green shadows. He glanced around again. Yes, there, another. And two more farther on. He heard a faint rustle of leaves from overhead and marked its position without bothering to look. There would be at least one person posted halfway up a tree—either a lookout or someone with a bow or a sling.

Mikiah had run away without his sword, without even a knife. He'd found a sharpish rock two nights ago and used it to tear off enough strips of bark to set a few snares, roasting his small catch the next morning over a tiny fire. It wasn't much, but it had kept him from starving, so he'd kept the rock just in case he needed it again. But it hardly counted as a weapon, and it wouldn't do him much good in a fight.

On the other hand, he was very obviously carrying nothing of any value. Possibly the robbers would let him just go by. He started running again, as if he'd only been momentarily spooked, but had reassured himself that nothing was there.

"Hey!" a voice shouted suddenly, and Mikiah bit back a curse. "Isn't that the guy that got Tubal killed?" A dirty figure with leaves in its black hair scrambled out onto the path ahead of him, pointing with an accusing finger.

"It is!" another voice called. "It's him! Get 'im, boys!"

Mikiah's fists clenched around damp palms and his heart pounded against his throat as he broke into a sprint. He would leave them all in the dust, if he could just get past them. Bodies boiled out of the underbrush, shouting angrily, and for every one he'd spotted, there was another that he hadn't. He ducked around a descending club and punched its owner in the throat. The man staggered back, dropping to one knee as he suffocated, and Mikiah used him as a springboard, leaping over the head of the man behind him. His hand flew at the top of his jump, and the rock spiraled through the air with deadly accuracy. A moment later there was a terrified scream as the man hidden in the tree branches fell with a crunching thud. Ahead, there were only two men between Mikiah and freedom. For a moment, he almost thought he would make it.

A thrown club slammed into his knees from behind, tangling with his feet, and he fell hard. He twisted as he fell, rolling one shoulder to take the impact, and was scrambling to his feet again when something hard smashed into his leg. Mikiah bit down on a cry of pain as he felt bone fracture under the blow. Running was no longer an option.

The broken bone stabbed pain at him, but he didn't have time for it. He spun desperately upright on his good leg and grabbed a club that was coming at him, wrenching it away from his attacker. That man went down under a blow from his own weapon, and Mikiah spun again, using the liberated club to block a savage attack aimed at his head. He was surrounded now, with no chance of escape. Even as he blocked, another club crashed into his right forearm, shattering both bones. He screamed, the club falling from fingers suddenly made of fire, and Mikiah felt another club smash brutally into his left side. The blow cracked against his ribs like a boulder and sent him flying, half-blind with agony, straight into another robber's descending weapon. The badly aimed swipe glanced off his skull as he fell, setting white stars flashing behind his eyes.

He felt the impact with the ground as just one more attack among the rain of clubs that beat at him. Hard kicks from every direction set his injured body aflame with agony. He cried out, curling into a ball of anguish, helpless to escape, death beating closer to him every moment. His weakening cries of pain only made his attackers more savage. After a time, dizzy and choking on blood, he stopped feeling the individual blows, aware only that his whole being was pain. Eventually, even that awareness left him, and he found his way into blessed oblivion.

There was a time of blackness. There was a time of bloody light digging into his mind, washing his dreams in fire. He surfaced once or twice, felt the intense, throbbing agony that was his body, and slipped under again without regret.

"I think he's still alive." The words looped and warbled in Mikiah's ears, dragging him back toward the pain. He struggled against the pull, trying to get back into the soothing blackness, but footsteps fell close beside him and someone was kneeling next to him. "Yes, he's breathing!" The hand that fell on his back was gentle, but still woke stabs of pain from fractured ribs. "He's freezing!" The touch withdrew, and a moment later something soft and warm was laid over him. Experimentally, Mikiah tried to open his eyes. One of them responded, but the swirling colors and shapes refused to resolve into anything he understood. The effect made his head spin and stirred nausea in his belly. He closed his eye again.

"He's in bad shape," another voice said. The sound of it stirred a memory, but it bubbled as if heard through water, and Mikiah couldn't place it. "And whoever did this to him might still be around. Can we move him, do you think?"

"I think we'll have to," a third voice said, and Mikiah was sure he should recognize this one as well. "He won't get any better lying there on the cold ground. Let's see if we can make some kind of stretcher for him."

For a while, the three men were silent, working, and Mikiah drifted away without their words to hold him there. The pain still assaulted him, but it was a distant thing, not quite connected. He wondered vaguely who the men were, where he had heard those voices before. He couldn't seem to focus his swimming mind enough to track down the memory of them.

"Ready?" The voice beside Mikiah's head jerked him back to awareness, and he felt three presences close around him. Then hands grasped at his arms and legs, cradled his head, and he let out a choked cry of pain as they pushed at him, rolling him onto his side. That single motion seemed to take forever, a wave of unendurable agony for every hairsbreadth of movement. He blacked out again with the pain of it.

There was silence when he came to, though it had felt like only a moment passed. Silence and stillness. He felt the three men still close to him, but motionless as if they'd been turned to stone. Mikiah opened his good eye, but the information it gave him was still too confused.

"Merciful heavens," someone breathed. "Aaron, it's—"

"I know." The voice was grim, and Mikiah's heart failed him at the hardness in it. Of course. Aaron. Muloki. Ammah. If there'd been a deity he believed in, he'd have cursed god for his luck. Bad enough to run into the remains of Tubal's herdsmen, driven from the land of Ishmael, but now the very Nephite preachers he'd tried so hard to have killed. With nothing else he could do, Mikiah braced himself to die, anger and hatred filling his heart until it pushed out even fear. He only hoped the Nephites would make it quick.

"What should we do?" Mikiah recognized Ammah's whisper this time. He sounded almost . . . frightened. There was a pause.

"We came here to save them," Aaron said finally. "All of them. As many as we can. Even him." There was another pause, and Aaron's voice seemed wryly amused when he continued. "Perhaps *especially* him. Were any of us any better than he is? But God saved us, after everything we'd done. It's only right we should do the same, isn't it?"

Mikiah didn't quite understand that, but he felt the surface shift beneath him, and his body flew into the air, jerking and swaying dizzyingly with the motion of the stretcher. When he finally succumbed to the motion and slid back into unconsciousness, he was surprised to be almost certain that he would eventually wake up again. Though it defied all logic, he felt that he was, for some unknown reason, safe with these men whom he'd been so determined to kill.

TEN

LAND OF NEPHI, 90 BC

HE BECAME AWARE OF THE SOUND OF BIRDS. THERE SEEMED TO BE an unholy cacophony of them screaming in his ear, and his head throbbed with the sound. He was lying on something wonderfully soft and warm, a gentle cradle for his battered body. He could still feel the pain of broken bones, but it had receded to a dull ache. He strongly suspected that would change if he dared to move. Something was wrapped tight around his chest, and a hard, flat something had been strapped to his right arm. There was a wonderful smell of baking bread coming from somewhere nearby, and the sound of someone moving around tugged at his curiosity.

Mikiah opened his eyes—or his eye. The other one was bandaged shut. The world swayed and twirled slowly, but he thought he recognized a shape. He tried to focus on it, and gradually the room steadied around him. The shape turned out to be a stool, close beside his bed, with a bowl set on it. He blinked, and everything swam around, forcing him to go through the process again. Focus. Steady. Where was he?

His bed sat in a corner, and a patterned cloth was strung from the ceiling not far away, giving him some privacy. Light and birdsong came in through a narrow window beyond the foot of the bed. The walls and ceiling were built of wood, worn smooth and dark with time. Aside from the bed and the stool, his little corner held no other furnishings. The blanket that covered him from toe to neck was woven of brightly colored wool, thick and warm and wonderfully soft. He moved his fingers just slightly to appreciate the texture and hissed in annoyance as the motion woke pain in the shattered bones of his arm.

Footsteps came from beyond the curtain, a hand pushed the cloth back, and Mikiah found himself staring into deep gray eyes set in a face the color of chocolate. The woman couldn't have been much older than Mikiah, but there was a feeling of strength and maturity behind her welcoming smile. "Oh, good," she said. "You're awake."

She came to his side, still smiling, and her light footfalls were soft enough that even Mikiah's aching head didn't notice them. She bent over to place a cool palm against his forehead, and a long fall of black hair spilled past her shoulder. "How do you feel?"

Mikiah made a small noise that would have been a grunt if his ribs hadn't hurt so much. "Not dead," he whispered. "But not far from it."

The woman laughed. "That's not surprising. When they brought you in, you looked like someone had been using you for a kickball. You'll be happy to know that you'll probably survive it, especially since you've woken up again. We were worried for a while that you wouldn't, with all those knocks to your head."

"And what else?" Mikiah didn't want to move another muscle until he had a better idea of how much it was going to hurt.

The woman's eyes darkened and a small crease appeared between her brows. When she spoke again, her voice had lost its light teasing. "You'll have already noticed the ribs. Four of them were cracked, but you're lucky they didn't break entirely and go into a lung or something. All the bones in your right arm are broken, and the left shoulder was dislocated. We snapped it back into place, but you'll need to keep it still and let it heal, or it'll pop back out again. Your left ankle is fractured as well, but not badly. The thing to worry about is internal bleeding. You've got some solid bruises on your stomach and back, but so far no unusual swelling. You'll probably find blood in some strange places, but if we're very lucky, it'll stop after a few days. All things considered, I'd say you got off easy." She frowned at him then, as if he was a puzzle she wanted to solve. "Apparently, you know how to take a beating."

"And the eye?" he asked, ignoring the questions in her gaze.

She bit her lip, and his heart sank at the sympathetic look she gave him. "I'm sorry," she said. "There's too much damage. I don't think you'll be able to see much out of it, even if it heals properly."

He closed his good eye, and his throat worked convulsively, swallowing the surge of pain and loss. It wasn't entirely crippling, he reminded himself. He could still see. He could speak and hear. His hands would still work, eventually. He'd be able to walk and to run. He could find a way to live with this.

Then he remembered that he was likely to die soon, anyway.

"Where am I?" he asked abruptly, opening his eye again, his blue gaze intense and demanding. "How long has it been?"

The woman looked startled by his sudden vehemence. "You've been asleep since they brought you in two days ago," she said. "They had to carry you for most of a day to find someone who would take you in. Aaron and his friends being obviously Nephites, and with you an Amalekite and unconscious, they couldn't *prove* you weren't one of them. They brought you to my cottage, just outside the city of Nephi."

It's too late, Mikiah realized. The Nephites would have gone straight to King Laman, and any chance Mikiah had had of convincing the king not to listen to them was long gone by now. The man had already been half convinced by Ammon. It was too much to hope he would have seen sense before Aaron got to him. Which meant there was only one thing left for Mikiah to do.

But not right now. Not right away. A man who was planning to assassinate a king would need to be able to stand. He would need to wait, to give his body time to heal, to give himself the best chance of completing his final mission—before he died.

The patch of sunlight had moved up from the floor and was creeping slowly up the curtain, making the brightly colored fabric glow like fire, when Mikiah woke to the sound of familiar voices.

"It was wonderful, Ashir!" Muloki was saying, sounding as though his whole being were suffused with joy. "It was everything we've been praying for!"

"Tell me!" The woman, Ashir, sounded nearly as excited as the Nephite. "Sit down. Let me get you a drink, you must be parched. But tell me!"

Carefully, biting his lips to keep from groaning, Mikiah began working his way into a sitting position. He wanted to be able to see this conversation.

"We weren't sure what to expect when we went to see King Laman," Muloki said. "We knew he'd met Aaron's brother, and that it was King Laman himself who sent word to Antiomno to release us from prison. So we knew there was a chance he might be willing to listen. All the same, I don't think any of us were expecting the reception we got!"

"He started asking questions almost before we got through the door," Ammah put in. "It was like he wanted to know everything, all at once. I think he got a little impatient when Aaron had to go back to the beginning and explain the basics before he could answer the questions the king had actually asked."

Muloki laughed. "No, it was when Aaron kept stopping to ask if he believed what we'd just told him. Finally, he told Aaron to just assume he believed everything Aaron taught, and to get on with teaching it!"

Mikiah had managed to ease himself agonizingly to his good leg, using the wooden wall for support, and now he leaned heavily against it as he half-hopped the few steps to the curtain. There was a gap wide enough to look out, but now his head was swimming again. Carefully, trying to control the rasp of his painful breathing, he slid down the wall to sit beside it, leaning his head back so he could continue to peer through the curtain into the larger room.

Muloki, Ammah, and Ashir were perched on stools around a wooden table, leaning together in their excitement. Mikiah could see Ashir's eyes dancing in the afternoon light. "And did he believe it?" she asked breathlessly. "Truly?"

Ammah nodded. "He did. But that's not all. Aaron asked him to pray, you see, and—"

"And as soon as he did," Muloki interrupted, too full of exhilaration to hold back. "As *soon* as he did, it was like the Spirit of God was just there *waiting* for him!"

"It was too much for him, of course," Ammah sighed. "There was some . . . excitement when it came over him." He saw Ashir's questioning look. "Well, it doesn't really look good when the king suddenly falls down and doesn't move. Hard to blame the servants for panicking, really."

"What did they do?" Ashir asked.

Ammah sighed again. "They ran and got the queen. She reacted about as you'd expect, seeing a bunch of Nephites standing there, and her husband on the floor. She told the servants to kill us all, and when they were too afraid to even try, she sent them to get reinforcements. Things *might* have gone pretty badly if Aaron hadn't decided to speed things up a little. He woke King Laman up just before the servants came back with a mob."

Muloki nodded, his face still alight with joy. "Seeing that the king was all right helped everyone calm down, and then *Laman* started teaching the people everything he'd just learned. Not just what Aaron had taught him, either, but everything he'd learned through the Spirit as well. And before long, he had all of us helping him teach. And most of them *believed it,* Ashir! Believed it as they never would have if it had just been us going out there and quoting scripture at them." A look of self-reproach flashed across his face. "The time we wasted . . ." he muttered to himself.

"But the king *was* converted. *And* all his family, at least those who were there. *And* all his servants!" Ammah said. "Aaron's still there teaching them, and their families, and anyone else who'll listen."

"That's wonderful!" Ashir said. Mikiah, in his corner, thought he might be sick. Killing the king wouldn't be enough, not anymore. If Laman's sons were all converted as well, whoever inherited could give the kingdom to the Nephites just as well as their father. The Amalekite spy balked at the thought of all those deaths, the blood of children on his hands. Could he do it? Could he slaughter an entire family? The idea of killing the king had been bad enough.

"It *is* wonderful," Muloki replied to Ashir. "But it isn't even the best part. King Laman sent out a proclamation. Of course, he couldn't just command everyone to change what they believed. We wouldn't have let him, even if he'd wanted to. But he *did* say that we have the right to go anywhere we choose and teach the gospel in any city. People may still disagree with us, but at least we're not likely to be thrown into prison again." His mouth twisted into a crooked smile. "At least, not legally."

Behind his curtain, Mikiah gave up. The Nephites had won. Despairing, hardly caring about the pain it cost him, he crawled back to his bed and curled into its softness, struggling with his splinted right arm and left leg as he pulled the blanket up over his ears. He didn't want to hear any more.

The next morning, the two Nephites were gone, off to continue their mission, now that it had become so much easier. They had asked about Mikiah at one point, but the Amalekite had pretended to be asleep. He didn't know what to say to them, his gratitude for their rescue at war with everything else he thought of them. He still didn't understand why they hadn't just left him to die. He was sure it must be part of their greater plan, but he couldn't see what they gained by it. There was a part of him that worried and wondered—had he been wrong? It was a tiny part, but it was there, nagging at him. And then, was that doubt exactly what the Nephites had hoped to create in him with their unexpected kindness? Perhaps they had even set up the ambush on purpose to give them the opportunity to plant that seed of uncertainty. He didn't know, and not knowing, he couldn't decide what to do. The thought of dealing with the Nephites again made him feel like he was picking his way through a bog, never sure what was solid ground and what was bottomless mud. He was relieved when they left without insisting on speaking to him.

That left him with Ashir, who seemed to live alone when she didn't have visitors or patients to care for. She pulled back the curtain only a few minutes after the two men had gone.

"All right, they're out of earshot. You can stop faking now."

Surprised, Mikiah opened his eye to see her grinning down at him. "How did you know?"

Ashir clicked her tongue at him. "That's my secret. And you're a man who knows about keeping secrets, aren't you?" His face went blank, which was, he realized, nearly as good as a confession. "Never mind. You can keep your secrets and I'll keep mine," she continued cheerfully. "But we can share breakfast, because everyone knows about that."

Mikiah laughed. He couldn't help it. True, he gasped in pain a moment later as the motion seemed to push coals against his ribs, but it felt so *good* to be surprised into laughter. To have something, even such a ridiculously small something, to laugh about.

She helped him sit up in bed, and he was pleased to find that his head didn't spin as much as it had the day before. It still ached, of course, as if the ghosts of all those kicking feet were still beating against it, but at least he was more or less sure which way was up and which was down.

The breakfast she brought him wasn't much, just a bit of bread and water, but Mikiah doubted he could manage much more than that, anyway. His abdomen throbbed as much as his head, and he knew a large meal would probably just come back up again.

"So, tell me your story," Ashir said as she settled on the stool beside him, passing him a hunk of light and fluffy bread. "The story you tell people who want to know about you. What brings you to the land of Nephi?"

Mikiah took a bite and his eye lit up with pleasure. Ashir's cooking more than lived up to the promise of its smell. But she was waiting for an answer, her gray eyes dancing with a teasing sort of challenge.

"I'm a message runner for King Ashoram of Jerusalem," he said, wondering if it was wise to tell those sharp eyes anything at all. "I was carrying a message to King Laman."

"Hmm. Must have been an important message, to make those robbers beat you up for it," she said innocently, biting into her own bread, which was covered with honey. "Did they steal it from you?"

Mikiah shook his head, his eyes going dark. "No, but it doesn't matter. It's too late now, anyway."

"Will you deliver it, though, when you're better? Even if it's late?"

Mikiah paused. Would he, or wouldn't he? "I . . . don't know." He sighed.

Ashir gave him a long, calculating look. Then she tossed her head, seeming to shake her thoughts away. "Well, you've got some time to think about it. You won't be going anywhere for a week, at least. And then only on crutches."

"I know," Mikiah said. "And thank you.

Her eyebrows lifted. "For what?"

"For taking me in. I'd offer some kind of payment, but . . ." He gestured helplessly. He wasn't even carrying any money when he'd fled Jerusalem, and the thieves would have taken anything he had.

Ashir waved that away. "Not to worry," she said cheerfully. "I have plenty to share. Now finish that up and I'll help you outside for a bit. The sun will do you good."

Ashir was humming to herself, the sound harmonizing with the buzzing of the bees in her garden as she pulled weeds from around the roots of her plants. Her long, black hair was pulled back in a loose braid, which trailed over one shoulder to dangle its tail among the green leaves, and the hot sun beat down on her bent head and brown shoulders. Her eyes held a look that was both far away and slightly melancholy and yet full of joy at the same time. Mikiah, weeding quietly a few rows away, wondered what she was thinking about.

He'd spent five days either in bed or resting outside in the sunlight. Ashir had a horrible-tasting concoction that she forced him to drink once a day, and another foul-smelling brew that she used to clean and poultice his wounds and bruises. He had to admit it helped, though. After nearly a week of inactivity, he was ready to scream with boredom and frustration. Finally, Ashir agreed to let him help in her garden, provided he promised not to strain his left shoulder and not to use his broken arm and leg at all.

The moist earth felt good against his legs as he sat among the plants. He hadn't done anything in a garden since he was a small boy helping his mother, but he enjoyed the smell of the dark soil, the dampness of it in his hands, even the black half-circles of it visible beneath his fingernails. It felt solid and real in a world that was becoming more and more confusing.

He still hadn't decided what to do about King Laman. It seemed pointless to even try turning him against the Nephites, now that he'd made his conversion and support so public. The king was known for his stubbornness. Even if he changed his mind, he'd have a hard time with the idea of actually retracting an order he'd already given. It would make him seem unsure of himself and shake the confidence his people had in him.

So that left the back-up plan, which became less and less palatable the longer Mikiah thought about it. The Amalekite spy was certain he had the ability to kill King Laman—and his entire household if necessary. What he didn't have was the stomach for it, especially when he was almost certain that it wouldn't change anything, anyway. The Nephites had gotten too great a foothold now. Even with a different king on the throne, even if it was someone who was actively against the Nephites, the only thing they could do was slow down the spread of the infection. There would always be some who believed, and those believers would convert more.

There, his thoughts ran straight into Ashir again. The woman puzzled him almost more than anything else in his whole confusing world, and that included the incomprehensible behavior of the Nephites themselves in saving his life. Ashir was a highly intelligent woman; he'd seen that from the start and had it confirmed over and over as the days passed. She was a competent healer, skilled in a number of other areas as well, and obviously knew her own talents as well as her own mind. Mikiah found that both intimidating and obscurely attractive. He was certain she'd seen through every attempt he'd made at evasion, and that she knew or guessed far more about him than he would prefer. Mikiah suspected that Ashir could spot a lie just as easily as he himself could.

But Ashir believed the Nephites, and Mikiah couldn't understand it. How could someone so intelligent believe something so obviously absurd? He was willing to admit that the Nephites were very good liars, very good at acting as if they believed it themselves, but even so, their lies were so ridiculous, even a child should see through them! But Ashir, who saw so much, for some reason couldn't see this.

Mikiah dug the weeds from around the next plant in row, his brow furrowed in a thoughtful scowl, and his mind wrestled with one unsolvable problem after the next. He wished he could ask someone for advice, for something that would make it all come clear. But his father was dead, King Ashoram far away. His friends, even his sister, none of them could help him now. The only person he *could* talk to was out of the question. If Ashir could be so willfully blind as to believe in the Nephite religion, there was no way he could trust her advice.

But he could weed her garden. And he could heal. Maybe by the time he was well again, he'd have some kind of answer.

"So here he comes up out of the pond, looking like something a monster had chewed on and spat back out," Ashir laughed. "And the child looks up at us all laughing at him, covered in pond slime as he was, and says 'Well at least I still have my fishing pole!'"

"Ashir! Are you there?" The familiar voice cut through the story the woman had been telling Mikiah while she prepared their evening meal.

"Aaron!" Ashir dropped her mixing spoon in the bowl and hurried to the front door, her face lighting in a welcoming grin. "Come in, you rascal. Of course I'm here. Where else would I be but waiting right here for you to *finally* come tell me what's been happening?" She ushered the Nephite inside, laughing as he held up his hands in playful surrender.

"Mercy! Mercy!" he begged. "I'll tell you whatever you want to know!" She chased him to one of the stools at the table across from Mikiah, and this time there was no way for Mikiah to pretend, or avoid the Nephite's grinning eyes. He'd have to find some way to talk to the man. Aaron turned his gaze back to Ashir, widening his eyes and turning the corners of his mouth down pathetically as he appealed to her. "Do I have to talk on an empty stomach, though?"

"Ha! And you, a man of God!" Ashir mocked. "Isn't fasting supposed to be good for you?"

"Oh, it is," Aaron assured her. "And I've been fasting all day, just so I'll be sure to truly appreciate the generosity and care that you put into each and every meal."

Ashir laughed again. "All right, you horrible beggar. I'll have to go dig a few more potatoes if I'm going to feed your bottomless pit." She went out into the garden, leaving Mikiah alone with the Nephite.

Aaron turned to greet him with a friendly smile. "Well, you're looking better than the last time I saw you," he observed.

"Yes," Mikiah said, mentally gritting his teeth. "Thank you."

"Do you mind if I ask you a question?" Aaron asked, casually helping himself to one of the berries set in a bowl on the table.

Mikiah shot him a surprised look but nodded reluctantly.

"What's your name?" Mikiah felt his unbandaged eyebrow rise. That wasn't a question he'd been expecting. "I've been wondering for days, now," Aaron continued. "It'll be so much easier if I have something to call you, other than 'that one Amalekite.'" He grinned sheepishly. "Not that my friends don't know who I mean, anyway, but . . ." He trailed off, studying Mikiah expectantly.

"It's Mikiah," the Amalekite admitted. Then he couldn't resist showing off just a little. "And you're Aaron, one of the sons of the Nephite king."

Aaron's smile faded a bit and his eyes darkened. "I wish people wouldn't keep going on about that," he said. "It's not like it matters."

Mikiah stared at him. "It *doesn't matter* that you might rule the Nephites one day?" he said, incredulous.

Aaron quirked one corner of his mouth. He snagged another berry and began playing with it, rolling it across the tabletop under his index finger. "If I'd wanted to rule, I'd already be doing it," he said. "My father died a few years back, shortly after we left to come here. And I'm—well, I'm actually the eldest." He sounded almost embarrassed to admit it. "If I'd wanted to take the throne, I could have. But I didn't want it. None of us did." He smiled again, a little sadly. "We'd already proved that kind of power was bad for us, you see."

Mikiah's thoughts moved like lightning, putting the pieces together. "That's what you meant," he guessed. "The day you found me, you said you'd been as bad as I was." He decided not to waste time arguing that he, Mikiah, hadn't actually done anything wrong, that he'd only been trying to protect his people. The Nephite wouldn't see it that way. "What did you do that was so wrong?" he asked, curiosity briefly overcoming his solid dislike.

Aaron blew out a breath. "Let's just say that when a king's sons decide to be rebellious, they have a lot more influence to do it with." He looked at Mikiah and seemed to read the unsatisfied question in his face. Another soft smile lifted one corner of his mouth. "I'm not sure you'll be able to understand, Mikiah. You don't believe in God, do you?"

"Not really, no." Mikiah shook his head. "My father did, and some of my friends, but I've never seen anything to convince me there's anything beyond this life." He felt a pang, admitting it, remembering the light that had gone out of his father only a few days before. He wished he could believe that had been Minek's soul, that something of his father still remained, somewhere.

"Then you'll just have to accept that we *do* believe in God, that we *know* He's there, or this explanation won't make any sense to you." Aaron looked down at his hands, rolling the berry in a small circle. "We believe in God as our Heavenly Father, as a parent who loves us—and by 'us' I mean every person ever born—with a love as strong as any earthly parent ever had for their children. Stronger. Can you accept that?"

Mikiah nodded, though he couldn't really, just so Aaron would continue.

"Well, what we were doing, it was like—like taking a man's children away from him." Aaron shook his head, face lined with regret. "Have you ever known a father whose whole purpose and joy in life was to *be* a father? I mean, some men find pride and pleasure in their work, or in hunting or playing games or something, but there are some men who truly devote their whole being to their family. That's just who and what they are. Imagine a man like that—and we were taking his children away from him, turning them against him, convincing them that he had never loved them, that he was just using them. Like we were putting his children in a cage that only he had a key to, and convincing them that he would only hurt them if they let him pull them out. Imagine a man like that, watching us tear his family apart, and still loving them, and—and still loving *us* as well, because we're his children too." There were actually tears standing in the Nephite's eyes now, and Mikiah stared at him, affected in spite of himself.

"What made you stop?" he asked quietly.

Aaron gave a watery laugh. "Now that, I already know you won't believe."

"The angel?" Mikiah said, more of a statement than a question, and Aaron nodded.

"I saw him, Mikiah," the Nephite said, looking straight into Mikiah's eye with a strange fervor shining behind his face. "I really did, and so did my brothers. It wasn't a hallucination, and it wasn't a trick. He shone brighter than the sun, and his voice shook the earth. And I'm not talking about a little trembling, either—we couldn't stay on our feet. There's no way to fake that. I know it sounds crazy to you—for that matter, it sounds crazy to me half the time—but it *happened.* I *saw* it."

Mikiah stared at him for a long moment, recognizing the raw truth behind his eyes. Either Aaron was the best actor Mikiah had ever seen, or he wasn't lying. He truly believed what he was saying. That didn't mean *Mikiah* had to believe it, but . . . "I think I understand how you converted Ashir, now," he said finally.

Aaron leaned back and laughed, breaking the moment. "Her?" he chortled. "We didn't convince *her* of anything. She was already converted when we got here!"

"What?" Mikiah glanced at the door that led to the garden. "How?"

Aaron laughed again. "That's her story, I'm afraid. You'll have to ask her. She'd never forgive me if I told it wrong."

"As if you'd be able to do anything else," Ashir said, coming in from the garden with another handful of dirt-covered tubers. "You've never told a proper story in your life. But if you want to see anything to eat on that table, you'd better *start!*" She glared at him, her gray eyes dancing as she attacked the potatoes with a knife.

"All right, all right!" Aaron spread his hands innocently. "I don't know what Muloki and Ammah already told you, so I'll start at the beginning."

Mikiah listened intently as Aaron related his first meeting with King Laman in much greater detail than his friends had done, and as he listened, he felt the confused battle inside him grow even more violent. Where was the truth in all this? And above all, what should he do about it?

Like his friends, Aaron moved on the next morning, but it was a few days before Mikiah found a way to ask Ashir for her story. For one thing, he wasn't sure he wanted to know. Talking with Aaron had only troubled him more, and he doubted Ashir would do anything to ease his mind. But his curiosity was piqued, and his days were bare of anything to do except think. Increasingly, he found himself thinking of her—and what might have been if she wasn't a Nephite convert. He might not want to know, but he did want to understand. To understand *her,* specifically.

They were in the garden again, harvesting cherries this time from trees that Ashir had trained into a low hedge beside the vegetables. Mikiah was beginning to hobble around on crutches by now, but Ashir had insisted that he sit and go after the lower fruit. The small cherries gleamed bright red and plump in the sunshine, and Mikiah couldn't resist eating a few of them while he dropped the others into his basket. He knew Ashir, on the far side of the hedge, had seen the minor theft, her eyes laughing at him while she studiously appeared *not* to notice. He wasn't surprised when she started humming again—working in the garden seemed to pull the music from her somehow. But this time, working so close to her, he realized that she was singing words to the tune as well.

In years to come, they'll know Him then
He'll live on earth and walk with men
But I know Him now.
The angels then will sing His birth
The Son of God at last on earth
But I hear them now.

In the shade of the hills, in the glow of the sky,
I know Him.
In the warmth of a touch, in the breath of a sigh,
I know Him.

They'll feel His hands, His healing reach
And burn with light at what He'll teach
But I feel it now.
His death and life will change their fate
Unlock the door and break the gate
But He frees me now.

In the shine of the stars, in the dance of the trees,
I know Him.
In the peace of my heart when I fall to my knees,
I know Him.

The words were soft, almost inaudible, and Mikiah found that he had frozen, hardly even breathing, so he could hear them better. When the song ended, Ashir was silent for a moment before she continued humming to herself, apparently unaware of the Amalekite listening a few feet away.

Mikiah let out a long breath. "You really do believe it, don't you?" he said quietly. There was something in her voice, in the way she sang, that had convinced him of that more fully than anything else could have done.

Ashir glanced at him, surprised. "Well, yes," she said simply.

"Why?"

"Because I found out the truth for myself."

Mikiah raised one eyebrow. "That's it? No stories of divine intervention or angels appearing?" He'd accidentally let a trace of sarcasm slip into his voice, and felt a stab of guilt as she leveled her gaze at him, piercing right through him and into his heart.

"I could tell you one of those," she said, and her voice wasn't angry but quiet. "And then you could try to find a rational explanation for it and go on just as you are now. Until you know for yourself, nothing will change."

He met her gaze for a long, thoughtful moment. "Tell me anyway," he said finally, the stillness of his voice matching hers in an unspoken apology.

Ashir hesitated, considering. "All right," she said. "But not here. Come sit down, and I'll tell you."

She led Mikiah to a shady bower a little way from the house and garden, where a couple of chairs looked out into the sun-dappled green shadows of the surrounding forest. The shade felt cool and pleasant after the hot sunlight in the garden, and the woven wood chair was surprisingly comfortable. The two of them sat in silence for a while; Ashir didn't seem to know where to start, and Mikiah was willing to give her time to find her own words.

"This house belonged to my father before me, you know," she said, looking around at the fluttering leaves and bright flowers that surrounded them. "My sister and I grew up here. You won't meet Abish—she lives in Ishmael now, with her husband. Actually, you remind me of him, a little." She smiled a secret smile, the one that said she knew something Mikiah didn't know, and she wasn't going to tell him what it was, either. "When our father died, it was just us two. There weren't any brothers or cousins or uncles to take it, so this place became mine, and Abish stayed with me until she met Zerimhi and followed him home to Ishmael. It would've been maybe five years ago, about half a year after our father died, Abish and I were sitting right here in this bower one evening, watching the stars come out. That's when it happened."

"What?" Mikiah asked when she paused.

"We heard someone speak, very close. It was a man's voice, which startled us, of course. We hadn't heard anyone, and you would if someone was just walking up to talk to us—the leaves make a lot of noise.

"So we jumped up—I thought of using the chair as a weapon if I needed to—but the voice spoke again, and this time I recognized it. It was our father's voice, and he was saying our names. And when I looked closely, there he was, standing just there." She pointed to a place beside one of the rustling trees. "He waved to us, and it seemed like he wanted us to come see something, and when we came closer, he showed us a path through the forest." She shook her head. "Don't ask where it is. It wasn't there before he showed us, and it wasn't there the next day. But it was there then, a narrow, twisting path, lined with white stones. I was terrified, of course. I couldn't understand what was happening, and I didn't want to set one foot on that trail until I knew what it led to. But Abish just went ahead and walked down it, so of course I had to go with her. And our father—well, our father's spirit—went right along with us, except he was walking through the forest instead of on the path, which just made me even more jumpy because he didn't make a sound the whole time.

"After a while, we came to a wall with a gate, and the gate opened for us. Inside was—" She broke off, her face echoing the wonder of the memory. "It was like a dream, it was so beautiful. There were trees and plants like I've never seen, and everything was so much brighter. It was like the colors themselves had come alive and glowed from somewhere inside. There was a building there—huge and so white it nearly blinded me—and there was a waterfall pouring out of the building. Oh, that waterfall . . ." She drew in a deep breath, marveling. "It sparkled like it was made of jewels instead of water," she continued. "And there was—somehow there was music in it, like all the songs in the world, sung together in perfect harmony." She stopped talking for a while, lost in memory, but eventually she shook herself and continued.

"That was when I noticed our father wasn't there with us anymore. He'd stopped at the gate, and I saw that it was open for us but closed for him. Of course, I went back to him. It was hard—*hard*—to turn my back on all that, but he was my father, and he was locked out. If I was going to enjoy that place, I wanted him there with me. But he told me—" She lifted both her hands and let them fall again. "He told me he couldn't come in yet. He said he'd been wrong all his life, and now he saw what he'd missed before. But he didn't have to be locked out forever. He said that soon the Nephites would come to us—to Abish and me—Nephites who knew the Son of God and carried His light with them, and they could give us the power to open the gate and let our father in. And then—" Ashir sighed deeply. "I opened my eyes and I was back here sitting in my chair, covered in dew. It was nearly dawn. There was no path, there was no sign of my father, there was no evidence that any of it had been anything more than a beautiful dream." She looked Mikiah straight in the eyes now, challenging. "Except that if it was a dream, Abish had exactly the same dream at exactly the same time."

"That's . . . hard to believe," Mikiah said, trying to be honest without sounding insulting.

Ashir smiled at him. "Isn't it, though? And I *didn't* believe it for a quite a while. Abish did, though. She got pretty frustrated with me about it too. I kept looking for some explanation, for something that made *sense.* It actually wasn't until Abish told Zerimhi about it that I had any idea what to do about it all."

Mikiah blinked, his eyebrows rising. "Zerimhi? What did he do?"

Ashir laughed. "It turns out, his father had been one of the guards King Laman sent to guard the Nephites—you remember, when that group of them lived in the land of Lehi-Nephi and Shilom for a while. So Zerimhi had been around the Nephites as a child and knew a little bit about their religion. He told me that if there was a Son of God, like my father had said, then obviously there was a God for Him to be the Son of, and the Nephites taught that anyone can pray to God and ask to know the truth." Ashir smiled widely, a smile that held confidence and joy and, yes, still that hint of a challenge. "And *that* was when I got the explanation I'd been looking for. True, I suppose it isn't what you would call rational, and you'd probably say it doesn't make sense, either. But I *know* what the truth is, and to me it makes perfect sense—because I found it out for myself."

Mikiah swung on his crutches down the path that led from Ashir's house through the trees to the main road. He'd been practicing with them, down to the road and back, and was beginning to feel far less helpless as his mobility returned. He stood in the road for a while, looking one way and then the other. One way would lead to the city of Nephi and the court of King Laman. He knew now that he didn't want to go there, that he would avoid it if it was possible, and go only after every other option was closed to him. The other direction—he turned to face that way down the road. That would take him back to Jerusalem and King Ashoram. He didn't know what would happen when he got there, but there was a strong chance he wouldn't enjoy it.

He almost wished—glancing back at the path he'd come down—that he could just stay here with Ashir in the peaceful retreat of her house and garden. He wasn't sure how he felt about her faith anymore. He couldn't explain what had happened to her and Abish, and he couldn't explain Aaron's angel either. But then, *they* couldn't really explain it. He'd considered asking why the loving father that Aaron described would lock Ashir's father out of paradise, but he knew they'd have some kind of glib answer for it. When it came right down to it, the fact was that they believed and he didn't, and nothing he or they could say would change that. He would always have questions, and they would always have answers that satisfied *them* but didn't satisfy Mikiah, and that would always be a barrier between him and Ashir.

On the other hand, having met the Nephites and spoken with them, he no longer felt the burning hatred and suspicion he'd been taught for so long. If they believed, he was willing to let them believe. They might be deluded fools, but their delusions weren't hurting anyone. He could still hate their religion, but he didn't hate *them* anymore. And that very softening would be what put Mikiah in danger if he went back to Jerusalem.

Mikiah sighed deeply, turning to go back up the path. He wouldn't be fit to travel for days yet, but the time was coming. His fractured ankle was already nearly healed. Very soon, he'd have to make up his mind.

"Is that—?"

"It is! Mikiah! *Mikiah!*"

Spinning in surprise at the sound of those familiar voices, Mikiah found Eliah and Shehum running down the road from Nephi toward him, both of them laughing and grinning with sheer relief at the sight of him.

"Where have you been? We've been looking everywhere for you!" Eliah was babbling. He would have jumped on Mikiah with an exuberant hug, but Shehum held him back, noticing the crutches, the bandages that still supported the Amalekite's ribs, the splints along his right arm, the bandage over one eye.

Shehum frowned at the injuries. "What happened?"

"I ran into the remains of Tubal's herdsmen," Mikiah said, pulling Eliah into a cautious one-armed hug. "I guess Lamoni finally drove them out of Ishmael. Unfortunately, they remembered me." He gripped Shehum's shoulder tightly in greeting. "It's *good* to see you both. What are you doing here?"

"Looking for you, of course!" Eliah answered. "Ashoram sent us to find you, but then you weren't at King Laman's court, and we didn't know where you'd gone. It's been weeks!"

Mikiah raised his eyebrows. "Ashoram sent you? Why?"

"To stop you from doing what he told you to do," Shehum said. He gave a grim chuckle at Mikiah's confusion. "Oh, if you'd been able to keep the Nephites away from King Laman—or if we'd been able to—Ashoram would've been delighted. But since we couldn't, he wanted us to keep you from doing anything . . . hasty."

Mikiah measured his friend with his gaze for a moment. "I think you'd better come back to the house," he said finally. "It sounds like there are some things I need to know."

"I heard what Ashoram said, of course," Shehum said, once Mikiah had introduced Ashir to his friends and settled them around the table. Ashir had tactfully withdrawn into the garden to give them some privacy. "He wasn't exactly keeping his voice down, and the windows were wide open. When I saw you run out of there like that, I just—well, I admit I waited for a little bit—gave the king some time to cool down. But then I went to him and . . . I'm afraid I might have spoken to him more bluntly than what he's used to."

Eliah snorted. "The way I heard it, you started out by telling him he was an idiot, continued to tell him categorically what he'd done wrong, and finished up by saying that if he didn't do something about it—and quickly—the whole kingdom of the Lamanites would know that he was both an idiot and a traitor."

"It wasn't quite that bad," Shehum protested. Eliah raised an eyebrow at him, and a slow grin stole across his face. "All right, maybe it was," he admitted. "Honestly, I don't think Ashoram had realized exactly what he'd said, or how you'd take it," he told Mikiah. "I just explained it to him, and reminded him of his oaths of fealty to King Laman, and that I wasn't the only one who'd been able to hear through the windows. Even if you weren't caught—which forgive me for saying, but you probably would have been—if anything happened to Laman now, everyone would know exactly who was to blame. And that's assuming you didn't just tell them who sent you if they took you alive, which Ashoram hadn't actually told you not to do."

"I wouldn't have anyway," Mikiah said, then remembered the turmoil his thoughts and emotions had gone through since he left Jerusalem. "Probably." He sighed. "To tell the truth, I'm not sure

I would have gone through with it even if you hadn't found me. It seems so . . . pointless."

"At this point, it probably would be," Eliah agreed.

Shehum made a derogatory noise in his throat. "It would've been pointless any time, unless you could find some way to put the blame on the Nephites. Even then, with so many people knowing what Ashoram told you, that wouldn't have lasted long. It probably would have driven King Laman's heir right into the Nephites' arms."

Mikiah's eyebrows rose in surprise. Shehum was normally quiet and reserved—a decent spy, but he'd never shown such understanding of strategy before. The Lamanite saw his surprise and winked at him. "Just because I don't talk much, doesn't mean I don't think."

"Obviously," Mikiah said, impressed. "Sounds like I should ask your advice more often." Shehum grinned and ducked his head, embarrassed. "So, should I go tell Ashir we're leaving today? We'll have to take it slowly. You might have noticed, I'm not exactly fit for a long run."

Eliah jumped up, ready to go that instant. "I can run ahead and tell Ashoram you're coming," he said eagerly. A slightly worried look passed over his face. "It took us a lot longer to find you than we expected. He'll be getting impatient."

"And you'll want to tell Nabeth you found her brother, no doubt," Shehum observed with a wry smile.

Eliah grinned widely. "No doubt," he agreed. Then he took off at a run before anyone could say another word.

Mikiah found himself laughing, as much with relief as at his friends' banter. The decision he'd worried about so long was lifted from his shoulders. "I'll go tell Ashir," he said and went out into the garden, still chuckling.

Ashir knelt in the turned earth, half-hidden by a row of pepper plants, her dark hair lying in a shining wave over her shoulders. The laugh died in Mikiah's throat as he saw her, and suddenly he realized that he was leaving, that he might never see her or hear her humming voice again. He would miss this place, the peace and simplicity of it, and he would miss Ashir, who was the center and source of that tranquility.

"It's time for you to go?" she said quietly, not even turning her head to look at him.

"Yes," he said, and his voice was equally soft.

She nodded, staring at the leaves in front of her. "Travel won't be pleasant, but you'll be all right with your friends to help you. As long as you go slowly and treat yourself gently. Stay off the foot for at least another week, and make sure a healer looks at that eye before taking the bandage off."

"Shehum will take care of me," he reassured. There was a pause. "I'll miss you."

She smiled at that, turning her head just enough to glance at him with one gray eye. "Will you deliver your king's message to King Laman?"

He shook his head, feeling the rush of relief again. "Turns out King Ashoram doesn't actually want that message delivered. That's what my friends came to tell me. We'll just be going home." He thought of Nabeth, left all alone to mourn their father. "I've been away too long already." He would see his sister again, but he suddenly wished he could bring her here to meet Ashir, sure that the Lamanite woman could somehow offer a kind of comfort that he himself never could.

She turned to him then, and her lips smiled, but there was an unusual brightness in her eyes. "I'll wish you a safe journey, then," she said, strangely formal. "And if you're ever passing back this way, you're welcome to stop here."

Mikiah felt the formality as though she were drawing herself away from him, and his good eye darkened. "Thank you," he said. "I will. And—if there's anything I can do for you . . ."

She stood, looking out at the trees for a moment. "There's . . . maybe one thing," she said hesitantly. He waited. "If Aaron or Muloki or any of them should come to Jerusalem," she began. She seemed to sense his stiffening in rejection already, because she continued hurriedly, "I don't ask you to believe them, or even let them into your home." Her eyes pleaded with him now, staring up into his. "Just—I know even with the king's proclamation, some places will still be dangerous for them. Just make sure they aren't hurt while they're there. That's all."

The nod he gave her was stiff and unwilling. It wasn't that he wished any particular harm to the Nephites—not anymore. But for some reason he couldn't define, even to himself, he wished Ashir had asked him for something else, something that didn't have anything to do with the Nephites or her obvious fondness for them, or theirs for her. But . . . "I will," he said. "For your sake."

The smile she gave him was the only reward he could have wished for, and he carried the memory of it with him as he left.

Eleven

City of Jerusalem, 90 BC

The journey back to Jerusalem took more than twice as long, going at the easy walking pace that wouldn't worsen Mikiah's injuries, stopping to rest early and often. Luckily, they didn't run into Tubal's men or any other bandits, and even the weather cooperated, staying bright and sunny most days. When clouds did block the sun, they never offered to drop rain on the travelers, and the shade was a welcome respite from the heat.

It was frustrating, traveling at less than half his normal speed. Mikiah kept wanting to push himself, to get home faster, but Shehum cheerfully overrode him, holding them both to the slower, easier pace. "We'll get there faster if we *don't* have to stop halfway to make sure you don't die," he said over Mikiah's protests. "You won't do anyone any good by killing yourself."

It was on the final day, when they both knew they were slightly less than a half day's normal travel from home, that Shehum let Mikiah's impatience speed them up. When Mikiah left his crutches behind that morning and set out at a brisk walk, Shehum didn't rein him in. Mikiah kept that pace the entire day, although his leg and arm began to throb with a dull ache and his ribs stabbed him with pain more frequently than before. By the time they reached the walls of Jerusalem late that afternoon, he felt the last of his energy waning and suspected that the word "haggard" might have been applied to his appearance.

Shehum, surprisingly, seemed pleased by this. "Ashoram cares about you, at least when he's thinking straight," he said. "Showing up looking battered and bedraggled actually ups your chances that he won't blame you for getting beat up in the first place, or taking this long about getting back here."

"It was ten against one!" Mikiah protested. "What does he expect of me?"

Shehum laughed. "Superhuman strength, skill, and cunning, of course. The ability to defeat a dozen armed enemies with your bare hands, disappear like smoke in the trees, travel for days on broken legs without feeling the pain, and think ten steps ahead of anyone else."

Mikiah snorted, which made his bandaged ribs twinge again. "I'll have to work on that. I'll let you know when it happens."

"Probably right after you convert and become a Nephite," Shehum teased.

Mikiah shrugged. "Well, Ammon had to learn it somewhere. Maybe he'd be willing to teach me how it's done."

Their banter had brought them to the base of the palace steps, and Mikiah, looking up at the entrance to Ashoram's throne room, found himself swallowing down a surge of nerves. After the last time, he wasn't sure what to expect from his king. His feet were reluctant on the steps. What if Ashoram *did* blame him?

But when Mikiah finally stepped into the throne room, limping slightly, the king greeted him warmly. "Mikiah, I'm so relieved! When Eliah told me what happened—Are you all right? You look exhausted." His gaze lingered on the bandage over Mikiah's eye.

Mikiah bowed, hiding a small twitch of a smile. Shehum had been right. "I was impatient to get home, O king," he said. "I'm afraid I pushed myself more than I should have." He let just a trace of his weariness tinge his voice.

"Well, sit down, man. Sit down!" A servant brought in a stool at Ashoram's command, and then withdrew as Mikiah sank gratefully onto it.

"And I have to apologize as well," Mikiah continued. "I was unable to reach King Laman in time. I couldn't keep the Nephites from—"

Ashoram interrupted with a wave of his hand. "No, I'm the one who should apologize," he said. "Sending you out of here like that—and just after your father died—it was not the act of a man, or of a king." He laid his hand gently on Mikiah's shoulder and gave it a comforting squeeze. "I expected more of you than you had to give, and I'm sorry for it."

"But the Nephites—" Mikiah began, but Ashoram interrupted him again.

"Yes, they've got their hooks firmly into King Laman and his family," he said grimly. "And that proclamation means they'll be even more insidious than before. Luckily, thanks to you, I already have a shield in place." Mikiah raised his eyebrows in question, and Ashoram chuckled. "The Nephites might be willing to attack on their own, but if half their plan was to use their converts to surround us . . ." He lifted both hands in the air, palm up. "I doubt Lamoni will be willing to attack the man who holds his favorite daughter hostage, and she's King Laman's granddaughter as well." He shook his head. "No, as long as I have Temisah, I'm safe, at least from that side. And if the Nephites attack on their own, endangering her, it might just be enough to make Lamoni—and maybe even Laman—see sense."

Mikiah, looking up into Ashoram's face, saw the grim determination behind his hazel eyes, but also something else. He didn't know what to call it, but he knew that anything he said in defense of the Nephites, even his own observations and belief that they weren't lying or planning any kind of attack, would be wasted at best and twisted to fit Ashoram's assumptions at worst.

So he didn't bother. He bowed his head, his eye sinking wearily closed for a moment. "Yes, my king," he said quietly. He would just have to trust that Ashoram knew what he was doing.

TWELVE

CITY OF JERUSALEM, 87 BC

THE LINE OF BRIGHT GOLDEN FLAMES WOUND THROUGH THE VELVET darkness of the night, an earthly mirror of the glittering silver stars above. Mikiah walked beside his sister, holding her hand, aware of the tension in her fingers, the moist warmth of her palm against his. She was smiling widely as they walked, apparently unable to help herself, and her breathing was quick and light. The pulse that beat against his hand was faster than the slow march of their progress would account for, and her round cheeks were rosy with excitement and nerves. Delicate pink flowers decorated the soft brown waves of her hair. Jewels glinted from her ears and throat. The gown she wore had taken months in the creation. And none of that mattered, because she outshone them all. Mikiah had never seen her look more beautiful.

They arrived at the house where Eliah waited with his family and the rest of the guests. This would be the new home for the young couple, a place to grow together and build their own family—and apparently Eliah was looking forward to a large one, if the size of the building was any indication. Mikiah smiled at the thought, but wondered if he would be lonely, all alone in the house he'd shared with his father and sister all his life.

He walked Nabeth ceremoniously up to stand in front of her groom. With a respectful bow to his friend, Mikiah reached out and placed Nabeth's hand in Eliah's, holding both their clasped hands with his own for a moment, before he stepped back and became just another member of the crowd.

Eliah and Nabeth stood looking deeply into each other's eyes, haloed by the surrounding torchlight. They both wore remarkably silly grins—not that anyone cared, least of all them. They barely seemed to notice when the high priest of Eliah's synagogue joined them in the circle of torchlight.

"Brethren," the old man proclaimed, raising both hands above his head in blessing. "Here stand two young people bound together by love and devotion. Here stands a man who will care for his wife, who will provide for her needs and safeguard her happiness. Here stands a woman who will comfort her husband, who will raise his children and give him all honor. Will you both swear so to do?"

A murmur of "Yes" came from both bride and groom, and the high priest glanced around.

"Who brings the gift of the children?" he asked.

Eliah's mother gave her youngest daughter a push forward, and the little girl came up to her brother, blushing furiously, stiff and wide-eyed at finding herself the complete center of the whole crowd's attention. Eliah gave his sister an encouraging smile and nod, and the girl reached up to hand Nabeth a large bouquet of wildflowers. Nabeth took them, nodding grave thanks to her new sister, who scampered back to hide her face in her mother's skirts, task successfully accomplished.

The priest raised his hands again, drawing eyes back to himself. "Brethren," he intoned again. "Here stand two young people bound together by joy and acceptance. Here stands a man who will protect his wife, who will spend his life that she might live. Here stands a woman who will be a helpmeet to her husband, who will rejoice with him in his success and mourn in his failure. Will you both swear so to do?" He waited for the affirmative response before lowering his hands. "Who brings the gifts of the parents?"

Eliah's parents came toward the couple, bearing a new cloak and skirt for Nabeth. Mikiah's heart felt squeezed for a moment, and tears stung his eyes as he stepped out of the crowd again, taking the place of his father. Nabeth's own parents should have been here to offer the bridal gift to Eliah. Instead, Mikiah stood in Minek's place, and—he cast a concerned look at the woman who stepped out of the shadows with him—Temisah took the place of their mother. It was the queen's place to fill, if there were no other female relatives to fill it, and Nabeth had wanted her there, but Mikiah was uneasy about it. He hadn't been this close to the girl since . . . well, since three years ago when he took her from Ishmael and her family. Now, looking closely, he was shocked at the change. Her face was wan and miserable, dark half-circles hovered under her eyes, and her hands trembled slightly as she reached up to clasp Eliah's new cloak on. She seemed brittle, the fire within her burning low, the rebellious spirit that had once attracted King Ashoram's notice now almost broken.

Mikiah gave himself a shake, jerking his attention away from the queen. This was his sister's wedding, and he had a part to perform. He gave Eliah a welcoming grin as he bent to strap on the new sword that was a father's gift to his daughter's husband. By the time he and Eliah's parents stepped back into the crowd, Mikiah had lost sight of Temisah and nearly put her out of his mind.

"Brethren," the old priest called, raising his hands for a final time. "Here stands a man who will be a husband. Here stands a woman who will be a wife. I confer upon them the gift of the ancients and proclaim that these two shall henceforth be one in the eyes of the law, of the land, and of the people. So let it be known!"

Eliah, eyes dancing with a gleeful mischief that belied the maturity of a married man, swept Nabeth into his arms and kissed her both enthusiastically and thoroughly. Nabeth wrapped her arms around his neck and responded with equal enthusiasm, drawing a cheer from the crowd.

As Mikiah joined in with the baying, joyful shouts, he felt a deep sense of relief and unadulterated happiness. Yes, before long he'd have to go home and face a house that no one now lived in but him. And yes, the political situation was still teetering on the brink of violence, and he had no idea what to do about it. And he should probably try to find out what made the queen look so ill. But all that was in the future. For right now, all of it fell away, and Mikiah found himself embraced in a single perfect moment—even as perfect as if his mother and father were standing there beside him, rejoicing at their daughter's marriage. For that one moment, it was enough.

As the cheering died away, the smell of roasted meat, fresh bread, and spiced vegetables wafted over the crowd, and the women disappeared to bring out the feast they'd prepared. The men began spreading tanned hides across the ground, laughing and joking with the newlyweds. The feasting would go on all night, unless the ridiculously large amount of food somehow ran short, and then Eliah and Nabeth would begin their married life with at least four days spent alone together in their new home.

Mikiah found himself stepping back, blending into the shadows, away from the joking and revelry. He still wanted to savor the moment. He stood there in the dark, watching his sister laugh, her shining eyes, the way she held Eliah's hand in hers. Lost in the beauty of it, Mikiah didn't notice Shehum coming up beside him until the quiet Lamanite was already there. The eye Tubal's men had injured was healed enough to appear normal, save for a thick scar above Mikiah's eyebrow, and he got some use of it in daylight, but he was practically blind on that side at night. His friends were kind enough to pretend they didn't notice. Even that reminder wasn't enough to shake his sense of perfect joy, though. "He will take care of her, won't he?" Mikiah said, watching his new brother. It was a statement more than a question, tinged with wonder at the strange neatness of life's order.

"Definitely," Shehum said. "You just have to look at them to know that. And she'll take care of him. What I want to know is," the Lamanite scowled at nothing, "who's taking care of Temisah?"

Mikiah sighed, reluctantly letting go of the bright glow of happiness. "You noticed that, did you?"

"Kind of hard to miss. I've hardly seen her for the past three years, and now . . . What happened to her?"

"I don't know." Mikiah looked over again at Nabeth, imagining his bright, stubborn, beautiful sister in the queen's place, with all the lively spirit drained away, and felt an inward shudder run through his core. "But I think someone needs to find out."

Mikiah trailed home with the dawn, yawning and stumbling. The feasting had gone on all night, and he was stuffed full of good food, glowing with good wishes, and nursing the beginnings of a monstrous headache. He had plans—things to do with the house now that it was his alone, things to find out now that his curiosity had been roused. But right now, what he wanted was his bed and a long period of blissful sleep.

What he definitely did *not* want was to see two Nephite preachers walking down the city street across from him. His feet stumbled again, losing their rhythm in surprise at the sight of Muloki and Ammah, and he staggered to a complete halt as he stared at them. The Nephites didn't seem to notice him, continuing down the street, and Mikiah found himself engaged in an internal struggle. Three years ago, he'd promised Ashir he'd look after her Nephites, but did he *have* to do it *right now?* Surely, they wouldn't get into too much trouble in just one day? Just long enough for Mikiah to sleep off the effects of the wedding feast?

He heaved a deep, long-suffering sigh of annoyance. He knew his people, and knew that the first day in Jerusalem would actually be the most dangerous for the Nephites. If he could keep them from getting themselves lynched or stoned today, the people would probably have time to remember King Laman's proclamation. Hopefully that would help cool any anger the Nephites would inevitably inspire.

Grumbling to himself and cursing the Nephites for their stubbornness and awful timing, Mikiah reluctantly sent himself trudging along in their wake. His bed would just have to wait, as would his other plans. He'd made a promise, and the very last thing he wanted to explain to Ashir—the next time Ashoram sent him in the general direction of the land of Nephi—was why the Nephites had been killed while he slept.

The noise of the crowd was growing, and the mood was getting ugly. Mikiah estimated it would take only a few wrong words to turn the peaceful square into a cauldron of mindless violence. Actually, he was impressed at how well the Nephites had handled themselves; they'd managed to avoid rousing the mob for far longer than he'd expected. It had helped that they hadn't just stood there preaching, but had been mingling and talking quietly with individuals and small groups instead. It had taken the true hotheads a while to notice.

But now it looked like *someone* was going to have to do some preaching to the crowd, or the day would end bloody.

"*Enough!*" Mikiah's voice snapped out over the square, startling the incipient mob into momentary silence. Most of them turned to look as Mikiah hoisted himself up on the lip of the well so they could all see him. "Listen to me," he called, gathering every eye, including those of Muloki and Ammah. He saw the two Nephites recognize him, and the way their faces froze on a sudden surge of worry, and one corner of his mouth quirked at the irony. "You're angry that these Nephites are here," he continued to the crowd. "That's all right. I'm not too happy about it myself. And if you want to argue with them or ignore them, be my guest. *But that's as far as it goes!*" He layered his words again with the intensity of any battle commander. "Do you understand? Remember King Laman's proclamation. Lay a hand on those men, and we'll all suffer his displeasure."

There was a low rumble from the crowd, but the anger of it was fading. They might not like it, but most of them were coming back to thought and considering consequences. Most of them.

"Shame on you, Mikiah!" someone shouted. "Defending Nephites? Your father would have—"

"My father killed himself with his unthinking hatred," Mikiah snapped, giving the speaker a one-eyed blue glare. "You'll forgive me if I choose not to follow his example. You don't have to listen to the Nephites if you don't want to. You certainly don't have to believe them. But unless you want to face King Laman, you do have to let them be."

A few more grumbles came back, resentful, but no one dared to push the point. Not this time. Sighing wearily, Mikiah sank back down to sit beside the well. He knew this wasn't over—not even close—and wondered how many times today he'd be forced to call the mob back to its collective senses.

Muloki and Ammah were watching him. For a moment, they looked like they might have come to talk with him, but his hot glare warned them away. Ammah gave him a cautious nod of acknowledgment and thanks, and the two Nephites turned away from him again. Mikiah leaned his aching head back against the stone rim of the well, letting his eyes sink closed for just a moment. *Not today, Nephite,* he thought. *You saved my life, and I promised Ashir I'd look after you, but I'm not ready to talk to you. Not today.*

Mikiah stopped with one foot inside his door. Even his good eye was blinded by the evening shadows, and his mind was clouded with fatigue, but he knew something was wrong. Something out of place.

"That was a very decent thing you did back there."

A small light blossomed in the darkness, a bright orange flame at the end of a length of straw, kindled from the carefully banked embers of Mikiah's hearth fire. The intruder moved around the room, lighting lamps until he stood in flickering half-light.

It took Mikiah a moment to recognize the man. "Cherom?" he said finally, stepping fully inside. "What are you doing here?"

The old spy from Middoni smiled. "Nothing, so far. I haven't had to. You did it for me."

"You're—wait, you came with the Nephites?"

Cherom lifted both hands, moving them up and down as if comparing weights. "Well . . . yes and no. Muloki and Ammah don't actually know I'm here. But King Antiomno was worried about them. Antiomno doesn't like to worry—he says it causes disease and invites misfortune. So he sent me to look after them."

Mikiah grunted. He'd heard that the Nephites had converted Antiomno and most of his people in the last year, no doubt with Cherom's help, the duplicitous weasel. "Great job so far," he said, oozing sarcasm. "If I hadn't been there this afternoon . . ."

"Hmm," Cherom nodded in agreement. "I've never quite gotten the hang of calming a mob," he admitted. "And I don't know the people here like you do. If I'd needed to, the best I could have done would be to get them out alive. That's why I came to see you." He gave Mikiah a piercing look, as if trying to read his heart. "We seem to have a similar goal. We could work together, if you're willing. But I'm curious as to why."

"Why what?"

The Middonite raised his eyebrows. "Last time we met, you were doing your level best to get these same men killed. And don't tell me you were just following your king's orders. *You* wanted them dead." He cocked his head slightly to one side. "What changed?"

"It doesn't matter," Mikiah said, turning away. He began pushing his furniture into the new arrangement he'd planned out, grouped more closely toward the main door. Cherom was still watching him expectantly. "I made a promise," Mikiah finally told him, just to stop the man's gaze burning into his shoulder blades. "To keep them safe while they're here."

Cherom remained silent for a moment, and when Mikiah turned to look, he found the older spy deep in thought, staring off into the shadows. Eventually, he seemed to reach a decision. "All right, then," he said briskly, pushing himself to his feet. "I'll take the night watch. The way I understand it, Aaron and his brothers are protected, but these two are taking their chances. I can make sure they aren't murdered in their sleep, if you'll keep them from getting mobbed during the day. What do you say?"

Mikiah shrugged. "Sounds like as good a plan as any. I don't have any message runs for a few days," he said, his tone almost dismissive, though in truth he was wondering what Cherom meant that Aaron was "protected." Protected how? Or by what?

Cherom grinned and headed for the door. "And while you're there anyway," he said as he left, "you might want to try actually listening to what they're saying—and think about what it would mean if it turns out it's all true." He disappeared into the night before Mikiah could form a response.

If it were true . . . Mikiah mused the next day, sitting once again in the square and watching the antics of the Nephite preachers. But it was so obviously *not* true. Even a fool could see that. What was the point of even considering it? And yet . . . Ashir was not a fool, even if the Nephites were. She saw through Mikiah quickly enough. And he knew that—foolish or not—the Nephites truly did believe what they taught. *If it were . . .*

A loud, challenging voice called Mikiah out of his contemplation. The ebb and flow of the crowd had brought Muloki closer, near enough for Mikiah to hear the conversation the Nephite was having.

"God! That's what you want to talk about, young man? Let me tell you something about God!" An old Lamanite man stood before the Nephite, leaning close with one finger raised and waving about like a weapon. "You look at the world. Just look! There's hunger and sickness and misery and death, and it's everywhere. All around us! How d'you account for that?" Muloki opened his mouth to answer, but the old man rode right over the top of him. "You can't, that's how! Just look at my life. Look at my wife, sick in bed for the last five years, and me barely scraping enough to pay the doctor. Going hungry myself so she can eat. Look at my daughter, like to be just as sickly as her mother, and probably never marry because of it. Look at my boys, both of them dead in wars with *your* people. The end of my family. Look at my brother—his house destroyed in a fire, so he and his family had to move in with *us*, and our house barely big enough to cover us. You look at all that, and tell me—what kind of God would allow it to happen? Tell me that, young man, standing there with your health and youth and full belly. Because it's no God that *I'd* ever want to know!"

The old man stopped, glaring, and Muloki's head bowed for a moment. When he looked up again, Mikiah was surprised to see tears in his eyes. "You've had a hard life," he said. "You've gone through a lot of trials, and I'm sorry you had to." He hesitated a moment, searching the old man's eyes, as if wondering how best to continue. "There *is* an answer to your question," he said finally, "if you're patient enough to hear all of it. I think if I tried to give it to you in just a few sentences, it'd only give you another reason to be bitter. Will you sit with me, and let me share what I know?"

Mikiah thought the old man looked confused and a little off balance, like a man who punches a wall and discovers it's made of air. Mikiah wondered if he'd been expecting the Nephite to argue with him. He seemed more surprised than anything to find himself sitting down beside the missionary, on a bench not far from Mikiah.

"Fine!" he grumped, trying to disguise his interest. "Tell me what you think you know that'll make everything all better." He glared at the Nephite, arms folded tight across his chest, obviously prepared to reject every word.

"For a question like yours," Muloki said, "I'm afraid I have to go back and start at the very beginning, or the answer won't make sense. I hope that's all right with you?"

"Start wherever you like," the man said. Mikiah, listening, shut his jaw tight. He knew what was coming. He'd heard it before, when Ammon taught Lamoni, and he didn't expect to like it any better this time.

"I suppose the most important thing to remember as we go through this is that you and I and every person who ever lives, we all existed as spirits before we were born, and we'll all continue to exist after we die. The scriptures teach us that, and I suspect you already know it in your heart."

"Oh, do I?"

Muloki nodded. "I think maybe you do. Don't you still love your sons?"

The man looked away, scowling, but gave an unwilling nod.

"I know I still love my mother. She died when I was only ten years old, but even now I sometimes find myself talking to her as if she were there. Sometimes I feel that she *is* there, listening, and still loving me as I love her. And I know that death isn't the end of life. That I'll see her again someday. And if death isn't the end, then I also know that birth isn't the beginning. We lived before we came here, and we knew our Heavenly Father *as* a father—a loving father who wants us to grow, to learn to be everything we're capable of being."

"See, that's where you lose me," the man said. "Why would any loving God, or Father, or whatever, send us to *this?*" His outflung arms took in the whole world and all the evils in it.

Muloki sighed, but not impatiently—more in sorrowful agreement. "I know. It seems hard. The best way I can give you to think of it is this. When your sons were very small, they had a lot of energy, didn't they? And a lot of curiosity. And I bet they wanted to do everything you did."

The man nodded, this time with a look of wistful remembrance on his face.

"Did you let them run and play, even when you knew they might fall down and get hurt? Did you let them try to help you, even when you knew something was a little too big for them?"

"Well . . . yes, of course."

"Why?"

"Because that's how children learn. You can't keep them wrapped in feather blankets all their lives."

"And if they keep trying, hurt and failure can become success and joy?"

"Yes, but that's children!" the man protested. "That's a bump on the head or a skinned knee! It's completely different!"

"From a baby's point of view, a bump on the head is the end of the world. And from God's point of view, we're all still just children, barely learning how to walk."

"So that's it? That's your answer?" the man scoffed. "Life's full of pain, get used to it?"

"No, that's just part of it." Muloki said. "A very small part. Let me go back again. As I said, we lived before this life, spirit children of our Heavenly Father. We wanted to grow and learn, just like any child, and our Father wanted that for us as well. That's why He created the earth for us, because He knew this was the only way for us to learn—to truly learn from our own experience—and that *only* by learning from our own experience could we ever understand what it means to be happy. That was the choice our first parents made in the Garden of Eden—to know good from evil, to take the joy with the sorrow. Without that choice, none of those evils you talked about would ever have entered the world, but neither would any of the good things."

Muloki's words had begun to come more quickly in his excitement, and the man was drawing back a little, confused again. "I . . . don't think I understand that," he said.

Muloki sat back, shaking his head and smiling wryly at his own exuberance. "Sorry. I get a little carried away sometimes. It's just that this is very important to the question you asked. I know, because I asked that question myself, more than once." His eyes darkened for a moment in memory, and Mikiah thought back to his own conversation with Aaron and what he'd said about the missionaries' past. Muloki must be remembering those times, when he had fought against what he now believed so fervently. Even if it was a load of rubbish, Mikiah could see that the Nephite *did* believe it, believed it so strongly that it shone from his face and glowed behind his eyes. Mikiah turned his head away from the conversation, firmly directing his gaze elsewhere, but he couldn't block out Muloki's voice. "I probably still don't have the whole answer," the Nephite continued, "but I really want to give you as much as I do have. So let's talk about the Garden of Eden for a while.

"In the garden, our first parents, Adam and Eve, were in a state of complete innocence and lived without any of those awful things you mentioned. They were never hungry, or sick, or miserable, and they would never die. *But.* They also weren't really learning or growing, and they couldn't be truly happy. They were like children wrapped up in feather blankets, like you said, with everything provided and nothing to challenge them. They didn't know good from evil, because they'd never experienced evil. They didn't know joy from sorrow, because they never experienced sorrow. You might say they weren't really living yet, just *being.* Does that make any sense to you?"

"Not really," the man admitted. "You'd think someone without any problems would be happy."

Muloki chuckled. "You'd think, wouldn't you? And yet—do you know, I never really knew how good it was to sleep in a proper bed until I spent a night up in a tree? And food never tastes as good as it does when you're *really* hungry."

"So . . . you're saying they were happy, they just didn't know it?"

Muloki considered that for a moment. "In a way, I suppose," he said. "They *couldn't* know it, in their innocence. And if they'd chosen to stay in their innocence, that would have been the end of our Heavenly Father's plan. Adam and Eve would have stayed in the garden, not miserable but not truly happy, and never would have had children, and the rest of us would still be spirits, waiting for our chance."

"So what happened?" the man asked, and Mikiah pressed his lips together as he heard the unwilling fascination in the Lamanite's voice. "What changed?"

"What happened was that they made a choice. Tempted by the devil to do it, yes. But in the end, a choice that will provide the path to eternal happiness for them and all their children," Muloki said. "You see, when God first created Adam and Eve and placed them in the Garden of Eden, He gave them commandments. Two of them, in fact. The first was to be fruitful and multiply, but the second was to not eat the fruit of the Tree of Knowledge of Good and Evil, because if they did, it would bring death into the world, and they wouldn't be able to live in the presence of God anymore. When they ate that fruit, that's what we call the Fall."

"You mean they knew what would happen and they still ate it? Just how dense were these people?"

"I know. It sounds like an easy choice, doesn't it? Stay here and have everything provided for you, and never die—or be cast out into a hard, uncaring, transient life. But you could just as easily say it was a choice between staying like children forever and never really living, or going out and discovering the world, giving themselves the chance to meet the challenges it would throw at them." Mikiah found his gaze drawn back long enough to catch the crooked smile Muloki gave the man. He jerked his eyes away again, told himself not to listen, told himself he *wasn't* listening. But the rage he'd used to block out Ammon's words to Lamoni was gone or fading, smoothed over by the Nephites' rescue and Ashir's kindness. He heard, whether he wanted to or not. "I don't think many people would choose to remain children forever," Muloki continued. "To stay wrapped in feather blankets. But there was still that problem—that by eating the fruit and gaining that knowledge, they became mortal and couldn't stay in the presence of God, just as He'd said. That would potentially mean that they would be lost forever, never able to return to their Father, in this life or the next. In this life, they would have sorrows, sicknesses, unfilled needs, and hard work, but also joy, compassion, triumph, and family love. They chose that. But they had also chosen death, physical and spiritual, the whole of mankind lost and fallen for all eternity. Doesn't sound much like eternal happiness, does it?"

"Not by a long shot," the man agreed. "You're not going to tell me it's better than something even worse, are you? So we should be happy for it?"

"No, I couldn't tell you that," Muloki chuckled. "Because I can't think of anything that could be worse. But remember what I said, that the most important thing to know is that we are children of our Heavenly Father, and that He loves us. All of His work wasted and His children cut off? He wouldn't let that stand, any more than you'd let your own children die if you could prevent it. If He did, He'd stop being God. And, since He *is* God, He knew from the beginning that this was going to happen, and He planned for it. He prepared a way for us to return to Him and to be saved from death."

"What do you mean? Everybody dies. Nothing's going to change that," the man protested.

"Yes, everybody dies," Muloki responded calmly. "But because of the Atonement of the Son of God, everybody will also live again. It's also true that we all sin and make mistakes, and because we do, we're unfit to return to the presence of our Heavenly Father. But because of the Atonement of the Son of God, the way is open for us to repent and be washed clean."

"You keep using that word—Atonement. I've never heard of it. What does it mean?"

"It means that God will send His Only Begotten Son, the only truly perfect man who will ever walk this earth, to suffer and die and rise from death, so that we can live again." Muloki's voice had gone soft with an almost painful wonder, and Mikiah's gaze drifted back without him noticing. He saw the emotion on the Nephite's face—the impossible mixture of overwhelming joy and intense sorrow. The sight held him against his will.

"He's the only one of us who won't deserve any punishment at all," Muloki said, still hushed with reverence, "and He'll be the one who takes all of our punishments on Himself—all of our pains and sicknesses, all the unfairness of the world, all the consequences of our sins. He will be the one to make all of that right—but only if we let Him. In the same way that we make the choice to sin, we also have to make the choice to let Him take those sins away from us. That's what repentance is all about. That's why we keep talking about it.

Because it allows our Savior to bring us back into the presence of God." He gave the man a soft, sympathetic smile. "So, why does a loving Heavenly Father allow bad things to happen to good people? Because He knows that His children need the experience in order to grow. And He's provided a way so that we can be truly happy, in spite of all the hurts."

"And that's it? That's the best you can do?" the man scoffed. His scorn broke through the spell, and Mikiah blinked, growling to himself as he shook it off. It was a very tempting fantasy, but still a fantasy. Mikiah was grateful—he told himself he was grateful—to see the old Lamanite sneering at Muloki. "All the poor, miserable people should just put up with it because they'll be happy after they're dead?"

"No," Muloki said quickly. "You should work to improve your life, if you can. But the most important thing about the Atonement is that you don't *have* to wait until after death. The joy of the Gospel can bring you happiness *now,* in whatever circumstances you may be in."

The man snorted. "Easy to say, when you've never had anything to complain about."

Muloki broke into a cough at that, a valiant attempt at disguised laughter. He looked up, over the man's shoulder, a small smile still playing around his mouth, and met Mikiah's gaze. The Amalekite got the impression Muloki had known all along that he was listening. "Mikiah," he called. "Perhaps you could tell my friend here—has everything in my life been easy?"

Mikiah glowered at him, determined not to be ensnared again. "No," he said, the word clipped and harsh. He wanted to leave it at that, but Muloki's relentless gaze and almost teasing smile pulled at him. "I've seen this man sleeping in a stable in a bed of straw, because the inn wouldn't take a Nephite," he said to the old Lamanite, though his eyes never left Muloki's. "I've seen him unable to help the people he loved when they were hurt. I've seen him in prison, beaten and starved. I was the one who put him there, and I did my best to have him killed. No. Things have definitely not been easy for him all the time."

"They haven't," Muloki agreed, his voice soft with remembered pain. "Did I want those things to happen to me? Of course not. And

I did my best to stop them happening. But even in the worst times, I had the peace that can only come from God." A small smile twitched at the corner of his mouth. "Maybe you're right—I can't say I was full of glee in the middle of all that. But I *was* full of peace, and even then I had the comfort of the Holy Spirit and of knowing I was doing my Father's work. And if Mikiah *had* managed to have me killed—" He looked up to meet the Amalekite's eyes again, and Mikiah felt a stab of guilt that shattered the feeble walls of anger he'd built up. "I know I would have been taken home to God. And I would have seen my mother again."

The Lamanite sat in thought for a long moment, staring off into the distance. After a while, he drew in a deep breath and climbed to his feet. "It sounds like a decent way to think about life," he said, looking down at the Nephite. "And I don't doubt it's brought you some comfort. But as for me"—he shook his head—"I think I'll go on wishing your Adam and Eve had just gone ahead and stayed in their garden."

The man walked away, his face resettling into its bitter lines, and Muloki stood, gazing after him. "There goes a man who's been deeply blessed and doesn't recognize it," Muloki said. He turned and saw Mikiah's look of confusion. "He's got a home, which is more than his brother has. He's got his health, which is more than his wife and daughter have. He has a wife that he obviously loves and cherishes, and a family that loves him. He has the ability to help those who love him, as well—his wife and his brother's family. There are those who would give anything for the opportunity to do that. But he doesn't see it."

"Hmm," Mikiah said, neither agreeing nor disagreeing. "He didn't ask the question I was thinking."

"What question?"

"Where did all this come from?" Muloki asked. "The whole story about Adam and Eve and the Garden of Eden and the Son of God and everything. Who told you it was true?"

Muloki blinked, surprised. "It comes from the scriptures."

"And who wrote them?"

"The prophets. They all speak of the Son of God, one way or another. But I suppose the earliest record about the Creation and Fall would have been Moses."

"And how did he know? He wasn't there, was he? How do you know it's not just a pretty story he made up?"

Muloki smiled at the challenge in Mikiah's voice. "He knew because God told him," he said, leaning down to pat Mikiah's shoulder. "And God *was* there. And I know it's true because God told me. Same as He'll tell you, if you ask."

"Sure, I'll get right on that," Mikiah said sarcastically, brushing the Nephite's hand away. "In the meantime, though, no offense but you'd better go." Muloki raised his eyebrows, and Mikiah glared at him. "I promised Ashir I'd keep you two safe," he said quietly. "And that mob-calming trick of mine stops working if people see us getting too friendly."

Muloki's mouth formed a surprised "O," but then he nodded stiffly and walked away, his back held straight as a rod, as though he'd just been deeply offended. Mikiah, to his own surprise, snorted a brief laugh at the Nephite's theatrics, before he regained control and intensified his scowl. Hopefully no one had noticed.

The conversation stuck with him, though. It replayed in his mind over and over as he sat in the square, watching Muloki and Ammah being repeatedly rejected by the people they approached. Some spoke with them for a while. Some ignored them entirely. Some yelled obscenities. Mikiah was only forced to stand up and stop the mob once that day. It gave him far too much time to think.

His biggest problem was that—as he'd told Muloki—he didn't dare be seen talking to the Nephites, not even if he was obviously arguing with their doctrine. He had to be completely neutral if he wanted the people to feel that he was one of them, only upholding King Laman's proclamation. All the questions and arguments that spun through his mind were completely useless, and he found himself wishing he could talk to Ashir about it all. And then, thinking of Ashir, he remembered the aura of palpable peace that had infused her home, that still hung about her every time he visited, and wondered if that was the peace Muloki had been talking about. If it was, and Mikiah—against all probability—did convert, would *his* home become a similar kind of serene haven?

He snorted at the thought, shaking his head at his own foolishness. Not likely. It was ridiculous to even think about it so much. He decided firmly to put it all out of his mind.

But the conversation still niggled at the edges of his thoughts, no matter how many times he banished it. There was something about it that wouldn't leave him alone. Now that he'd let himself actually listen to the Nephites' doctrine, no matter how unwillingly, he found himself agreeing with something Nabeth had said years ago. He could see how believing it—if you truly did believe it—would be a nice kind of fantasy to have. And then Cherom's challenge would come back to him again: What would it mean if it were true? And then he would decide—again—not to think about it anymore, and the whole thing would start over.

It wasn't until nearly sunset that Mikiah found his solution. He had watched the Nephites out of the square, seen Cherom lurking unobtrusively behind them as they went, and acknowledged the old spy's subtle nod. What he really needed, Mikiah thought, was someone who believed, but who wasn't going to try pushing anything on him, someone he could talk to without raising suspicion. At the thought, a slow grin stole across his face. He knew where to take his questions, knew someone who probably wouldn't even *want* to convince him it was true, given how much she hated him. He'd promised himself a visit to Temisah anyway.

He found her in the Queen's Garden, a small cloister of flowers and trees surrounded by gray stone walls with one side open to the steep cliffs over the sea. Ashoram had had the garden built especially for Temisah, in one of his infrequent attempts to force her to be happy with him. It was a beautiful place, the cascades of flowers shining like jewels in the sunlight, the ocean breeze fluttering the leaves on the trees so that they appeared to shimmer like light on water. It was one of the few places Ashoram would allow his queen to be without her guards, and Mikiah knew she often retreated there to find some solitude. But the fact was, she could be left unguarded here because the stone walls kept her in. The illusory freedom of the wide view over the ocean was just that—illusion. The cliffs here were sheer and unclimbable, with jagged rocks at their base, a long drop to certain death. Like the rest of Temisah's life, the Queen's Garden was nothing but a beautiful prison.

Temisah was sitting on a stone bench in the last puddle of evening sunshine, drooping like a broken lily. The long fall of her hair hid her face from the world and her feet drew listless patterns in the dirt before her, but her hands were clenched tight on the rim of the bench. There was still some slight spark of fire left in the girl, even after her years of captivity.

Mikiah paused just inside the gate, guilty for intruding on her privacy and obvious mourning. He might have turned around and left again, if Temisah hadn't chosen that moment to look up, pushing her hair back from a tear-wet face. Her eyes widened when she saw him there, then narrowed into the glare of disgusted anger she'd always given him.

"What do *you* want?"

Mikiah found himself standing like a rabbit in sudden light, frozen and tongue-tied.

The glare intensified. "*Well?*"

"I—" He couldn't ask her. He didn't even know what he'd wanted to ask in the first place. And now, finding her here in tears, he felt like the lowest of all mortals for even presuming he could ask her anything. "I'm . . . sorry," he said to his feet. "I shouldn't have—I'll just go."

"*Hold it right there!*" The command seemed to snap straight into his brain, freezing him in place again. Temisah rose from her bench and stalked toward him like a she-panther. Anger snapped in her brown eyes and crackled in an almost visible aura around her. "*What* did you say to me? You're sorry? *Sorry?!*" She came right up to him, glaring up into his terrified eyes. When she spoke again, her voice was no more than a harsh whisper. "Do you have any idea how much you've done to be sorry for?"

Up close, he could see clearly what torchlight had only hinted at the night of Nabeth's wedding. She was pale beneath her dark complexion, and her skin had an almost waxy sheen to it. The dark circles under her eyes were even more apparent, a mottled purple-blue still glistening with recent tears. Her eyes were red as well, bloodshot with too many hours of weeping. She was far too thin, the delicate bones standing out beneath the brittle covering of her skin. Three years ago, Mikiah could have circled her arm with one hand. Now he could do it with just his thumb and small finger, with room to spare. And—he flinched at the sight—in the last sunlight, he could see the evidence of old bruises on her face and arms.

"Temisah," he said softly. "What's happened to you?"

"What happened to me?" she hissed. "*You* happened to me. The king of *pigs* happened to me!" She started to cry again, her voice rising on the sobs. "And I—I can't—I can't let that man have—" She broke off, whirling away from him, but took only a few steps before she fell to her knees in the soft earth among the flowers, her face buried in shaking hands.

Mikiah sank down beside her and laid a comforting hand on her trembling shoulder. She jerked at his touch but didn't shake him away. "You can't let him have . . . what?"

"My child," she breathed into her fingers. "He'll take my baby away from me."

Mikiah drew in a sharp breath. "You're—you're with child?"

She nodded, the slightest dip of her head. "I tried not to," she confessed. "There are plants that can stop it. But I ran out. And he—" She hugged herself tightly, huddling around the precious spark of life within her. "That man is no true king," she said finally, her voice dark with bitter condemnation. "And he is no true father, either. I *won't* let him take my child."

"Does he know?" Mikiah asked.

Temisah shook her head. "Not yet. Do you think he'd even let me come out here, if he even suspected?"

Mikiah sighed. He'd lost his boyish hero worship for his king three years ago, though he'd shoved that loss to the back of his mind. "No, probably not," he admitted. "Temisah, I'm—I'm sorry. Truly. I was wrong to steal you back then, and Ashoram was wrong to ask me to. And he's wrong to treat you the way he does."

She looked up at him again, and something seemed to flare behind her swimming eyes. "Then do something," she said.

Mikiah blinked. "What?"

"*Do* something about it," she said again. "Don't just sit there telling me how wrong you were. *Fix* this!" She widened her eyes at him, pleading, her fists clenching tight around the flower stems under her knees. "*Take me home*," she begged, the longing raw and shivering in her voice.

"I—I don't—" he fumbled. He'd never even considered it before. He didn't know what to say.

"You stole me from my father," she insisted. "You *must* be able to steal me from my husband."

He hesitated for a moment, his mind racing. "Temisah . . . I don't know if that's a good idea."

Her face hardened again. "I knew it," she spat. "You're just as bad as *he* is."

"No, wait." Mikiah held her there when she would have climbed to her feet and run from him. "Listen to me. I'm not saying I won't do it. But there are reasons—good reasons, some of them—for you to stay here. If you still want to go, once you understand the consequences—" He took a deep breath, committing himself. "Then—I'll help you."

She gave him that same measuring look again, searching behind the mask for any sign of falsehood, before she gave him a grudging nod. "Fine," she said. "Tell me your 'good reasons.'"

"I guess the most important one is—Do you know what Ashoram thinks the Nephite missionaries are?" Her brow wrinkled, and Mikiah nodded. "I didn't think so. According to the king, the effort to convert us all to the Nephite religion is nothing more than the opening move in a war of invasion, the Nephites attacking from one side, while their 'converts' attack from within."

"What? But that's crazy!" Temisah protested. "The Nephites have never—and anyway, everything they teach is against—they'd be going against their own faith!"

"Yes, but Ashoram doesn't think they actually believe what they're teaching. No one who wasn't either stupidly gullible or insane *could* believe such obvious lies."

"He's wrong!" she said. "They do believe it. They *know* it. And so do I!"

Mikiah sighed. "Yes, I know. But Ashoram doesn't, and won't. In his mind, the only thing that's kept the Nephites from attacking already is that he has you."

Temisah blinked in surprise. "Me? What do I have to do with it?"

"Come on, Temisah, think!" Mikiah said. "Take what I've told you, and think about it from *his* perspective. If Ashoram has you as hostage, your father won't attack Jerusalem, and it might even keep King Laman from attacking as well. If they won't attack, then the Nephites won't either, not without the second prong of their two-prong plan. Do you understand? If you're gone, I wouldn't be surprised if Ashoram decides to attack *them* before they attack him. Remove at least one half of the threat. And I couldn't tell you which half he'd go after—the Nephites, or your father. Do you see? Your escape could be the spark that ignites a war Ashoram has been preparing for three years."

Temisah was staring at the ground now, digging small holes with her fingers while fresh tears leaked down her cheeks. "I do see," she whispered, a deep sorrow in her voice.

Mikiah bit his lip, wondering if he should continue. "There's also . . ." he began hesitantly. "I'm sorry, but I have to say it. Are you sure your father will welcome you back?"

She frowned at him. "Why wouldn't he?"

"You *are* a man's wife, Temisah, even against your will. You're carrying his child. The chances of you being able to marry again are next to nothing. Not every father would be exactly overjoyed to have his daughter back again under those circumstances."

She stared at him for a long moment, her eyes shocked and lined with tears. But then her lips firmed. Her thin fingers closed into fists, nails digging into her palms. "Maybe not every father would," she agreed. "But *my* father will! He'd want me free of that man, even if it means he has to go to war because of it." She stood and walked a few paces away, head bowed, hugging herself with trembling arms. "If it was just me," she said softly, "maybe it would be right to stay, to try to prevent that war. But it's not, is it?" She turned to face Mikiah again, and he read decision in her eyes. "This child doesn't deserve the life it'll have if I stay here. And neither do I. Please, Mikiah. Take us home."

Mikiah let out a long breath he hadn't noticed he was holding. His eyes fell closed for a moment, his thoughts racing in the darkness. It looked like he'd have yet another secret to shove to the back of his mind. "All right," he said. "I'll need a day or two to plan." He opened his eyes again to level a hard look at her. "In the meantime, *you* have to make sure Ashoram doesn't suspect anything. Don't try to get anything ready to take with you. You escape with the clothes you wear, or not at all. You can't even hint that anything might have changed. You have to act just the way you've been behaving for the last three years. Understand?"

Temisah nodded, smiling widely, her eyes glowing with a hopeful fire that would give them away in an instant if Ashoram saw it.

Mikiah glared at her. "You're going to have to do better than that," he growled.

Instantly, Temisah's smile vanished, and she shrunk into herself, drooping. The light in her eyes couldn't go out completely, but it dimmed to a mere sparkle. "Sorry," she whispered, her voice layered with long despair. "Is this better?"

"It'll do," he grunted. "Just give me a little time." He stood and went to her, laying a hand on her drooping shoulder. "I'll get you home, Temisah. I will."

Somehow, I will, he added to himself as he hurried from the darkening garden. Now he just had to figure out exactly *how* he could do it. Preferably without Ashoram finding out that it was his favorite spy who had helped the girl escape.

Mikiah stole silently through the midnight streets of Jerusalem, swathed in the folds of a dark cloak with the hood pulled far forward to hide his face. He was absolutely confident that he would be stopped before he reached his goal.

He paused for a moment on a doorstep, his hand brushing the frame as though he might go in, but then he shook his head and moved sideways around the building. By the time he reached the window there, he'd picked out the ghostly footsteps behind him, but only because he was listening for them. It wasn't until his hands were actually on the window sill, ready to pull himself inside, that he felt the prick of a knife point against his back and heard the whisper, "And where do you think you're going?"

The deep hood hid his grin. "Oh, *there* you are, Cherom," he said, keeping his voice barely above a breath. He didn't want anyone else to hear them.

The older spy let out a grunt of surprise. "Mikiah?" he said. "What're you doing here, man? I might have killed you!" There was the soft snick of a knife returning to its sheath, and Mikiah finally turned to see the dark silhouette behind him.

"It seemed like the easiest way to find you," he said. "I need help. And I don't have anyone else I can ask."

"Hmm. Your new brother is still enjoying his time with your sister, but as far as I know, your other friend is free."

Mikiah shook his head quickly. "I can't involve them in this."

"I see," Cherom said. "So this isn't a task your king gave you. Should I assume it's something he wouldn't care for, if he knew you were doing it?" He tilted his head, one eyebrow raised.

Mikiah bit his lip. "Yes," he breathed.

"And you think it's something *my* king *would* care for?" Cherom asked.

"That depends," Mikiah said. "How does Antiomno feel about the captivity of women and children?"

There was the slow hiss of an indrawn breath. "I'd say he's generally against it," Cherom said. "Especially in the past year. Why don't we sit down and you tell me what kind of help you need?"

So Mikiah told him.

"After that, it'll be up to you," he finished a few minutes later.

Cherom sat in thoughtful silence for a while. "There's just one problem," he said eventually. "You know no matter what we do, Ashoram's going to blame these two." He jerked his head back at the building where Muloki and Ammah slept. "How do we get your girl out, and still keep them out of trouble?"

"You could try asking for our help," a voice said from just inside the window. Mikiah and Cherom jumped to their feet, whirling to find Ammah grinning down at them, starlight glinting from his eyes.

"You two holding your super-secret spy meetings in public, now? I'm not sure that's an idea that'll ever catch on."

Cherom's mouth had dropped open. "You're supposed to be asleep!" he protested.

"We're not complete idiots," the Nephite said, his voice teasing. "Although we *did* volunteer to come teach the gospel to a bunch of heathen Lamanites, so you could make the argument. But we've been taking it in turns to keep watch." He lifted his hands. "Not that we don't trust you, Cherom, but it seemed prudent while we're in Jerusalem."

The Lamanite spy made a disgusted noise. "You've known I was here the whole time?"

"Oh, don't worry. You weren't obvious or anything. Muloki just has a good memory for faces. So what kind of trouble are we talking about?" He leaned his arms casually against the windowsill, his eyes glinting in the darkness.

"King Lamoni's daughter," Mikiah told him. "She wants to go home."

Ammah raised his eyebrows. "And she convinced *you* to help her?"

Mikiah flinched as though Ammah's judgment were a lash. "I'm the one who stole her in the first place," he admitted, his voice very low and head bowed. "Ashoram wanted her, but—" He forced himself to meet the Nephite's eyes in the dark. "I wish I hadn't done it."

Cherom reached out to give his shoulder a sympathetic squeeze. "We've all done things we wish we hadn't," he said. "So now we'll help you make it right."

Ammah nodded. "And count us in, too," he said. "Lamoni's been a good friend to us, and I know he misses his daughter. He would have fought for her, I think, except that he was convinced she went willingly. So if she wants to get home, Muloki and I want to help."

Mikiah shut his eyes for a moment, feeling a stir of relief even as his mind spun quickly, revising his plan. It wasn't over yet. It had barely even begun. But he had allies now, and the new plan might work even better. "Thank you," he said finally. "If you both—all three—really mean that, then here's what we'll do."

Mikiah was in Ashoram's throne room when the guards came running in a blind panic.

"She's gone!" one of them yelled as soon as he was over the threshold. "King Ashoram, the queen! She's gone!"

Ashoram shot to his feet, his dark face going pale and then red with rage. "*What?!*"

The guards slid to their knees at the foot of the throne, more breathless with fear than with the run. "She's gone, my king," the other one said. "She was in her garden longer than usual, so we just glanced in to check, and she wasn't there!" He gulped in air. "My king, I swear we didn't leave our posts, not even for a moment! I swear by my life we didn't!"

"Show me," Ashoram barked, already striding toward the door. He glanced over his shoulder. "Mikiah, come!" he commanded, a peremptory gesture summoning his lackey to heel. With a well-practiced lack of expression, Mikiah followed him.

The Queen's Garden was empty, just as the guards had said. Ashoram glared at the gray stone walls, kicking uselessly at bushes that couldn't possibly have hidden a child, much less a woman the size of Temisah. He gave a small yelp when one of them punished him for the abuse with its hidden thorns.

Mikiah, meanwhile, was studying the ground. He knew what he was looking for, because Cherom had snuck in earlier, before Temisah normally came to her garden, and very carefully arranged for it to be there. The trick was to find it at just the right time—not too quickly, but before Ashoram accidentally put his foot in just the wrong place. He watched the king out of the corner of one eye.

"Tell me again," Ashoram demanded of the worried guard. The man stood in the garden gate, wringing his hands and watching his king as though Ashoram were a dangerous animal that might attack at any moment. "Tell me *exactly* what happened."

"Well, she came to the garden as usual, maybe just a little earlier than normal," the guard said. "We checked before she went in, like we always do, and there wasn't anyone in here. After that, we went and stood guard out here. But it got late, much later than she's ever stayed before. Normally, she'll come inside during the hottest part of the day. So we just thought we'd peek in to make sure, and she was gone!"

"Just gone," Ashoram echoed. "Just like that? Did you at least hear anything?"

The guard shook his head. "No, she was quiet. She normally is, in there. Quiet as a cat when she wants to be."

Ashoram glared at the garden. "So how did she get out?"

"I think I know," Mikiah called, beckoning the king over to where he knelt in the soft earth. "See these?" he said, pointing out two deep gouges in the dirt. "She didn't get away on her own. Whoever helped her had a ladder. It wouldn't have taken much time to get in here with that, and the guards wouldn't have been in a position to see anyone outside the walls here, not with the angle of this corner."

"Who would dare?!" Ashoram hissed, and then drew in a long breath. He stood frozen for a moment, staring at the ladder marks, the evidence of conspiracy, and Mikiah already knew what conclusion the king's mind was racing toward. "The Nephites," he said. "They're not here to preach. They never were. Temisah was the one thing that stood in the way of their plans, and now they've got her."

"For now," Mikiah interjected. "If we can find them—get her back before Lamoni learns she's escaped . . ."

Ashoram nodded sharply. "You're right, Mikiah. Come on! They may be hours ahead of us already!" Beckoning for Mikiah and both guards to follow him, he jogged out of the garden. "Call for the huntsmen, the message runners, all the guards. We can't spare a single man from this!"

Mikiah, following his king, smiled sadly. His plan was working, and he couldn't wish it wasn't, but he felt a flash of guilty nostalgia, mourning for the young man he'd been three years ago who would have been horrified by the thought that he could ever betray Ashoram this way.

"Yeah, I saw two Nephites go out this way about midday," said the guard at the gate. "Headed north. Good riddance to 'em. They didn't have any girl with them, though."

"What about some kind of box or container that might have been big enough?" Mikiah asked. "That's how we got her out of Ishmael. She might have tried the same thing."

"Yeah, they were hauling a bit of luggage, now you mention it," the guard said, scratching his head. "Didn't bother to look inside it, but it could've held a girl, maybe, if she was smallish."

"But why go northward?" Shehum said, turning to Ashoram. "Ishmael is south of here. They'd have to swing around through the wilderness to get there."

Ashoram was standing at the head of a small army, ready for the hunt. "They're not going to Ishmael," he said, his voice hard. "It makes sense. I held Temisah to keep Lamoni from attacking us. The Nephites will hold her to ensure that he does. They won't take her back to her father—they'll take her to Zarahemla and keep her there." He scowled in thought for a moment. "Mikiah, Shehum, go back and get captain Hanan to assemble the men of Jerusalem. Then go to the cities of Helam and Amulon and ask them to join us as quickly as they can. If we don't catch up with the Nephites before they reach their own lands, I want to have an army behind me when I march in there and take her back."

Mikiah made a careful observation of the whole area before he went back into the Queen's Garden. All it would take was one stray set of eyes to ruin the whole thing and send Mikiah straight to his execution. But there was no one there. Ashoram's entire household had been called out to join the pursuit, and the palace stood empty.

He strode silently toward a certain corner that held just another bed of flowers, the bright green stems standing out sharply against dark, freshly turned earth. Cherom had done a perfect job. Even knowing what he was looking for, Mikiah couldn't see it.

"Temisah," he called quietly. "Come out. It's time to go."

Small scuffling noises came from the flower bed, and the dirt began to stir. Slowly, a mound of earth pushed itself up at one end of the bed, revealing a dark hole. Temisah's thin hands emerged, encrusted with black dirt, and Mikiah took hold of them and gently pulled the girl free of her hiding place. The whole process barely disturbed the leaves of the flowers planted across the leather and wood frame that concealed the pit Cherom had dug the night before. If they carefully replaced the earth Temisah had just moved, no one would know it wasn't solid earth—at least not until the frame rotted and collapsed.

"Ashoram's gone," Mikiah told her. "Most of the men of the city are getting ready to follow him to war with the Nephites." Temisah ducked her head guiltily, squeezing her lower lip with her teeth. Mikiah nodded. "I did warn you that would happen."

"You did," Temisah said in a small voice. "And I accepted it. What do we do now?"

"Now comes the hard part," Mikiah said. "Now we get you out of the city."

"How? If everyone's looking for me . . ."

"Everyone's looking for you somewhere else. They won't expect to see you here, and that gives us an edge. After that . . ." He gave her a considering look. Still thin and petite, not showing her motherhood yet. With a few changes, he thought they stood a good chance. "How good are you at running?" he asked.

The city gate was a scene of chaos. The army was gathering outside the walls, swelling slowly as the men came to join it. It wasn't just the army crowding the gates either. They all had families—wives and children who wanted to stay with their husbands and fathers as long as they could, knowing they might never return. There were more than a few tears visible, and many faces were smiling a little too brightly, trying to hide the fear.

One of Ashoram's messengers pushed his way through the middle of the chaos, scowling at the delay. The harried guard at the gate could see that Mikiah was in both a hurry and a bad temper. A Lamanite boy followed in his wake. The boy was barely into his adult years, if the paleness of his newly shaved head was any indication, and he seemed to glow with a kind of terrified excitement. The excitement was obviously for his first steps into his adult life, learning the trade that would allow him to see so much more of the world. The cause of the terror was equally obvious.

"No, not like that," Mikiah barked as they finally cleared the gates and broke into an easy run. "You'll be lame in half a day, running like that." He rolled his eyes at the gate guard, who smiled sympathetically. The guards all knew Mikiah hated training new runners, and to pull the duty when he had an urgent message to deliver would just make him more irritable. "You run on the whole foot, not just your toes, or you'll sprain an ankle for sure." He watched the boy's form for another moment as they made their way around the city walls toward the road that would take them to the city of Helam. The last the guard heard was Mikiah bellowing, "*No!* You don't pound the road with your heels like that either! Are you *trying* to break something?"

THIRTEEN

LAND OF JERUSALEM, 87 BC

"ARE YOU SURE HE'LL COME?" TEMISAH WAS FRETTING, RUNNING A hand repeatedly over her shorn head. It had been a shame, shaving off all that long, dark hair, but between that and the change of clothes, she was hardly recognizable. In all the clamor and shove of the city gates, no one had thought to look twice and realize the "boy" was nothing of the sort.

"He'll be here," Mikiah assured her. Cherom had said he'd meet them before sundown, and the red-gold light of evening was already streaking the forest around them.

"You hardly know him. What if he turns us in?"

Mikiah grunted. "Stop worrying," he said irritably. "I promised to get you home, and that's what I'm doing."

That silenced her, but he could tell she was still on edge, her hand continuing to rub at the skin of her scalp. She still had dirt from the garden under her fingernails. Mikiah's mind, racing with his own nerves, overlaid her delicate fingers with the memory of Ashir's strong, work-callused hands in the cool, damp earth.

"Do you think I could change?" he asked abruptly. He cursed himself as soon as the words left him, feeling blood heat his cheeks. Pale skin was a distinct disadvantage when it came to hiding blushes.

Temisah's eyebrows twisted upward, and then she snorted. "You? Not likely."

Mikiah's head dipped, his lips pressed together. He turned away from the girl, scanning the surrounding forest for any sign of Cherom. "Yeah. I didn't think so either."

"Wait." He looked back to find Temisah twisting her fingers together, scowling at nothing. "I'm sorry," she said, looking down at the carpet of fallen leaves beneath her feet. "I didn't mean that. And if I did, I should be ashamed of myself." But the look she gave him was still deeply puzzled. "What brought this on?"

"Nothing. Forget I said it." She continued to gaze at him, and finally he tossed his head uncomfortably. "It was just something Muloki said. About the Son of God."

"What about him?"

"He said the Son of God would take the punishment for our sins, if we repent."

"Yes?" she prompted when he paused.

"It's just . . . 'repent' means 'change,' right? But what if . . . what if you can't change?" He shook his head, trying to find the right words. "What if you try to change, and you end up right back the same way you always were?"

"Then you try again," Temisah said softly. "And again and again. I'm not an expert—I didn't have time to learn all I wanted to know about what Ammon was teaching. But if I understand it, repentance isn't always just a one-time thing. Sometimes it takes a lot of time and trying, and sometimes you don't notice the change until you look back to where you were."

"But what if you keep trying, and you never do change?"

Temisah was silent for a time, deep in thought. "I think," she said slowly, "I think God blesses you, even for trying." She looked up at him, meeting his eyes with a sympathetic frankness that startled him. "And yes, Mikiah, I do think you can change. If you really want to." A corner of her mouth quirked, and she waved a hand at the forest around them. "Just look at where you are now—what you're doing. A few years ago, you would have thought it was insane even to try."

Mikiah snorted. "I think it's insane now."

"But you're doing it anyway." She cocked her head at him. "Why?"

Mikiah opened his mouth, and then stopped, unable to find a good answer. A pair of gray eyes flashed in his thoughts, but he refused to believe he was risking his life just because of a woman he sometimes dropped in to visit when he was in the area. At the same time, he was certain that Ashir *would* want him to do exactly what he was doing.

He was rescued from the question by a distant rustle in the undergrowth. He spun toward the sound, a quick gesture cautioning Temisah to silence. The leaves whispered again, and soon he could see motion, a dark body moving through the deepening shadows. He breathed a sigh of relief as the Middonite spy stepped into view.

"Finally," Mikiah said by way of greeting. "What kept you?"

"Making sure Muloki and Ammah got off safely," Cherom said easily. "But now I'm all yours." He was grinning as he bowed deeply to Temisah, and her cheeks dimpled, her eyes dancing. In that moment, she proved that she could be just as lovely as ever, even shaved bald and wearing boy's clothes. Rising again, Cherom clapped Mikiah on the shoulder. "And you'd better get running if you're going to make it to Helam in time to keep Ashoram from suspecting anything. Unless you want to change your mind and come with us for good?" His raised eyebrow was half teasing, half inviting.

Mikiah shook his head lightly. "Not today," he said. "Keep her safe, Cherom. Take her home."

"I will," Cherom promised.

To Mikiah's utter astonishment, Temisah came to him and kissed his cheek in parting. "God bless you, Mikiah," she said softly. "Whatever else you do with your life, God bless you for this."

He carried the warmth of those words with him as he jogged all through that night, running on the road to war.

FOURTEEN

WILDERNESS SOUTH OF NEPHITE LANDS, 87 BC

THERE WAS AN ARMY COMING TO MEET THEM. MIKIAH WAS ALMOST relieved to see it. He'd caught up with Ashoram without any problem, but the hunters had lost track of the two Nephites within half a day—Cherom's handiwork showed in that. While the strip of wilderness between the two nations had narrowed in recent generations, it was still a pathless forest stretching for days in every direction. Any sign of civilization was welcome after that, even if it was Nephite civilization.

It was obviously an army coming toward them, but in truth, there wasn't much of it. Or perhaps he should say there wasn't much *left* of it. As they drew closer, he could see men in the ranks wearing bloodstained bandages over their wounds. This was something unexpected.

King Ashoram grunted as he reached the same conclusion. "One of you, go see what those fools think they're doing," he said, pointing at the remnants of the Nephite army.

"I'll go," Mikiah said quickly, mostly to keep Eliah from volunteering first. His Lamanite brother had insisted on joining the army, though it was only days after the wedding, and he should traditionally have been given more time alone with his wife before they re-entered the world. For Nabeth's sake Mikiah wanted to keep him out of danger as long as possible.

He felt terribly exposed as he jogged cautiously out of the forest's shelter into the meadow of waist-high grass. Someone in the approaching army gave a loud yell as they caught sight of him, and a scattering of arrows flew harmlessly into the grass from panicky warriors. Mikiah ignored them. He wasn't anywhere close to their range. He just hoped they'd get over their nerves before he got close enough for them to get a lucky shot.

"*Save your arrows, you idiots!*" someone bellowed from behind their ranks. "*You stupid grunts couldn't hit the side of a mountain at this distance!*"

Mikiah barely made out a softer, smoother voice responding. "Don't scold them, Keb. It's no wonder they want to kill a Nephite, after what we've been through."

"I'm no Nephite!" Mikiah called back, wondering what the Nephites had done to make these people so angry—or frightened.

"What?" The first voice sounded surprised.

"I'm no Nephite!" Mikiah repeated. "I'm an Amalekite!"

"He says he's an Amalekite, Keb," the softer voice said, and Mikiah caught a slight edge of mockery in the tone.

"Yeah, well, he would say that, wouldn't he?" Keb grunted. "But what's an Amalekite doing *here?*"

"A valid question," the other conceded. "And one I'd like to have answered without all this yelling. Some of you—go collect that man and bring him here to me."

A large group of angry-eyed men detached itself from the ragged army and came toward the lone Amalekite. Mikiah raised his open, empty hands as they approached. Too many of them looked like men who only wanted an excuse, and he wasn't going to give them one. He didn't struggle as they grabbed him roughly by the arms, took his sword away, and carried him back to shove him to his knees before their leader.

The man was tall and handsome, powerfully built, with pale blond hair and bright blue eyes. He gazed down at Mikiah with a kind of speculative caution. The man beside him—Keb, Mikiah assumed—was thin and wiry, slightly shorter, and his ragged black hair hung over deep-set eyes that glittered with solid hatred. His right forearm was wrapped tightly with a blood-stained bandage. A knife blade gleamed in his fist.

"Good afternoon," said the leader pleasantly. "My name is Amlici, which I'm sure you'll want to know, if you don't already. This, as you may have gathered, is Keb." He gestured elegantly to the man beside him. "May I have your name?"

Mikiah raised his eyebrows at the exquisite manners. "Mikiah," he said, and then because it didn't seem to matter, added, "From the city of Jerusalem." He cocked his head curiously. "What did the Nephites do that makes you want to kill them on sight?"

"Ah, I don't blame you for being inquisitive on the subject," said Amlici easily. "But you'll forgive me for satisfying my own curiosity before I answer yours. I am, as you may see, in a state to be cautious, and in the present circumstance, it seems prudent to be quite sure of who I'm speaking to before speaking. After all, there's no point in lengthy conversations with a dead man." Behind Amlici, Keb flexed his muscles threateningly, giving Mikiah an evil smile. "So tell me," Amlici continued, "what is an Amalekite from the fair city of Jerusalem doing so far from home in Nephite lands?"

Mikiah paused, cautious. "Hunting," he said finally.

Amlici lifted one eyebrow. "It seems like an awfully long way to come just to slaughter some poor, defenseless animals. Couldn't you hunt closer to home?"

"That depends on what you want to hunt," Mikiah said. "And I suspect your men might know a little about how 'defenseless' these particular animals are."

"Ah," Amlici responded, drawing the sound out long. "It's true, we have encountered some very vicious animals this day. Over ten thousand of my people didn't survive the experience. And you think your 'hunters' can do better?"

"It's possible," Mikiah said cautiously, but Keb was already protesting.

"Amlici, you can't seriously be thinking of trusting him," he said. "What proof do we have that he's what he says he is? It's just the story a Nephite spy would spin, to lead the rest of us into a trap." He glared at Mikiah, who met his eyes with a bland calmness that he didn't quite feel. "You should let me kill him and be done with it."

"Not quite yet, Keb," Amlici said calmly. He gave Mikiah a questioning look. "Keb does have a point though. What proof do you have that you are in fact an Amalekite and not a Nephite spy?"

Mikiah snorted. "What proof would you accept?" He shook his head. "The only proof I have is the army of Lamanites coming behind me."

Amlici smiled broadly. "Now that, I should very much like to see. If there *is* a Lamanite army in the vicinity, why, I can see no reason why we shouldn't be allies. Even friends. I'm certain I and my people share similar goals with the Lamanites, especially on the subject of Nephites. Perhaps, just to prove that such an army exists, you might be willing to conduct a—shall we say, a return envoy back to your own leader?"

Which was how Mikiah found himself accompanied by Keb as he made his way back to his own camp.

"I warn you," the Amlicite said in a low voice as they neared the forest edge, "if this is some kind of trick, if Amlici dies because of you, the first thing I'm going to do is spill your guts on the ground. Even if it's also the last thing I do."

Mikiah just sighed. "You might want to put that knife away, or our sentries are liable to think you're threatening me. You won't be able to protect your leader with an arrow through your neck."

The two men measured each other up like a pair of strange dogs, cautiously friendly but alert for any threat. Mikiah would have laughed at the image if he hadn't felt the stretching tension, lingering on the edge of war. He could almost see the turned-back ears and raised hackles. They were near opposites physically. Ashoram's half-Lamanite heritage gave him the dark hair and complexion of his mother, contrasting with Amlici's pale blond. While they were similar in height, Ashoram was much thinner than Amlici, all sinew and narrow muscle rather than the broad-shouldered, stocky build. Yet there was something in Amlici that reminded Mikiah strongly of his king, the powerful charisma that had once led a young man to believe that whatever Ashoram wanted must be right. He wasn't surprised by the devotion he sensed from Keb and the other Amlicites.

Amlici broke the silence with a friendly smile. "Well. One of us is going to have to speak first, and since I'm obviously in the weaker position in terms of sheer numbers, I suppose I'll have to accept the onerous task. Your man Mikiah tells me you're planning to do some hunting. If that is the case, we may be of use to you."

"Of use." Ashoram sneered. "A ragtag bunch of walking wounded, apparently running for your lives. How could you possibly be of use to us?"

Mikiah, watching closely, saw the flash of anger in Amlici's eyes, but it was quickly hidden behind a smooth smile. "Ah, you see clearly, O king, but you see only half. Yes, it's true my men were defeated today, but the Nephite armies did not escape entirely unscathed themselves. We bloodied them well for you. More importantly, we know where they are." His eyes narrowed in deep satisfaction. "And where they are not." Ashoram drew in a sharp breath, his eyebrows lifting, and Amlici nodded. "If you were to allow us to lead you toward the city of Zarahemla just now, you might find something to your benefit. With your innumerable host, the remnants left in Zarahemla would stand no chance against you." Amlici's voice had dropped slightly, low and persuasive. "Once you hold the city, what's left of Alma's army would be helpless to take it back from you. And there you would be, perfectly positioned to take control of all the Nephite lands." He looked away, examining his fingertips with studied indifference. "We would have only one—small—request to make in return."

"And what's that?"

"Why, to let us join you, of course. I admit, we were heading in your general direction anyway, hoping for refuge, once the Nephites drove us from our proper lands and deprived us of what should have been ours. I've heard that some of your people have a similar background, so I hoped we might find sympathy among you."

Ashoram grunted. "You wouldn't be the first refugees the Lamanites have taken in."

"Yes, with all their professions of religious tolerance, the Nephites do have a striking tendency to drive out anyone who disagrees with them."

"More Nephite lies. How surprising," Ashoram said drily.

"You'd think they'd at least make a pretense of believing what they preach," Amlici said. He was watching Ashoram intently, gauging his reactions.

"It's possible they think they don't need to anymore," Ashoram growled. "If their plan works, they'll finally have everything they want."

Amlici's eyebrows went up. "Plan? What plan?" Mikiah thought it was the first time he'd seen the man truly surprised.

Ashoram grimaced. "They have my wife," he admitted. "And they'll use her to start their conquest."

"They kidnapped your wife? Shocking," Amlici said, shaking his head. "But I wouldn't put anything past that Alma. The so-called 'chief judge of the Nephites' would do anything to hold onto power—or grab a little more. I should have been king over the Nephites, if it weren't for Alma's greed and lust for power." There was a hidden viciousness in his voice when he mentioned Alma's name, something ugly glowing deep within the vivid blue of his eyes. "You're wise to make this kind of preemptive strike. A man like Alma won't stop until someone *makes* him stop." He glanced aside, a carefully timed hesitation. "Alma lives in Zarahemla, of course," he remarked casually. "*His* wife will be there, and his children. If you truly wanted to have something to hold over the Nephites . . ." He trailed off suggestively, and Mikiah saw a cruel light blossom in Ashoram's eyes, ignited by Amlici's smooth hatred.

"My king, may I speak?" Mikiah said, stepping close to Ashoram, his voice low. Amlici drew himself up, indignant at the interruption, but Ashoram nodded for Mikiah to continue. "Are you sure this is what you want to do?" Mikiah asked. He'd turned his back to Amlici, excluding the former Nephite from the conversation. "Attacking the Nephites is one thing, but if you follow this man's counsel, you'll be making war on nothing but women and children."

Ashoram's expression was thunderous, and Mikiah's heart sank. "And what else did *they* do, using my wife against me?" the king growled. "No, Mikiah. I don't blame you for your scruples—they show an honorable heart—but this is not the time for them. This time, we give the Nephites back all the wrongs they've done to us. This Alma can have his family back once I have mine—just before I cut his heart out!"

"And don't worry, young Mikiah," Amlici put in smoothly. "You'll have your chance to fight the armies of the Nephites as well, to carve glory from their ranks as much as you wish. This will merely give us the greatest advantage over them in battle. And may I say, O king," he continued, turning his attention back to Ashoram, "while I recognize your infinite superiority in numbers, there is just *one* other request I'd like to make of you before we join our forces."

"What is it?"

Amlici smiled, and the mask of cultured civility dropped for just a moment, so that Mikiah could see the naked greed, ugly with unthinking hatred and bloodlust, that Amlici worked so hard to keep hidden. "I want to kill Alma myself."

"Stop moping, Mikiah," Eliah said cheerfully as the army marched in the direction of Zarahemla, guided by the Amlicites. "I don't know what you're so upset about anyway. Ashoram's only giving the Nephites back as good as he got. It's no more than they deserve, after what they did."

"What *they* did?" Mikiah raised an eyebrow at his brother. "What they did isn't so different from what *we* did, if you remember. What if Lamoni did what we're doing? Came attacking while we're all away and captured Nabeth? Your mother and sisters? What would you think then?"

Eliah's eyes widened. "That's—he wouldn't—that's completely different!"

"No it isn't," Shehum contradicted, his deep voice slow and mild as always. "But there's nothing we can do about it, so maybe you two could shut up about it."

Mikiah followed Shehum's eyes and found Keb marching not far away, watching them. There was no telling how much the Amlicite had heard. "Shehum's right," he said. "There's no point in discussing it. We'll do what Ashoram tells us to, just like we always have."

Except that I haven't, he added to himself, remembering Temisah's kiss on his cheek and her blessing in his ears, remembering his promise to Ashir and the doubts that had begun in her home. He'd seen the blind loathing that truly drove the Amlicites, no matter what they told themselves about the "injustice" the Nephites had heaped upon them. Amlici's hatred was too vicious, too delighted by his own cruelty, to be rational. Listening behind the words, Mikiah would bet the true story was one of aggression from the Amlicites and simple defense on the part of the Nephites. A man like that wouldn't stop at merely conquering a city full of women and children. He'd burn it to the ground—and all the better if the women and children were trapped inside.

And it would be Mikiah's fault. He cringed inwardly, but he couldn't avoid the truth. He'd known how Ashoram would react when Temisah disappeared, but he hadn't counted on this. Any atrocities Ashoram or Amlici committed would be at least partly on Mikiah's head. But what could he do about it?

"You think maybe we can bring it down?" Eliah asked suddenly, plucking at the bow over his shoulder. Mikiah jerked out of his thoughts, realizing he'd been staring into the sky, tracing the sweeping pattern of a bird against the blue. "Fresh meat for dinner would be a nice change."

Before Mikiah could answer, the hunting falcon stooped, dropping from the sky like lightning toward a flock of birds that had risen above a clump of trees away to the west of the Lamanite army.

Eliah sighed, releasing his bow. "Too late now."

Mikiah was still staring at the trees, his eyes narrowed in sudden speculation. "Maybe not," he said slowly. "*Something* scared those birds."

Mikiah and his friends crept silently through the underbrush in the grove, following the quiet murmur of voices. Mikiah eased forward, feeling the scratch of small branches and brush of green leaves across his skin, the ground soft with green moss and leaf mulch beneath his feet. The voices were closer; even quiet as they were, he could almost make out what they were saying. He moved a final branch gently out of the way and found himself looking out, still hidden by the bushes, at four Nephites less than a stone's throw away. They were obviously in the middle of taking a short break to rest and eat and relieve themselves, but by the small packs they carried and the stains of travel, they'd already come a long way and intended to go even further. Mikiah's eyes narrowed again as he saw the weapons ready to their hands and the marks of recent battle—cuts and bruises and blood-spattered clothes that could only have been obtained in one way.

Four Nephite warriors—which meant four Nephite spies sent to watch the camp of the Amlicites.

"I still think we should go now," one of them was saying. By the looks of them, he was the youngest, but he didn't seem to have any problem with expressing his opinion.

"We need at least some idea how many there are," the next oldest said, impatient with his junior's persistence. "What's the matter, Manti? Afraid of a few Lamanites?"

Manti glared at him. "Zeram, if you think Alma will thank you for trying to fight the entire Lamanite army all by yourself and getting yourself killed, instead of coming to warn him, like we *should,* you go right ahead."

In the shelter of the bushes, Mikiah turned his head slightly to raise one eyebrow at Shehum. "Nothing we can do about it?" he said, no more than the breath of a whisper. Shehum's eyes went wide as he understood what Mikiah was asking. He stared at his friend for a thoughtful moment before giving a single nod. Mikiah turned the same questioning look to Eliah, who shook his head, not understanding. Mikiah pulled the Lamanite close, his mouth right next to Eliah's ear. "Amlici is using Ashoram to get his own revenge, and we both know it," he whispered. "The king would never have done this on his own. I don't know about you, but I came here to fight the Nephite army, not to slaughter children."

Eliah drew in a sharp breath and pulled back, his eyes searching Mikiah's. He worried his lower lip between his teeth, his eyebrows drawn together. A long, silent sigh seemed to pull the decision from him. "All right. Do it."

Mikiah nodded, jaw clenched, and handed his sword to Shehum. "Try not to let them kill me," he whispered, and stepped free of the concealing bushes, hands raised in token of peace. He seemed to be making a habit of walking up to armed men who wanted to kill him today.

The youngest Nephite let out a surprised yell at the sight of him, scrambling for his weapon, and before Mikiah could blink, he was surrounded by swords and spear points. He held very still, surprised by the depth of his awareness of his own mortality. "Calm down," he advised. "If I wanted to kill you, you'd already be dead."

"Then what *do* you want?" the oldest of them asked, scowling, sword point still held uncomfortably close to Mikiah's belly.

"I want to ask you why you're still *here?*" Mikiah demanded. "The Amlicites have joined forces with my king. They're—*we're*—headed for Zarahemla. You have to know that Amlici is insane. I don't think he sees anybody besides himself as a real person. Do you have any idea what a man like him will do once we get there? You've left your city completely unguarded, and you're sitting here worrying about getting a *headcount?!*" He shook his head. "You have to warn your people as soon as possible. If the Nephite army doesn't stop us, Amlici is going to wash the streets of that city with blood, and my king won't bother to hold him back."

"Then why would *you* bother?" the man called Zeram asked. He glanced at the eldest. "Don't listen to him, Limher. He's a Lamanite. If what he says it true, why would he tell us? He's trying to trick us."

"No tricks," Mikiah said, raising his empty hands. "I'll swear it by anything you like. The Nephite preachers saved my life once. I'm just repaying the debt. Besides," he shrugged, "I don't like killing women and children." He glanced over his shoulder, toward the passing army. "I have to go. They'll miss me if I stay longer."

Zeram growled, raising his spear. "You'll stay until we're through with you," he said threateningly.

Mikiah met the Nephite's hot glare with a level calm. "No," he said. "I won't." There was a rustle as, behind him, Shehum and Eliah rose from their hiding places, weapons held ready. Eliah's bow was already drawn with an arrow on the string, and Mikiah's sword flew into his hand as Shehum tossed it to him. The Nephites fell back in surprise, which gave Mikiah just enough opening to slip back into the undergrowth. "I warned you," he said, just before he disappeared. "If your wives and children die now, it'll be on your heads, not mine."

"I don't care what any of you say," he heard Manti saying as Mikiah and his friends left the same way they'd come. "Whether he's telling the truth or not, Alma needs to know what's happening. I'm going now, even if I go alone."

Mikiah smiled grimly to himself as he stole through a clump of sharp, long-leaved plants. He'd done all he could. Now he just needed to survive.

FIFTEEN

BORDERS OF ZARAHEMLA, 87 BC

"JUST OVER THAT LAST HILL," AMLICI SAID, POINTING AHEAD. "WE'LL be able to see the river Sidon, and a bit further along its course, Zarahemla." The former Nephite had lost none of his cultured superiority over the long march, but he'd abandoned the mask of controlled outrage. He no longer pretended to upright indignation or that his goal was anything more than revenge for his thwarted ambition. He was vicious, savage, and he had unleashed that savagery on the people of the Nephites. The small towns and farms they'd passed lay behind them in ruins. Amlici had incited his men to atrocity, pillaging and murdering all they found. While Ashoram hadn't actively encouraged his own men, he hadn't stopped any of them who wanted to join in. Mikiah regarded the hill that blocked them from view of Zarahemla with anything but anticipation, his stomach clenched tight on apprehension. If the Nephites didn't arrive in time, it would be more of the same—but on a much larger scale, and neither Amlici nor Ashoram were bothering to pretend otherwise.

"King Ashoram! King Ashoram!" One of the forward scouts came pelting back toward the army, waving his arms and pointing behind him, stumbling slightly in his panic. "The Nephite army! They're here! They're crossing the river!"

"*What?!*" Amlici's blue eyes blazed with a rabid light, and he gripped Ashoram's arm urgently. "We've got to hurry! If they get their whole army across that river, they'll be ready for us. We've *got* to hit them while they're still crossing."

Ashoram turned to Hanan, his chief captain, catching Amlici's excitement. "Sound the charge!" he cried. "We'll catch them in the water and slaughter them all!"

Hanan nodded stolidly, but the signal he called for was a quick advance rather than a charge. When Ashoram would have protested, the captain just gave him a hard look. "With all respect, my king, I've been doing this a long time. If our men go running up that hill, they won't be good for anything when they reach the other side. Time enough for charging once we're over the top."

The armies of the Lamanites and Amlicites poured over the crest of the hill like a wave breaking over a rock. A wide, fertile plain stretched into the distance, the dark streak of the river meandering through the golden fields. Farther up its course from the hill, the river Sidon made a sharp bend, curving back toward the east, and on the far side of that bend stood the walled city of Zarahemla. Closer, the river widened, spreading out into shallows that could be forded, no deeper than a man's chest in the center. Those fords had bottlenecked the Nephites, with a fraction of the army on the west side, or crowding through the river, and most of them still on the east, waiting for their chance to cross.

As the Lamanites came to the crest of the hill and spotted the Nephite army below them, each man dipped his fingers into a pouch at his side and drew them across his forehead, leaving an arc of red above the left eyebrow. It was a symbol, a silent war cry. It meant, *I am going to shed blood today.* Since there were so many Amalekites and Amulonites in the army, as well as the Amlicites, it would also help to distinguish friend from foe. Mikiah's thumb across his brow was no more hesitant than any of his companions, the red streak covering the scar above his bad eye.

"Remember," Eliah murmured beside him, "you asked for this."

"Better than the alternative," Mikiah replied grimly.

As the army pooled around him on the far side of the hill, Ashoram gripped his sword tight with anticipation, his eyes shining. "*Now* can we sound the charge?" he asked his chief captain.

The older warrior just nodded, unfazed by the sarcasm. "Yes, my king," he said. "Now we charge."

"Good!"

With the high, howling scream of their war cry shattering the moist air of the river valley, Ashoram's army thundered toward the Nephites. But the Nephite army was well trained. The small band of men on the west of the river didn't panic or run. They'd seen their enemies coming and turned to meet them, standing tightly clumped with braced spears. The first wave of Lamanites found themselves running into a forest of sharp points and most of them died instantly, unable to stop with the crush of people coming behind them. Their bodies did some good, hindering the weapons of those who'd killed them, but there were more, always more Nephites pushing forward as they gained the west bank of the river. With such a narrow battlefront, the bulk of the Lamanites couldn't even reach anyone to fight, making their numerical advantage useless for the moment. The Nephites' own distinctive war cry rose to meet the Lamanites, a hollow, almost metallic barking, meant to imitate a jaguar's snarl.

"Archers!" captain Hanan shouted, stabbing a finger at the men in the water. "Bring them down!" Flights of arrows answered him, raining down on the unprotected heads of the Nephites, and bodies began sweeping away from the battle down the river, impaled by feathered shafts. The men on the east of the river howled with anger, pushing forward even more eagerly, flooding into the ford as quickly as they could.

"Push them back!" Hanan shouted. "Don't let them cross!"

But the Nephites weren't willing to be pushed. They formed an impassable barricade of men and weapons, holding the west bank of the ford. Though the bodies began piling on top of one another, both Nephite and Lamanite, there were always more ready to take the place of those who fell. The Nephite line held—and began to advance. They came slowly, painfully, paying for each step with the lives of their men, but they came, and they took as many lives as they gave for their advance. More corpses floated down the river as the

Nephites threw their dead enemies into the water to clear the way for those who were crossing.

Ashoram wasn't willing to stay back and direct the army. It was his first battle, and he'd insisted on taking part personally. Nonetheless, his guards did manage to keep him away from the front lines, safely behind the actual fighting. Mikiah stood beside the king, ready to act as a messenger if Ashoram needed to talk with his chief captain. He could feel the repressed energy radiating from the Amulonite, and felt the growing fever of battle himself, the tension of waiting, the almost overwhelming need to *do* something. Mikiah felt like a bowstring pulled back and vibrating with the need to snap forward.

Even in their excitement, both Mikiah and Ashoram were pictures of serenity compared to Amlici, who stood beside them. He was almost dancing, swaying back and forth and craning his neck as he tried to see around or over the heads of the men around him. As the Nephites pushed the front line back, their men siphoning through the shallows of the river like grains of corn through a funnel, the battle became more widespread, and Amlici soon found what he was looking for.

"There!" he exclaimed, pointing toward the center of the Nephites battle front. "I see him. Alma is there! The fool—he's right out in the open, if I can just get to him!"

Ashoram grinned at his guards. "My friends," he said, "our ally has an appointment with the ruler of the Nephites. Let's escort him there!"

The king and his guards, Mikiah among them, forged through the Lamanite army like a spearhead, aimed at the heart and soul of the Nephite resistance. Mikiah had fought before, but this was his first battlefield, and he was surprised by the way he could feel the impact when their spear hit the Nephites. "Alma!" Amlici screamed, charging toward a dark-haired man, whose clothing was still dripping from the river crossing. "Prepare to pay for your crimes!" He fell upon the Nephite leader, sword raised to strike. He was the picture of righteous justice and outraged majesty—unless you looked at his eyes, which were wide and wild, seeing nothing but the chance for blood.

Mikiah didn't have attention to spare for Amlici or Alma after that. He found himself face to face with a man half a head taller than him, big and powerfully muscled. The Nephite was already gripped by battle fever. He swung viciously at Mikiah, the edge of his cimeter slicing the air where Mikiah's head had been a moment before. Mikiah threw himself to one side, and his own blade whirled under the giant's guard, ripping his shirt and drawing a thick line of blood across his ribs. The Nephite roared, the pain only fueling his anger, and Mikiah was forced to jump out of the way once more. His opponent was big—but also slow, and ruled by the heat of battle. Mikiah danced back, his sword flashed to the right, but it was his left foot that connected, smashing full force into the Nephite's knee. The snap of breaking bone was drowned by the cry of pain, and the Nephite stumbled. Mikiah looked into his eyes for only a moment, and saw the despair dawning there. The Nephite knew he was finished, that Mikiah could kill him. The next moment, the giant lurched toward him with a sobbing war cry, cimeter raised high above his head. Mikiah moved almost without thinking. His free hand snapped out, blocking the descending blow, and his sword rammed home in the Nephite's chest. Mikiah found himself staring into the man's eyes only a hands breadth away, unable to look away from the shock and fear that filled them. And something else—something he had no time to name—lurking deep in those eyes. His eyes were pale blue, almost gray, and as the life slipped from them, another pair of gray eyes flashed in Mikiah's mind. He nearly lost his grip on the bloody hilt of his sword as the dead Nephite fell away, and he felt a surge of deep revulsion as he tugged it free. He wanted to retch, but he didn't have time. Another Nephite was already attacking.

Mikiah lost himself for a time, his world narrowing to the need for life, to kill or be killed. He didn't know how many lives he took, and he barely felt the pain of his own wounds, bloody and ugly, but not enough to hinder him. The dim vision from his half-blind eye was more of a handicap. Several times he noticed motion on his blind side with just enough time to duck or block the weapon swinging at him out of the chaos. The battle swirled around him, and the whole world seemed to move with it. Without noticing how he got there, he found himself fighting at Amlici's shoulder, facing one of Alma's guards.

The Nephite leader didn't have the uncanny fighting ability of Ammon. In fact, he was barely holding his own against Amlici, and obviously tiring, his breath coming in harsh gasps. Sweat trickled into his brown eyes and plastered black strands of hair to his forehead. His sword swung truly in spite of his fatigue, barely fast enough to block the wild frenzy of Amlici's blows. Amlici grinned savagely as he fought, his very insanity lending him strength that the Nephite couldn't hope to match. With a lightning thrust, he broke past Alma's weakening guard. Alma, twisting desperately away from the blow, overbalanced and fell with a cry of pain, but he'd gained himself a few seconds. Amlici's sword, rather than plunging into his chest, only sliced along his side, opening a deep gash. Amlici stood over his fallen enemy, savoring his moment of triumph as he raised his sword high for the killing stroke.

In that moment, Mikiah jumped sideways, avoiding a barely-seen blow from his own opponent's club that would have crushed his skull. He crashed right into Amlici. The former Nephite cursed savagely as he stumbled, but Alma was already making use of the distraction, crying out in prayer. "O Lord, spare me!" he yelled, turning his gaze to the vivid blue sky above them. "Let me save this people!"

The next instant, he was on his feet, and his sword rang like a bell against Amlici's again and again. Mikiah, just glancing at him, saw the same strange emotion in Alma that had lurked hidden in the eyes of his first opponent, but now in full blaze. Mikiah was startled when he recognized what it was. Hope. In the middle of this field of pain and death, Alma dared to be filled with hope. Amlici snarled at it, beat against it with both sword and hatred, but he couldn't break it. Alma beat him back, and further back, and then the Nephite leader's jaw clenched, his eyes hardened, and he lunged, sword darting past Amlici's guard in an all-or-nothing attack that held nothing in reserve. The sword point punched through Amlici's throat, and the former Nephite fell. His body landed with a squelching thud in the grass, mingling his blood with that of the lives he'd wasted in his pointless, useless war.

Alma stood there for a moment, panting, his hand pressed against the wound in his side as he gazed down at the man he'd killed. He should have been completely unprepared for Ashoram's sword striking at him from one side. But he wasn't. Somehow, Alma's own weapon was there, blocking the blow that should have finished him, the blade ringing with a harsh clamor of metal against metal. He stood ready, facing the Lamanite king with a righteous fury blazing from his brown eyes—the attitude Amlici had tried so hard to project and failed. Alma's sword flashed toward Ashoram, who was still off balance after his failed sneak attack. The Amulonite king barely managed to twist out of the way in time and the tip of Alma's blade sliced the cord that held his leopard skin cloak, rather than impaling Ashoram's throat. Ashoram fell back, stumbling over his fallen cloak, one hand clutching at his neck as if to be sure it was still whole. He'd gone very pale, his eyes wide and white. For just a moment, he seemed to freeze solid with the chill and sudden understanding of his own mortality. Then he turned and ran from the Nephite leader, plunging back into the safety of his army.

"Kill him!" Ashoram shrieked at his guards as he fled, his voice laced with panic. The guards closed ranks behind him, doing their best to obey, but they found themselves blocked both by Alma's own guards and the Nephite leader's unnatural strength. Mikiah felt the Lamanite army beginning to give way, infected by their king's cowardice. There was space opening behind him as those in the rear fled, and others pushed forward much less eagerly under the eyes of their captains. The Nephites, sensing victory, surged against their enemies with renewed zeal.

Mikiah, all his attention bent on keeping Alma's guard from smashing his head in, wasn't expecting an attack from behind. The widening of the Nephite's eyes, a slight flick of his gaze over Mikiah's shoulder, was all that saved his life. Mikiah dropped where he stood, falling out of the way of the slicing sword. Without even looking around as he crouched in the trampled grass, his face almost level with the ground, he swung his leg out in a sweeping kick that took his attacker just behind the knees. He saw the dark-haired figure stumble forward, arms grasping for balance, and then Keb's sword was buried almost by accident in the Nephite guard's gut. Keb regained his balance and pulled the sword free without so much as a second glance at the dying man. He whirled to attack Mikiah again, swinging wildly with the fury of a berserker. Mikiah leapt backward from his crouch and landed on his feet a few paces away, avoiding the attack and giving himself room to move. He didn't know why Keb was trying to kill him, and he didn't have time to think about it. The Amlicite was already lunging for him, and Mikiah found himself barely holding back a hard rain of vicious, unpredictable blows. His body jarred each time his sword met Keb's, and he felt the harsh vibration of the hilt numbing his palms, the slow-burning ache in his arms. He needed just a moment—half a moment—to catch his breath, gather his strength again, and Keb, fueled by his mad fury, wasn't going to let him have it.

He saw the blow coming, Keb's sword hacking at him, but he couldn't move fast enough. His aching muscles dragged his arms through air that had become thick as honey, far too slowly to stop the deadly blade. He was too late to block it, but he felt his sword glance off of Keb's, knocking the blow down and to the side.

Mikiah screamed as the sword bit deep into his thigh. His fingers loosened, dropping his own weapon, and a moment later he followed it to the ground. He lay in the grass, clutching helplessly at the bloody gash in his leg, choking on the pain of it, his face contorted and glistening with sweat. Keb loomed above him, the point of his blade ready to plunge into Mikiah's unprotected chest.

"I told you," the Amlicite said, his voice coming to Mikiah through a dark, watery veil. "If he dies, you die." He gathered himself to drive the blade home.

The point of a sword erupted from Keb's chest. The Amlicite's body froze in shock, eyes and mouth gaping, and then he toppled, dead before he hit the ground. Behind him, Alma jerked his sword free, grimacing. As he turned away, his eyes met Mikiah's for half a breath and something like recognition flitted across his face. Then he was gone, and Mikiah curled himself around the slash in his thigh, panting in spreading shock as he tried to hold the wound closed. He lost himself to the pain for an unknown time, sinking beneath a gathering darkness.

"Mikiah!" He roused as a rough hand grabbed his arm, tugging sharply. "Get up, Mikiah, we've got to go!"

Lifting his eyelids took tremendous effort. Eliah's frightened face hovered somewhere above him. "Can't," he whispered. "You go. Tell Nabeth—"

"Don't be stupid," he heard Shehum say sharply. Mikiah cried out as the Lamanite hauled him upright and slung him over one shoulder. "Come on," Shehum said, breaking into a heavy run. Mikiah passed out with pain and blood loss before his friend had carried him more than half a dozen steps.

SIXTEEN

WILDERNESS OF HERMOUNTS, 87 BC

HE WOKE TO DARKNESS AND RAIN. WATER PATTERED FROM THE SKY, gathering and dripping from the leaves of trees, soaking the leaf mulch beneath. Mikiah twitched as a cold droplet hit his cheek. He was propped against something hard and uneven, the wide base of a tree. His whole body hurt, his leg throbbing with angry heat, and he clenched both fists and teeth to keep from thrashing against the pain. A groan slipped away from him, and something nearby rustled in response.

"Mikiah? Are you awake?" Eliah's voice came out of the darkness. A groping hand gripped Mikiah's shoulder.

Mikiah's mouth felt dry, and his voice was no more than a harsh whisper. "Where—where are we?" he asked.

"Some forest northwest of Zarahemla," Shehum said from his other side. "I think I heard one of the Amlicites call it Hermounts." Something soft bumped against his hand. "Here. Drink."

Mikiah found the neck of the wineskin and managed to bring it to his mouth, swallowing thirstily. Hopefully, it would help dull the pain. "Where's Ashoram?" he asked, lowering the skin. "The army?"

"Scattered in the trees somewhere," Shehum said. "We heard shouting for a while, people trying to find each other, but with the dark and the rain . . ."

"And there's something else out there," Eliah put in. "We spotted tracks before the light went. Some kind of animal. We don't know what they are, but they're big." A terrified scream echoed in the distance. "And they're hungry."

"All right. First thing we need to do is get out of here, as soon as it's light." Mikiah's thoughts were already churning, plotting a route home. "How bad am I?" There was an awkward silence that stretched far longer than Mikiah liked. "That bad, huh?"

"It doesn't matter," Eliah said. "We'll carry you all the way back to Jerusalem if we have to."

"The real problem's going to be getting past the Nephites," Shehum said.

Mikiah shook his head in the darkness. "No, that won't be a problem."

"You have a plan?"

Mikiah drew in a deep breath that rattled in his throat, his eyes sinking closed against the pain. "I always have a plan."

By the time dawn began to creep around the enshrouding trees, Mikiah was gripped by fever, barely conscious, groaning in pain at the slightest motion. His friends lashed together a litter to carry him and shifted him onto it as gently as they could.

"Which way?" Eliah asked, picking up his end.

"South," Shehum replied, but there was doubt behind the decision. He cast a confused gaze around the trackless wilderness, the layer of clouds that blocked the sun. "If we can find south in this place."

"No," Mikiah whispered. "Out of the forest. Then south."

His friends stared at him. "But—won't the Nephites—?" Eliah protested.

"Like bees," Mikiah told him. "If you don't bother them, they won't bother you."

"He's raving," Shehum said, shaking his head.

Mikiah reached out for him, gripping his wrist and shuddering at the cold dampness of his skin. Mikiah felt chilled from his bones out, but he knew he was actually burning with fever. "Trust me," he said. "Out of the forest. Then south."

Mikiah lay on his litter, staring up at a sky studded by fluffy clouds, ribbons and spots of blue showing through the gaps, and tried not to think about the sick feeling churning in his throat. He'd gotten a look at the wound in his thigh that morning. Dark blood still seeped from the gash, and the flesh around it was red and swollen, warm to the touch. A cloudy pale liquid was beginning to mix with the blood. Mikiah had seen enough to recognize a wound going bad when he saw it. The chances of his surviving it were maybe half and half—*if* they could get him to somewhere it could be treated in time.

Eliah, supporting the litter at Mikiah's feet, stumbled over the uneven ground, and Mikiah gasped, body clenched at the throb of pain. "Sorry," the Lamanite muttered. He'd been staring off into the distance, his eyebrows pushed together in worry and confusion. "Why aren't they attacking?" he asked.

"What?"

Eliah nodded to his left. "We've passed three farms and a village so far. All right, it was a small village, but there's only three of us. Why aren't they coming out to finish us off?"

"They don't want to," Mikiah told him. His voice was weak, but steady enough.

"What? How d'you figure that?"

"History. Attacking the Nephites may be like kicking a wasp's nest, but they've never attacked *us.* It's always been defense."

"But what about Temisah? Wasn't that—?"

"Wherever Temisah is, I doubt the Nephites had anything to do with it, no matter what Ashoram thinks," Mikiah said, perfectly truthfully. "And I doubt those preachers are trying to get Lamoni to attack us, either."

"But, didn't Amlici say—?"

"No, I'm with Mikiah on this one, Eliah," Shehum said. Craning his neck, Mikiah could see only his friend's broad back and tail of black hair as Shehum trudged along, supporting the head of the litter. "Amlici was a madman, but he understood the odds of battle as well as anyone. Without us, Amlici never stood a chance of winning, and he knew it. He would have said anything, told any lie, to get Ashoram on his side. That colored every word he said and everything the Amlicites did."

And if that's true of the Amlicites, Mikiah thought, but chose not to say, *what does that say about other groups that left the Nephites?* Mikiah's father had always said the Amalekites dissented because they couldn't live with the lies and hypocrisy anymore. But Minek himself had been killed by his own unthinking hatred, and Mikiah had already seen for himself that not all Nephites deserved the accusations the Amalekites and Amulonites heaped on them. In fact, he was staking his life and the lives of his friends on it. That was a risk, but some deep instinct told him the Nephites could be trusted.

And that fact terrified him far more than the war ever had.

Mikiah was freezing, drenched in fever sweat, cringing from the chill touch of the night breeze against his skin, and too exhausted even to shiver at the cold. His friends slept on either side of him, providing some shelter from the air, but it wasn't enough. They didn't dare risk a fire, no matter how tolerant the Nephites had been so far.

A particularly bright star winked at him through the leftover wisps of cloud blowing across the night sky and the branches of the forest edge they had been following. Mikiah opened his mouth, then paused, rolling his head so he could glance to either side. Eliah and Shehum breathed deeply and slowly, motionless lumps of shadow in the darkness.

"Well, here I am," Mikiah said, so quietly even he could barely hear himself, staring up at that bright point of light. "They all tell me I have to find out for myself. I guess that means prayer. I never prayed to anything before, so you'll just have to put up with it if I don't do it right." He paused, feeling awkward, but he'd gone this far. It'd be even more stupid to stop now. "I don't know if you're real," he admitted. "I don't know how you'd let me know if you are. I don't know what kind of proof I'd accept. But we're in trouble, and it's going to get worse. The army is still coming from Helam; they'll probably reach the Nephite lands tomorrow. It's likely the Nephites won't be so tolerant once that happens. We've got days of wilderness to get through, and the only certain path back is the one the army'll be coming straight down. I don't want Eliah and Shehum getting caught in another battle, and if we meet the army coming, they'll be forced to join it. And I think—I think I'm probably dying." He brushed the festering wound in his thigh with one hand and drew in a deep breath, blinking several times as he stared up into eternity. "So if you're there," he whispered. "If you're listening—if you care about us at all, I'm asking you to get us home. Let me live, get us all home safely, and that will be proof enough."

He waited in the dark, not knowing what to expect. Possibly a dream of some kind. He remembered hearing that Father Lehi had had some kind of dream. An angel had come to Aaron. Ashir had seen a vision. If it was true, anything might happen.

And if it is true? A thought whispered in his head, in a voice that sounded like Muloki's. He could almost see the Nephite's gently challenging look. *If He saves your life and brings you safely home, what will you do then?*

"Then I'll believe," Mikiah breathed. "Then I'll do whatever you ask of me. I'll change, if I can."

Something shifted. The chill receded slightly from his bones, and Mikiah's heart lifted, like a bubble of air rising from deep water. It wasn't an angelic visitation, nor a vision the way Ashir had described. If it was a dream, it was a very strange one, with no sensation of drifting off or awakening afterward, the vague disconnection from the physical world. He felt something, warm lips pressed against his cheek, and heard a voice without anybody there to speak. "God bless you, Mikiah," it said, a woman's voice, soft and familiar. Then a second voice spoke, another voice he knew. "If you want to find healing, come and find me," Muloki told him.

Tears trickled from Mikiah's eyes, lines of wet heat down his cheeks, and he let them fall. "I will," he whispered into the night breeze. "I promise I will." He knew he was making a commitment not just for his immediate future but for his entire life. At least that meant that his life stood a better chance of extending beyond the immediate future. He knew now where he needed to go: south—directly south, to the land of Ishmael.

Seventeen

City of Ishmael, 87 BC

Days later, two very weary, very hungry, very disreputable-looking Lamanites stepped out of the wilderness north of Ishmael, carrying a third man in a makeshift stretcher. All three were dirty and ragged with their long journey through the forest, the clinging underbrush and low branches and sharp-thorned plants leaving their marks in skin and clothing.

"Well, there it is," Eliah said dubiously, in spite of his relief at seeing the end of their journey. "Are you sure this is where you want to go, Mikiah? We did steal the man's daughter, after all."

Mikiah roused from a half stupor, squinting against the midday sunlight, bright in his eyes now that they'd left the shelter of the trees. "Are we there?" he asked hoarsely, rolling his head to either side, but unable to see ahead. Eliah nodded. "Good. I know someone here who can help."

"If you say so." Eliah jostled the litter slightly, resettling his grip, and Mikiah gasped aloud as it jarred his damaged leg. The wound was swollen with infection after so long, oozing pus and tender to the slightest touch. "Come on, Shehum," Eliah continued, his voice light to hide the worry clouding his eyes. "One last push, and then we won't have to carry this useless layabout one step farther."

Shehum just grunted, trudging along with the same steady pace he'd kept since he carried Mikiah from the battlefield.

Mikiah woke with a sharp gasp and lay panting for a few seconds. In his dream, he'd been drowning, struggling to reach a surface that only moved farther and farther away. He was warm, a sensation he'd nearly forgotten. Also, he seemed to be resting in a bed, covered with woven blankets, and he thought he might have been bathed. Certainly, the wound in his thigh had been cleaned and rebandaged. He looked around, recognizing the golden stone walls of the room. He'd reached King Lamoni's palace. The room was simply furnished, one of the guest rooms such as those he'd stayed in during Ashoram's first attempts to negotiate for Temisah's hand. Sunlight shone in at one window, casting a square of brighter gold on the far wall, the flat angle of early evening. In spite of the comforting atmosphere, he was bothered by the sweetly cloying scent of something rotten in the room.

Mikiah heard a familiar voice humming nearby, beyond the open doorway, and his eyes widened in surprised disbelief. "Ashir?"

The humming cut off abruptly and a Lamanite woman came in. She did look like Ashir, but this woman's eyes were brown and soft rather than Ashir's piercing gray. "Not Ashir, I'm afraid," she said gently. "Abish."

"Ashir's sister," Mikiah said, remembering. "You were with her when . . ." He trailed off, too out of breath to finish.

"Yes." She came to him and helped him lift his head so she could hold a cup of cool water to his mouth. He swallowed a few times, but the motion seemed to punch at his throat, and he lay back even more exhausted.

"Where's Eliah and Shehum?" he whispered.

"Gone." Abish frowned. "They took one look at Temisah and said they had to go. Temisah, on the other hand . . ." A gentle smile replaced the frown. "Temisah took one look at you and insisted you had to stay. She's had the best physicians here to care for you."

Mikiah shook his head, rolling it against the pillow. "Physicians can't cure me," he said. "Not now." He'd seen his leg when she lifted him, the fiery streaks beginning to extend their tendrils from beneath the bandage, reaching for his heart. Even clean and newly bandaged, the wound smelled of death. "Muloki," he whispered. "The Nephite preacher. Is he here?"

Abish's eyebrows flew upward. "Yes." she said, startled. "Yes, he is. How did you—?"

"Go get him," Mikiah commanded, but then shook his head again. That wasn't the way to beg for one's life. "I mean, please go ask him if he'll come to me."

"I'll bring him," she said. She straightened his blanket one last time, then hurried from the room. He heard her footsteps break into a run just past the threshold.

Mikiah drifted back from his thoughts to the sound of voices, indistinct with distance and echoes but growing closer. They cut off before they got near enough for him to make out what they were saying. He felt his heart beating against his ribs as he waited. He was watching the door, but he still didn't see the Nephite arrive. He blinked, and Muloki seemed to appear in the room, already halfway to the bed. Abish was peeking around the door behind him, but drew back quickly when Mikiah met her eyes.

Muloki settled himself at Mikiah's bedside, concern making a crease between his eyebrows. He glanced at the Amalekite's wounded leg. "What did the physicians say?" he asked quietly.

"I don't know," Mikiah answered. "It doesn't matter. I know a dying man when I see one." He paused, panting for a few breaths. When he opened his eyes again, Muloki had shifted without him noticing, leaning closer. Mikiah realized he must be cutting in and out of consciousness. "I wanted to tell you . . . I'm sorry," he said.

Muloki raised his eyebrows. "Tell *me?*" he repeated. "Aaron and Ammah deserve the apology more than I do."

Mikiah nodded. "They do. And they'll get it. But . . . you can heal me. If you will."

He watched the expressions flit over Muloki's face as the Nephite stared at him, first in surprise, quickly shifting to speculation, and then compassion. "It's not a question of if I will or not," Muloki said.

"It's a question of faith. Do you have faith, Mikiah? Faith enough to be healed?" His eyes were piercing, searching for truth behind Mikiah's words.

"I don't know," Mikiah whispered. "But I'm willing to find out. If God wants me, He can have me—" He broke off, clenching his jaw at a sudden stronger throb of pain. A bead of sweat trickled from his hairline across one temple. He panted for a moment when the pain eased off. "One way or another."

"Then let's find out what our Father has in store for you." Muloki reached out to lay his hands on Mikiah's sweaty brow. They were cool and slightly rough, but Mikiah felt a wave of warmth spread from them as soon as they touched him. He drew in a long, shaky breath.

"Mikiah, son of Minek," Muloki began, "the Lord has a work for you to do. You will be the means of saving many souls. The Father has accepted the promise you have made and bids me to command you, in the name of the Son, to be healed."

If Muloki said anything after that, Mikiah didn't hear it. He was instantly plunged into the deep, comforting blackness of a dreamless sleep.

For three days, Mikiah slept without waking, not even stirring when the physicians came to change his bandages or when dead flesh sloughed from the wound, revealing healthy new tissue below. For three days, Muloki, Ammah, and Temisah neither slept nor ate, fasting and praying for the man who had both wronged them—and saved them. They took over the room opposite Mikiah's, taking it in turns to pray aloud, begging the Lord for his life and health, pleading that his heart would be softened.

On the morning of the fourth day, they heard feet taking hesitant steps across the stones of the corridor, and Mikiah stood in the doorway, pale and weak but alive and on his feet. "I'm ready," he told them, his voice thick with disuse. "Teach me what I need to know."

The sun shone high overhead, sending brightness cascading over the fields, flashing from the leaves of the nearby forest, glittering on the ripples of the waters of Sebus. Mikiah could feel it baking his shoulders as he sat once more atop the hill where he'd once watched Ammon take apart Tubal and his men. Ironically, it was also the place Mikiah had been baptized the day before. He remembered the coolness of the water as it engulfed him, Muloki's hands supporting him beneath the surface for a moment, then the water pouring off of him as Muloki raised him up again. In spite of the added weight of water clinging to him, there had been a feeling of lightness that filled him as he scrubbed the long hair back from his face.

An echo of that feeling still lingered with him now, buried at his core. Thanks to the power of God, he'd regained his life, and for an added wonder, he was seeing the world clearly through both eyes again, the years-old damage to his vision completely healed. The view over the water was lovely; the day itself seemed to be rejoicing in its very existence, but Mikiah's thoughts didn't quite match it, in spite of his joy at being able to see it. He sat in the sunlight, frowning as he gazed into the distance, and into the future.

"May I join you?" Mikiah looked around in surprise at the voice. A tall Lamanite man he'd never met before stood at a polite distance, offering Mikiah a friendly smile.

He must move like a cat, Mikiah thought, surprised he hadn't heard the man coming. Aloud, he said, "It's a free hilltop. Go ahead."

The man settled down at a comfortable distance beside him, smiling gently as he turned his face to savor the green-scented breeze. "So. How's the leg?" he asked.

Mikiah gave him a puzzled glance. "It's fine. I could go home tomorrow if there were any way to explain how I recovered so quickly. Anything that didn't involve the word 'miracle,' that is." The man nodded with a sympathetic grimace. "How did you know about that?" Mikiah asked.

"Abish," he answered succinctly. "I'm Zerimhi, her husband. I think you've met her sister as well?"

"Oh. That's right, Ashir told me about you. Did they miss me at the palace?" Mikiah had left without telling anyone, feeling the need to be alone with his thoughts, and he'd probably walked farther than was wise so soon after his recovery.

Zerimhi shook his head. "I saw you leaving. You looked like a man trying to figure out what to do with the rest of his life." He shrugged. "Cherom told me that there might come a day when I'd be able to offer you some . . . insight."

Mikiah gave the man a sharper look at that. Of course. The silent way he moved, the clear alertness of his eyes, the relaxed readiness of his stance. Another spy. "Ashir learned it from you, didn't she?"

"Learned what?"

"That way she has of seeing through people. You taught her that."

Zerimhi just smiled, and Mikiah knew he'd never get an answer to that question. "So tell me what's bothering you," Zerimhi said instead. "A man who's just received his life back and found that God exists should at least be at peace, if not overjoyed." He followed Mikiah's gaze, down to the water, and his voice grew more serious. "You're not feeling guilty about Tubal and his brigands, are you?"

Mikiah didn't even bother asking how Zerimhi knew he'd been the cause of all that. The man was a spy, after all. "Not entirely. Maybe a little," he admitted. "Men died that day because of me. Partly because of me." He shrugged. "The same thing probably would have happened eventually, but I made it happen sooner."

"And because of what happened, Lamoni was converted, along with most of his people."

"True." Mikiah plucked a few stems of grass, letting them blow away in the breeze.

Zerimhi eyed him speculatively. "That's not what's really bothering you, is it?"

"No." Mikiah shook his head, still gazing out over the water, his eyes dazzled by the light shining off the ripples. "I'm more concerned with the future than the past just now."

"Hmm, yes, that can be a tough one," Zerimhi agreed. "You've just converted to the cause of Christ—now what? And you've got it worse than I ever had because you serve an Amulonite king." He raised one eyebrow at Mikiah. "You know Ashoram will kill you as a traitor if he ever finds out, right?"

Mikiah nodded glumly, tossing a few more bits of grass into the wind. "The way I see it, I've got a few choices. I could stay here, settle down, maybe find myself a wife." Ashir's face floated before his mind's eye, but he banished the thought with a quick shake of his head.

"The quiet life. Doesn't seem too appealing, does it?" Zerimhi said, possibly misinterpreting the head shake. "And what a waste of all those years of training. Though with the right woman . . ." He grinned. "I'm proof that life doesn't have to stop with marriage."

Mikiah ignored that, though it was something he wanted to ponder later. "Or I could stay here," he continued, "give King Lamoni the same service I've given to Ashoram. Or . . ." He trailed off, gnawing at his lower lip. The third option was both tempting and dangerous.

"Or you could go back," Zerimhi finished for him. "Go back, pretend to still be someone you're not anymore, serve a king who despises what you believe—knowing that you being there to hear Ashoram's plans might save all our lives. And that it might cost yours."

"Yes," Mikiah sighed. "There's not really a choice at all, is there?"

"There's always a choice," Zerimhi said quietly.

"No, there's not," Mikiah said. "Not if it's a choice I've already made." He looked down at the water's edge again, remembering. "Enough lives have ended because of me. From now on, I'm going to find out how many I can save."

Zerimhi nodded, and a wry smile pulled at one side of his mouth. "Good. Because you're about to get the chance. Your friend Shehum is back with a message from Ashoram, and King Lamoni could use your advice. We need to prevent another war."

Mikiah groaned, rubbing at his forehead with one hand. "He just can't let it go," he sighed. "All right. Let's go see just how badly we've managed to anger the king of Jerusalem."

Mikiah's eyebrows rose as he scanned quickly through the roll of parchment Shehum had delivered. He was aware of Lamoni and Zerimhi watching his reaction, Lamoni's fingers tapping almost silently on the table top. They hadn't dared let Shehum catch a glimpse of his miraculously healed friend, so Lamoni brought Ashoram's message into a small meeting room hardly bigger than a cupboard.

Judging by the tone of the letter, they had made Ashoram very angry indeed. He demanded; he threatened; he blamed; he demanded again. That wasn't what made Mikiah blink in surprise, though.

"He's bluffing," Lamoni said as Mikiah reach the end of the message. "He must be. There's no way he can wage another war so soon, not after the way the Nephites routed his army. He has to be bluffing."

"No," Mikiah said, and his voice was dark with worry as he rolled the parchment together. "He isn't bluffing. He's panicking."

Lamoni reared back in his seat, staring at the Amalekite. "*Panicking?*"

Mikiah nodded. "Did Temisah tell you what Ashoram believes about Ammon and his brothers, O king?" Lamoni nodded, and Mikiah pressed his lips together. "It'll be even worse now. He's lost his hostage. His army is weakened. In his mind, there's nothing to keep you from running right over the top of him. Worse, this was Ashoram's *first* war, and Alma frightened him—frightened him badly—and his warriors know it. He's got to do something to make them forget his cowardice. To regain their confidence." He held up the rolled parchment. "All that bluster in here, that's what it is. He's terrified, and he's trying to make sure no one knows he is."

Zerimhi was nodding thoughtfully. "So he'll start a war he's not ready for, to convince his warriors that he's not a coward, and to keep us from getting the jump on him." He shook his head in helpless disgust. "Nothing more stupid than a man who's desperate to prove how brave he is."

King Lamoni was starting to look harried. "Isn't there any way to stop him?" he asked. "I mean, I have plenty of reasons for hating Ashoram, but that doesn't mean I want our people to go out and slaughter each other. Even if my side would win in the end, that kind of victory is too much like losing!"

Zerimhi snorted. "Sure, I know what'll satisfy him. Complete surrender!"

Lamoni turned his questioning gaze on Mikiah. "Should we start preparing for war, then? *Is* that the only thing he'll accept?"

Mikiah gnawed on his lower lip for a moment. "Maybe not," he said slowly. "I think, maybe, he'd believe an oath."

Lamoni cocked an eyebrow. "An oath? Like, I'll promise not to attack you if you promise not to attack me?"

Mikiah smiled. It sounded almost childish, put that way. "Something like that," he said. "Ashoram does honor his oaths. If you write to him, O king, and swear with an oath that you won't wage war on Jerusalem, but make it obvious at the same time that you're prepared to defend yourself if Ashoram attacks, I think that might be enough. At least for a while." He smiled again. "Especially if it's Shehum delivering the message. He's been known to talk his king back into reason occasionally."

Lamoni nodded and a small smile tugged at his mouth as he glanced at Zerimhi. "Yes, a useful sort of servant to have around," he said. "And it's not a bad plan. I'll need to spend some time drafting a proper response, something that shows restraint but not weakness. And maybe there's something more to be done as well. If Ashoram honors his oaths, he's sworn to obey my father. If King Laman were to order him . . . ?"

"I think he'd obey," Mikiah agreed. "But it's a two-week journey to Nephi and back to get that order. Ashoram might not give us that long."

"Which is why I'll write my own letter, as you suggested," King Lamoni said. "As you say, it should at least slow him down a little. But you," he said, turning to Zerimhi, "you'd better get on the road to King Laman as soon as possible."

"Could I take the message?" Mikiah blurted out, and then blushed as both men turned surprised and questioning eyes on him. "Sorry, it's just—" he stammered, feeling about twelve years old. "I normally stop in and visit Ashir when I run to Nephi, and I wanted to tell her what's happened to me and . . ." He trailed off, far more flustered than he had any right being.

Zerimhi was watching him with a sudden speculation in his eyes. "Perhaps we should both go," he said slowly. "Abish is visiting her sister. We could surprise them." He bowed to King Lamoni with a questioning glance. "If that's acceptable to you, my king?"

The Lamanite king waved them away, pulling a fresh sheet of parchment toward him. "Fine, fine. It's probably a good idea to get Mikiah out of the way for a while. I've told your friend you're at a healing place in the wilderness, but he doesn't seem like the kind of man who misses much, even if he keeps his mouth shut about it." He gave Zerimhi a mock glare. "Just get back soon enough that I'm not forced to follow up on the threats I'm about to make." He leaned over the parchment and began working on his epistle to King Ashoram, ignoring the two spies as they bowed themselves out.

EIGHTEEN

LAND OF NEPHI, 87 BC

MIKIAH STARED AT THE PEACEFUL LITTLE HOUSE, FEELING HIS HEART hammer against the base of his throat, trying to wipe away the clammy dampness of his palms. He'd sent Zerimhi on to the city of Nephi without him. He wanted to talk to Ashir alone. He'd traveled five days to get here, and the last fifteen paces seemed like the longest part of the journey. Ashir would laugh at him if she knew how nervous he was about talking to her, but that was the problem, wasn't it? What if she laughed at him? What if she gave him that pitying look reserved for those who dream far beyond their abilities? What if she was disgusted?

It wasn't supposed to be like this. He was supposed to talk to his parents, who would talk to her parents, who would talk to her. Unfortunately, neither of them had any parents left, which meant he was forced to act for himself, and he'd been wrestling with doubt the entire way here. Zerimhi hadn't gotten much conversation out of him, he'd been so wrapped up in his own mind. He'd faced the battlefield with more courage than he could muster to face a beautiful woman who wore peace like a shawl. After five days of running to get here, he was on the verge of turning around and going back. He might never have made those last fifteen paces if Ashir herself hadn't come around the corner of the house and seen him.

"Mikiah!" she said, hurrying to greet him with a welcoming smile and hands outstretched. "What brings you this time? Another message for King Laman? Come inside and sit down."

He let her take his hands, but held back when she would have led him inside. "Ashir, I want to talk to you. Privately. I know Abish is visiting; is there someplace . . . ?"

Her eyebrows rose, but she nodded without asking all the questions that leaped into her eyes. Instead she led him toward the little glade where she'd told him about the vision of her father. "What did you want to talk about?" she asked casually as she settled into one of the chairs. Her gray eyes affected Mikiah like bright sunshine, warming his skin and difficult to look at. He shifted nervously in his own seat. He realized suddenly that this was the first time he'd seen her clearly with both eyes. She was even more beautiful than he remembered.

"I came—well, first I came to say thank you," he said. "You were the start of making me a better man. And—I wanted to tell you I found out for myself."

Ashir's mouth dropped open. "Seriously?"

"Seriously." He nodded. "I'm a believer now. A Nephite. Whatever."

"Mikiah, that's wonderful!" Then her smile froze and faded. "What are you going to do about Ashoram?"

Mikiah drew in a deep breath and held it for a moment. "That's the other thing I wanted to talk to you about," he said. "I'm going back. Ashoram needs watching, and I'm the only one who can do it. If there's even a chance I can prevent more deaths—I have to go back. The only thing is, I—I keep thinking about you, Ashir." He said it quickly, like diving into cold water. "You've stuck in my heart. Every choice I make, I find myself thinking about which way *you'd* want me to decide. I know what that means. I know what I want. But—I can't take you back to Jerusalem with me. It'd be too dangerous for both of us—raise suspicions, with you coming from Nephi. If you say yes . . . Even if I survive, you'd be a widow to this job I've given myself—maybe for years. I don't have the right to ask that of you. But I thought—maybe I don't have the right to make the decision for you either. So, here I am, offering you the choice."

She was staring at him with her mouth open, her eyes wide and soft with surprise. He watched a tear form and trickle down one cheek, but still she didn't speak—possibly couldn't speak.

"Please say something," he begged. "No, yes, I'll even accept a maybe. Just say something. Please."

She closed her mouth, blinking quickly. Another tear splashed onto her bare arm, and she seemed to notice suddenly that she was weeping. She wiped quickly at her cheeks. Mikiah saw the familiar dark lines of earth under her fingernails. She stared at the moisture across her fingers and gave a small laugh. Mikiah's heart sank. It swelled again a moment later, though, as she leaned toward him, pressed her still-damp cheek against his, and whispered in his ear.

"It took you long enough."

"Are you nervous?" Zerimhi asked the next morning as Mikiah tried to help prepare for his wedding. There wasn't a lot to do, in truth. No gifts from parents, no torchlight procession. Zerimhi had found Aaron preaching in Nephi and brought him to conduct the ceremony, and Nephites married by daylight. Aside from Abish and Zerimhi, there wouldn't be anyone else there to witness. Ashir and Abish had made a feast anyway, which was filling the air with the smell of baking, and Zerimhi promised to celebrate enough for a whole mob.

Mikiah shrugged, not looking up from the flower stems he was threading into a woven circlet. "It doesn't matter if I'm nervous or not. It's not like I'm going to change my mind now." Zerimhi just raised an eyebrow, and Mikiah shrugged. "All right, I admit I wasn't expecting this to happen *today,* but Ashir says she's been waiting three years, and she's not going to wait any longer." He grimaced at a lopsided white plumeria. "To be honest, I'm trying not to think about it. That way my mind probably won't catch up until after the deed is safely done."

Zerimhi barked a laugh. "That sounds like nervous to me," he said, reaching out to squeeze Mikiah's shoulder. "That's all right. I'd respect you less if you weren't. And since you're going to be my brother, I'd rather respect you more." He laughed again. "After all, I'd hate to lose my faith in Ashir's judgment."

Mikiah grinned weakly, thankful for the Lamanite's teasing. It reminded him of Shehum and Eliah. He wished they—and especially Nabeth—could have been there. "How long can you stay, before you have to run King Laman's message to Ashoram?" he asked, changing the subject.

"Not long," Zerimhi admitted. "King Lamoni needs that order, and soon. But I'd rather run through tonight to make up the time than miss a single moment of today."

Mikiah nodded. "I won't be far behind you. I need to be there too. If I can turn Ashoram's mind in the right direction . . ."

Zerimhi scowled. "You'll stay at least a full day, you hear me?" He brandished a flower at Mikiah, who laughed and pretended to cower, using his wreath as a shield. "If you let politics ruin Ashir's wedding, Abish will never forgive me. And that means I'll never forgive you!"

"Are you two ready?" Aaron's amused voice pulled them both around. The Nephite stood watching them from the entrance to Ashir's glade, where the ceremony would take place. He nodded as Mikiah held up the completed flower circlet. "Good. I think we can begin."

Mikiah was surprised at how calm he felt as he took his place beside Ashir and settled the crown of flowers on her head. She reached for his hand and held it tight, her eyes looking twice as big and deep as normal. There should have been butterflies cavorting in his stomach, shouldn't there? His heart should have been up in his throat, pounding fit to burst. But all he felt as he stood there with Ashir's hand in his was a sensation of warmth and joy and love so strong he didn't think he could contain it. He wondered if it made his blue eyes glow as brightly as Ashir's gray ones.

Aaron smiled at them, and his breath came out in a little laugh. "I think I'm actually more nervous than either of you," he said. "I've never done this before. Still, I guess if you're willing to put up with an inexperienced priest, I'll give it my best try." He chuckled again. "First, let me say a few things. Although I'm not married, so I don't know how qualified I am to be giving advice. But our Father knows all about marriage, and all about the two of you. That means the best thing you can do is to always make sure God is there in the marriage with you. He'll give you better advice every day than I ever could. He wants this marriage—this family—to succeed, and I know He'll make that happen if you let Him. When you have hard days—because you definitely will—turn to him for comfort and counsel, and turn to each other as well. Talk together and dream together. Honor and respect each other." His smile grew a bit mischievous and his eyes twinkled. "And remember that no matter how well you think you know each other right now, you're going to be in for a few surprises.

"Now." Aaron took a deep breath. "Today you're going to be making a covenant, not just with each other, but with your Heavenly Father. Covenants should never be taken lightly, so I want you to really think about the things I'm about to ask you." He turned to Ashir, his eyes searching hers. "Ashir, will you covenant to take Mikiah as your husband and give yourself to him to be his wife? Will you cleave only to him, forsaking all others, and be his wife in the eyes of God and all men?"

Tears stood in Ashir's eyes as she nodded. "Yes," she said, her voice soft but firm. "I will."

"Mikiah, will you covenant to take Ashir as your wife and give yourself to her to be her husband? Will you cleave only to her, forsaking all others, and be her husband in the eyes of God and all men?"

"Yes," Mikiah said, then hesitated. "With the exception that I *can't* let them know in Jerusalem, not if I want to stay there and keep an eye on King Ashoram. So it can't be quite *all* men. But I can promise that I won't ever say I'm *not* married to Ashir. Will that be enough?"

Aaron just looked at him for a moment, his eyebrows raised and one corner of his mouth twitching. Abish let out a long breath, and Ashir's eyes were dancing again. "Yes," Aaron answered, and there was a hint of laughter bubbling behind his voice. "I think that'll be fine." He reached out and laid a hand on their shoulders. "Then by the holy priesthood, which I hold, and the authority given to me by King Laman, I bless you, Mikiah and Ashir, as husband and wife, that you may be fruitful, and have great joy in fulfilling the measure of your creation." He dropped his hands and grinned at Mikiah.

"Now, I think you'd better kiss her so we can all go find out what's been smelling so delicious all morning!"

As Mikiah's lips met Ashir's, an amazing surge of warmth and love made him feel almost dizzy with the rushing joy of it. Whatever else happened, he knew he could face it all if he could just hold to the memory of this one glorious moment.

NINETEEN

CITY OF JERUSALEM, 87 BC

NEARLY A WEEK LATER, MIKIAH SAW THE WALLS OF JERUSALEM coming into view through the trees and had to consciously unknot the tightening muscles of his back and shoulders. He'd never before come home with such a sinking heart. He knew then that Jerusalem wasn't home anymore, not really. That name could only be given to a small cottage on the borders of Nephi, now, where a Lamanite woman with gray eyes lived.

He paused on the edge of the forest, looking out over the cleared farmlands around the city, the sun glinting on the blue stretch of ocean beyond. He was aware of eyes watching him. "Zerimhi?"

There was a faint rustle, and the Lamanite spy dropped out of a tree onto the path beside him. "Glad to see you were smart enough to circle around," he said. "Make it look like you're coming from Ishmael instead of Nephi."

Mikiah snorted. "I may be in love, but I'm not stupid." His gaze turned to the city again. "How did Ashoram take it?"

Zerimhi shrugged. "He wasn't happy." He gave a short bark of a laugh. "Actually, he was furious. But I think you read him right. He'll stick to his oaths—for now, at least." He shrugged again when Mikiah raised an eyebrow at him. "When I left, he was still trying to find a way around it. And trying to figure out what Lamoni and King Laman are up to. Your king is a very . . . determined man."

"Go ahead and say stubborn," Mikiah said. "And sharp enough to cut himself. I used to admire that about him." He shook his head. "He's latched onto this idea and refuses to accept anything that might go against it."

"Yes, he did seem like a man who was searching hard for the worst possible explanation for everything," Zerimhi said. "If he keeps that up for long enough, he won't even need a reason for hating us anymore. He'll just need an excuse."

Mikiah shivered. It wasn't that long ago that he'd been headed in the same direction as Ashoram. "I'd better go," he said. "He'll want to see me."

Zerimhi nodded, reaching out to squeeze Mikiah's shoulder in parting. "Be careful, Brother," he said. "I'll stick around for a few days, just in case. If you need me."

Mikiah returned the grip, smiling. "I hope I won't. But thanks."

Zerimhi disappeared into the bushes as silently as he'd come, and Mikiah drew in a breath and stepped out of the forest shadows, striding wearily toward the city that had once been his home.

In the dark splendor of Ashoram's throne room, Mikiah sank to one knee slightly more awkwardly than he needed to, favoring the leg that had been so brutally wounded. "My king," he said in a hoarse voice. "I'm so glad you're safe."

"And I'm glad to see you so well recovered. Eliah and Shehum said you looked like death when they left you in Ishmael," Ashoram said, raising from his throne to come and grip his spy's shoulders and help him rise. "I'm going to need you now more than ever." A shadow passed over his face. "And actually, it's just as well you still have some contacts in the land of Ishmael."

Mikiah frowned, his eyebrows drawing down. "Why? What did I miss?"

Ashoram gave a mirthless laugh. "Where do I start? You knew Temisah is back with her father?" Mikiah nodded, and Ashoram's eyes flashed angrily. "If I ever find the person who helped her, I swear I'll kill him myself. She's started a bloody war!"

"A war? But—forgive me, my king, but I didn't see any preparations for war in the land of Ishmael. Everything was peaceful as I came through."

"Oh, of course it was." Ashoram snorted, waving his hand irritably. "And I have Lamoni's *sworn word* it'll stay that way." His voice dripped scornful disbelief. "He's got his father on his side as well, of course. King Laman *ordered* me not to attack, even if they are keeping my wife from me." He drew in a deep breath through his nose, straightening his shoulders. His eyes flashed as he glared. "Well. I can see what they're up to."

"What?" Mikiah asked, wondering what explanation Ashoram had invented.

"Isn't it obvious? The Nephites have always wanted legitimacy, from the very beginning! That stupid story about how Nephi was the rightful ruler!" He whirled away from Mikiah, pacing around his throne room like a caged animal as he spoke, his hands gesturing in time to his words. "Lamoni wants me to attack first, you see? That way the 'converts' will be able to say they were just defending themselves. No matter what kind of provocation they give me, if I attack first, they can say it's *my* fault!" His hazel eyes were wide and gleaming, the pupils shrunken. He ran his hands restlessly through his hair.

"They want you to break your oath to King Laman?" Mikiah said. "But they must know you'd never do that."

Ashoram growled. "There's no telling what they think, with their heads full of Nephite lies. But they've made a mistake this time—especially Lamoni, swearing not to attack. If I take him up on it, there's nothing they can do. King Laman is an old man. He can't live for many more years. When he is no longer king, the whole situation will change. All they've done is give me time—time to prepare for the war that's coming." He smiled, a hungry predator's smile. "When the time comes, we'll be ready."

Mikiah could only pray that King Laman would live long enough for Ashoram to come to his senses—but looking into the king's wild, hazel eyes, he had a hard time believing that would ever happen.

TWENTY

CITY OF JERUSALEM, 81 BC

"ALL RIGHT, PELONTI, PUT IT RIGHT HERE." MIKIAH CROUCHED down, holding out one open hand to his nephew, and a small fist smacked into his palm. Mikiah's other hand darted out, and Pelonti squealed with laughter, squirming away from the tickling fingers attacking from the side. Mikiah grinned. "Now the kicks," he instructed. "Over to the side." A dirty little foot hit his hand. "And the front." Pelonti thrust the ball of his foot toward Mikiah's face, and Mikiah only just got his hand in the way in time. "And now up high." He held his hand up, and Pelonti jumped, hopping on one foot so he could bring his other heel down on Mikiah's cupped palm. Mikiah grabbed the foot and lifted, his fingers wrapping around the three-year-old's ankle. Pelonti crowed as he tipped over backward, his uncle catching him before he hit the ground and tickling him mercilessly. The boy squealed with laughter, twisting like a contortionist as he tried to get away.

When Mikiah finally let him up, he scrambled to his feet and fell back into the ready position Mikiah had taught him. "Again!" he demanded, grinning.

Mikiah laughed. He'd been inventing a different, unarmed way of fighting for the past six years, and his nephew thought it was a wonderful game. "All right, then. One more time. Punch!" He held his hand up for Pelonti's fist, but this time his tickling attack met a sharp little elbow jabbing at his fingers. "Oho! Getting clever, are we?" Pelonti giggled loudly and went on giggling as he tried the side kick and Mikiah grabbed his foot again. With one leg held gently but inescapably in the air, Pelonti was helpless to dodge his uncle's rapid tickling, and soon he collapsed into a limp heap in the dust of the yard, weak with laughter.

"That's enough, you two," Nabeth said, grinning at her brother and son as she stood in the doorway of her house. "Come in and eat." Six years of marriage and three of motherhood hadn't aged her visibly, but there was a sadness hidden in the corners of her eyes now. Pelonti was the only child she'd carried long enough to deliver alive, and Mikiah knew each loss had broken her heart a little more. It made her only son even more precious.

"You hear that, Pelonti?" Mikiah scooped the boy up in his arms. "Your mother wants to feed me again! She thinks I don't know how to feed myself. She thinks I'd starve to death without her."

Pelonti whooped as Mikiah held him up high, spun him around once, and set him back on his feet. The boy ran to his mother, grabbing a fistful of her skirt and tugging to get her attention. "Uncle 'Kiah gonna starve to death!" he told her, nearly shouting like he always did when he thought something was funny, even if he didn't quite understand the joke. "An' he tried to get me, an' I *stopped* him!"

Mikiah, following more slowly, ruffled his nephew's dark brown curls. "You'll be a great warrior someday," he said. "Just make sure you fight for what you believe in, and you'll make your uncle a proud man."

Nabeth pressed her lips together in a smile, her eyes dancing. "No doubt. But right now, you great warriors have some dinner to do battle with. Shall we see who can kill the most potatoes?" She pushed her son ahead of her into the house, where the boy ran to his father and started chattering so quickly that Mikiah only caught one word out of every five. He thought it might be something about a bug Pelonti had seen that day. Eliah bore the onslaught with the ease of long practice, nodding and murmuring a word or two while he settled Pelonti on his lap and reached one-handed for the dish of stew Nabeth set in front of him.

"You were teaching him that weird thing, weren't you?" Eliah asked, looking at his brother over Pelonti's head.

Mikiah shrugged. "It might come in useful someday."

"It's a waste of time," Eliah told him, more teasing than arguing. "Who seriously fights without weapons?"

"Well, I tried to, once, and Tubal's men nearly killed me." Mikiah blew softly on the stew to cool it before taking a bite. "Things might have gone differently if I'd known how to defend myself."

Eliah snorted. "Things might have gone differently if you hadn't run off without your sword."

Mikiah shrugged again. "No harm in knowing both ways." He grinned at Pelonti, whose cheeks bulged with an overlarge mouthful he was trying to chew. "Besides, he likes it. Don't you, Pelonti?"

The boy's answer was garbled through his food, but the tone sounded generally positive.

"You're so good with him," Nabeth said, smiling at her brother as she settled down beside Eliah. "I don't know why you don't find yourself a wife and have a few children of your own."

Mikiah started to answer, but stopped at the sound of running feet approaching the house.

"Eliah!" a voice shouted. "Mikiah! Come quick!"

"Shehum?" Mikiah sprang to his feet and was at the door in time to meet his friend. Shehum sprinted up, stopping himself against the outside wall, and grabbed Mikiah's arm, wide-eyed and panting.

"Mikiah! You have to come! Hurry!"

"What is it?" Eliah set his son down and stood, looking over Mikiah's shoulder. Mikiah made room for him, the three of them clustered in the doorway.

"King Laman is dying. He's named his eldest son king in his place, and he's summoned all the kings to acknowledge his son king over all the land."

"So? What's the problem with that?"

"He's named his son King Anti-Nephi-Lehi!"

Eliah drew in a sharp breath, and Mikiah's eyes widened in surprised understanding. He'd heard the name before. The word meant "Like unto Nephi and Lehi," and it was what the converted Lamanites had chosen to call themselves. Calling the new king by that name was a statement, declaring that the converts were no longer associated in any way with the people who called themselves Lamanites.

"Ashoram isn't going to go, is he?" Mikiah said, already knowing the answer.

Shehum shook his head. "He's ordered the messenger from King Laman whipped."

Mikiah felt the blood drain from his face, his heart suddenly speeding. Without wasting time on another word, he ran, dashing toward the king's palace at his top speed, his friends no more than half a pace behind him.

Mikiah froze in the doorway of the throne room when he saw the face of the man kneeling on the floor, blood trickling from the lash marks on his back and dripping onto the dark stone. Zerimhi. Two guards held the Lamanite's arms, while a third swung the whip. Mikiah hid a flinch at the wet snap of it across bare flesh. He met Zerimhi's eyes for just a flicker of a moment, read the pain-filled recognition, and didn't dare answer it. Eliah prodded him in the back, and Mikiah strode into the throne room as if nothing had happened, expressionless as a stone, ignoring the beaten messenger. He didn't even glance in that direction again, though he stood within a few paces of the guard wielding the lash, the sound twitching at the skin of his own back. The need to do something, to save his brother, burned like fire in his gut, but he held himself back with an iron discipline that was the only reason he'd survived the past six years.

Ashoram stood like a statue beside his throne, scowling at Zerimhi, and Mikiah could sense the king's building rage as soon as he walked into the room. It was like the heaviness of the air before a storm. Ashoram's fists opened and closed convulsively, and the hazel of his eyes had shifted to a bright, flashing green. A roll of parchment sat on the king's throne, half unrolled and tossed sloppily across the seat. The king held up one hand, and his guard paused, whip still held ready.

"Let this be the punishment for anyone who ever again mentions that name in my presence," Ashoram said, and Mikiah felt a chill at the deadly calm of his voice. It reminded him inescapably of Amlici. "I haven't moved against the traitors in all these years, because I swore an oath to King Laman. If Laman is no longer king, that oath no longer holds me, and I *will not* bind myself again to any man who spits on our people's freedom. I—will—not!" He bit off each word, spitting them out like poison. "Any man who calls himself *Anti-Nephi-Lehi* will never be a king of mine. I'll spill a river of blood before I allow *him* the rule of the people."

The king turned his brilliant glare on Mikiah and his friends. Mikiah was sure he saw Eliah cringe back under that green gaze, but he met it levelly, without the slightest slip of emotion to betray him. "You three will go to the land of Helam, Amulon, and Midian. Our allies are ready. This is what we've waited for. Call them out to battle, and we'll crush both the Nephites *and* their brain-dead puppets."

"As you command, O king," Mikiah said, bowing low, his mind racing. He had to stop this, find some way to convince Ashoram—

"But first," the king went on before Mikiah could think of anything, "I want the world to know how I deal with traitors." He nodded to his guard, his face ugly with bloodlust as he stared down at Zerimhi. "Whip that dog until he's dead." The guard raised his lash again.

"No!" Mikiah's control broke and he jumped at the guard, wresting the whip from his hand and pushing him violently away. Ashoram's sword rang from its sheath at the sudden outburst, and Mikiah fell to his knees before the king, desperate pleading showing naked on his face. "Please, King Ashoram, don't kill him."

The point of Ashoram's sword came to rest under Mikiah's chin, pricking his throat as he swallowed, and Mikiah looked up into the oncoming storm of outraged majesty. "Tell me why," Ashoram said in a low, threatening voice. "Quickly."

Shehum spoke before Mikiah could answer, holding out a placating hand to both of them. "Ashoram—my king—please, don't be hasty," he said.

"Hasty!" Ashoram protested. "It's hasty to punish betrayal, is it?"

"Once before, you let your anger drive you to do something you regretted later," Shehum reminded him. "Give yourself time to think. Once he's dead—either of them—you can't take it back."

Muscles bunched in Ashoram's jaw, but he drew in a long breath through his nose and stiffly lowered the sword from Mikiah's throat. "Very well. You've been right before, Shehum. But I doubt Mikiah was trying to save me from my own temper." He narrowed his eyes, the sword still ready in his hand. "You will explain yourself, Mikiah. Now."

"I—I was trying to save my friends," Mikiah admitted. "Please don't kill him. Think of the consequences—think of what would happen to those who serve you."

"What? What consequences?"

Mikiah bit his lip, not daring to raise his eyes above Ashoram's ankles. "If you kill him to send a message to King Laman's son, you know it won't be enough just to kill him. You'll have to send his body back. That means sending *your* messengers to King Laman's court—when you've just had *his* messenger killed." Mikiah glanced sideways at Zerimhi, but the Lamanite's eyes were closed, his lips moving in silent prayer. "Whatever you do to this man will come down on the head of whoever you send." He swallowed. "It wasn't my place to contradict your order. I know that. I did it to save my friends. If I was wrong, then—then let me carry his body back to King Laman myself."

The silence stretched for what felt like an eternity. Mikiah could feel his heart hammering against his ribs, and hear the throb of his pulse behind his ears. If this didn't work, he'd be forced to do something drastic—something he couldn't survive. He refused to just stand by and watch Zerimhi be beaten to death.

Ashoram's sword scraped as he returned it to its sheath, and Mikiah risked looking up at the king. He was still frowning, but some of the fire had died down. The green of his eyes was fading back to hazel. "Have it your way," he said. "Give him another twenty strokes," he told the guard. "Then strip him and throw him out of the city. Let him make his own way back to his so-called king. And you three"—he scowled at Mikiah again, and the Amalekite spy saw the crumbling edges of the king's trust in that glare—"get going. We have a war to fight!"

"As you command, O king," Mikiah said, lowering his head. He left the room with Eliah and Shehum but sent them on ahead, leaning against the wall just beyond the door, out of sight of Ashoram and the guards. He listened, counting the strokes, hands clenched into trembling fists, flinching at each crack of leather across bare skin. He didn't move until he heard the whipping stop and the heavy tread of the guards, weighed down by Zerimhi's body as they carried him from the throne room. Only then did he steal away, cursing himself that he could do nothing more.

Eliah had already come and gone by the time Mikiah came to bid farewell to Nabeth and Pelonti. Mikiah found his sister in the garden beside her house. She stood quietly, watching Pelonti chase after a flight of little moths in the red-gold light that always pooled there just before sunset. Coming silently into the yard before she noticed him, he saw the strain that tightened the skin around her eyes and mouth.

"Nabeth?" he said softly, laying a hand on her shoulder. She turned to him with a jerk, as though the touch had released her from something that held her frozen. She wrapped her arms tight around his chest and pressed her face into his shoulder. He returned the embrace, holding her while she just shook.

"I'm sorry," she said. "I know you have to go. It's just—" She choked, then drew in a sobbing breath. "I heard you talking before you left, and—and King Ashoram wouldn't make all of you run through the night if it wasn't important, and—" She pulled away enough to look up at him. She wasn't crying, but tears hovered in her eyes. "It's war again, isn't it?"

"Yes, I'm afraid it is."

She nodded, stepping away from him and wiping at her eyes. "I couldn't ask Eliah. I didn't want him to see me crying when he had to go." She gave a watery laugh. "So now I'm doing it to you. I'm sorry. Don't worry about me. You've got a long run to get to."

Mikiah shook his head. "It's half a day's journey to Midian. A few minutes won't make that much difference."

She sniffled, scrubbing her face again. "Oh—Why can't the Nephites just leave us alone?" she burst out.

"I think you already know the answer to that," Mikiah said. "Or you did many years ago when you tried to help Temisah."

"I was an idealistic child!"

Mikiah raised both hands. "So are the Nephites. Idealistic, I mean. They're here because they're working toward their ideal world—one where they can believe as they choose without the Lamanites trying to kill them for it." He paused, then shrugged. "And also because they know what they're teaching is true, and they don't want anyone to suffer in eternity or be cut off from the presence of God."

Nabeth snorted. "You're talking like you believe them."

"Yes, I am, aren't I?" Mikiah replied, a small smile curving one corner of his mouth. Nabeth whirled, staring at him, but Mikiah ignored her, pouncing on Pelonti as the boy ran past and scooping him up into a bear hug. "There's my favorite nephew!" He arranged the boy against his hip so they could look each other in the face. "I have to go away for a while, Pelonti," he said. "It might be a long time before we see each other again. Will you do something for me while I'm gone? It's something very important."

Pelonti nodded wordlessly, wide-eyed and serious.

"I want you to remind your mother every day that I love her, all right? And you remember I love you too. Can you do that?"

Pelonti's face broke into a wide grin. "Sure, that's easy!" he said. "I can do that, Uncle Mikiah!"

"There's one more thing. You have to wait until I'm gone to tell her this, understand?" He put his mouth close to Pelonti's ear and whispered to him for a few seconds. Then he set the boy down again and came back to his sister.

"What did you—?" she began, but broke off as Mikiah hugged her one last time.

"Goodbye, Nabeth," he whispered. He was running as soon as he released her, sprinting away without looking back. He didn't think he'd have the strength to go if he turned to see her watching him leave.

"What did he tell you, Pelonti?" he heard her voice fading in the distance.

Pelonti's reply was loud and excited, easy to hear even as Mikiah disappeared around a corner. "He said I have some other cousins, and he hopes I get to meet them someday!"

"*What?!* You mean—*Mikiah, you get back here this instant!*"

Mikiah grinned at his sister's shouted demand, but he kept running.

Mikiah made only one more stop before he left Jerusalem for the last time, ducking quickly into his own house to grab the bag he kept packed and ready for long message runs. He cast his gaze one last time around the house he'd grown up in, the home where both his mother and then his father had died, where he and Nabeth had been children together. He'd made changes when it became his alone, turning half the main room and most of the garden into a sort of exercise area where he could practice his new way of fighting without weapons. But it was still the same house, and his memory populated it with the ghosts of his parents, the echoes of times long gone.

He gave his head a quick shake, banishing the memories. He didn't have much time. Was there anything more he'd need? He caught up a warm poncho Nabeth had woven for him, rolling it quickly into a tight bundle and stuffing it in on top of everything else. There was a pebble with sharply glittering bits that Pelonti had given him because the boy thought it was pretty. Mikiah added that. Pelonti's other treasures would have been crushed—a blue eggshell, a dried flower, a snakeskin—but Mikiah could keep this one memento. He looked around again. There was nothing else. Nothing but the leaving.

Blinking quickly, he looped the bag over one shoulder and jogged out the door into the fading red light of sunset.

Zerimhi had made it as far as the shelter of the forest before he collapsed. Mikiah found him beside the path in the gathering dusk, half-hidden by bushes. The guards had stripped his clothes from him, and by the smell of it had doused him in ocean water for good measure. He lay on his face, breathing shallowly, and flinched at Mikiah's gentle touch.

"Easy, Brother. It's me."

"Mikiah?" the Lamanite breathed. "Oh, thank God."

"Amen to that." Mikiah hissed as he pulled the branches aside and saw the bloody welts across Zerimhi's back. "We need to get these bound up," he said. "I can't do it here; I need more light—a fire. Can you walk?"

Zerimhi grunted. "Sure, I'm just lying here because it looked comfortable." He groaned, trying to lift himself. "Help me up and I'll try."

"It's not far." As gently as he could, Mikiah pulled the Lamanite to his feet, lending Zerimhi his shoulder for support as they staggered deeper into the trees.

There was a little hollow with a tiny spring trickling through it, hidden from view of the city by a small hill. As children, Mikiah and his friends had made a kind of secret playground of it, pretending they were deep in the wilderness. It wasn't much, but the discreet fire he started wouldn't be visible, and there was water to bathe Zerimhi's wounds.

"Here, put this on," Mikiah said, pulling the poncho out and tossing it over the naked man. Mikiah rummaged in the sack some more. "Ashir always makes sure I've got some basics in here." His hands found a roll of soft bandages and a small pot full of ointment that released a nose-tickling herbal scent when he lifted the lid. "Lie down. This is going to sting."

Zerimhi complied, hissing as Mikiah gently washed the blood away with a dripping cloth then carefully slathered Ashir's sticky paste over the welts. "Do you know where we go next?" Mikiah asked, trying to distract Zerimhi from the pain. "Back to Nephi, to warn the king, right?"

"No," Zerimhi gasped, shaking his head sharply. "King Anti-Nephi-Lehi is waiting in Ishmael." He turned his head enough to give Mikiah a tight grin. "Why else would it be me running this message? Lamoni loaned me to him."

"What's he doing in Ishmael?" Mikiah finished with the salve and got Zerimhi to sit up so he could wrap the bandage.

"Let's just say he won't be surprised by our news. He wanted to be close in case something like this happened." He flinched slightly at the first touch of the soft cloth on his back. "Ammon and his brethren are supposed to meet him there."

Mikiah finished with the bandage, frowning as he tied it off. "He knew it might be a suicide mission, and he sent you anyway?"

Zerimhi shrugged, then grimaced. "Somebody had to do it. I volunteered." He met Mikiah's eyes, his dark face highlighted by the dim, orange glow of the fire. "I wanted to get you out of there. If Ashoram's going to war, I don't want you trapped in Jerusalem."

Mikiah just grunted, digging through his bag again. He handed Zerimhi a chunk of dried meat. "Here, eat that, and then we'll go. You'll need your strength."

Zerimhi took the food, but didn't eat, regarding Mikiah steadily. "You'll go faster if you leave me," he said.

"Forget it," Mikiah growled. "Not going to happen."

"But—"

"I said, forget it." Mikiah glared at the Lamanite. "I'm not leaving you here alone, and there's no way you can make me. So eat, and let's get going."

"Someday you're going to find someone who can out-stubborn you," Zerimhi said, gnawing obediently at the tough meat.

"I already did," Mikiah smiled. "I'm married to her. And she'd reach whole new levels of stubborn if she found out I left her sister's husband wounded in the wilderness. So if you're looking for someone to blame, Brother, you can blame this one on her."

Twenty-One

City of Ishmael, 81 BC

Mikiah was waiting on the steps to Lamoni's palace two days later when the entire group of Nephite missionaries arrived. He'd nearly carried Zerimhi the last few miles and delivered him, protesting, into the hands of his wife.

"I have to report to King Lamoni," Zerimhi had insisted, trying feebly to crawl out of the bed where Mikiah and Abish laid him down. "And Ammon and his brethren. I have to tell them—"

"No, you don't," Mikiah said, holding the tall Lamanite down with one hand. "That's what you have me for."

"And if you don't lie still now," Abish added, glaring, "I swear I'll knock you out!"

The two kings had been less than pleased when Mikiah told them Ashoram's plans. Now, as Mikiah lifted a hand to greet the Nephites, he saw several sets of raised eyebrows at the loud voices ringing from the windows.

Aaron grimaced as he came up to Mikiah, nodding in greeting. "I was afraid of this. They're arguing about what to do, aren't they?"

"Actually, they're not." Mikiah couldn't make out the shouted words, but he'd been listening to Anti-Nephi-Lehi and Lamoni all morning. "If you listen to what they're saying, they're actually agreeing with each other. They're just doing it loudly."

Ammon surprised Mikiah by chuckling, shaking his head wryly. "We'd better go see what they're agreeing about, then. Come on!" With the ease of long practice, he took the stairs two at a time, leading his brothers into the throne room. Mikiah trailed along after them, curious.

"—we're either fools or hypocrites!" Lamoni was shouting as Mikiah came in. The two kings faced each other over a table spread with maps. "I don't know which is worse!"

His brother gestured vigorously. "How do you argue with that? There's no way we can prove—"

"We can't prove *anything!*" Lamoni threw his hands up at the futility. "Proof doesn't work for something like this! It's a matter of—"

"And even if we *could,*" Anti-Nephi-Lehi yelled, "they'll never believe the Nephites aren't—"

"How can they? *I* barely believe it, after everything we've done!"

"They'd have every *right* to—"

"But we don't." Both kings jumped in surprise as Ammon's calm, powerful voice broke over their loud discussion. "No one has a right to hatred. But we do have a right to defend ourselves."

Lamoni and Anti-Nephi-Lehi welcomed the Nephites, making room for them around the maps that covered the table. "If we're talking defense," Anti-Nephi-Lehi began, "the first thing to figure out is where they'll attack from. If they muster their armies here . . ."

Mikiah stopped listening, his attention drawn by movement in the doorway that led to the private chambers where Lamoni's household lived. A small girl peeked one hazel eye around the doorframe at him, wisps of black hair curling against her cheek. A pudgy brown hand beckoned when she saw him looking, and he came obediently.

"Sebbita?" Mikiah squatted down across from the child, most of her still hidden behind the door frame. "What is it?"

"I lost a tooth," the girl whispered, as though imparting a great secret.

Mikiah put on a look of intense fascination. "Really? How exciting! But aren't you a little young to have your baby teeth fall out?" Temisah's daughter was barely five years old.

"It didn't *fall* out," Sebbita said, insulted by the very suggestion. "I was chasing Kish, an' I jumped an' caught him, an' he fell down, an' I fell on top of him, an' his elbow hit me in the mouth." Mikiah stifled a laugh as she peeked a little further around the corner to smile at him, revealing a swollen lip and a gap where her front tooth had been. "An' Grandfather said I was just like Mother all over again," the girl continued. "An' Mother said she wasn't that bad, an' Grandfather said she was too, an' I was no more than she deserved. An' then Mother said it's a good thing she *was* that bad, or she wouldn't be here now, but I didn't understand that. An' then Grandfather squeezed us both, *hard,* an' I laughed 'cause I couldn't breathe. An' then—"

"Sebbita, come back here," a woman's voice interrupted. "Now's not the time to bother your—Oh! Mikiah!"

Still crouched down, Mikiah looked up at Temisah as she smiled to see him. The fiery girl he'd once stolen was gone, as was the beaten prisoner, both now replaced by a young woman full of joy and strength. The bright glow still burned at her core, but it had mellowed a little over the years to a welcoming warmth, less likely to scorch anyone who touched it. As she gathered her daughter up, a few words of the conversation around the map table caught her ears, and the smile slid from her face. "They're going to fight, aren't they?" she asked.

Mikiah stood, looking over his shoulder at the other men. "Yes, I think that's the plan."

Temisah sighed wearily, worry drawing lines in her face. "How many people will have to die this time, for one man's pride?"

The words struck at Mikiah like a slap, though he knew she didn't mean them for him. A chill shivered through him.

Before he had time to think beyond that first shock, he heard Anti-Nephi-Lehi calling for him. "Mikiah? Come here; you'll need to understand this so you can explain it." He pointed at the map in front of him as Mikiah came closer. "We want Antiomno to position part of his army here to block the easiest pass toward Nephi. We'll have to evacuate Ishmael, I'm afraid, but that'll give him extra men to defend Middoni. And then we'll have our main army here in the city of Nephi. That's where they're most likely to attack. The other Anti-Nephi-Lehi lands are shielded by Middoni and Nephi. You understand?" Mikiah nodded, feeling the muscles of his face tighten as his thoughts raced. "Then I want you to go to Middoni," the king continued. "Antiomno needs to be ready."

Mikiah bowed his head for a long moment, wrestling with himself. Then he looked up and met Anti-Nephi-Lehi's questioning eyes. "No," he said quietly. "Forgive me, but I will not."

"Mikiah, we have to defend ourselves!" Aaron protested, but Mikiah noticed Ammon staring at him with something more like speculation.

"No," Mikiah said again. "I won't do it." He gestured vaguely at the door where Sebbita and Temisah still stood. "That little girl cost thousands of men their lives. That's not her fault, and it's not Temisah's. It's mine. I was so wrapped up in my own arrogance, so fascinated by the challenge that I never stopped to think about the right and wrong of it. By the time I saw the consequences, all I could do was keep it from killing more thousands of women and children. Repenting for that nearly killed me. I can't do it again."

"There's no sin in defending yourself, Mikiah," Muloki said gently. "Or fighting to save your own wife and children."

"Isn't there?" Mikiah shook his head. "Maybe not for the Nephites, but with so many innocent lives already on my soul, I won't risk adding more. Besides," he added, "I have friends on the other side. I grew up in Jerusalem. My sister lives there with her family. Should I help make her a widow? Her son fatherless? Should I send my friends into death so totally unprepared?" He shook his head again. "I won't do it. I'd rather die myself."

There was a long, shocked silence, and Mikiah could feel the pressure of half a dozen startled people staring at him. He held the king's eyes and saw the growing horror there as Anti-Nephi-Lehi realized how close he'd come to leading his people back into their worst sins. The king turned away abruptly, almost convulsively, bracing himself against the map table, hands widespread and gripping the edge. The room seemed to hold its breath as he stared at the map in front of him, head bowed, black hair hanging across his face. Then one hand flew, dashing the maps away. The rolls of parchment flapped like ungainly birds as they fell across the golden stone of the floor. The king breathed in deeply as he straightened, squaring his shoulders.

"You're right, Mikiah," he said. "I wasn't thinking. After all we've done, and all we've been through to obtain a forgiveness, we daren't risk any least approach to the same kinds of sin." He shook his head. "We *dare* not. And we won't." The king gripped Mikiah's shoulder. "Gather the people to the land of Nephi," he said. "That's where our brethren will come with their armies, and that is where we'll meet them with nothing but our faith. If God decrees that we should live, he'll soften their hearts. If not, it's better that we should die than to condemn our brethren." He met Lamoni's eyes across the table. "And *that* is how we prove it," he said quietly.

TWENTY-TWO

LAND OF NEPHI, 81 BC

IN SPITE OF EVERYTHING, MIKIAH COULDN'T HELP GRINNING AS HE jogged up the bush-lined path, the trees closing in behind him to shut out the world. All too soon, reality would intrude even here, but for now he felt nothing but simple excitement at the prospect of seeing his family again. He paused as he emerged from the shade of the trees, basking in the sight of the house and garden, the deep scent and color of the flowers, the familiar clamor of the birds, the way the sunlight filled the little clearing with a warm pool of gold. The place had always seemed like a perfect dream to him, more deeply rooted and at the same time somehow less real than the rest of the world.

His grin widened as a little girl with bare feet and a mass of black hair came running from the house. "Father!" she yelled, her high-pitched squeal piercing the stillness. "Father!"

"There's my girl!" Mikiah bent down to catch the flying body as his daughter jumped into his arms. He held her high above his head and spun her around before wrapping her in an exuberant hug. A sticky kiss landed on his cheek and small arms threatened to throttle him. "I missed you too, Nadai," he said, pretending to gasp for air. "But please let your father breathe!"

Nadai giggled and released him, sitting back in his arms. "Guess what! I taught Giliel how to somersault!"

"Really? Last time I saw him, he was just learning to walk."

"Well, he's running now," Ashir told him, arriving more slowly in her daughter's wake. "And likely to kill himself—if he doesn't kill me first!" Bearing children had thickened her body a little, but she still carried the same beauty and soul-deep stillness that had attracted Mikiah in the first place.

"You said the same thing when Nadai learned to walk," he said, moving his daughter to one side so he could hug Ashir with his free arm. He looked down and saw the little man clinging to Ashir's skirt with a pudgy brown fist and staring up at him. Giliel had inherited his mother's wide gray eyes with a fringe of long black lashes, and at only a little over one year old, his face and arms were still dimpled with baby fat. Mikiah thought he was perhaps the most adorable little boy he'd ever seen.

Nadai saw her brother and squirmed to get down. "It's Father, Giliel!" she told him, wrapping her hand around one of the little fists and pulling him forward. "Don't you remember Father?"

A crease appeared between Giliel's eyebrows. "Pah-dah?" he said. Nadai giggled.

"I wouldn't expect him to remember me, Nadai," Mikiah said, smiling as he crouched down to greet his son. "I've been gone for months. Babies don't remember that far back."

But when he held his hands out, Giliel toddled forward. "Up!" he demanded, and Mikiah was more than happy to comply, lifting the boy and spinning him as he'd done with Nadai. Giliel squealed, clutching at Mikiah's wrists as he flew through the air. When Mikiah set him down, he retreated behind Ashir again, but he was giggling now as he peeped out at his father from the shelter of her skirt.

"Looks like you won't have any trouble getting reacquainted," Ashir said, smiling down at the toddler. "Come inside. How long can you stay this time?"

Mikiah wrapped her hand in his, the smile fading from his face. "This time, I'm not going back, Ashir," he told her, and saw her eyes widen. One hand flew to her mouth. "Ashoram declared war as soon as King Laman gave up the throne. He won't acknowledge King Anti-Nephi-Lehi. His army is probably already gathering." Mikiah shook his head, his mouth tight. "I couldn't stay. Not now." He shrugged as though he was rolling something off his shoulders. "Besides, I think he got suspicious when I talked him out of killing Zerimhi."

Ashir was still staring at him. Tears welled up in her eyes and spilled over as she caught her breath in a sob. "You—you're—" She choked again and pulled in another gasping breath. "You're staying?' she whispered. Mikiah nodded, and Ashir burst into tears, throwing herself into his arms.

"Mother? Mother, what's wrong?" Nadai pressed close around their knees, reaching up and standing on her toes to pat her mother's elbow and back with quick, light smacks. Giliel, understanding only that his mother was crying, began wailing in sympathy. Ashir gave a breathless laugh and broke away, bending to scoop the toddler up and cuddle him close.

"Is Zerimhi all right?" she asked, finally taking in everything else he'd told her. "What's King Anti-Nephi-Lehi going to do?'

"He's fine, more or less," Mikiah said, his eyes going dark with memory. "In fact, we need to get the house ready for visitors. He and Abish should be here in a few days."

"They're coming *here?*"

Mikiah's mouth quirked. "Ashir, *everyone* is coming here. King Anti-Nephi-Lehi wants to address all the people. He's sent runners out to all the cities of the Anti-Nephi-Lehies to gather them all to the land of Nephi. Before long, we're likely to have more guests than we know what to do with. That's why Anti-Nephi-Lehi sent me on ahead. He wanted to warn his father what he's planning before he tells everyone else."

"Then—you haven't heard?" Ashir gave her head a quick shake. "No, of course you haven't. You must have been on the road for the last week." She looked up at him, her eyes dark as oncoming thunderheads. "King Laman died four days ago."

The news hit Mikiah like a punch in the gut. He'd known the old king's life was fading, but he hadn't really accepted it. The irascible, stubborn old man had seemed so *permanent*, like a boulder in a stream, too headstrong to die.

Mikiah let out a long, slow breath, feeling the hollowness of distant grief in his core. "Then it'll be up to us."

Mikiah and Ashir sat on a blanket on the grass at the base of the tower, craning their necks to look up. Mikiah held Nadai snuggled in his lap and Ashir was playing hand games with Giliel to keep him quiet. The boy giggled as his mother twisted her fingers into a kind of grotesque face and "nibbled" at his arm.

The tower was tall enough for someone on the top to see over all of the land of Nephi and a good portion of Shemlon, and right now the whole population of seven lands and cities was gathered around its base. People farther back in the crowd probably had a better view, but Mikiah and his family were more likely to hear the words directly from the king's mouth, rather than waiting for the written proclamation. That was worth a little neck strain.

A slow hush fell over the vast carpet of people as King Anti-Nephi-Lehi climbed into sight atop the tower. By now, every person in the multitude had heard that the armies were on their way. Mikiah wasn't surprised by the fear and defiance he saw in the faces around him, but he also wasn't surprised by the calm acceptance and pure trust that showed—sometimes in the same faces. These were people who would do the right thing, no matter how much it frightened them—and no matter what the consequences.

"I'm thankful today, my people," the king's voice rang out over the crowd. "I'm thankful to God that he has sent these Nephites to us, to teach us the truth." All of the Nephite missionaries stood with him atop the tower, and he gestured broadly to them, exaggerating the motion so everyone could see. "I'm grateful that God has shown us how wicked the traditions of our fathers are and that He's softened our hearts so that we could learn from these, our Nephite brothers." He paused a moment, head bowed. "We have committed many sins . . . many murders, because of the traditions of our fathers, and though it costs me great pain to know that, I'm grateful that I do. Because knowing that, I also know that God has offered us the chance to repent, through the gift and sacrifice of His Son. He's taken away our guilt and removed the stain of our sins."

Anti-Nephi-Lehi swept the crowd with his eyes, and Mikiah knew he wasn't the only one who felt as though the king looked directly at him. "You all know an army is coming to destroy us, every last man," he said. There was a low murmur from the audience as he finally said it out loud. "The men of that army are no more guilty than we ourselves were. They are our brothers and our brethren. After our many sins, you know that it took all we could do to repent enough that God would remove our guilt and wash our weapons so that they are no longer stained with blood. If we stain them again—if we fight and kill our brethren—it's possible that even the blood of the Son of God won't be able to wash them clean again."

He drew his sword and held it up, laid flat against his palms, the edge glinting bright in the sun. His voice was a trumpet call. "I proclaim here that I will not fight, and I will not kill! Who of you that hear it will stand with me?"

Mikiah, still holding Nadai in his arms, was one of the first to rise, and Ashir stood beside him. "I think he was talking to the men," Mikiah whispered, but Ashir shook her head, her lips set in a stubborn line.

"You think the men will be the only ones to make sacrifices to this?" she murmured. "No. I'm standing with you."

Beyond her, Mikiah saw Zerimhi and Abish also climbing to their feet as the rustle of shifting bodies swept across the field. Within less than a minute, all those that were within earshot of the king were on their feet, and there was a distant murmur of voices as those behind passed the word to the outlying people who hadn't heard.

Anti-Nephi-Lehi, watching as more and more of his people stood to join him, was weeping openly. "Thank you, my people," he said, his voice thick with tears, but still carrying loud and clear across the assembled throng. "If our brethren come to destroy us, let them come. We will not fight them. We will even bury our weapons as a testimony and a covenant that we have never used them since our conversion, and that we never will use them." He lowered the sword, and his gaze passed slowly over his people again. "If our brethren destroy us all, it's better for us to go to our God and be saved than to murder and be damned."

The huge hole in the ground took a full day to dig, and the diggers required a ladder to escape it once it was done. Mounds of moist earth stood around it, taller than Mikiah's head. The smell of it under the morning sun pulled his mind back to Ashir's garden. He only hoped what he planted here would someday lead to the same kind of peace for all of them.

Zerimhi looked into the depths and whistled. "When King Anti-Nephi-Lehi makes a covenant, he doesn't do it halfway, does he?" he said. "Anyone who wants his sword back is going to have a long, hard dig to have second thoughts in."

"We don't want them back," Mikiah said. "That's the point. And it isn't King Anti-Nephi-Lehi making the covenant. It's all of us. The *Anti-Nephi-Lehies*."

One side of Zerimhi's mouth twisted up. "You still can't say that without looking over your shoulder to make sure Ashoram isn't listening, can you?"

Mikiah shook his head. "Six years of habit. Give me time. I'll get over it."

Zerimhi sighed, grimacing. "I'll give you all the time you want. Ashoram won't."

"Unless you count eternity."

"There is that."

The two brothers fell silent as the king made his way up to the edge of the pit. Anti-Nephi-Lehi rested one hand on his sword hilt, his knuckles whitening as he gripped it tight. His mouth was a flat, straight line, and a deep groove had drawn itself between his eyebrows. The edge of the blade grated against the sheath as he pulled it free. Mikiah recognized the sword. It had belonged to King Laman and probably the King Laman before that as well, spanning back who knew how many generations. Mikiah had seen it years ago when King Laman threatened to kill Ammon with it. The rumors might have even been true that this was the legendary sword of Laban, carried by the Nephite kings until the Lamanites had conquered the land of Nephi a hundred years ago. There was no telling how many lives that sword had taken.

Anti-Nephi-Lehi held it up, staring at the blade for a long moment, his face unreadable. Then he drew his arm back and let it fly, flashing as it whirled end over end until it hit the loose dirt at the bottom of the hole. The men around the hole stood hushed in such reverence that the soft *thud* of the sword landing was easily audible. Without looking down, the king unfastened the sword belt and sheath as well and tossed them after the sword. His eyes closed, his head bowed in silent prayer and promise for a long moment. When he looked up again, his expression had softened, still as determined and immovable as water, but no longer frozen. He turned and walked away from the pit without a word. Behind him, other men stepped up to the edge, and more and more swords and cimeters, spears and shields, rained down into the earth.

When it was Mikiah's turn, he threw his sword in without any regret. Its point pierced the dirt and it stood there, rocking slightly, hilt pointing toward the sky. The blade shone bright against the dark earth.

"Show off," Zerimhi muttered as he chucked his own weapon into the hole. It clanged off of Mikiah's upright sword and tumbled to lie flat against the earth.

Mikiah frowned. "Sure. It's easy for you. Take your sword away and you're defenseless. But *I've* spent the last six years figuring out how to fight with nothing but my bare hands. How am I supposed to bury that?"

Zerimhi clapped him on the shoulder as they turned away to go find their wives. "I guess you'll just have to be a shining example to all of us in resisting temptation."

Ashoram's army came into view, marching down the road toward the city of Nephi. Mikiah, standing with the rest of the Anti-Nephi-Lehies in the fields around the city, saw the familiar gesture the men made, drawing one finger across their foreheads, leaving a crimson line. He shivered slightly, feeling the morning breeze cool against his damp skin.

"We are doing the right thing, aren't we?" he murmured. Beside him, Zerimhi watched the advancing army with resigned eyes. Cherom stood next to Zerimhi. The spy from Middoni had somehow shouted down both his king, who'd wanted to stand in the front lines, and his fellow spies, who'd tried to convince Cherom to stay back as well.

"If we're not, it's too late to do anything about it now," Cherom said, and Mikiah resisted the urge to try once more to convince him. No one with that much gray in his hair belonged this far forward.

An unexpected warm body pressed in on his other side, and a long-fingered hand inserted itself delicately into his. "Yes," Ashir said. "We're doing the right thing."

Mikiah whirled, staring at his wife, panic rising in his throat. "Ashir! What are you doing here? You're supposed to be back with—"

"No." She cut him off without raising her voice, and her hand squeezed his until it almost hurt. "I'm supposed to be right here. I've watched you go off without me for years. This time I'm staying with you."

"What about Nadai and Giliel?" Mikiah protested. "They'll need you."

"They're with Abish. She'll take care of them."

Mikiah floundered, grasping for arguments, anything that would convince Ashir to go back into relative safety with the other women and children, behind the line of men. His heart beat at the base of his throat, choking him, and the words he reached for fled from his mind. He clutched Ashir by the shoulders, his fingers digging in hard enough to leave bruises.

"Please, Ashir," he gasped. "You can't—you don't know what you're asking."

"No more than you asked of me all those years."

Mikiah's head bowed, his eyes closed in pain. "I don't think I'm strong enough to watch you die," he whispered.

Her hand brushed his cheek, and he leaned into the caress. "Then pray for strength."

Mikiah gave a defeated, despairing groan and dropped to his knees, clutching at his head with clawing fingers. There were times when Ashir became utterly immovable, not with anger or defiance, but with peace. Mikiah had learned long ago that when she did that, he might as well try to keep the sun from rising as try to change her mind. She was going to die beside him, and there was nothing he could do to stop it. The advancing army suddenly seemed far too close and far too large. There was no way to stop it, not with nothing but faith to fight it with. The whole idea suddenly seemed utterly reckless. Absurd. What had he been thinking? His breath came short and his vision dimmed around the edges.

Ashir knelt beside him, and a moment later Zerimhi and Cherom joined them. Then the men around them, and those beyond that. Without command or discussion, they all sank down in prayer, until the whole people of the Anti-Nephi-Lehies were on their knees in the dew-wet fields, pleading with their God for deliverance.

The ranks of the advancing army rippled, a murmur of voices rising above the sound of marching feet. "They're not even armed!" someone said, loudly enough for Mikiah to hear.

"Of course they're armed!" another voice screamed. "It's a trick! Are you going to let these fools make fools of you? Get them! Kill them all!"

That was enough. For men already primed with anger, it was enough. The ground beneath Mikiah's knees trembled as the army charged, and the many-voiced war cry shattered the air. Some of them still hung back, caution or compassion slowing their charge. Others, mostly Amalekites and Amulonites sped up, spurred by their blood hunger and easy prey.

"You do believe it, don't you?" Ashir whispered in Mikiah's ear as the ragged line of the army bore down on them.

He drew in a harsh sob. "Yes."

"Then trust."

Mikiah nodded, but he also gathered his wife into his arms so he could protect her with his own body. His whole being trembled with the desire—the *need*—to move, to act, to fight as he'd trained himself, to defend those he loved. He was only one man; he knew he couldn't fight a whole army, but the terror coursing through his muscles insisted that he try. He ignored it, only holding Ashir closer. As the running beat of footfalls drew near, Mikiah turned his head and looked up to meet the eyes of the man who had come to kill him.

Eliah stumbled, his face going pale and wide-eyed. "*Mikiah?*" He skidded to a halt, staring down at his brother. His sword sank to his side in loose fingers. Mikiah's eyes pled mutely with him. Then Eliah's jaw clenched, his eyes narrowed, and he clutched his sword in a white-knuckled fist. "You're one of them!" he hissed. Mikiah flinched at the venomous hatred glaring from his brother's eyes. He could hear screams of agony now from either side, mixing with the battle cries. Some of the Lamanite soldiers were hanging back, hesitating as they realized the Anti-Nephi-Lehies truly were unarmed and willing to die for their religion, but there were more than enough that didn't hesitate. Only a few feet away, one of the charging Amulonites gave a wild whoop as he jumped high in the air and brought his sword slashing down on Cherom's bowed head. The old spy's last cry was a word of prayer, but his attacker didn't pause to hear it, jerking his sword free as he turned toward his next victim.

Cherom's death hit Mikiah with a hammer of grief, the price of his faith more real than ever before. He felt death all around him, thick enough to taste, coming to claim him in the weapon of his friend—the sword Mikiah had given him when he married Nabeth. In a frozen moment, he watched Eliah's sword rise above his head and held Ashir closer. His brother's hand and arm trembled, wiry muscles tight and bulging, and his face contorted as he met Mikiah's gaze.

With a wild, despairing shout, Eliah brought the sword slashing down. It stabbed into the dirt at Mikiah's knees. Eliah jerked it free and slashed again, and again, tears streaming down his twisted face as he beat at the earth. He leaned against the hilt as it stuck up from the ground, breathing hard, and Mikiah could almost see the long-taught hatred pouring away from him, the first glimmer of true light beginning to shine. With a final sharp tug, Eliah pulled his blade free and threw it away. It whipped through the long grass, leaving ripples in its wake, and skidded back to earth far from Eliah's reach. Mikiah released Ashir enough to hold out one arm, and his brother lurched helplessly into his embrace.

Several paces away, another Lamanite flung his sword away and fell to his knees. Then another, and Mikiah was shocked to recognize the old man Muloki had taught in Jerusalem years ago. Spreading across the battlefield, or what would have been a battlefield if both sides had been willing to fight, more and more Lamanites fell where they stood, tossing away swords and cimeters, clubs and spears, and dropping to kneel in the damp grass.

"NO!" Mikiah heard Ashoram screaming across the field. "Kill them! They're not even fighting back! *Kill them!*"

Another voice rode over Ashoram's, the chief captain's bass bellow cutting through all the noise of battle. "Fall back!" he commanded. Most of his soldiers stopped in their tracks as though that voice had taken control of their muscles. A few of the Amulonites ignored it, too lost in bloodlust to hear. The man who had killed Cherom snarled rebellion, ramming the point of his sword into the unprotected chest of one of his former comrades. "I said, *fall back!*" Hanan roared, somehow achieving even more volume than before.

With some reluctance, the Lamanite army pulled away, regrouping on the far side of the field, in the shade of the forest trees. Though not one of them had even been injured, they'd lost nearly a tenth of their men, who were still on their knees among the Anti-Nephi-Lehies.

"Over a thousand dead."

The morning had worn away into late afternoon, and the Lamanite army still occupied the edges between the field and forest, but they hadn't attacked again. The full count of the slain was only now sifting through the ranks of the Anti-Nephi-Lehies.

"One thousand and five," Zerimhi said more exactly. He was sitting on the grass now beside Mikiah, with Eliah and Ashir gathered close. The wives and mothers waiting in the rear had sent food forward, and there would almost have been the air of a picnic about it if it weren't for that number passing from mouth to mouth, the smell of spilled blood, and the blanket-wrapped bodies carried back behind the lines, Cherom's among them. "And another fifty-seven wounded who'll probably survive," Zerimhi continued. "But nearly two thousand Lamanites joined us."

Eliah shook his head, shredding a morsel of bread in his fingers. "I doubt that'll be much comfort for all those families that just lost husbands and sons."

"Maybe not, but it'll be *some* comfort," Mikiah said. "And it's a huge relief to me, personally, having you here instead of over there trying to kill me."

The smile Eliah gave him was almost painfully forced, and the Lamanite's eyes glistened more than usual. "Shehum is still over there," he said. "Nabeth and Pelonti are . . . I don't know what I'm going to do. Nabeth swore an oath. She can't let me come home without breaking it, and that's assuming I could get there."

Mikiah reached out and gave Eliah's shoulder a tight squeeze. "She made a few vows to you as well, remember? And those ones weren't made under duress. If she's forced to choose between them, I think I know which set of promises she'll decide to keep." Eliah's attempt at a smile was more convincing this time. "Anyway, she's been harboring a Nephite sympathizer for years now, with all those persistent invitations for me to come eat with you."

"Years . . ." Eliah shook his head. "I still can't believe it. When did you start believing?"

"Amlici," Mikiah said simply, and Eliah's eyes widened. "I should have died then," Mikiah continued. "You knew it as well as I did, whether you admitted it or not. An infected wound that far gone—there's no way I should have walked away from that." His mouth lifted in a crooked smile. "Apparently God had something important for me to do."

The sound of raised voices drifted across the field from the Lamanite camp. Two men shouted over one another, each voice obscuring the other so the listeners couldn't make out either.

"You think they'll attack again today?" Zerimhi asked, gazing at the distant mass of men. Mikiah lifted both hands in ignorance, but Eliah shook his head.

"Not today," he said. "Ashoram got everyone riled up by telling us the Anti-Nephi-Lehies were planning to conquer us and force us all into slavery."

Mikiah snorted. "He'll have a hard time convincing anyone with that one after today."

"Right." Eliah nodded. "The men over there aren't stupid. They know he lied to them. He might be able to get the Amalekites and Amulonites to follow him now, but if he does, he'll lose even more of the Lamanites." He shrugged. "Captain Hanan knows his men. He won't let Ashoram give that many of them away."

Mikiah let out a long, considering hum, his eyes narrowing as he stared across the field.

"You sound like you don't much like that," Ashir said, studying him with a very similar look.

Mikiah shook himself out of his thoughts enough to give his wife a reassuring smile. "It's probably nothing," he said.

"Oh, no. You don't get to give me that one. What were you thinking?" she demanded.

"It's just . . . If Ashoram can't get his army mad enough to attack *us,* who *can* he get them angry at?"

Ashir frowned, following his line of thought. Her eyes widened and she drew in a sharp breath. "You think they'll attack the Nephites?"

Mikiah stared across the field again, and felt something settle into his heart like certainty. "I think they need watching."

Twenty-Three

City of Ammonihah, 81 BC

Mikiah sat in the dark, the smell of old straw tickling his nose and the rough stone of the prison wall pressed against his back. He didn't know how long he'd been there, he didn't know what the Nephites had planned for him, and most of all, he didn't know what he'd done wrong.

The bar on the door grated and the door swung open with the scrape of wood across packed dirt. Mikiah squinted against the sudden rush of daylight, trying to see the man who stood over him, a dark silhouette blocking the light. Brown eyes sneered down at him from beneath heavy brows, and as Mikiah's sight adjusted to the glare he realized just how large the Nephite was. The man must have stood a full head taller than Mikiah and had a chest like a barrel, running slightly to fat. His clothes were finely woven in bright reds and golds, and gold rings glinted from his ears and fingers.

"You must think we're idiots," the man said. "You think we're stupid enough to fall for your lies?"

"Lies?" Mikiah asked, his voice hoarse with hours of silence. "What're you—?"

The man cut him off with a backhanded blow across the face. Mikiah's head snapped back, bashing against the stone wall, and he blinked dizzily on stars. A trickle of blood ran down his cheek from a gash the man's ring had cut. Anger flickered, but Mikiah pushed it down, reminding himself of the covenant he'd made. He wouldn't fight back, not even if this man killed him.

"You prophets and your doom-laden whining," the man said. His voice took on a mocking nasal drone. "'Thus saith the Lord, Repent or the Lamanites will come destroy you.' Always the same story." His hand flashed again, and Mikiah grunted as the blow knocked him sideways, nearly falling into the dirty straw. A second stream of blood joined the first. "Well, we're still here!" the man continued, throwing his arms out as though inviting the world to do its worst. "And where are the Lamanites? Where is your God? What use are your so-called prophecies now?"

He hit Mikiah again, his heavy fist crashing against the side of the Amalekite's head in a red-white flash of pain. When Mikiah could see again, he found himself face down in the straw. He levered himself up a few inches, swirling pain throbbing in his head. He tasted blood.

"I'm no prophet," he whispered. "I was trying to warn you."

"We don't need your warnings!" A foot slammed into Mikiah's side like a club, lifting him from the ground and bashing him backward into the wall again. "Whatever threat you dreamed up, it can't hurt us."

Mikiah lay curled in the dirt, gasping in pain. When the man kicked at him again, his hands acted without conscious thought. He caught the foot a hand-span before it connected with his head, got a firm grip, and pushed upward. The man staggered backward, arms windmilling for balance, and Mikiah took the opportunity to stand, hands and shoulders resting against the wall to prop up his aching body.

"I'm not a prophet," he repeated more loudly. "I'm not here to preach repentance or anything else. I came to warn you about something I saw with my own eyes, not in a dream. There's a Lamanite army marching toward this city *right now*. I've been following them for days, and when I figured out where they were headed, I ran all night to get ahead of them." He sighed, his eyes sinking closed as he wrapped an arm around his bruised ribs. "I was trying to warn you," he said again. He heard the first screams begin in the distance. The prison was on the south side of the city, and the wall there was barely more than a fence. He covered his eyes with one hand and groaned at the sounds of death rushing nearer. "There's no time now."

"Antionah!" The large man jerked around at the shout from beyond the prison door. Another Nephite dashed inside in a blind panic, nearly tripping over his own feet as he clutched at Antionah's tunic. "Antionah! The Lamanites! They'll kill us all!"

Antionah just stared, slack-jawed and frozen with shock, his florid face changing to pasty gray. The sound of screams was almost at the door now, the slap of running feet drowning in the high, howling war cry of the Lamanites. "It can't be," he whispered.

His companion shook him, terrified beyond reason. "Antionah! Do something!" he shrieked. "*Do something!*"

Antionah jerked himself free of the smaller man's grip and ran toward the door. Mikiah didn't know if he was trying to escape or simply needed the proof of his own eyes before he would believe. In the end it didn't matter. A Lamanite arrow took him full in the throat before he'd gone a single pace into the open. He fell back, choking, clutching at the feathered shaft. His knees thumped onto the dirt floor. Slowly, like the majestic fall of an ancient tree, he tipped over, crashed to the ground, and lay still.

Mikiah and the other man stood for a breathless moment, staring at the corpse. Then the other man looked around, his eyes wild as a cornered animal, and seemed to realize that the windowless prison had turned into a death trap with only one way out. With a terror-stricken, despairing cry, he ran, stumbling out the door into the chaos that had been a proud city only minutes before.

Mikiah didn't follow. He glanced quickly around the single-room prison, his mind churning with fear-whipped speed. He knew that if any of the attacking army found him, they'd kill him without a second thought. After losing control of the situation during the abortive attack on the land of Nephi, Ashoram would have stirred his men into an unstoppable frenzy of bloodlust before turning them loose here. He wouldn't be satisfied until this city was razed to the ground and everyone in it was dead. Mikiah's only chance now was to hide.

The smell of blood hung thick in his nostrils as he bent over the dead body. He grimaced as he touched one shoulder with hesitant fingers, feeling the remnants of life beneath his hands—the residual body heat, the firm muscle under taut skin. He didn't have time to show the man the respect he deserved. With a grunt, Mikiah got his hands under the corpse's armpits and lifted his shoulders, dragging him into the room, toward the furthest, darkest corner.

Mikiah let the corpse flop back to the ground. He heaved a deep breath and wiped his face with his forearm. Any limp body was difficult to shift, but Antionah really had been a huge man. Mikiah didn't have time to rest, though. He could hear the battle raging just beyond the prison walls, and it would only be a matter of time before someone came to check inside. With another grimace, he rolled Antionah onto his side, his face toward the prison door. Then he kicked all the dirty straw into a pile behind the man and laid down, his back pressed against the corpse's, and pulled the straw over himself. With the smell of blood and moldy straw threatening to gag him, Mikiah lay still and waited. There was nothing more he could do.

Mikiah held his breath as he heard the prison door scrape open, trying to shrink further behind the body and remain utterly motionless at the same time. He didn't know how long it had been since he took cover here, but the daylight that had filtered dimly past the partially open door had faded and been replaced by the even dimmer glow of flickering firelight. This was the fourth time he'd heard someone look in.

"Hey, come here!" a voice shouted. "I think I see someone hiding back there!"

"Is this the prison?" a second voice responded, growing nearer.

"Yeah, I think so. Hey, you!" the first called. "Come out of there if you don't want to die in jail!"

Mikiah stayed still, every muscle tense, his heart hammering. He bit his lip to keep from breathing.

"Have it your way, then," the first voice said, and an arrow sprouted from Antionah's gut with a meaty thunk. Mikiah cringed as he felt the impact ripple through the body at his back. "Personally,

I would have chosen to die a free man under the stars," the archer said, as though discussing the merits of different foods.

"Hmm, I don't want to disappoint you," the second voice said, "but I'm afraid you might've just killed a corpse. See the blood there?"

"Oh. Yeah." The first voice grunted. "Oh well, what's one arrow more or less? It wouldn't be the first corpse I've killed today."

"Should've known you can't make a decent shot unless the target's already dead. I don't know why captain Hanan lets you carry that thing."

"Because I'm even worse with a sword."

The second man snorted. "You're more dangerous than the enemy."

"Hah! That's not saying much, the kind of spineless, sorry excuses for warriors this place had. I've never seen so many overfed weaklings."

Another voice interrupted, shouting from the distance. "Hey, you two! Hurry up! Scouting party found us some provisions, and some prisoners to cook 'em up into a decent meal for once!"

"What? Really?"

"Really! There's fresh meat for the stew pot tonight! Don't expect me to save any for you!"

Without another word, the two men ran off into the darkness, and Mikiah let out a long, cautious breath, telling his heart to calm down. He forced himself to count slowly to one hundred before he moved, listening for any slightest sound of motion nearby. There was nothing.

His arms and legs protested with sharp aches after lying still for so long. Mikiah cautiously stretched them out before rolling up to his knees, crouched behind the body that had sheltered him. He laid a grateful hand on Antionah's shoulder and bent low to whisper. "Thank you. In life, you weren't a righteous man, that much is obvious. But I've done as much to others as you did to me, and you saved my life, even if you didn't mean to. I hope you find some forgiveness in the next life."

That was all the honor he had time to give the dead. Leaving the body where it lay, he crept on silent toes to the door and peered out into the flame-lit night.

The forge that had once stood across from the prison was a smoldering heap, lighting the street with a red glow. It was a miracle the fire hadn't spread. The hissing embers cast black, twisted shadows that shifted like ghosts and demons in the smoke. Bodies lay like discarded piles of rags in the dust of the street. Just a few steps from the door, Mikiah recognized the Nephite who had come to warn Antionah. He had a gaping hole where his heart should have been.

The sounds of celebration carried over the dead city from the Lamanite camp. It sounded like they'd set up around the city gates, and victorious howling echoed through the empty streets. Mikiah wondered if anyone else had survived the massacre. One of the soldiers had mentioned prisoners, hadn't he? He worried at his lower lip. Now would be the best time for Mikiah to slip away safely, while the Lamanites were distracted by food and wine and triumph. But if there were prisoners, now would also be one of the most dangerous times for them—and the best time for someone to slip into the Lamanite camp to help them.

He stole out of the dark prison and began making his way toward the sounds of revelry.

Getting in was dangerous but not difficult. He'd lived among these people his entire life, and he knew how to act like one of them. He cringed as he dipped his fingers in a puddle of blood and swiped the dark red smear across his forehead over one eyebrow. In the darkness and firelight, it would look just like the mark all the Lamanites used in battle. It was almost ironic that the mark would also serve to disguise the scar over what had once been his bad eye. All he had to do was stroll into the heart of the Lamanite camp as though he had every right to be there. The greatest danger was that he might meet someone who recognized him.

Luck, fate, and the grace of God were with him. The chief captain had posted a minimal guard around the camp, but most of them were only barely keeping to their assigned posts, whooping and shouting with the rest of the men and paying almost no attention to anyone who might be coming or going. Mikiah walked through the crowds of shouting, dancing men without a single challenge.

The smell of roasting meat drew him toward the center of the camp where a huge bonfire roared. Dark figures danced around it, the golden light gleaming from sweat-lined skin and faces painted in blood. Mikiah shied back from the light. He saw Ashoram, standing close to the flames, arms wide and head thrown back as though to embrace the golden heat. The Amulonite king's face was flushed and his body was streaked with perspiration. He'd abandoned his fine clothing to stand nearly naked, as close to the heart of the fire as he could go without burning himself. There was something viscerally compelling about the sight, Mikiah admitted to himself, something that spoke to the most basic, primitive nature of mankind. He turned away from it, a sour sickness churning in his gut.

The scent of cooking came from other, smaller fires nearby. It looked like the scouting party had slaughtered an entire herd of cattle, and hungry men surrounded at least a dozen spitted carcasses over the fires, hacking off hunks of meat as it roasted. The smell spoke directly to Mikiah's stomach, reminding him that he hadn't eaten all day. He drew closer, cautiously scanning the faces in the firelight for anyone he knew. It wasn't until he came close enough to reach the roasting carcass that he realized he might stand out for a different reason.

He wasn't carrying a weapon. No sword or club to wave victoriously in the air, no spear to shake at the heavens. He didn't even have a knife to cut off a piece of the meat—the Nephites had taken it from him when they threw him in prison. That problem wasn't insurmountable, though. Mikiah joined the crowd of laughing, jostling men, pushing eagerly toward the sizzling roast. The man beside him never even felt the knife disappear from his belt, and when Mikiah had used it to slice off a well-cooked slab of meat, he returned the borrowed knife just as easily.

Mikiah tore into the meat, dropping his guard for just a moment in sheer pleasure. He closed his eyes to savor the taste, the hot fat dripping down his chin and coating his fingers. When he opened his eyes again, he found himself caught in the gaze of a small, wrinkled Nephite woman. She was methodically turning the spit, her thin fingers wrapped around the handle as she pulled back and pushed forward in steady rhythm. She was so tiny, she had to put her entire body into the effort, and wisps of gray hair clung to her damp forehead, but she barely seemed to notice the work, instead staring steadily at Mikiah.

Mikiah's mouth went dry, and his appetite disappeared. If this woman was from the city, the blood on his face might have been her husband's, her child's, or even her grandchild's. He continued eating anyway, not daring to break character now, but he took a closer look at the other cooking fires. Each one had a Nephite prisoner turning the spit, and there was a group of children nearby, preparing vegetables for cooking. The only men were either old and frail as the woman he'd seen first, or stripling boys barely ready for their first sword. Mikiah guessed that the scouting party hadn't spared anyone who might be able to fight back. He frowned as he finished his meal, watching the prisoners with worried eyes. They were too spread out for him to protect them all, and he couldn't keep up the pretense forever. Eventually, someone would recognize him.

He began circling the cooking fires, prowling through the dancing shadows, and slowly a plan coalesced. It wasn't perfect. There were a dozen ways it could go wrong, with deadly consequences. The fact that none of the prisoners were able-bodied men was a serious hindrance as well. But there were ways around even that.

It seemed to take forever for the celebration to die down. The dancing and howling continued long into the night, until the roasted carcasses were picked to the bone, the wineskins were all empty, and most of the Lamanite army had collapsed from sheer exhaustion. When the last few tired Lamanites came to round up the prisoners, none of them questioned the presence of one more Nephite. True, the man was young and strong, obviously accustomed to hard work, but his left arm was splinted and bound up in a sling, and he moved with a stoop-shouldered, plodding monotony that implied he had to think about everything he did well before he did it. There was no threat there, and none of the Lamanites noticed the intelligence that glinted in the blue eyes hidden behind a long curtain of greasy blond-brown hair.

The Lamanites herded their prisoners together, clearing a space for them near the center of camp by the simple expedient of kicking, rolling, or carrying their sleeping comrades out of the way. There were no walls to keep them in, or even a tent for shelter. Most of the

Nephites were too exhausted with work, shock, and terror to even think of escape. They simply lay down in the cleared space, held their loved ones close, and hoped sleep would somehow make the world better.

Mikah curled up on the hard ground, pulling his long limbs in close to his body against the cooler night air. He jerked in surprise when he felt a smaller body snuggle in next to him, a warm but bony back pressed against his.

"You're not a Nephite." The voice was quiet so only he could hear it, cracked and high-pitched with age. He realized it must be the old woman who'd stared at him so intently earlier. "Not a Lamanite, either. Amlicite?"

He shook his head, watching as the Lamanite guards settled down around the embers of a fire, laughing and yawning. They'd notice if someone tried to run for it. Anything less would be lost in the haze of victorious exhaustion. "Amalekite," he murmured. "Or used to be."

"Hmph. What kind of Amalekite doesn't carry a weapon?"

"One who's trying to be something else."

"Well, you've convinced that lot you're a Nephite. I take it that was on purpose?"

"Yes." Mikiah couldn't help smiling a little at the bite in her tone. She reminded him of Nabeth. "I wanted to help you, if I can." His voice darkened and he swallowed on sudden bitterness. "There was nothing I could do for the city. I tried, but . . ." He shook his head helplessly at the darkness.

"Son, there was nothing anyone could have done for Ammonihah." Her sharp voice had gentled, and he felt a soft-skinned hand pat his leg. "That city's been headed for destruction for a long time. Better men than you have tried to save it and couldn't. It's sad, but I can't say it's surprising that God brought the Lamanite army here."

Mikiah lay silently for a while, troubled by her words. "I . . . don't think I understand that," he said, his eyebrows drawn down tight. "I thought God was a loving Heavenly Father. Why would a loving Father destroy a city full of His children?"

The woman at his back sighed, and Mikiah felt the heavy rise and fall of her ribs. "There have to be consequences," she said in a small voice. "And you obviously don't know what the Ammonihahites did."

"What could *possibly* have been bad enough to—" Mikiah broke off as the woman shushed him and he realized how much his voice had risen.

"You're a father, aren't you? I can tell," she said. "Being a parent gives you a different look at things, and mostly it's better. But you don't really know what Ammonihah was like. Even the most loving father in the world might be forgiven for not protecting his child—or even killing it himself—if that child had gone mad and was killing his other children."

Mikiah couldn't help applying that thought to his own children, and shuddered. "What happened?"

She sighed again. "I don't much like talking about it," she said. "And I like to talk, so you know it must be pretty bad. What happened was that Alma came to the city, preaching, like he does."

"Alma? The—what was it? Chief judge?" Mikiah vaguely remembered the man who'd once saved his life, killing the Amlicite who'd been on the verge of finishing Mikiah off.

"Well, yes and no. Alma gave up being chief judge so he could leave Zarahemla and spend his time teaching. When he came to Ammonihah, they pretty much just threw him out. He was about to give up on them, but as he was leaving, an angel appeared and told him to go back."

"Really? Another one?"

She chuckled. "Same one again, the way Alma tells it. So anyway, he goes back and finds out one of the Ammonihahites *also* saw an angel, and he's all set to help out with the preaching. I guess either there's strength in numbers, or the new preacher—Amulek was his name—knew just the right things to say to get through to them, because the second time they actually had some success. Not a huge amount, mind you, but there were people listening and believing—changing their lives, like Alma and Amulek taught them."

"And?" Mikiah prompted when she paused for a long while. "Is this the bad part?"

"Yes." She sniffled. "Bad enough. The rulers of Ammonihah didn't much like people following anyone else, you see. So they rounded up all the men who believed and threw them out of the city. Would have stoned them to death if they hadn't run fast enough. And then they got all their women and children together, and—" She broke off, sniffling again. "And they killed them all."

Mikiah was shocked speechless. "They killed *children?"* he whispered, feeling ice in his spine and sickness in his gut.

"Burned," another woman said out of the gloom. "Not just killed. They burned them all alive. And they made Alma and Amulek watch."

"That's Naomarah," the woman at Mikiah's back whispered. "Alma and Amulek stopped at her farm on the way to Sidom after they escaped from Ammonihah. She got the whole story first hand."

"Are none of you actually from the city?" Mikiah asked.

"No, thank heaven. There's a little corner of the land of Noah that sticks down between Ammonihah and Sidom. That's where we're from. We don't rely on Ammonihah for anything."

"Didn't," Naomarah's voice corrected bitterly. Mikiah wondered which of the lumps in the darkness it belonged to. "We're slaves to the Lamanites now. We'll have to rely on them."

The silence beat harshly in their ears for a long moment. Mikiah bit his lip at the despair in the woman's voice. "Does your chief judge know what's happening?" he whispered.

"We think so," the woman behind him whispered back. "Some of the men were in the fields; we think they escaped. They'll warn Nephihah." She grunted a small laugh. "And even if they don't, someone else will. We've had generations to learn how to handle this kind of thing."

"And this Nephihah will send an army?"

"Yes."

Mikiah nodded with a feeling of squaring his shoulders to accept a burden. "Then all I have to do is keep all of you safe until they show up."

A sobbing laugh came from Naomarah's direction, but Mikiah ignored it. This was something he *could* do.

Twenty-Four

Wilderness West of Nephite Lands, 81 BC

Ashoram moved the Lamanite army the next morning, with much grumbling and moaning from the soldiers. The Nephite women were again in charge of preparing the food, but a large portion of the army was in no fit state to eat it, and instead they spent their time losing the meal they'd been so enthusiastic about the night before. From the sounds of retching, their stomachs were just as enthusiastic about getting rid of it.

In spite of it all, Ashoram and Hanan managed to get them on their feet, packed up, and stumbling along before the sun was more than a few handspans above the horizon. The Nephite prisoners had no choice but to go along, trudging beneath heavy burdens the Lamanites didn't feel like carrying. They headed west briefly, their shadows stretched long and black across the desolate fields in front of them. When the jungle swallowed them again, they turned south, following the line of wilderness that ran between the Nephite lands and the western sea.

That first day was the hardest for Mikiah. The men were still aching with the effects of their overindulgence, and took vicious pleasure in tormenting their captives. There was a limit to how much they could do while on the march, but Mikiah took the brunt of the physical punishment. In his disguise of dim-witted laborer, his face carefully hidden by the mask of his long hair, he walked deliberately into the feet that hooked out to trip him. He stumbled and fell to hard shoves, supposedly meant to hurry him along, and endured the beatings the guards used to get him up and moving again. He whimpered, cradling the splinted arm in its sling, and that only inspired the Lamanites to find any excuse to bump into him and jar the "injured" arm.

The women and children were spared most of that. Even after the slaughter of Ammonihah, the men of Ashoram's army wouldn't go so far as to torture women. Kill them outright, perhaps, but not torture. They had no qualms whatsoever, though, about verbal abuse, and the Nephite prisoners were subjected to a rain of insults, rude jests, and mockery. Mikiah gritted his teeth and bore it, reminding himself that there were more serious things to protect them from. The prisoners, white faced, walked along in tight silence, though they had to restrain some of their older children from answering back.

Mikiah was surrounded by laughing, jeering Lamanites, stumbling as they shoved and hit him back and forth between them like the ball in some child's game, when he saw a dark-haired Nephite woman trying to pull away from one of the Amulonite soldiers, who held her arm in a tight grip. Reeling from a glancing blow, Mikiah stumbled toward the confrontation, only to be met by another shove.

"Let me go!" the woman gasped. Mikiah recognized Naomarah's voice, panic rising to hysteria as she struggled. "Don't you dare touch me! My husband will kill you! He'll bring the Nephite armies and he'll kill you!"

The man's face twisted. "Your husband's dead!" he said. "And if he isn't, it doesn't matter. You'll never see him again."

Naomarah drew in a sharp breath, almost a sob. The harsh words seemed to break her fear into a flare of anger, and her eyes blazed for just a moment. She wrenched her arm free of the Amulonite's hand. "I *will* see him again," she said, as if the power of her faith could etch those words in stone, in the bedrock of the world. Then the moment passed and she closed her eyes, trembling, a tear falling down her cheek. "I will," she whispered.

The Amulonite laughed, loud and mocking. "You just go on dreaming that, Nephite," he said. "But you're going to spend the rest of your life serving *us* now. And don't think you're going to be rescued, either. We've got orders. First sign of any Nephite army, you all die." He grabbed her arm again, pulling her toward him, and she shrunk away from the evil glee in his eyes. "So you'd better learn to—Hey!" He staggered as Mikiah barreled into him, propelled apparently by an ill-placed kick from one of the Lamanites. Mikiah clung to the Amulonite, struggling for balance and nearly pulling the man down with him, while the Lamanites behind him called laughing apologies. By the time the Amulonite knocked Mikiah to the ground and delivered a kick to the ribs for good measure, Naomarah had escaped, disappearing into the crowd of wearily marching prisoners.

Twenty-Five

Wilderness South of Nephite Lands, 81 BC

On the evening of the third day, they reached and crossed the river Sidon where it flowed through the southern wilderness that divided the Nephites and Lamanites. Mikiah collapsed, sopping wet, when he reached the eastern bank for the last time. The Lamanites had set him to carrying loads across the river—shallow enough here to wade across. They hadn't interfered with him while he was hauling anything. They didn't want their things getting wet. But every time he turned back for another load, he found himself tripped or shoved face first into the rushing water. His knees were bloody and his feet bruised by the stones in the river bed, his eyes and nose stung with the repeated dousing, and his long, unbound hair was plastered to his head and face. He huddled miserably on the ground and shivered at the brush of a warm evening breeze.

"Come on, get up!" a voice barked at him, and a rough toe prodded his back. "We're making camp. You can sleep when that's done."

Panting, Mikiah lumbered to his feet and plodded in the direction the Lamanite guard pointed him. A small, wrinkled hand slipped into his, and he looked down to see the old woman peering at him with worried eyes. She'd eventually gotten around to telling him her name—Zerubah.

"Are you all right?" she asked.

He nodded heavily, but winked at her through the curtain of his hair. "Better than I look," he whispered.

"That's good, because you *look* like someone begging to be put out of his misery. Was this part of your plan?"

"None of you have been attacked so far." His eyes narrowed as he scanned the darkening trees. Something tickled at the back of his mind.

"And we're grateful for that, no question," Zerubah said. "But you can't keep this up forever."

Mikiah suddenly chuckled. "Looks like I won't have to," he said. He straightened, rising out of his dull slouch and pulling his shoulders back, letting out a relieved groan as he stretched the cramped muscles of his neck and back. He slipped the makeshift sling off, unbound his splinted arm, and used both hands to scrape his wet hair back, pulling it up away from his face and tying it there with a strip of raw leather. "Signal the others."

Zerubah gaped at him, barely understanding, much less believing. Then a wild light dawned behind her eyes and she drew in a sharp gasp. She scanned the dark trees eagerly. Her face fell slightly when she didn't see anything, but a glance up at Mikiah reassured her. With a quick nod, she pursed her lips, and a shrill whistle rang out over the Lamanite camp like the cry of a hunting bird.

Everything seemed to happen at once. All over the camp, Nephite heads popped up from whatever task they'd been set, their faces ranging between hope, fear, and disbelief. In a ragged wave, they dropped their loads and began running, converging on Zerubah and Mikiah. Mikiah heard a horribly familiar voice call out, "*Mikiah?* What're you—?" He turned to see Shehum standing a few paces away, his mouth hanging open, frozen in shock. Someone near the forest screamed as an arrow appeared buried in his gut, and then the air was filled with the buzzing whir of flying shafts, the panicked cries of the Lamanite army, and the hollow shrieks of the Nephite war cry.

"I'm sorry, Shehum," Mikiah said. He took two swift paces, jumped, whirled, and smashed his heel into his friend's face. Shehum dropped like a sack of clay, safely unconscious before he hit the ground. "But I'm saving lives." An arrow speared through the space

Shehum's body had occupied a moment before, and Mikiah shivered. "Including yours."

He turned quickly back toward the huddled prisoners. "Get down!" he snapped. "Flat on the ground, all of you, now!" The Nephites didn't need telling twice. They dove for the leaf-strewn forest floor, clinging to any scrap of cover they could find. Mikiah crouched down next to them, but didn't dare obscure his vision by hugging the ground. His eyes tracked the chaos that had engulfed the Lamanite camp, watching for anything that would threaten his charges.

The Nephites had chosen the perfect time for their attack. The Lamanites were tired and footsore from marching all day, their minds wrapped up with the expectation of food and sleep. They were in the middle of making camp—neither marching or resting, the time when they were paying the least attention to their surroundings. In the fading twilight, the Nephites were hidden in the shadows of the forest, while the Lamanites formed dark silhouettes against the open river, making them perfect targets and rendering their own archers useless. Completing the perfection of the surprise, no one had expected the Nephite army to be *ahead* of them, waiting for them to arrive. All of Ashoram's scouts had been watching their back trail, expecting pursuit. Even Mikiah couldn't understand how the Nephites had known exactly where and when to hit them, though he'd at least sensed the attack coming.

"Charge!" captain Hanan's voice echoed through the screams. "Don't just stand there and take it, you idiots! Into the trees! Get them!"

It took a few moments before anyone obeyed him, and the charge started out as more of a stumble. Most of the first Lamanites died as they ran toward the archers in the trees, cut down before they got within striking distance. When Hanan managed to gather enough of his warriors for a concerted assault, struggling through the storm of arrows, they met with an even more deadly storm of swords out of the shadows. The Lamanite charge fell back, locked in fierce battle with the Nephite front, but they'd at least succeeded in stopping the flights of arrows.

Mikiah had no more time to watch the battle. Several Lamanites came pelting back toward the cluster of prisoners. The weapons in their hands said they weren't trying to run away. Beyond that, they might have been looking for hostages, or they might have been obeying the order to prevent the Nephites being rescued at any cost. Mikiah didn't know and didn't care. They were threatening the people he was there to protect, and that made them his problem.

He started to run at the attacking Lamanites, and the image of his sword cut through his mind, its point embedded in a dark pit. But he also remembered Ammon repeating, "There's no sin in defending yourself." Mikiah reached the first of the Lamanites, facing the armed man with empty hands. *I made a covenant not to kill. I never said I wouldn't fight.*

The man lashed out, his sword striking down like a falling thunderbolt, but Mikiah wasn't there. He slipped sideways, twisting his body like a snake. He grabbed the Lamanite's arm and pulled. Mikiah's knee drove into the soldier's midriff, leaving him coughing and gasping for air. He doubled over and Mikiah wrenched the sword from his hand and let him drop. The next behind him skidded in leaf mold, suddenly confronted by a man with a sword instead of an unarmed prisoner, but Mikiah threw the sword away almost as soon as he touched it. He wiped his hand against his leg and whirled again, ducking under a swinging club and bringing his fist up into his attacker's chin. The man's head snapped back and he fell backward, scrambling away crabwise on his hands and feet. He'd dropped the club, and Mikiah kicked it away, then whirled to confront another attacker, weaving around a thrusting spear to ram the spearman with one shoulder.

He'd never before had the opportunity to use his own style of unarmed fighting in a full melee. There was a kind of glory in it, underlaid with a sparkling edge of danger, like the sharply ragged edge of a broken quartz crystal. He spun through the battle, a lion among wolves, but the memory of his discarded sword still hung in his mind.

One of the soldiers—an Amalekite—tried to get around him, to reach the prisoners. Mikiah grabbed one of the others, swung him around, screaming and flailing, and sent him skidding into the Amalekite. Both men fell, arms and legs tangled together. Mikiah twisted again, ducking away from something that flashed toward his head, and lashing out with a kick at one of the men in the crowd surrounding him. The Lamanite fell back, but his wildly flailing sword struck Mikiah's unprotected leg, drawing a thin line of blood. Mikiah jerked back, the pain jarring his concentration, and he was forced to block a swinging club rather than dodge it. The length of rough wood scraped a glancing blow along his upraised arm, and he flinched again at the pain.

He didn't dare let himself slow down. Gritting his teeth, he forced himself to ignore the throbbing ache, the flow of blood. He struck back with renewed ferocity, arms and legs flying in a deadly dance, and now he barely even felt the blows that fell on him. His mind focused itself down to the need to simply survive and keep moving. Lamanite soldiers fell away from him, clutching at broken limbs and dislocated shoulders, crushed noses and swimming heads. Someone grabbed him from behind, pinning his arms to his sides as a blade swung toward him. Desperate, he snaked one foot back, hooked an ankle, and heaved. Both he and his captor fell backward, and the sword passed harmlessly over their heads.

Mikiah landed heavily on top of the man who held him, heard the breathless grunt, and felt the creak of straining ribs. The man's grip loosened, and Mikiah rammed an elbow into his gut and rolled free, leaving the Lamanite gaping after air as the man tried to convince his lungs to function again. Mikiah came to his feet in one smooth motion and launched himself at the first soldier he saw. The man was only a shape in the gathering darkness, faceless and inhuman. Long-trained instinct took over. Mikiah screamed a war cry as he attacked the soldier with all the single-minded violence with which he'd once attacked the straw men in his training yard. One arm knocked a weapon out of the way while the bunched knuckles of his other fist rammed toward the dark shape's unprotected throat, ready to crush the windpipe and leave the man to suffocate.

Mikiah came to his senses at the last moment. Too late to stop the blow entirely, all he could do was redirect it, and he felt the man's collarbone crack with a sickening noise beneath his hand. The Lamanite fell, screaming. Mikiah froze, his breath coming short as icy horror rose up to choke him.

I might have killed him!

He no longer cared that he was surrounded by enemies. He no longer heard the noises of battle, the shrieks of the dying, the shouts of the victorious. Even the Nephite prisoners faded from his mind in that moment of pure, burning self-reproach. Mikiah's body went limp, and he dropped to his knees beside the man he'd so nearly destroyed. It saved his life, a cimeter slicing through the space he'd occupied a heartbeat before, but he didn't even notice. He curled in on himself, and a soul-wrenching groan rumbled in his throat. He'd come so close to the edge; he didn't dare move for fear he'd slip over it and be lost forever.

There was movement around him. Huddled there in the fallen leaves, Mikiah braced himself, expecting any moment to feel the sharp pain of a sword thrust, the crush of a club against his skull. A part of him wondered if he deserved it. He only hoped Ashir would forgive him for not coming back.

"*Get away from him!*"

Mikiah's head jerked up at the wild scream, his mouth falling open as he looked around and saw the tiny figure of Zerubah menacing the group of Lamanite soldiers, a captured sword held in both hands. Behind her, the other prisoners had armed themselves with whatever they could find—lengths of firewood or fist-sized rocks mostly, but a few had picked up discarded weapons. Mikiah saw the sword he'd thrown away from the first Lamanite attacker trembling in Naomarah's fist.

"You may think we're just women and children, but we know how to fight!" Zerubah continued, shaking her sword at the Lamanites. She looked like something out of a campfire scare-tale, with her wild eyes glowing in the twilight, her wispy hair flying loose around her head, and her wrinkled lips pulled back from a nearly toothless mouth in a grimace of terrified rage and defiance. The Lamanites around Mikiah fell back a step or two, staring at the apparition. "We fight for our homes!" she shrieked. "We fight for our families! We fight for the dead that *you* have slain!" She threw her arm out, pointing the sword at the Lamanites, and Mikiah saw several of them take another step back, as though afraid the blade might come to life and fly at them, pierce them dead where they stood. Zerubah must have seen it too. Her voice dropped to a menacing, unearthly whisper, like something echoing out of the tomb. "Leave now—or face us!"

The Lamanites weren't cowards or fools, but the night was closing in and the Nephite army had already spooked them with its uncanny attack. The soldiers hesitated, exchanging nervous glances. Behind them, the screams of dying Lamanites mingled with the victorious war cries of the Nephites. "Now! They're breaking!" a Nephite voice shouted from the depths of the forest. "Hit them *now!*"

One of the Lamanites cursed softly. "Not worth it," he muttered. He jammed his sword into its sheath and took to his heels, disappearing into the deepening shadows. His flight broke the others' stasis, and soon they were all gone, running like rabbits from the Nephite armies—and a crazy old woman with a sword.

Zerubah grunted, letting the sword point drop until it dug into the leaf mulch. "Huh. I didn't think that would work." She stumped over to Mikiah, dragging the sword behind her like a plow through the fallen leaves of ages. "You hurt, boy?"

Mikiah snapped his gaping mouth closed. He had to try twice to get his voice working. "How did you do that?"

She chuckled. "My sons liked it when I told exciting stories," she said. "I figured, those boys were already scared, barely knew what to do with you even once you were down. Wouldn't take much to set 'em going, you know?"

"What would you have done if it hadn't worked?"

Zerubah shrugged. "I'd rather die fighting than cowering," she said, staring off into the dark forest. The golden sparks of torches drifted through the trees now, and Nephite voices called to each other. The Lamanite army was gone, leaving the Nephites to deal with the dead and wounded from both sides. Zerubah shook herself and let the sword fall, reaching down to touch Mikiah's shoulder. "Never mind," she said. "You're not hurt, then. What stopped you?"

Mikiah looked at the ground. The man he'd almost killed had scrambled away with the rest of them, but Mikiah could still feel the crack of bone beneath his hands. He shuddered. It would have been so easy. "Trying to be something else," he said in a hoarse, tight whisper.

"You are that," she agreed. "Never seen anyone fight like that."

He shook his head. His body felt loose, almost drunk with the aftermath of battle. “I hope you never have to again.” He staggered to his feet, swaying, feeling now the collection of bruises and cuts he’d ignored in the heat of the moment. The one on his leg was the worst, a dark wash of blood trickling steadily over his calf. In the deep blue twilight, it looked like tar. His whole body felt like one long bruise, and his muscles groaned in protest at every movement. He shook his head again, trying to jog his thoughts back into place. “Shehum,” he muttered to himself. “Where’s—?” He turned, stumbling, and managed two steps toward the place he’d last seen his friend, but even in the dark he could see that Shehum was gone. Mikiah stopped again, swaying slightly. “I have to go,” he said. “The army—they might attack again, somewhere else. I’ve got to—” He took another step, and his legs collapsed beneath him.

Zerubah caught him, grunting as she held him on his feet. The tiny old woman was stronger than she looked, but Mikiah struggled to support his own weight, afraid he was going to crush her.

“Get off her!” A hard hand rammed into Mikiah’s shoulder, spinning him away from Zerubah, and he found himself sprawled on his back, looking up the length of a shining blade at the dark silhouette of a Nephite warrior. “Coward!” the Nephite spat. “Attacking an old woman!” He shoved Zerubah behind him and raised his voice. “Father! Lehi! I found them! Are any of you hurt?” he asked the gathered prisoners as answering shouts echoed from the forest. Mikiah tried to move, but the sword point pressed against his throat and he froze again. “You! Lamanite!” Mikiah couldn’t see the Nephite’s face, but his voice was thick with contempt and hatred. “Either run away now, or pick up your sword and fight me.”

Mikiah wanted to go. He would have. But after three days of near-constant abuse, and then the river crossing, and then the battle, his body overruled him. He couldn’t move. The last of the fear-fueled energy he’d used to fight the Lamanites had drained away, and it was almost more than he could do just to prop himself half off the ground. He stared up at the Nephite, breathing heavily.

There was a low murmur coming from the group of former prisoners, a strange blend of confusion and anger. “No, sir, we’re none of us hurt,” Naomarah’s voice rose above the low rumble and she stalked out of the crowd. "But only because the man you're threatening has spent the last three days protecting us all with his own body." She knelt beside Mikiah and laid a possessive hand on his shoulder, glaring up at the Nephite. "If you drive him off, I for one am going with him." A number of voices rose in agreement behind her.

The soldier gaped at the women and children as though they'd all gone mad together. "*Him?* But—but he's a Lamanite!" he protested. "The Lamanites are the ones who *attacked* you! Why would he—"

"I'm not a Lamanite," Mikiah said. He wanted to say it clear and firm, but his voice came out as more of a croak. He cleared his throat and tried again. The sword point still hovering near his chest didn't help. "I'm not one of them. We gave ourselves a new name—Anti-Nephi-Lehi."

"Anti—" The Nephite stumbled over the long name. "What's that supposed to mean?"

Zerubah stepped free of the man's restraining arm. "It means a Lamanite who's trying to be something else," she said. She knelt across from Naomarah, resting her own hand on Mikiah's other shoulder.

Mikiah smiled at her. "It means your last king's sons are doing some good."

The Nephite drew in a sharp breath. "The sons of *Mosiah?* They're still alive?" he exclaimed. Mikiah nodded, though the man might not have seen in the darkness. The warrior wavered for a moment, then withdrew his sword, ramming it into its sheath with a decisive click. "I think you need to talk to my father."

Zoram, the chief captain of the Nephites, wasn't a large man, but he moved with a decisive quickness that spoke of a sharp mind and focused self-control. He found Mikiah sitting on a fallen log, to which the combined mass of freed prisoners had carried him and settled him down with a certain amount of firmness. "You're not going anywhere until you've had a rest and I've had a chance to bind up that leg of yours," Zerubah told him. "So you might as well get comfortable." She was still cleaning the wound by the light of the Nephite torches when Zoram appeared.

"My son Aha tells me you've got an unbelievable story for me, Lamanite," the man said. He stood with folded arms, looking down at Mikiah as though he were something Zoram would need to scrape off the bottom of a boot. The word *Lamanite* sounded like a curse in his mouth.

Mikiah grimaced as Zerubah's wet cloth hit a particularly tender spot. "What do you want to know?"

"You told Aha the sons of Mosiah are still alive?" Zoram asked. Mikiah nodded. "And they're . . . free?"

"As of a few days ago," Mikiah told him. "They haven't seen the inside of a prison in years."

Zoram grunted, his mouth twisting. "When they didn't come back, I figured they were captured—if they weren't dead. I always said it was a bad idea, letting them go."

Mikiah cocked one eyebrow. "You didn't believe the Lord would keep His promise to King Mosiah?"

Zoram's eyes widened slightly. "Not many people know about that," he said. He shook his head. "It's not so much that I didn't believe, but you can be alive and rotting in prison. Then again, if they fell away from the truth, of course so would the blessing fall away from them. A lot can happen in ten years." He snorted. "So they're still alive and playing at being preachers, and much good it's done. The Lamanites still haven't stopped attacking us. I've told Nephihah a hundred times—we ought to just go up and wipe them all out."

Zerubah made a noise in the back of her throat, and Mikiah saw her lips white and pressed together, her eyes narrow as she wound a length of cloth around his leg. She didn't say anything, but the force with which she didn't say it made her opinion clear. Zoram, standing behind her, possibly didn't notice.

Mikiah groped for something to say. He was beginning to think he didn't much like this man. "I take it Nephihah disagreed with you?"

"He did. And so did Alma before him. And King Mosiah before that, as a matter of fact." Zoram glared again at Mikiah as though he was the source of the Nephite rulers' stubborn peace mongering. "But that won't stop my men from killing any Lamanite we find in our lands. And you can tell your chief captains and rulers that. With my compliments."

Mikiah drew in a sharp breath as Zoram all but called him a liar and a spy. Zerubah shot to her feet. "Young man, I don't care who you are, don't you *dare* insult this man to his face! Don't you dare!" She shook one finger under Zoram's nose, and the chief captain actually fell back a step. "He's the only reason we're all still alive for you to 'rescue.'" Her voice dripped scorn at the word. "Did your men even *think* about us while they were aiming those arrows? Did you even consider sending someone to protect us? Because the Lamanites surely sent people to kill us, and if Mikiah hadn't stopped them, we'd most of us be dead now!" She glared up at the captain. "He did your job for you, and you'd better show him some respect or so help me, you'll regret it!"

Zoram stared down at the tiny old woman panting with rage before him. One eyebrow quirked, and he looked over her head to meet Mikiah's eyes. "It appears I must apologize," he said formally. "If what you say is true, I suppose it's good news there are at least a *few* Lamanites who won't attack us."

Mikiah met the man's gaze and held it in steady challenge. "A few thousand, actually."

The chief captain's eyes bulged and he looked like he'd swallowed his tongue. "*Thousands?*" he choked. "They—they converted *thousands?* The sons of *Mosiah?* But—" He gave his head a sharp shake. "But they were just a bunch of rebellious boys!"

Mikiah's eyebrows drew together, and then he blinked in surprised comprehension. "People can change, you know."

Zoram threw that comment away with one hand. "I know, I know. It's just—"

"Forgive me," Mikiah said gently. "I think you know, but you don't entirely believe. The sons of Mosiah may have been rebellious boys, but now they're men of God. The Lamanites they converted may once have been your enemies, but now we are not."

Zoram gave him a long, considering look, his lips pressed together and his forehead wrinkling with deep thought. "I think," he said, "Nephihah will want to talk with you."

Mikiah shook his head. "I can't spare the time now." He gestured toward the dark trees. "The army's gone, but they could still attack from the wilderness somewhere else. I need to—"

"My spies are taking care of that," Zoram interrupted. "If they attack anywhere in Nephite lands, we'll be ready for them. Besides that, I can't afford to let you go now, even if I was willing to assume you're telling the truth. I know, you say he saved your life," he said, holding up a hand to forestall Zerubah's outburst. "But rescues can be faked. I'm not saying he did, but I can't say he didn't either, and that means he comes back to Zarahemla with me." Zoram's eyes were hard, glinting in the torchlight as he stared at Mikiah. "The question is whether he'll come willing or bound hand and foot."

Mikiah sighed deeply as he rose from the fallen log. Standing, he found himself looking down to meet Zoram's eyes. The captain was half a head shorter than Mikiah, which was almost surprising. The man had such a forceful personality that Mikiah had actually forgotten his physical size. Mikiah broke the challenging stare to give Zerubah a weary smile. He patted her shoulder, a gentle thanks for her care. "I'm sorry," he said.

She snorted, but her hand came up to cover his. "Don't be. Some people just can't be talked into reason."

Mikiah jumped, his legs whirling, and his heel connected squarely with Zoram's jaw. He was running before the Nephite captain hit the ground, and he vanished into the concealment of the night and the thick bushes, leaving the pursuit to thrash in the undergrowth behind him.

Twenty-Six

Wilderness East of Nephite Lands, 81 BC

Mikiah woke early the next morning to a hard hand clamping over his mouth, the cold kiss of a blade against his throat. He jerked in surprise, then froze as the knife bit. His eyes flared open and he stared up at the dark silhouette crouched over him, the false light of early dawn giving only the vague suggestion of shape and features.

"Mikiah? That is you, isn't it?" The hoarse whisper was close enough for Mikiah to feel the breath against his face. He drew in a sharp breath, feeling the edge of the knife press harder on his neck, the first trickle of blood as the skin parted. "I should kill you now for a traitor," the voice growled. Mikiah's pulse pounded, throbbing close to the trembling blade, and he felt the twist of terror and despair in his gut. He knew that deep, steady voice. In the breathless darkness before dawn, the two men paused, motionless, hovering on the edge of decision. Mikiah's captor drew in a long breath. "But first I want to know why."

Both knife and muffling hand withdrew, giving Mikiah enough room to raise himself on one elbow, his hand clutching at the slow seep of blood from his throat. "Shehum?" he gasped. "Th-thank you."

"Don't thank me yet," the Lamanite said, his voice hard. "I should still kill you. What did you do to Eliah?"

Mikiah shook his head. "Nothing. I swear. When you all attacked, he found me on the field. He wouldn't kill me." Mikiah coughed slightly. It hurt to talk. "He's probably brought Nabeth and Pelonti back to the land of Nephi by now. With my wife."

"Your wife." Shehum drew in a breath and let it out slowly. "It's that Lamanite woman, isn't it? The one who took care of you. She turned you against us."

"No."

"Is that when all this started? As far back as that?"

"No. It wasn't her," Mikiah insisted. "Though she *is* my wife now. It was . . . Amlici. Muloki and Temisah." Shehum drew in a sharp breath at that name, and his spine straightened. "And—and God."

Shehum grunted. "God," he repeated in an unreadable voice. "Are you going to tell me you saw an angel?"

"No." Mikiah coughed again. "But I saw a miracle. And . . . I saw the truth." He looked up at his friend, his gaze piercing even the darkness to study Shehum's face. "And I think you saw it too."

Shehum reared back in surprise. "What?"

"You're always listening, Shehum. It's part of who you are. You listened to Ammon in Ishmael, didn't you? I was trying not to, but you listened. You listened to Amlici and recognized his madness. You helped me keep him from slaughtering Zarahemla. And now you're listening to me. A part of you knows where the truth is. You *want* to be convinced."

Shehum scrambled away, shaking his head. "No! I don't—I *can't*—"

"You can," Mikiah told him inexorably. "Anyone can change, if I could. And I *did* change after the Amlicite war, didn't I, Shehum? You must have seen it, even if I fooled everyone else." The dark shape that was Shehum flinched, but Mikiah didn't let up. "Was it a change for the better?"

He waited while his friend wrestled with himself. After a long pause, Shehum's voice came out of the darkness. "Yes," he whispered.

Mikiah sat up and reached out to squeeze his friend's shoulder. "Shehum," he said, and the Lamanite flinched again at the gentle love in his voice. "What are you so afraid of?"

Shehum drew in a sobbing breath. "I'm a Nehor," he said. "I've always been a Nehor. I have my own religion, but I'm a good person, aren't I? Isn't that enough?"

"Is it?" Mikiah asked. "I won't force you to do anything, Shehum. If you kill me, I won't even fight you. But after the city you slaughtered, after the Lamanites you killed in the land of Nephi, is it really enough?"

Another gulping breath came out of the darkness, and Mikiah could feel the shoulder shaking under his hand. "I didn't do any of that, you know," Shehum said. "I was there, but I didn't—I didn't actually—" He broke off with a deep sigh. "But I didn't do anything to stop it either," he admitted slowly. "And—no, that isn't enough. I've been a coward. I was too afraid to make a decision."

"And now?"

"I—I don't know." Shehum held up his hands and let them fall again. "I'm sorry, Mikiah. I can't just—just change my mind—myself—all at once."

Mikiah's mouth quirked. "I know the feeling. I think you and I think too much for it to come easy. There's no shame in that. The thing you should consider, though, is what you're going to do once you've found the truth for yourself." He glanced around at the slowly lightening forest. The Lamanite army had settled down in a narrow canyon the night before, the steeply rising rock walls leaving Mikiah with no way to camp far enough from them to be safe. He'd found a little hollow, sheltered by rock on one side and thick trees on the other, choked with a tangle of bushes and vines. It should have deterred any curious eyes—any but Shehum's, apparently. Mikiah barked a soft laugh. "And you might want to consider what you're going to do with me now."

Shehum snorted, fumbling his knife into its sheath. "What are you even doing here?"

"Well, I thought I was spying on the Lamanite army, but if you found me this easily, I guess I wasn't doing a very good job."

"It helps if you don't curl up under a bush and start snoring," Shehum told him. "That kind of thing echoes in this canyon."

Mikiah sighed, feeling the ache of fatigue-heavy muscles, each bruise and cut adding its own layer of pain. He dabbed at the fresh wound on his neck. "It's been a hard few days."

Shehum scrubbed at his eyes with the heels of his hands. "I don't know what to do," he groaned. "Ashoram is wrong. He's been wrong for years, and I'm not the only one who knows it. But—he's the king. I can't obey him—and I can't disobey him." He let his breath out slowly between pursed lips, drooping slightly as he deflated. "I'm not going to kill you, Mikiah," he said. "I'm not going to turn you in. Just—just go. Leave. Go back to your family. Maybe someday I'll join you. Maybe not. I have too many questions to answer first."

Mikiah regarded his friend for a moment, picking out the familiar features in the graying light. "The army won't move today," he said. "Ashoram pitched his tent last night. You have wounded, and he needs time to figure out what to do next. He won't move until tomorrow at the earliest." He leaned forward to squeeze Shehum's shoulder. "I'll rest here until then. Then I'll go. If you need me, I'll be here."

Shehum gave the ghost of a laugh, but he nodded. "Goodbye, Mikiah," he whispered, and left, disappearing into the underbrush with barely a rustle. Mikiah sat for a long time, staring at the spot where his friend had vanished.

He spent the day hidden in the little hollow of bushes, waiting for something to happen. He didn't know what it was, but a dark foreboding pressed on his heart. The feeling of something coming crawled over his skin like the heaviness of an oncoming thunderstorm, and he couldn't help glancing up at the blue sky again and again or twisting to look over his shoulder into the empty woods. By the time a red sunset began mellowing into dusk, he was so keyed up he could barely sit still.

The commotion of shouting from the Lamanite camp broke the stillness and jerked Mikiah to his feet. He was moving before he even thought about it, running toward the noise, and his heart pounded hard with some unknown dread. Whatever he'd been waiting for, it was happening now.

The Lamanite camp was like a kicked ant hill, swarming with confused activity. A clump of men formed the center of the chaos, a huddled group of frightened Lamanites, with a frothing ring of Amulonites and Amalekites surrounding them, pushing and crowding, slowly herding them toward the great bonfire just being lighted near Ashoram's tent. As Mikiah watched, the pile of wood and dry brush flickered, glowed, and sent a torrent of flames toward the treetops, bathing the canyon walls in molten gold. The Amulonites sent up an echoing howl of triumph as the fire caught. The captured Lamanites shrank back in terror, and questioning shouts hurled back and forth from men running to see what was happening.

Mikiah saw Shehum, one of the running crowd, but he was going in the wrong direction. The lit bonfire had drawn the army's attention, pulling them toward it, but Shehum pushed past them, away from the light, heading into the shadows of the forest. As he came toward Mikiah, still hidden in the trees, the Lamanite's breath came in frightened gasps, his face contorted with fear and desperation. He let out a little scream as Mikiah's hand shot out, catching his arm as he passed, and pulling him into hiding.

"Shehum, what are you doing?" Mikiah demanded. "What's going on?"

Shehum clung to his shoulders, head hanging as he panted in near-panic. "I came to find you!" he gasped. "Mikiah, you've got to do something! You've got to stop him!"

"Stop who?" Mikiah gave his friend a shake. "What's happening?"

"Ashoram!" Shehum's eyes were wide and pleading, reflecting tiny sparks of firelight. "I said I wasn't the only one who knew he was wrong. Mikiah, there are *converts* in the army! After everything that's happened—they started believing!"

Mikiah drew in a sharp breath. "And Ashoram found out?"

Shehum bit his lip, and his hands clutched tightly on Mikiah's arms. "I think he's going to burn them!"

Mikiah's eyes sank closed, his breath stopping as his mind raced. He couldn't let it happen, but what could one man do against an entire army? Unless . . . He opened his eyes and looked up, judging the distance to the nearest tree branch. "No, he's not," he said. "I just need to get up a bit higher."

Shehum's brow was still furrowed in doubt, but a hint of hope twitched at the corners of his mouth. "You always have a plan?"

"Yes." *But they don't always work,* he didn't say, *and if this one doesn't, I don't know if I'll live to make another.* He shook his head, tossing the thought away. "Boost me up."

In the center of the Lamanite camp, the bonfire flared behind King Ashoram, casting his face into black shadow as he stood in judgment over the converted. The Amulonites crowded close around them, shouting for blood, but beyond them most of the Lamanites stood quietly, and there were more frowns than eager expressions on their faces. Ashoram didn't appear to notice the difference. His voice rose in rolling condemnation above the shrieks of his followers, though the words were indistinguishable from where Mikiah listened at the edge of camp.

If the king was oblivious to his surroundings, his army was not. A growling, metallic scream echoed back and forth from the canyon walls, and men whirled, wide eyes searching the darkness, hands clutching instinctively at weapons. The call came again, many-voiced and sourceless with the confusing echoes, and somebody screamed in agony out of the night.

"The Nephites!" a voice cried in panic. "It's the Nephites!"

Ashoram's unwilling audience dissolved into chaos, Lamanites running blindly in any direction, scrambling toward any kind of cover they could find. Shouted curses and screams of terror filled the canyon, drowning out the sound of the Nephite war cry that had sparked the pandemonium.

Mikiah didn't regret that no one would be able to hear it again. He'd nearly torn his own throat out producing that sound. He had no idea how the Nephites managed it. With a deep breath, his eyes busily calculating distances, he took two swift steps along the branch he'd perched on and jumped. His heart pounded against his throat as air whistled past his ears, but then his hands caught on another branch. The rough bark lacerated the skin of his palms as he swung his body in a wide arc and dropped again. He landed on the backs of two fleeing Lamanites, all three of them crashing to the ground in a tangled pile of fresh bruises.

Mikiah rolled to his feet amid a flashing confusion of shrieks and yells, shadows and firelight, men running, tripping, rolling, and wrestling in the dark. The two men who'd broken his fall didn't stop to find out what had attacked them, scrambling to their feet and disappearing into the crowd without looking back. Mikiah was possibly the only person in that canyon who knew what was happening and where the enemy was, and he joined the running, shoving throng, the bonfire like a beacon ahead of him.

The Amulonites still stood in a firm ring around the fire, trapping the converts, but they were as confused as everyone else, weapons clutched in their hands as they searched the shadows for the Nephite attack. Mikiah chose his target, his eyes narrowing as he saw the swords raised and ready, the two Amulonites preparing to strike as he barreled toward them. A pace away, he dropped, hands punching into the ground, and the Amulonites just stared as his legs whirled around and took their knees out from under them. Mikiah launched himself through the gap before anyone noticed it was there.

He was just in time to see Ashoram shove a struggling, screaming Lamanite into the heart of the flames. And that one wasn't the first.

No more. There were about twenty Lamanites inside the circle. Their hands were bound behind their backs, but they were held there as much by their own fear and confusion as by the ropes. Mikiah snatched up a sword fallen from the Amulonite's hand and quickly slashed through one of the convert's bonds. He threw the sword at the man. "Get them out!" he barked. "Run!" Without waiting to see if the man obeyed, he whirled to face the Amulonites who blocked their escape.

There were too many. Most of them were only just realizing he was there, that the expected attack was already past their defenses. Even with that surprise, Mikiah knew he didn't stand a chance of holding them all off. All he could do was keep the way open as long as possible.

"*Mikiah!*" Ashoram bellowed behind him, audible in his rage over even the roar of the rioting army. "Stop him! *Kill him!*"

Mikiah ducked under a spear, grabbed the spear-bearer, and swung him around, knocking down the first wave of Amulonites charging toward him. He jumped over them, straight into the faces of the startled men behind. A blade scored his shoulder as he twisted desperately to avoid the weapons they held, and the only reason he didn't die in that moment was that none of the Amulonites had expected him to attack them. He dropped and rolled, knocking another bunch off their feet. He was surrounded now, angry yells and kicking legs raining down on him.

He grabbed a foot that came toward his face, pushing back against it to unbalance his attacker. Getting his feet under him again, he jumped into the gap as the man fell, only to leap away again, avoiding the sweeping slice of a cimeter toward his head. Strong arms caught at him from behind, wrapping around his chest and pinning his arms to his sides. He kicked off, pushing back against the man behind him to kick another attacker in the face. That man dropped, but another grappled with Mikiah's legs, more and more restraining arms wrapping around him until he was held helpless, suspended above the ground.

Mikiah stopped struggling, only twisting his head to see around the men who held him, trying before he died to see if the converts had escaped. He caught a glimpse of bound men, forced to their knees at spear-point, but there were fewer than there had been—barely half as many. As a sword flashed above him, Mikiah squeezed his eyes shut, expecting the death blow any moment. He'd saved some lives. It would have to be enough. He pictured Ashir, held her face laughing before his mind's eye like a talisman. He wanted that to be his last thought in this life.

"Wait!"

Mikiah flinched at Ashoram's shout, his eyes snapping open in surprise, and he wasn't the only one who twisted around to stare at the Amulonite king. Ashoram's smile as he regarded his former spy was not reassuring. Mikiah saw the burning branch in the king's hand, and knew that if death was coming for him, it wasn't going to be quick.

"Bring him!" Ashoram commanded, and the hands holding Mikiah carried him forward, dropping him at the king's feet and forcing him to his knees. Two men still grasped each of his arms, and a hand tangled itself in the long tail of his hair, pulling his head back to meet his former king's flat, hazel-green glare. Ashoram had returned to his leopard-skin cloak, but the fur was caked with dirt, and singed in places. His clothes were tattered, and a long, bloody slice ran along the side of his head from eyebrow to crown. Blood was matted into his black hair, and half his face was smeared with the dried brown flecks of it. His eyes held the madness of a wounded, rabid animal—no compassion—no humanity. Mikiah flinched back from the hatred in those eyes as Ashoram leaned closer.

"There is no Nephite attack, is there?" the Amulonite whispered. Mikiah said nothing. Ashoram's backhanded blow cracked across his face, and Mikiah tasted blood. "Is there?" Ashoram demanded.

Mikiah regarded him for a long moment. "Just me," he admitted.

Ashoram smiled again, that same hungry smile that twisted Mikiah's gut. "Captain Hanan!" he barked. "Can't you stop this riot? Are your men so cowardly that they'll run when no one is attacking?"

Hanan shook his head, though the look he gave his king had little of regret in it. "I could sound the all clear, but I doubt anyone would understand the signal, the way this canyon echoes. Best let them work it off. They'll come to their senses soon enough."

Ashoram snarled, but then grew calm again. "Fine," he said, thrusting the smoldering branch back into the bonfire. "A brief reprieve, then. I want the entire army to understand exactly what happens to traitors."

Mikiah swallowed, his eyes drawn with sick terror to the leaping flames, the bodies blackening at the heart of the fire. *Father, help me to endure it,* he prayed with silent desperation. *Give me strength to hold to the truth. Until the end.*

Slowly, the noise and confusion died to a frightened stillness. Questioning calls came out of the night as men crept out of whatever shelter they'd found. As time passed and no Nephite attack followed, the crowd around the bonfire began to reassemble. Mikiah, helpless in his captors' grasp, heard the low murmurs, the rustle of shifting feet, and felt the tension twist tighter as Ashoram's mad eyes stared relentlessly down at him. The king stood motionless, waiting, and the murmurs of the crowd grew, swelling like the sound of ocean waves. "Who is that?" someone asked, just near enough and loud enough to break Ashoram's tableau.

The king swung around, glaring at the crowd. "You want to know who this is?" he demanded, his voice dripping contempt. "*This* is what you were all running from, like the cowards you are. One Amalekite traitor! It's no wonder you can't win a single battle with the Nephites!" He spat in the dirt. "Cowards, all of you! And if not cowards, then traitors! Yes, traitors, like this weak-minded idiot!" His fist cracked across Mikiah's face again. Mikiah's head snapped sideways, and he grunted as pain flashed behind his eyes. As his vision cleared, he found himself caught in the gaze of one of the converts.

"I'm sorry," he told the man. "I tried." The Lamanite nodded, and while Mikiah could see fear in his eyes, it was swallowed up with something stronger. Sorrow. Compassion. Faith. A strange kind of gratitude. Mikiah drew strength from that gaze, strength enough not to cringe from the burning branch Ashoram snatched out of the bonfire again.

"Tell the truth, Mikiah," Ashoram said, holding the flame close to Mikiah's face. "How long have you been working against me?"

Mikiah gasped as the heat tore at him, the Amulonite hands bruising tight around his arms. The very air he breathed suffocated him, smothering hot in his lungs. "I stole Temisah from you, Ashoram, to save her from your brutality." Shaky as it was, he tried to make his voice loud enough for the army to hear. The king drew his burning torch back a bit, his mad eyes widening, and Mikiah found the breath to continue. "I warned the Nephites we were coming, when you and Amlici would have slaughtered the women and children of Zarahemla. I kept you from killing my wife's brother, and I would have fought you for his life. I warned the Anti-Nephi-Lehies that you were preparing for war with them, who had never done you any harm. I tried to warn the people of the city you massacred, and I kept your men from butchering the innocent women and children you took captive. If I worked against you, Ashoram, it is only because you are a coward and a murderer. You delight in the suffering of those less powerful than you, and you prey on your own people. You aren't fit to be king, or command the loyalty of any true man, and I would happily do all of it again to save these people from you." His voice was ringing now, loud enough to draw a slight echo from the canyon walls, and he barely knew what he was saying. Something else had taken over his words. Ashoram drew back even further, his hazel eyes wide, his mouth working soundlessly. "I tell you now, Ashoram, if you kill me, you will shed innocent blood, and it will be your final condemnation!" He stopped, out of breath, and sagging slightly as whatever had possessed him drained away. He felt hollow, yet filled with a kind of anguished peace. *Ashir. I'm sorry I won't come home again.*

Ashoram stared down at him, the torch in his clenched fist trembling. He drew in a long, slow breath, the muscles tightening along his neck and jaw. His hazel eyes had changed to the dark green of winter pine and were just as cold. "So be it," he said. "Tell me, Mikiah, how is that bad eye of yours?"

Mikiah screamed as Ashoram rammed the burning branch against his face, scorching over his un-scarred eye, the one that Tubal's men had not damaged. There was no way Ashoram could know that the bad eye was long since healed. The Amulonite king intended to blind his former spy before killing him. Mikiah's body writhed, trying futilely to escape the blazing, scouring agony. The torch withdrew only to lash back again, stabbing at the same target, and Mikiah choked on screams and blistering heat. The restraining hands loosed him, and he dropped to the forest floor, blinded by fire, pain driving the strength from his limbs. He shrieked again as the flames ate once more into him, burning over his heart.

"*NO!*" The deep-voiced shout echoed and re-echoed, bouncing from the canyon walls. Miraculously, the burning torch withdrew, and Mikiah, curled on the ground, managed to crack one blistered eye open. Through flickering darkness, he saw Shehum, sword drawn, advancing on Ashoram. "We've stood by and watched too long," the Lamanite said. He called out to the army. "How long are you going to let the Amulonites rule you? How many Lamanites did they slaughter in the land of Nephi? How many of our people would they have killed tonight? And for what? Religion?" He shook his head sharply. "The Amulonites *have* no religion! Today they kill us for believing what the Nephites preach. How long before they kill us for believing what the Nehors preach? Or any other belief? Or any reason at all, so long as it keeps *them* in power?" Angry murmurs began rising from the Lamanite army. "I say the Amulonites have ruled over us long enough!" Shehum shouted. "I say they don't get to kill any more of us! Not one more!" The murmurs rose to a roar behind him, and when Shehum jumped at Ashoram, he wasn't alone.

Mikiah, gasping in unrelenting agony, experienced most of that battle as a whirl of stomping, running feet going past him. He did see the moment when Ashoram, struggling and shouting, was lifted in the arms of those who had once followed him and thrown into his own bonfire. A howl of victory rose toward the heavens as the former king convulsed in the flames. Mikiah shuddered, shutting his eyes and curling around his own hurt as tears made painful tracks down his face. Ashoram had been an evil man, but Mikiah still remembered the powerful, shining king of his youth. He grieved for the death of that dream, and for the death of a child so unprepared to meet his Father.

Drifting in a haze of pain, Mikiah felt an arm lifting his head and the neck of a wineskin against his lips. He drank thirstily, tasting the bitter herbs mixed thick in the wine, and grateful for the relief they promised.

"That had to be the single stupidest thing you've ever done," Shehum's slow, deep voice said above him. "And that's including that time you decided to run naked through a tangle of needle bushes. I thought you said you had a plan."

Mikiah coughed weakly, feeling the binding bandages over his chest and half his face. "I never said it was a good plan." Talking made his face burn, and he hoped the drug would act quickly. "How am I?"

"You'll live." Shehum's voice was dark, almost angry. "Possibly you'll even keep the eye, though you're going to have a brilliant scar down your face on that side. You're lucky Ashoram wanted to kill you slow."

"Lucky you were there to stop him." Mikiah paused and shook his head slightly. "Not lucky. Blessed."

Shehum snorted. "Flattery will get you nowhere." He was silent for a moment, and Mikiah dared to crack his working eye open enough to see him gnawing on his lower lip, his head bowed. "I'm sorry I didn't come sooner," Shehum whispered.

Mikiah was starting to drift on the drugged wine, and his hand felt light and only vaguely connected as he lifted it to grasp Shehum's shoulder. "You came soon enough." He tried to raise his head, and hissed as he discovered there were some hurts the painkiller didn't numb.

"Idiot," Shehum caught him and helped him ease back down. "Lie still and let the salve work, or you'll have more than a scar to worry about." He looked into Mikiah's unbandaged eye and blinked slowly in surprise. He grunted. "Your eye," he said. "Your bad eye, all those years ago, it's—"

"Healed," Mikiah confirmed. "I said I'd seen a miracle." Shehum stared, but Mikiah ignored it. He tried again to look around, cautiously rolling his head sideways. "Where are we?" He saw a forest clearing, no canyon walls in sight, and a camp full of men—not enough to be the whole army, but more than the twenty or so he'd tried to rescue.

"A few hours' march closer to Nephi," Shehum replied, shaking off the surprise. "Hanan's in charge back there in the canyon. He'll probably end up king after all this. He's not openly hostile—at least, not yet—but he's not exactly welcoming either. We decided it'd be better to leave on our own before he kicked all the converts out."

"Converts?" Mikiah had to resist the urge to look around again. "All of them? But—there weren't this many!"

"And thank heaven for that, or you'd probably have thought of something even stupider to do." Shehum sighed. "Apparently, there were a lot of men who believed, but couldn't quite make up their minds to actual conversion. Seeing you willing to die for it—well, it was a strong inspiration."

"How many?"

"About a hundred more."

"And you?"

Shehum shook his head, a rueful curve at the corner of his mouth. "And me. I still have more questions than answers, you understand, but now at least I know who to ask."

Mikiah smiled, and then winced, which also hurt. "How long before that salve stuff works?" he asked, frustrated.

Shehum chuckled. "Don't worry. You'll be walking home this time." He offered Mikiah the skin of drugged wine. "Have some more of this. It'll put you to sleep for a while." Mikiah didn't argue. A period of drugged oblivion sounded like the third best thing he'd heard that day, right after Shehum's conversion, and the word *home.*

Twenty-Seven

Land of Nephi, 81 BC

Eliah and Zerimhi were sitting on a fallen tree beside the main road, just past where the path up to Ashir's cottage branched off. They appeared to be having an animated conversation, but Eliah broke off when he saw Mikiah rounding the bend in the road, and Zerimhi twisted around to see what Eliah was looking at. They jumped up and hurried toward him, both their faces tightened with concern as they saw the bandages on Mikiah's head and chest.

"Mikiah, what happened to—" Eliah broke off, his mouth falling open as he saw who was coming along behind Mikiah. "Shehum!" Eliah jumped at his friend, and Mikiah would have grinned if it didn't hurt so much, as Eliah lifted Shehum's feet off the ground in an exuberant hug.

Zerimhi still studied Mikiah's face, his eyebrows drawn together. "What happened?"

"Ashoram," Mikiah answered shortly. "It's not as bad as it looks."

"It *looks* like you've been dragged face down through a pile of sharp rocks," Zerimhi said. He reached out to finger a fringe of burned hair that hung over the bandage. His scowl deepened. "And then tossed into a fire pit."

"Ashoram did that?" Eliah released Shehum to look at Mikiah, hissing as he noticed the reddened skin visible around the bandage.

"He burned you," he said. Anger darkened his face, and his hands closed into white-knuckled fists. He shook his head, breathing hard. "If I hadn't just taken an oath not to kill . . ."

"You don't need to worry about it," Shehum said. "Ashoram's already dead. Hanan is probably king of Jerusalem by now."

Eliah grunted. "Good." Zerimhi raised an eyebrow at him, and he shrugged. "I know, I know. Charity. I'll get there eventually. It's just that I'll have to work up to it from where I am right now, which is being glad that the man who tortured my brother is safely dead."

"Did you lose the eye?" Zerimhi asked.

Mikiah shook his head. "Shehum says probably not." He clapped Eliah on the shoulder and gripped Zerimhi's arm, giving him a reassuring shake. "I'll be all right," he told them. "Really. I'll have some scars, but I'll live."

"And so will the people he saved while getting those scars," Shehum added. "We've just led over a hundred men to ask King Anti-Nephi-Lehi for help finding new places to live. All thanks to Mikiah." Mikiah shrugged uncomfortably, and the Lamanite grinned. "But I'll have to tell you about that later. Blushing probably hurts him right now."

Mikiah ducked his head, but the others chuckled. Some of the tension eased out of the atmosphere. "What are you two doing out here?" Mikiah asked.

Eliah chuckled again. "Our wives kicked us out of your house," he said. "Can't blame them, really, with how crowded it is." He looked at Shehum and Mikiah, smiling. "Not that we won't be grateful to have it even more crowded."

"Your wives?" Mikiah repeated, straightening. "You got Nabeth to come?"

"It was more a matter of keeping up with her, to tell the truth," Eliah admitted. "And it was Ashir's doing more than anything."

Mikiah's jaw dropped. "You took Ashir to *Jerusalem?*" He started to scowl, then flinched.

Eliah held up both hands. "Have you ever tried to stop that woman from doing anything she sets her mind on?" he protested. "She decided she was going to Jerusalem, and I could go along and keep her safe or not. She made me show her your house—your old house, I guess." He grinned. "She said if you tried to set up an exercise yard like that in *her* garden, she'd give you some *real* exercise. Then she wanted to meet Nabeth, of course." He grimaced, and a sudden worry stirred in Mikiah's mind.

"Didn't they like each other?"

"Well enough, eventually, but the introduction was a little . . . nerve-wracking. It was something like, 'Hello, Nabeth. Meet Ashir. She's been Mikiah's wife for about six years now, and they have two beautiful children. Also, I've joined the Anti-Nephi-Lehies, and I think you and Pelonti had better get yourselves packed up, because I'm pretty sure King Ashoram is going to take my change of allegiance badly, and he might take it out on you, so we're moving to the land of Nephi.'"

"And?" Mikiah prompted when Eliah paused. "What did she say?"

"I don't know," Eliah sighed. "About that time a volcano erupted, a hurricane rolled in, and the sea came up to cover the city. All I could do was hunker down and hope I was still alive when it was all over."

Mikiah's lips twitched against a grin as Zerimhi and Shehum both burst out laughing, but Eliah only raised his eyebrows at them. "Go ahead and laugh," he said. "It's going to happen all over again when they see Mikiah looking like an undercooked roast."

Zerimhi nodded, though he was still chuckling. "Nabeth and Ashir have both been worrying, the past few days, and had nothing to do with all that energy. It was Temisah who actually drove us out today. She said they were going to clean the house, top and bottom, inside-out, outside-in, and diagonally, and if that didn't work, she'd set them to polishing the fruit in the garden. They were still scrubbing the floors when we left. Except Abish. She's watching the children."

"Temisah?" Shehum asked. His deep voice was suddenly a few notes higher than normal, and a hidden tension rode on his shoulders. "She's here too?"

"Sure, the royal palace is as crowded as everywhere else at the moment," Eliah said. "And she and Nabeth used to be friends, didn't they? They've been talking nonstop since we got back. Pelonti practically worships Sebbita." He threw an arm around Shehum's shoulders. "Don't worry. She's calmed down a lot, and she says she doesn't hate us anymore for stealing her. She probably won't bite you this time!"

Mikiah, noting the faint blush under Shehum's dark skin, thought his friend might have a completely different reason to be nervous. Temisah's "husband" was dead now, after all, and Shehum had always seemed interested in the girl's welfare. He felt the grin tug at his lips again and sternly repressed it. "Come on, then," was all he said. "Let's go get the explosions over with."

A few minutes later, Mikiah understood what Eliah had meant. He had only a handful of seconds to savor the quiet cottage, the ripening garden, the laughter of children somewhere out of sight, before a scream shattered the peaceful scene and his sister came flying out the door of the cottage and came straight for him. She was like a force of nature as she threw herself at him, and Mikiah grunted in pain as her powerful embrace jarred the burns. He ignored the hurt, wrapping both arms around Nabeth and holding her tight.

"You utter *beast,* Mikiah!" Nabeth shrieked, pulling away and slapping at his arms. "How could you? If you'd died I would've—" She broke off, pulling him into another fierce hug. "Don't you *dare* do that to me again!" she said, banging a fist against his shoulder. It was like trying to hug a whirlwind, but he tucked her head under his chin and held on, savoring every moment.

A choked sob pulled him free of his sister. Ashir was on her knees in the door of the cottage, grasping at the doorpost as though it was the only thing keeping her from fainting. Her chest heaved with quick, gasping sobs, and tears rolled over her cheeks unheeded. She stared at Mikiah as he came to her, every breath shaking her body like a sapling in a gale. When Mikiah knelt beside her, she gave a wild cry and lurched into his arms, trembling as she clung to him, her face buried in his shoulder. Hysterical sobs still wrenched at her, and Mikiah could feel her fighting them, unable to stop.

"Hush, now. It's all right. I'm here," he soothed, whispering in her ear. He tightened his arms, again ignoring the pain as he pressed her to his bandaged chest. "I came home. Everything will be all right now. I'm home." She pushed away, smiling up at him through the tears she still couldn't stem. One hand reached up to gently caress his face, hesitant fingers brushing over the bandage. Mikiah let half a smile tug at his lips. "Yes. I look nearly as bad as the first time we met. But that didn't work out so terribly, did it?"

Ashir let out a gurgle of laughter nearly as uncontrolled as the weeping, and fell into his arms again. "I was so afraid," she whispered around a gasping breath. "It was like—something—something horrible—hanging over us, and I couldn't—" Her voice stretched thin and broke.

"I know," Mikiah said. "It might have been—it almost was—but Shehum saved me. Me, and over a hundred others. And now I'm home. I'm safe. We're all safe, now." He looked over Ashir's head at his friends—his family. Nabeth stood in the circle of Eliah's arm, watching Mikiah and Ashir. Abish and the children were just coming around the corner of the house, Zerimhi striding to greet them with a broad smile. Shehum was nervously approaching Temisah. Mikiah saw him bow low to her.

"Forgive me?" Shehum's quiet plea was barely loud enough for Mikiah to hear, but he saw Temisah's welcoming smile.

"Long ago," she said. She laughed as Sebbita came running and threw her small arms around her mother's waist. Temisah looked down at the child. "Sebbita, this is Shehum. He's Mikiah's friend—and mine." The last two words were said almost shyly, if Temisah could ever be shy, and they brought a delighted smile to Shehum's face.

"You know, Ashir," Mikiah said, squeezing his wife's shoulders. "Much as I love this place just like it is, I think we're going to have to build a few more houses." Her head came up, her eyes questioning, and he nodded slightly at the crowd of people around them, and saw her begin to smile, the tears finally drying. "Definitely one or two more," he said, and laughter danced in his eye as he saw Shehum crouched down, listening to Sebbita's chatter with every sign of fascination. "Possibly three."

Ashir wiped briskly at her cheeks, rubbing the remains of the tears away, then leaned in and kissed Mikiah firmly. "If you try building anything before you're fully healed, I swear I'll get Zerimhi to help me tie you down," she said, both hands on his shoulders so she could look him in the face. "And if you don't get inside right this minute so I can take a proper look at you, I'll clean those wounds out with maggots!"

Mikiah chuckled. "Yes, ma'am!" he said, and let himself be pulled to his feet and herded inside, grinning broadly—and wincing at the pain of it.

Twenty-Eight

Land of Shilom, 77 BC

Mikiah frowned as he came to a break in the trees and saw the thick column of black smoke against the sky. The old scar around his eye pulled the frown slightly crooked but didn't hinder his sight at all, and his eyes narrowed as he stared at the smoke.

They were at it again.

He picked up his pace, moving from a loping jog to a full sprint, knowing even as he did so that he was probably already too late.

Two of the houses in the tiny settlement were smoldering ashes by the time he got there, and tears stung Mikiah's eyes as he looked quickly away from the charred bones among the embers. Other bodies lay still in the streets, men and women cut down and left like piles of debris. There was no sign of the attackers.

It was a new settlement, one of those started by the Lamanite converts who'd lost their homes because of their conversion, not much larger than the little collection of houses Mikiah and Ashir now shared with Eliah and Nabeth, Shehum and Temisah. Mikiah shuddered at the comparison, imagining this destruction come to Ashir's peaceful clearing, his home burnt, the garden trampled, his own family . . .

He shook the thought away with a sharp toss of his head and was relieved to catch movement out of the corner of his eye. There were some survivors this time. A woman crouched over the body of her husband, sobbing. A boy who couldn't have been more than thirteen years old moved among the bodies, his face pasty gray, his eyes haunted as he checked for signs of life, for anyone who might still be saved. A few others huddled together—children, mostly, who were small enough to hide.

Mikiah approached the boy, his steps slow and steady, crunching in the gravel of the street. The young man looked up at the sound and started back with a cry, eyes wide with terror, when he saw a pale-skinned man coming for him.

"It's all right," Mikiah said, stopping and holding out empty hands. "I'm one of you. I promise I won't hurt you."

The boy still cowered, his breath coming in rapid gasps, and Mikiah wondered for a moment if he'd even understood the words. "You're an Amalekite!" the boy hissed. "There are no Amalekites among the Anti-Nephi-Lehies!"

Mikiah shook his head. "There's just one, and I'm him," he said gently. "Have you found any wounded? I might be able to help them."

"No," the boy said, though his steady gaze still spoke his distrust. "They killed anyone who didn't run fast enough. Except . . ."

"Except?" Mikiah prompted when the boy didn't continue.

"My sister. And Sarath. They're with child. They couldn't run. But the Lamanites didn't kill them. They—" His voice had risen, his eyes going blank as shock took over. "They *took* them, and—and I don't know—"

"Calmly, now. Calmly. Take a breath." Mikiah dared to reach out to the boy, gripping his shoulder, and felt him trembling. "Which way did they go?"

The boy raised a shaking finger and pointed westward, but he was already shaking his head. "That way. But there's nothing you can do! You can't fight them!"

Mikiah squeezed the young man's shoulder again. "I vowed not to kill," he said. "But maybe I can get your sister back without that. I'll try." The boy's mouth dropped open, and Mikiah could see something like hope dawning behind the shock and terror. "Stay here. See if there are any more survivors. Help the living. And—pray for your sister."

The boy nodded, biting his lip as tears brimmed in his eyes. "And for you," he whispered as Mikiah set off again, following the trampling footprints that led the way the boy had pointed. The roaming Lamanite gangs never bothered to hide their trail—not when they knew their victims weren't ever going to fight back.

It was a gang of about twenty, more Amalekites than actual Lamanites. They moved down the road in a whooping, hollering mass, pushing the two pregnant women along in their midst. They were headed north, toward Helam, and the women weren't all they'd plundered in their raid. Most of them carried bulging sacks, and many wore jewels and other finery, out of place with their rough clothes.

The women slowed them down, and Mikiah caught up with them quickly, moving silently off the road to circle through the fields and get ahead of them. They whooped and gabbled, almost incoherent with the heady rush of excitement. Hunting fever. They were all young, even younger than Mikiah had been when he first stole Temisah from her father. Too young to believe they could ever be beaten. When Mikiah stepped into the road ahead of them, he fully expected to have a fight on his hands.

The two men in the lead visibly jumped, stumbling back with wild shouts. One of them managed to get his sword out, and it waved vaguely in the dusty air as he nearly fell. The others cried out in echo, cowering as though Mikiah were a demon come to drag them to hell. Someone cursed. "It's The Scar!" a voice shouted. "Run!"

Mikiah blinked in surprise as the entire raiding party panicked and scattered, darting away into the fields beside the road and running like hunted rabbits. In their desperation to get away, they'd left behind their bags of loot and the two women. Mikiah stood a moment, tracking their progress through the long grass in case this was some kind of bizarre feint, but they kept going, only turning to circle back toward Helam when they were nothing but dots in the distance.

The women were on the ground when Mikiah came to them. One was on her knees, sobbing, and the other sat beside her, one hand cradling a swollen belly as she tried to comfort her friend. Mikiah approached cautiously and bent over them. "Are you hurt?"

The sobbing woman squeaked, and the flow of her tears dried up as she stared up at him with wide eyes. Mikiah did nothing, watching the slow return of reason to her eyes. She blinked. "You—you're—"

The other woman put an arm around her shoulders. "We're not hurt," she said, her voice soft, but unafraid. "Thank you."

Mikiah grimaced. "I wish I'd been here earlier," he said. "Can you walk? We should get you back to the village."

The more sensible of the two nodded and lumbered to her feet. Mikiah helped her lift the second woman from her knees. She was still staring at him, and she continued to cling to his arm once she found her feet. "How—how did you do that?" she whispered.

Mikiah cast his gaze after the fleeing Lamanites, long since disappeared toward their own lands. He shook his head, bewildered. "I don't know."

"Have they seen you before?" the first woman wondered.

"No. But they might have heard of me. This isn't the first gang I've driven off." He scowled, angry with himself. "Without weapons, without killing anyone. That's the kind of story that grows in the telling."

Twenty-Nine

City of Nephi, 77 BC

"It's getting worse," Mikiah told King Anti-Nephi-Lehi, delivering the results of his latest message run. "Ever since King Hanan attacked the Nephites again last year, he either doesn't care, or he's encouraging it. The raids are getting more and more frequent. And more brutal. I don't know what they were planning to do with those women, but it wasn't anything good."

The king nodded, his face pinched with worry. "I'm glad you were there." He saw the twist of Mikiah's mouth, more than was already caused by the scarring. "What is it?"

"I almost wish—" Mikiah shook his head. "It's not that I wish I *hadn't* helped them. It's just . . . Those boys were terrified of me, my king. Utterly terrified. That sickens me, but it also worries me—where that fear might lead. Frightened people do stupid things." He lifted his hands and let them drop. "I may have only made things worse."

The king grunted, chewing at his lower lip, and his fingers tapped quickly against the table. Unlike Ashoram, Anti-Nephi-Lehi never used a throne room, preferring to meet in smaller chambers of the palace. It showed how little he valued his own importance, but it also left him no room for pacing. He stared instead at the map laid out on the table, red markers spread across it like a rash, marking the escalating Lamanite attacks. His head bowed and his eyes sank closed, a look of pain etching his face. "We can't fight them," he said. "We dare not fight them. Yet it seems we can't live with them in peace, either." He opened his eyes to see the map again, his finger touching one red mark and then another. "If it were simply robbery, we might have some hope, but this—they're killing us for the sport of it now." He looked up at the third man in the room, who'd stood silently all this time. "Is there anything we can do but die?"

Ammon's eyes were dark with a pain that mirrored Anti-Nephi-Lehi's, the burden of thousands of lives. His finger touched the map opposite the king's, tracing a line north along the western coast. "There is one thing," he said. "We can go to the Nephites. All of us. Together. We can go to the land of Zarahemla and find a new home there."

The king shook his head. "They'll kill us as soon as we set foot there." He glanced sideways at Mikiah, and Mikiah knew they were both thinking of the Nephite chief captain who'd threatened to send his army after any Lamanites he found in the Nephite lands.

Ammon frowned. "I don't think they will. We'll be unarmed, and if my brothers and I—" He broke off with a sigh, seeing the refusal already in the king's face. "The Anti-Nephi-Lehies never do anything by halves," he muttered, almost to himself. "Including penance." He made a sharp gesture with one hand, challenging the king with his gaze. "All right. I'll ask the Lord. If *He* tells us to go to the Nephites, will you go?"

"Of course. We'll do whatever the Lord tells us to," Anti-Nephi-Lehi said, but his face was still grim. "If He commands us to go . . ." He scowled down at the map for a moment. "If He commands us to go, then we'll be the Nephites' slaves, until we've repaid them for all the harm we've done to them."

Ammon coughed, disguising a laugh. When he spoke, though, his voice was more sympathetic than amused. "I won't deny that there are probably a few misguided souls among my people who'd take you up on that. But far fewer than you might expect. Slavery has never been our way, and my father outlawed it entirely. If that's what you're worried about, you don't need to be."

The king shook his head, his mouth set in a stubborn line. "Ask the Lord. If He tells us to go, we'll go," he said. "If not, we may as well die here."

Ammon nodded, his steady gaze measuring something he saw in the king's face. "As you wish, my king," he said, bowing. As Mikiah watched the Nephite leave the room, a strong certainty settled into his heart.

"We'll want to gather in the land of Ishmael," he said. "Anywhere else, we'd have to go through Lamanite lands. From Ishmael, if we go by night, we may be able to get safely past them before they notice."

Anti-Nephi-Lehi raised an eyebrow. "You're that certain what the Lord will tell Ammon?"

"Ammon isn't the only person who can receive revelation," Mikiah told him, a soft smile curving his lips. "If you'd stop being so stubborn, you'd probably feel it too."

The king glowered at him but then snorted a laugh. "You may be right."

Mikiah bowed low. "If you don't need me for a few days, my king, I'd like to go tell Ashir."

"Yes, go, go." The king waved him away. "Even if you're right, it'll still take us some time to get everything sorted—even to draft a proclamation for you to carry. I'll send for you when you're needed." He was studying the map again as he spoke, clearly already working on the logistics of the problem.

As Mikiah turned to leave, he couldn't help smiling. If this worked—if they could get past the Lamanites—if the Nephites didn't kill them on sight. . . . It was the first time in years that Mikiah had felt even the possibility of a hope for true safety.

THIRTY

LAND OF ISHMAEL, 77 BC

FOR THE THIRD AND LAST TIME, MIKIAH STOOD ON THE HILL THAT overlooked the waters of Sebus and looked out over a very different landscape. Six of the seven cities of the Anti-Nephi-Lehies were empty, the farms and villages around them abandoned. The crowded sea of people covered the land of Ishmael, together with their flocks and herds and whatever provisions they could carry with them. People camped in fields that had once grown crops, the farmers no longer worried about trampling. Every building in the city was packed, and Mikiah knew King Lamoni had moved his family out of the city days ago, turning the golden palace over to those seeking shelter. He'd been living in a tent somewhere in the mass of humanity, along with Anti-Nephi-Lehi and Antiomno and the other kings.

As the sun lowered toward setting, a horn rang out from the distance, the signal repeated by other horns and carried over the whole land. Away in the north, King Anti-Nephi-Lehi had taken the first step of their journey. There was a murmur and a rustle through the crowd around Mikiah, some tardy people hurrying to pack the things they'd been using while they camped here the past few days, while others picked up their packs and slung them across their shoulders, overeager to be gone. This far back, they wouldn't see actual movement for a while yet.

Ashir's warm hand insinuated itself into Mikiah's, and he smiled down into her gray eyes, his free hand reaching out to gently touch the sleeping baby girl she carried on her back. Ashir didn't return his smile, studying him with pursed lips. "You're worried," she said quietly, so no one around them would hear.

Mikiah shook his head, but he wasn't really trying to deny it. "I just wish I could be in several places at once," he said, matching her soft voice. "The eastern flank—we should have scouts out there, watching for the Lamanite armies. Even if we can't do anything about it." He shrugged, a wry smile tugging at his mouth. "Then there's the king—or the kings, I suppose. If they need a messenger. And . . ." He shrugged, but his eyes went dark. "I hate to think what'll happen to anyone who gets left behind."

Now she smiled, eyes full of pride and love. "You should have been a king yourself, the way you care about your people."

A young voice rose behind them, sobbing with useless rage. "I won't! I don't want to go! I like it at home! Why can't we stay?" Nadai shouted, as she'd done at least once a day since they'd told her about the move.

Mikiah winced. "Heaven forbid," he answered his wife. "I've got enough trouble as it is." The two of them turned to find their daughter in tears, her whole body rigid with anger as she glared up at Shehum, daring him to try lifting her into the cart. Shehum glanced helplessly at Mikiah and Ashir, a wordless appeal for help. Ashir started to hurry over to calm her daughter—or at least try to—but Mikiah stopped her. "Let me do it," he said. "Maybe she'll listen to me."

Nadai transferred the glare to Mikiah as he approached, but some of the tension drooped from her shoulders, already sensing that her father wasn't going to give in. "I don't want to go!" she pouted.

"I know you don't," Mikiah said, putting an arm around her shoulders. "In some ways, I don't want to go either. Will you talk with me about it?" He led her away from the other children, who were watching from the cart. He could still feel the resistance in her shoulders, the reluctance of her dragging steps. He sat down beside her in almost the same place he'd first met Zerimhi, the green grass bathed in an orange sunset glow.

"If you don't want to go, why do we have to?" Nadai asked. "Why can't we stay here?"

"I think you already know the answer to that one."

"Because God told us to," Nadai said in the long-suffering singsong of a girl who had been told something repeatedly and still didn't really believe it.

"He did," Mikiah said. "But do you understand why?"

"Because he's bossy and mean." Nadai crossed her arms over her chest, the corners of her lips turned firmly down, obviously expecting to be reprimanded for saying such a thing.

Mikiah's mouth twitched as he repressed a laugh, but he saw the tears standing in his daughter's eyes and knew she'd never forgive him if he took this lightly. "Nadai," he said, giving her a searching look, "do you think you're old enough to understand the real reason?"

Her eyes widened, fear and surprise and hope mixed into her stare. "Yes."

Mikiah sighed, groping for a way to explain. "What do you know about the Lamanites?"

"They're bad people." Her answer was prompt, with all the simplistic judgment of a child.

"Some of them are," Mikiah agreed. "Some of them are good people who've been taught wrong. Some of them are just afraid. It's important to remember that. Sometimes people do bad things and really think they're not doing anything wrong." He scrubbed a hand through his hair. "When I was younger, *I* was a Lamanite, and I did things I shouldn't have done. People got hurt. You would have called me a bad person, but I didn't think I was." He looked out again at the waters of Sebus, remembering the blood and screams, his utter astonishment as Ammon took on a gang of robbers all by himself. "I didn't really think about good and bad until I met your mother. There are a lot of the Lamanites now that are like I was, and if you ever met them, you'd see that they're just people. They love their families. They have their dreams and their work and their homes. They want a happy life, just like we do."

"But they hate us," Nadai protested. "Everyone says so!"

"They hate us because they've been taught to hate us. Or maybe because they're afraid of the Nephites and that makes them afraid of us, because we believe the same things as the Nephites. And sometimes, when people are afraid of something, they'll lash out at it, to keep it from hurting them."

Nadai chewed on her lip. "You mean Heavenly Father told us to leave because the Lamanites might attack us?"

"Oh, Nadai." Mikiah reached out and pulled his daughter close, held in the shelter of his arm. "They already attack us. You know I travel around, carrying messages for the king. I've seen settlements—little places like ours—where gangs of Lamanites had been. They know our people won't fight back. There was nothing to stop them."

"They—" The little girl gulped. "Did they—?"

"Yes." Mikiah closed his eyes, holding her close as the pain of those memories shook him again. "There was no one left alive." Nadai gave a single choked sob and wrapped her arms around him, burying her face in his shirt. He rubbed her shaking back, trying to comfort the distress he'd caused. "That's why we have to leave, Nadai, even though we don't want to. I love our home—the cottage, the garden—I fell in love with your mother in that garden. But I love you and your mother and Giliel and baby Channisah more. I want you to be safe, and we can't be safe if we stay."

Nadai sniffled into his chest. "I wanted to be like Mother," she said in a small, lost voice. "I wanted to be a healer and keep the house and garden, just like she did. I was going to live there forever."

"We'll find a place for you both to plant a new garden," Mikiah promised. "You can plan it together, and your mother can still teach you all she knows about healing."

Nadai nodded, but her arms stayed around him. "What if the Nephites don't want us?" she whispered, almost too quiet to hear.

Mikiah shook his head. "I don't think Heavenly Father would have sent us to them if they wouldn't help us," he said. "But if they don't, we'll still follow God, and He'll lead us to a new home. It'll be all right, Nadai. I promise." She nodded, and he gave her shoulders one last squeeze. He looked up and saw the stirrings of motion in the crowds around the base of the hill, people and carts slowly beginning the long journey. "Now how about we get you loaded into the cart so we can get started?"

She let him go and went with him back to the others, but stopped short of climbing into the cart with Sebbita, Pelonti, and Giliel. "Can I walk with you?" she asked, slipping her hand into Mikiah's.

He smiled and squeezed the hand, so small and delicate, long-fingered like her mother's. "I think I'd like that."

EPILOGUE

LAND OF JERSHON, 76 BC

MIKIAH WAS IN ASHIR'S GARDEN WITH NADAI AND GILIEL, HELPING the children pull weeds while Ashir fed the baby in the shade of their new home. He was aware of the sound of a group approaching, but he didn't look up until he felt a cool shadow fall across him and heard Nabeth's voice. "Mikiah! There's a Nephite here looking for an Anti-Nephi-Lehi who used to be an Amalekite," she said, smiling down at him with a crease of worry between her brows. A young man stood behind her, with Shehum, Eliah, and Zerimhi behind him. "Someone gave him some vague directions and he ended up at Shehum and Temisah's house," Nabeth continued. "Shehum brought him to me, for some reason, even though he *said* he was looking for a man, and anyway I'm not an Anti-Nephi-Lehi precisely." Eliah made a small sound of protest and a dimple appeared in Nabeth's cheek. "Not yet, anyway. And then Shehum insisted we stop in at Zerimhi's house on the way here."

"Just being cautious," Shehum said. "Mikiah *did* punch out the chief captain of the Nephite armies once. People can hold grudges about things like that."

The Nephite had been studying Mikiah's face intently, eyes lingering on the red whorls of scarring, but at Shehum's words he suddenly broke into a wide grin. "It *is* you!" he said. "That's a relief! I was beginning to think you might have been killed in the land of Nephi. You have no idea how hard it is to get anyone to talk about you."

"They respect my privacy." Mikiah raised an eyebrow, sitting back on his heels and brushing dirt off his hands. "Do I know you?"

"You probably don't remember me. We did meet once before, though, and you might remember my grandmother, Zerubah?"

Mikiah's eyes widened, both eyebrows flying up. "Zerubah! From the land of Noah?" He stood, studying the young man more closely now. "You were one of the prisoners?"

The Nephite nodded, his blue eyes dancing as he noticed Giliel coming closer to study him from behind Mikiah's leg. "Your father saved my life once," he told the boy, then grinned when Giliel ducked back out of sight. He met Mikiah's eyes again. "I came to thank you," he said, offering Mikiah a respectful bow, hand to his heart.

"It's a long journey, just to give thanks," Mikiah observed.

"Well, I may have had another motive as well," the young man admitted. "You were amazing—what you did that night. I wanted to ask if—if you would teach me."

Mikiah felt his face stiffen and knew he must be scowling. "I don't do that anymore," he said. "I've given up fighting."

"Which is why you're here." The man gestured broadly with his arms. "So we can protect you. But—" He sighed, scrubbing a hand through his sandy brown hair. "War with the Lamanites is coming. War with the Lamanites is always coming, it seems like." He muttered the last sentence, low and almost rueful, as though he was talking to himself. "All I'm asking is the chance to learn as much as I can, before I go off to that war. I promise you, I'll fight with everything I have, so you and your family can live in peace."

Mikiah felt Ashir come up beside him and take his hand. He looked past the youth and met Shehum's eyes, then Eliah's, and Zerimhi's. His brothers and his friends, his wife and his sisters, and all of their children, all living here in safety thanks to men just like this young Nephite. He felt the future hanging in the balance somehow, teetering on this decision.

Mikiah sighed, shook his head, and then smiled. "Well, if you really want to learn, you'll have to help me get done weeding the garden before your first lesson."

The Nephite's eyebrows rose. "Weeding?"

Mikiah squeezed Ashir's hand and his lips twitched. "Yes, weeding. That's more or less how I started," he said. "There's no reason you should do any different."

The Nephite blinked and a slow smile spread across his face. "And, perhaps, while we're pulling weeds, you'll tell me how it helped you learn?"

"Perhaps." Mikiah returned the smile, his eyes twinkling, and reached out to clap the Nephite on the shoulder, ushering him into the garden. "You have a name, young man?"

The Nephite leaned his walking staff against a fence post and rolled up his sleeves. "Teancum," he said.

Discussion Questions

1. Sometimes the consequences of our good or bad choices aren't obvious right away. What are the long-term consequences of Mikiah's choices?

2. Mikiah and Ashoram start out with very similar attitudes. What are the things that lead to such different endings for them?

3. How does Mikiah's perspective help Lamoni and Anti-Nephi-Lehi avoid an "us vs. them" mindset? How does an "us vs. them" attitude keep us from having or developing charity?

4. How was the example of Ashir and the Nephite missionaries instrumental in Mikiah's conversion? What did they do or say that was most effective?

5. Many people tell Mikiah that he needs to find out the truth for himself. What might have been different if he hadn't had that personal revelation, and had just taken their word for it?

6. What was Mikiah's repentance process?

Pronunciation Guide

Key

a	*a*bout	ĭ	*i*t, h*i*m, h*i*story
ă	*a*sk, p*a*t, m*a*p	ī	*i*dle, f*i*ne, den*y*
ā	*a*ble, b*a*ke, w*ay*	ō	*o*ver, b*o*ne, kn*ow*
ä	*a*lms, f*a*ther, c*a*ll	ou	ab*ou*t
ĕ	*e*bb, m*e*t, s*e*cond	u	j*u*mp
er	p*er*mit	ū	r*u*le, b*oo*t, tw*o*

* Indicates Scriptural People and Place Names

*Aaron	ĕr'-an	*Anti-Nephi-Lehi	ăn'-tī–nē'-fī–lē'-hī
*Abish	ā'-bĭsh	*Anti-Nephi-Lehies	ăn'-tī–nē'-fī–lē'-hīz
*Adam	ăd'-um	*Antiomno	ăn-tē-äm'-nō
*Aha	ā'-hä	*Antionah	ăn-tē-än'-a
*Alma	ăl'-ma	Ashir	ă-shēr'
*Amalekite	a-măl'-a-kīt	Ashoram	ăsh-ōr'-um
*Amlici	ăm'-lĭ-sī	Channisah	cha-nĭs'-a
*Amlicite	ăm'-lĭ-sīt	Cherom	chĕr'-um
*Ammah	ăm'-mä	Eliah	ē-lī'-a
*Ammon	ăm'-un	*Eve	ēv
*Ammonihah	ăm-a-nī'-hä	Giliel	gĭl'-ē-ĕl
*Ammonihahite	ăm-a-nī'-hä-īt	Hanan	hā'-năn
*Amulek	ăm'-yū-lĕk	*Helam	hē'-lum
*Amulon	ăm'-yū-län	Hem	hĕm
*Amulonites	ăm'-ya-län'-īts	*Hermounts	her'-mounts
*Ani-Anti	ăn'-ī–ăn'-tī	*Isaiah	ī-zā'-a

*Ishmael	ĭsh'-mĕl
Jeromihah	jĕr'-um-ī-hä
*Jershon	jĕr'-shän
*Jerusalem	ja-rū'-sa-lĕm
Jubek	jū'-bĕk
Keb	kĕb
Kish	kĭsh
*Laban	lā'-bun
Ladon	lā'-dun
*Laman	lā'-mun
*Lamanite	lā'-mun-īt
*Lamoni	la-mō'-nī
*Lehi	lē'-hī
*Lemuel	lĕm'-yūl
*Limher	lĭm'-her
*Manti	măn'-tī
*Middoni	mĭd-dō'-nī
*Middonite	mĭd-dō'-nīt
*Midian	mĭd'-ē-un
Mikiah	mē-kī'-a
Minek	mĭ'-nĕk
*Mosiah	mō-zī'-a
*Muloki	myū'-la-kī
Nabeth	nā'-bĕth
Nadai	na-dī'
Naomarah	nā-ō-mar'-ä
*Nehor	nē'-hōr
*Nephi	nē'-fī
*Nephihah	nē-fī'-hä
*Nephite	nē'-fīt
*Noah	nō'-a
Pelonti	pĕ-län'-tī
*Rabbanah	ra-băn'-a
*Sam	săm
Sarath	sĕr'-ăth
Sebbita	sĕ-bē'-ta
*Sebus	sē'-bus
Shehum	shā'-ūm
*Shemlon	shĕm'-län
*Shilom	shī'-lum
*Shimnilom	shĭm-nī'-läm
*Sidom	sī'-dum
*Sidon	sī'-dun
*Teancum	tē-ăn'-kum
Temisah	tĕ-mĭs'-a
Tubal	tū'-bul
*Zarahemla	zĕr-a-hĕm'-la
Zerimhi	zĕr-ĭm'-hī
*Zeram	zē'-rum
Zerubah	zĕr-ū'-ba
*Zoram	zō'-rum

Song of Ashir

Words & Music by R.E.D. Richardson

12
Rec.
Vo.
I hear them now. In the shade of the hills, in the glow of the sky, I
he frees me now. In the shine of the stars, in the dance of the trees, I
16
Rec.
Vo.
know him. In the warmth of a touch, in the breath of a sigh, I
know him. In the peace of my heart when I fall to my knees, I
19
Rec.
Vo.
know him. I know him. I know him.
know him. I know him. I know him.

About the Author

R. E. D. Richardson spends a lot of time indoors writing about other people's exciting adventures, and when she wants to add variety to her life, she spends time reading about other people's exciting adventures. In between all this excitement, she's found time to earn a bachelor's degree in creative writing, and most of a second bachelor's in film and media arts. She was born and raised in Juneau, Alaska; served a mission in Jacksonville, Florida; and spent a year studying abroad in Essex, United Kingdom. She currently lives in Solitude, Utah, with her husband and a shadowcat.

Red has worked for a tutoring/testing center, a chiropractor, an assisted living residence, a phone book company, the Church Family History Department, a PBS television channel, a financial advisor, a company that makes quilting frames, and a company that sells replacement parts for power tools and appliances. She even spent a few months as a professional semitruck driver. Obviously, all of this is just an excuse to continue learning about lots of different subjects and people and has nothing at all to do with any kind of wanderlust.

Red cheerfully admits to being a geek, a weirdo, and an introvert, and while the social awkwardness has never been fun, there are a number of offsetting benefits. For instance, it's been years since the last time she was bored.

Scan to visit

redrichardson.wordpress.com